INTO His DARK

THE CIMARRON SERIES: BOOK ONE

ANGEL PAYNE

This book is an original publication of Angel Payne.

This is a work of fiction. Names, characters, places, and incidents either are the product of the author's imagination or are used fictitiously, and any resemblance to actual persons, living or dead, business establishments, events, or locales is entirely coincidental. The publisher does not assume any responsibility for third-party websites or their content.

Paperback ISBN: 978-1-64263-064-0

INTO His DARK

THE CIMARRON SERIES: BOOK ONE

ANGEL PAYNE

WATERHOUSE PRESS

For Thomas...you gave me the courage to fly on this one.

And I do mean HIGH.

I love you so much!

CHAPTER ONE

If opportunity knocks on a Saturday morning, am I still expected to answer the door?

The question powered my glare at my cell phone jingling its way across the kitchen counter. Technically, opportunity was ringing, not knocking—like *that* changed anything. There was still no reason to assume Harry Dane wasn't dialing from the middle of another hangover. It would follow the pattern of the other times he'd called in the year since we'd graduated from Chapman U—three of them, not that I was counting—all of them on Saturdays, all revealing nothing except that he was still with Beth, living in a craptastic studio apartment in Torrance, waiting for Hollywood to notice his directorial brilliance.

In short, a good occasion to be thankful for voicemail.

There was a time when I'd have pulled triple backflips to be the girl in that apartment with Harry. The days when life was going to be him, me, and destiny. We were going to change the world, one meaningful Sundance-film-fest winner at a time. Back in the days when I still thought we could all change the world by just believing we could.

The days before Beth.

Before I grew up.

Regrettably, my libido hadn't caught up to reality. The girl parts still tingled when Harry's face, a gorgeous blend of his Hawaiian mom and French dad, appeared in my phone's window. A tiny piece of my heart still ached to think of how our kids would've turned out. A little girl in a hula skirt with his dancing brown eyes and my long black hair, or a little boy as intense as his dad, resolute chin joined to my turquoise gaze.

A couple more rings and I could shove all that away again. Forget about Harry until after I'd finished my good-for-me self-help book, my shitty-for-me cereal, and my congrats-you're-a-human-again shower.

Which was why I reached across the counter and picked the damn thing up.

Too busy creating different ways to call myself an idiot, I forgot to greet the man properly. Probably why *his* voice came as a surprise. "Cam? You there?"

Wait. The surprise stemmed from something else. I actually understood him. Not a single sloshy word or half-blitzed burp.

"Hey. Hi. I'm here."

Whoosh of breath from his end. Relief? Dread? I had a second of static to contemplate that before he gushed, "Awesome. There's my rock star."

Wait. Whoa. *Gushed?*

"What the hell?" I blurted.

"What the hell what?"

"You're sober."

"Uhh, yeah. I am."

"You never call me unless you're drinking." *So why don't you act your age and drink more?*

He chuckled. *Damn it.* His chuckle was still really sexy.

"Okay, so..."

"Yeah, uh..."

"Harry." By the time it popped out, there was enough

rebuke in it to remind myself of my mother. *Ish*.

"Cam." It was all he said. But in a way, all he had to say. The syllable was...serious. For that reason alone...strange. Unless he was behind a camera dictating a shot, Harry wasn't serious about anything.

I stared at the marshmallow clovers still floating in the milk in my bowl, wondering if I was about to puke on them. "Harry?"

"Cam." Again, it was all he said. If my heart wasn't pounding so hard, I would've laughed at our exchange. This was so ridiculous it wouldn't even fly as a rom-com script.

"You said that already," I snapped. "What the hell's going on? Are your mom and dad okay?" I hadn't talked to Phillipe and Kalea Dane beyond emails in the last three months.

"They're fine. Everything's fine. Chill out, Camellia Diana, and that's an order."

I'd been about to rinse out my bowl and spoon. I left them behind in the sink, falling into a chair at my new Mission-style dining room table. Normally, I'd caress the polished surface in adoration—but right now, I barely noticed it.

"Shit," I rasped.

"What?" Harry laughed again. I really was going to deck him.

"*What?* You don't drop the 'Diana' bomb randomly, Dane. Spit it out. What kind of trouble are you in?" The money angle could be written off. Harry's parents weren't hurting. Even if they were, they'd sell their own limbs to help their son. "Ohhhh, crap. Beth—"

"Isn't pregnant." A smile tinged his voice. "Fuck. I *knew* you were going to go there."

I took a turn for a giggle. The relief of knowing he hadn't knocked up Beth—well, it wasn't like "opposites attract" ever had a prayer of reality with him and me—but even thinking of Beth having that lock on him, forever and always, was—

Not worth dwelling on anymore.

"Shut up," I razzed. "This is my logical deduction, not yours. Sober *and* serious. This means...you've either decided to really go for it and pursue the master's degree, or—"

I nearly choked.

He's never serious. Except when it comes to calling the shots from behind a movie camera...

"Come on, Camellia." His coax rose with confidence, on top of the world in an eerily calm way. "You're almost there."

"Holy freaking cow, Harry." It was damn near just a breath. I couldn't manage more. "Did you—"

"Get permission from the royal honchos of Arcadia to shoot my movie on their island and then score a boatload of financing from Pinnacle Pictures right after that? The answer to both of those would be yes."

"Holy shit!" A scream this time. "Harry! Seriously?"

His chuckle didn't drive me crazy anymore. It filled the line, warm and celebratory—and wonderful. "Wish I could see the faces on those assholes now."

He didn't have to elaborate. By *those assholes*, he meant *the* assholes: a group of five guys from our film workshop class who'd always labeled Harry's ideas as unrealistic, narcissistic, and way too ambitious for "the financial paradigms of the new Hollywood." Harry had really brought on their ridicule when, during a class discussion about dream location shoots, he declared he'd do a picture on Arcadia one day. The assholes had been relentless in their laughter before rallying the whole class in their merry quest. I'd remained silent but in some ways couldn't diss their reasoning, a truth I felt duty-bound to state again.

"Isn't Arcadia still an independent monarchy—with restricted airspace and sealed borders?"

"Yes, yes, and yes," Harry supplied. "I just happened to secure an exception."

"An exception," I echoed, "to bring in a whole film crew? To one of the most secretive societies in the world? Didn't some tool in the press even name them the Amish of the Mediterranean?"

"Very good, Watson," he drawled.

"Though I guess it's not hard to enforce that kind of stuff when you're an island."

"Actually, it *is* hard. Arcadia's been learning that lesson in some difficult ways over the last few years. Aside from a few strategic trade agreements for the island's helium supplies, which have helped carry the island's other economies, Arcadia has remained a shut-in from the rest of the world."

"Which means...?"

"That the world has moved ahead and they haven't." Oddly, the bummer words were delivered with Harry's growing excitement. "And I know it sucks ass for where they're at now, but Cam...it's been fucking awesome from a personal perspective. *Everything* happened the way I thought it would. You remember what I said that day in class, about the island's king getting ready to step down and all the changes his son was getting ready to make?"

I gave a wry hum. "How could I forget?"

"Well, I was right on the money." His knuckle crack of victory popped across the line. "King Ardent knew he was up against an old-school government who would never be open to the changes Arcadia needed to continue in prosperity, but he always hoped his children would find themselves under different circumstances, dealing with more open minds. I'm sure it was why he ordered they be schooled in England and France, not by Arcadia's tutors. I think one of them even went to high school in the States, somewhere near Boston."

"The guy who's king now?"

"No. Not Evrest. And he's not a 'guy,' Cam. He's a man. A king."

"Gah. Whatever you say, milord."

Loaded pause. "You *do* know who King Evrest is, right?"

Equally loaded snicker. "King Kilimanjaro's brother?"

"Crap." I pictured him indulging a face-palm. "Not *Ev-er-est* with three syllables. *Ev-rest* with two."

"Thanks. That clears everything up."

"Shit, Cam. Don't tell me you've been that far under a rock for the last year?"

"I've been *working* for the last year. As in, making the most of my scintillating double degrees in math and strategic comm. Concerned with shit like condo payments, groceries, health insurance. Being a grown-up. Any of that ring a bell?"

"Evrest. Cimarron." He stamped the words like pointing out I had a nose on my face. "Okay, when you're buying your precious groceries, do you ever glance at the magazines next to the register?"

"No." *Overtone of* ew, *activate magical powers.* "Okay, sometimes." Before he called me even more of a dweeb, I pulled over my laptop and tapped *Arcadia King* into the search string. "But seriously, I don't pay attention or..."

Anything.

The word never made it to my lips. Because it vanished from my head. Another took its place, filling every inch of my consciousness.

Everything.

Evrest Cimarron was absolutely everything that turned me into a hot, gooey, disgusting, lusty mess.

I recognized him now, of course. The American press didn't call him by his full name. They'd borrowed parts of it for snappy expressions like *Revvin' Ev, Get Your Ev-Watch Here,* and *The Cim is Simmering.* But I might have been completely wrong about those headlines because the second I saw the man on any magazine cover I forced myself to turn away. Concentrating on celery, toothpaste, and Nutella was my only chance of banishing the image of him, all thick black hair, brilliant Sultan eyes, and sleek, sculpted body, into the darkest pit of my mind. The shadows only visited when it was time to bring the vibrator out of the nightstand—and my fantasies out of their cage. The images of his bronze hands against my pale skin...

spreading me
exposing me
then filling me
with himself.

Not happening. Not right now. Damn it.

But he still dominated my screen, taunting me with his burnished beauty, penetrating stare, regal strength...and something else too. A strange echo in my pulse, as if a part of me actually recognized him...or at least the sight of him. With every moment I gazed, that cadence sprinted faster, commanding me not to look away, though my libido screamed with the sensual torment of it.

Ohhh, shit.

Definitely wasn't exiting this one unscathed. My dry mouth said as much. And my shallow breaths. And the aching throb between my thighs.

"Uh...okay," I finally stammered. "Yeah. He's...a little familiar. M-Maybe."

Wicked snort. A Harry special. "Ohhh, Cam."

"'Ohhh, Cam,' what?"

"Hey." I envisioned him holding up his free hand in protest. "I'm not hatin'. If I swung that way, he'd jump to the top of my dream fuck list too."

"Shut up."

"You need a moment alone with your laptop, honey?"

"Shut *up*."

"Okay, I have a better offer." The pause he took was too long for my comfort. "How'd you like to meet him in person?"

I closed my laptop with a vengeful thud. Focusing on the action helped me stay rooted in reality—not the wild idea he'd seemingly just proposed. "Meet who in person?"

His groan filled the line. "Maybe *you're* the drunk one today, yeah?"

Deep fume. "No. I just can't figure out what you're getting at. What the hell?"

He repeated the groan, dropping a register. "His Majesty, Evrest Cimarron of Arcadia. What would you say about meeting him?"

I considered myself a straight shooter when it came to conversation. When I received the same from others, I usually appreciated it. But Harry's turn at come-right-out-with-it didn't come close to the target. My belly twisted tighter. My nerves were icicles. "I...don't know what I'd say. I'm puzzled.

Did you get invited to some event with him now that you're going to turn his kingdom into a glamorous movie set? You need a date or something?" *And if so, why aren't you asking Beth?*

Harry didn't help things by chuckling again, piling on the indulgence. "No. I don't need a date. I need a production manager."

"Huh?" His words floated on my comprehension like leaves on water, refusing to sink in.

"And for that matter, a prop mistress, second unit liaison, accountant, and about six other job descriptions I won't name now, in order not to scare you off."

I took a turn to laugh. In disbelief. "Why would I be scared? It's an impossible proposition."

"Why?"

"Why?" I toyed with flipping the conversation to FaceTime, bed head be damned. If he saw the glory of my incredulity, maybe he'd believe it. "Because I have a life now, Harry, that's why. Responsibili—"

"Right," he cut in. "Responsibilities. Like that family you have to take care of?"

"Damn it," I muttered. He knew my parents as well as I knew his. Mom—aka Louise—was doing just fine, training for her fifth marathon and screening prospects for her third boyfriend in a year. And Dad? Well, Dad was...Dad, off in a part of the world where even if they had internet and cell reception, he wouldn't care. Bones and relics, the older the better, were the man's oxygen—likely reason number one behind Mom's quiet request for a divorce during my junior year in high school.

"Cam," Harry persisted, "you don't even own a dog."

"No shit." Time to let the snark fly. "I was seeing if I could keep plants alive first. You know what's going to happen to my plants if I run off to the Mediterranean with you?"

"Faye can check on them."

"No, she can't."

"Why not?"

"She's my boss, Harry."

"The boss who happens to think you walk on water."

He was right. Faye Mellencamp and I had formed a mutual admiration society from my first interview at her small but chic Newport Beach office. Landing a position with her had made purchasing this place possible. And the new car. And even a little bit of savings in the bank too. A decent nest egg...

For what?

To spend on who?

I swallowed against the ache that came with the demands, invading my chest and forming a lump at the base of my throat. If I didn't know any better, I'd have called the feeling loneliness. But I did know better—and I was proud of that. At twenty-four, I had already accomplished so much.

Including that whole changing-the-world thing. Right, girlfriend?

Frustrated growl. And the easy recognition that I directed it as much at Harry as the taunting voice from inside. "This is crazy. Traipsing off to Arcadia for eight to ten weeks is just—"

"Six."

"What?"

"Six weeks," he corrected. "That's all Arcadia is going to give us for the shoot."

Groan. "Then tell me we have more for preproduction." A significant pause. Another. "Harry?"

I swore his discomfort had its own special static. "Two

months for preproduction."

Harder groan. "I had to ask."

"*Now* do you understand why I need you? You're used to pressure like this." Thanks to the dozens of shoots I'd assisted him on during our years at Chapman, he knew I couldn't argue the point. "It's going to be tight, but we have no choice. Arcadia's given us the window, and we have to abide by it. As soon as we leave, everyone on the island will be wrapped up in a big-ass celebration—a week-long festival to celebrate Evrest's engagement."

"Oh." I sounded as nonchalant as a sixteen-year-old at a shoe sale—*and* just as gawky and confused—and eventually short on budget for everything I wanted. Stir in zits and I'd be dandy. "He's getting married?"

"That's the plan."

Harry sucked at containing his sarcasm more than I did with the little green monster. Cue the Cam Special: awkward laugh topped by a stab at glib. "*The plan?* Sounds like they're scheduling him for an execution instead of a wedding."

"Strong chance he'd agree with you on that."

"An arranged marriage?"

It was angrier than I intended. I had no place rendering an opinion on the matter. I wasn't naïve about this. Prearranged marriages were still acceptable, even normal, in many countries. But attempting to connect a gorgeous, worldly hunk like Evrest Cimarron with such a cold and archaic practice... Yeah, the gray matter threatened to implode.

"That part's a little more complicated," Harry answered. "But I can explain it in detail once we make it to Arcadia." A smirk sneaked into his follow-up. "I promise it's *very* interesting. You won't want to miss it."

"Bastard."

"*Adorable* bastard. You always forget the important part."

I tried to laugh as I rose again. Only the slightest surprise set in when my phone shook next to my ear—because of my trembling fingers.

Did I dare consider his offer?

I was still asking the question, wasn't I? Telling. Perhaps revealing. *Fine*; I still contemplated it. More than a little. Wasn't that understandable? A movie shoot. A *real* one in the *real* world, not a class project or a music video as a favor for one of Harry's friends. And not in just any setting. The island of Arcadia, seen by few outside eyes before. Even the business people who traded with the country had likely not seen it as we were about to.

In many ways, we'd be like explorers. Discovering a new land and, in turn, teaching them about ours. Columbus and the Native Americans, but with better plumbing. I hoped.

A chance to change the world.

Even if just a little.

But I couldn't lie to myself. As noble as that sounded, my intentions weren't all light, goodness, and Angelina Jolie. This was a chance to be near Harry again. I wasn't so delusional to think he wouldn't find a way for Beth to come as well—if he hadn't given her the lead in the movie already—but a pressure cooker like this could do strange things to people. And intrinsically, Beth wasn't "strange." She was actually pretty nice, to the point that I already knew she'd gracefully welcome me on the shoot and mean it. But that was because she had bigger things to focus on—like herself. It didn't make her bad. It just made her an actress.

Stick to the point, Saxon.

Fine. If Harry and Beth *did* decide to fill their free time during the shoot with the horizontal mambo, I had a great backup plan. His Majesty, King Dark and Sexy, would be perfect for some harmless mental swoonage. He'd be busy making engagement party plans, landing him smack in the file of beautiful but safe, meaning I could openly fantasize to my heart's content. Now I just had to put extra vibrator batteries— or an appropriate electrical adaptor—on my packing list. Crap. Were Arcadian maids the snooping type?

"Cam?" Harry busted into my thoughts—and the flawless, shirtless image of Evrest Cimarron that had broken in again. "You still there?"

"Hmm? Duh. Yes. Of course I am, bastard."

A fast *psshh*. Then with a shit ton of caution: "You're quiet. I hope that means you're talking yourself into this."

I bit the inside of my lip. Now that I was out of my imagination and back into my head, a thousand more protests attacked. I owed it to myself to voice the main ones. "Look, Harry—"

"Awww, no," he volleyed. "No, no, no, honey. Not the 'Look, Harry.' Not now!"

"For one thing, I'm not your honey anymore. But as long as you've conveniently brought up the subject—"

"Really? You're using *Beth* as your excuse to turn me down?"

I fought to ignore the lump of dismay in my chest—as well as my anger for indulging it to start with. "So she *is* going."

"Why does that even matter to you?"

I quashed a huff. Fine, I was jealous. A *little*. Why the hell that shocked him was beyond me.

Maybe because he's moved on and you haven't?

Shit. No matter how it got sliced, the truth stung. Sometimes right behind one's eyeballs, in the middle of what should have been a perfect Saturday morning.

Gritted teeth. The beginning of a headache. The kind that would cling all day. A stupid, stabbing reminder of reined-in tears.

"Damn it, Harry. It doesn't matter in the least and you know it!"

"Okay, okay. Of course I know."

But his tone was still skeptical. He released a measured breath, easing the headache at least a little. At least his gentlemanly side resurfaced.

"Look, Cam. You were the top name on my list for this call. All right, you were the *only* name. Nobody's qualified for this in the same ways. You know me. How I work. And hell, you nearly minored in film production. I really do need you."

I took a breath myself. *Time out.* We both needed it. And yeah, it felt good to savor what his confession did to my bloodstream. I'd forgotten what his reassurances felt like. They were nice. Damn nice.

A smile finally crept at my lips. "Okay, knock that off."

"Knock what off?"

"The sweet and sincere thing. It's easier when I can just call you a cocky ass."

"Call me whatever you want. Just follow it up with a screaming *yes*, and we'll be good."

"Didn't we just confirm that I don't scream anything for you anymore, Mr. Dane?"

Silken rumble. "God, Cam. I've missed you."

Shit. That officially screwed my resolve to save the swooning for King Evrest. Thank God for my dexterity with the mute button, engaged before Harry could hear my conflicted whimper.

Conflicted? Understatement. I felt like a rabbit who'd gotten used to the winter in my burrow, only to be told it was spring and I could run in the sun again.

And what about the woman who'd kept me safe in the burrow?

"Faye." I blurted her name after opening the line again. "What about her, Harry? I can't just up and quit, not after everything she's—"

"Who says you have to quit?"

"I don't understand."

"You haven't taken a single sick day since you started with her. You have at least a month of time off already on the books, and I'll bet she'd let you have the rest on credit."

Brain, picking up crayons—and connecting dots. Fast. "You bet she would, huh?" I didn't bother hiding the pointing finger in my tone. "And you just happen to know all about my work attendance...how?"

He snorted. "Don't pull a Sister Camellia on me, girl. Yeah, I called Faye. And I'm not sorry. And guess what? She's probably more excited about this than you are. I'm surprised *she* hasn't called *you* yet, ordering you to straighten out your files so you can turn them over to a temp."

I squirmed in my chair. Fought like hell to summon a proper snit at the bastard for daring to call my boss behind my back. I only managed to mutter, "I never said I was excited."

"You didn't have to."

Because you know me so well?

I left the retort unspoken. It'd be useless to voice it. Both of us knew the answer. Of course he knew me that well, because I knew him in the same way. Might've made us shitty lovers, but our friendship was quite the E-ticket spin—except at times like this, when he knew he'd ripped down the last of my viable defenses.

And for payback? Made him wriggle on the hook a minute longer, of course.

"So I assume there's pay for this gig, Dane?"

His combo of growl and groan roughened up the line. "Do you really, seriously, care?"

Of course I didn't—he probably knew that without a doubt too—but I relished the stringing-him-out-because-I-could element. Noticeably giggled, just to be sure he knew that. "How much, Mr. Dane? C'mon, I'm a homeowner now. The IRS has me on the grid, not to mention Audi USA Financing. I have to be a responsible girl and all."

"Responsibility is overrated."

"Says the guy about to have a mind-shattering load of it on his shoulders."

Funny. His answering grunt wasn't so derisive now. "Says the girl who's about to share that load with me."

"Not so fast, hot stuff. Contract? Paycheck? I can't work for Doritos anymore."

"Hmmm. Well, I managed to renew your card with the union even though you've been inactive for a while, so let's just say you'll be happy with the compensation."

"Hmmm." I was equally blasé about the echo. Harry didn't need to know that my heart raced so fast with excitement it pounded at the base of my throat—and that every neuron in my brain felt switched on for the first time in a year.

And that my stomach twisted with guilt for all of it too.

I owed Faye so much. She'd given me a chance I couldn't kiss her toes enough for. Financial stability like mine was enjoyed by few *people* my age, much less women. And yes, I liked the work, I really did—but advising millionaires how to become billionaires hadn't fed a shred of my soul. Forget about the hit it had taken on my social life. Even committing to an advance signup for cycling class at the gym felt like a risk, subject to destruction at the hands of some guy needing to liquidate assets to buy himself out of the doghouse with his wife, mistress, or both.

I missed being on a film set. Period. I missed the bad coffee and the buzz of excitement. I missed being on a team committed to creativity, working to combine light, sound, motion, and words into something completely new—and sometimes magical. Where if only for a little while, I felt part of a pretty cool family.

Changing the world.

If only by a little bit.

Damn.

The excitement turned into an ache. Twelve months of shoving this feeling aside took revenge on my composure in one blow. I forced the phone away while swallowing from the hit.

"Helll-lllo?" Harry's sing-song tease filled the line. "I know I need to just shut up and be grateful for the silences, but girl, you're making me a wreck."

Another giggle. It felt good. It felt right. "Oh, dear. We can't have you wrecked, Mr. Director."

"What does *that* mean?"

I tossed back my head as a grin spread across my lips. "It means you'd better tell me when we're leaving for Arcadia so I can get properly packed."

Including the vibrator batteries.

As Harry whooped, I almost laughed again. With my luck, the reality of Evrest Cimarron would be much different than the myth. Up close, he was probably a dog. Or a dick. Or both. But, as they said, a girl could dream. Especially when the adventure of a lifetime awaited.

CHAPTER TWO

Life suddenly feeling like a tornado? Check.

Production assistants tailing me like munchkins on crack? Check.

A "wizard" pulling too many strings behind the curtain and driving me crazy because of it? Check, capital freaking *C*.

Translation: it'd be a miracle if I didn't kill Harry before we left for Arcadia.

Fairness disclosure: it wasn't all his fault. Pinnacle had only given us the financial blessing for two months of preproduction on top of the six-week shoot. The time felt more like two seconds, despite some of the big tasks, like casting and shooting locations, being handled already. On top of that, I was still officially working for Faye, who'd be earning a halo and wings after all this was through. Harry's prophecy about her was more than right. She was thrilled about what she called "Cam's big-time movie adventure," only leveling one condition on my leave of absence. At least one of the Hemsworth brothers had to be invited to the premiere and seated next to her. Harry assured her he'd do everything he could. Hell if he didn't sound serious about it too.

Two weeks before "go day," I turned all my files over to a sweet UCI grad Faye had hired to fill in for me, who pounced into the work like a kitten on a laser dot. It was a little unsettling. I didn't remember ever having the same spark under me, even when first starting with Faye. The observation nagged during the drive to LAX for my flight.

Three flights and almost twenty-four hours later, our private charter plane dipped over the brilliant green foliage of an island so breathtaking, I wondered if I was still napping and dreaming. Made sense. I'd looked at so many photos of Arcadia over the last two months, my subconscious likely had them on autoplay. But if the pictures painted a thousand words, the real deal blasted a novel's worth of prose—and I couldn't access a word. I stared in awe as we circled on final approach to a landing strip stretched against a grove of banana trees. In the distance, a cluster of modest buildings and streets identified itself as Sancti, Arcadia's capital city.

Harry, seated across the aisle with Beth at his side, leaned over. "What do you think, rock star?"

I grinned. "Is there anything except *wow*?"

Beth narrowed her eyes in a playful tease. "Well, *I'm* thinking I should have listened to my instinct about an extra can of bug spray. And if I have to sleep on a cot with centipedes crawling up my leg—"

Harry stopped her with a raised hand. "Nobody's sleeping on cots."

I shrugged. "I'm siding with your woman on this one." When he hunched into his seat, I fired, "Simmer down, island boy. You and I both know what havoc Mother Nature can play on a shoot. And if she gets 'help' from her multi-legged friends—"

"Nobody's sleeping on cots." He slung a glare between Beth and me. "It's handled."

"Why the hell are you still playing secret agent about this? Damn it, Harry. I'm your production manager. If the security team on this rock isn't going to get over their shit and learn I can be trusted as much as you then we may have one hell of a—"

"*Cam. It's handled.*"

Ass.

Times like this, I was damn glad he was Beth's problem now. *Smirk.* I hid it against my palm while gazing out the window again—though it almost hurt to do so. The crystalline sea, the azure sky, the luxurious green trees... It was stunning, like flying into a postcard.

Wow.

In more ways than one.

My smile grew by a tentative degree. Emphasis on *tentative.* A huge part of my brain still couldn't believe I was here, really doing this. I hadn't even told Mom yet. As far as she knew, I was on a week's vacation with some college buddies. Not a total lie. I planned to call and give her the rest of the story once I couldn't easily step back onto a plane.

Another part of me, the part I'd started calling "Ms. Saxon," was doing everything she could not to let out a horrified scream and demand why I'd abandoned her. *Gah.* I'd just bought new dining room furniture! Faye had even upgraded my business cards. They were embossed now. I had a preferred card at the grocery store and had accrued nearly enough points to cash them in for a cast-iron skillet.

Then there was the other part of me. The giddy girl who'd just stepped out onto the craziest high wire of her life...

And loved the view.

Despite being so scared that her lips wobbled, her stomach churned, and her knees trembled.

But...loving that too.

None of this was going to be easy. I had no illusions about that. But I could handle this; I knew it with gut-deep certainty. Not just for Harry and the team. This was a little gift to me. For the first time in a year, adrenaline was my bestie again. I was pumped about the challenges every day brought. And for the first time in my life, I'd traveled thousands of miles from home. Was about to step foot into a land where no terrain, no road, no *anything* was remotely familiar.

So, *scared* was the go-to adjective for the moment. But so were *exhilarated, open,* and *excited.*

And *alive.*

The word resonated through me as the flight attendant popped open the door and let down the stairs. While everyone joined Harry and Beth in a group cheer, I only smiled like a dork. Then whispered words for my ears alone.

"Bring it on."

CHAPTER THREE

"Whoa."

I wasn't sure what else to say after climbing out of the sleek black Mercedes Sprinter that had just taken us on a thirty-minute journey from the airstrip, through Sancti's streets, up a cypress-lined hill to—

Where the hell *were* we?

"Whoa." Beth blurted the echo as she disembarked behind me.

Harry descended from the van after her. "*Now* do you believe me about housing being handled?"

I slid behind Beth to whack his shoulder. As he broke into a chuckle, Beth stammered, "Harry...it's a..."

"It's okay, sweetheart," he murmured. "Say it."

"Castle."

Accurate. But still the world's biggest understatement.

The complex before us was a combination of Spanish citadel, French chateau, and pop star crib, with Mediterranean touches to soften the imposing architecture. The entrance drive, made of gravel embedded with sparkling stones, ended at a stone bridge arching over a turquoise river, leading to a waterfall that cascaded in the direction of the sea. The castle's main hub was built into the cliff as well. Bracketing it were two majestic wings, sweeping to the left and right. Everywhere we looked, verandas with elegant stone balustrades were draped in magenta, purple, orange, and crimson flowers. In alcoves between the patios were statues of sea creatures, real and mythical, inlaid with colored glass that imparted the stone with movement every time sunlight filtered through the banyan, olive, and date palm trees.

Yeah. Dreaming. I was pretty sure of it now. But the breeze on my face, smelling of sea salt and lavender, felt wonderfully real. The crunch of the gravel beneath my feet, equally so. And Harry's hand on my shoulder, joined to the one he wrapped around Beth, was solid with confidence. "So does this beat a cot and some centipedes?"

Beth gaped. "We're staying *here*?"

His smirk widened. "Production offices will be here too. The whole north wing is ours for the next six weeks."

I shook my head. "But where is *here*? What is this?"

Harry stared like I'd asked who was buried in Grant's tomb. "You don't recognize it?"

"Should I?"

"This is Palais Arcadia. I sent you a file about it. Did you look at it?"

"At the specs, not the pictures. There were already so many photos to look at, I skipped the palais shots. All I needed to know was the space we'd be getting in the offices." To his eye roll, I snapped, "Remember me? The girl working two jobs before we left? Sorry I didn't pay attention to your entire travel brochure, Mr. Dane."

He squeezed my shoulder. "Chill. I'm about to repeat a lot of it anyway. Come on." Back to business. He never liked wasting time. "I've asked everyone to meet in the central atrium so we can go over some things and assign rooms."

As we entered the castle—the *palais*—the feeling returned, stronger than ever, that this was my brain's elaborate hoax and

I'd soon wake up in Lake Forest, peering out the window at June gloom clouds. But everything stayed solid as we walked beneath an ornate archway, past soaring oak doors, and through an entrance foyer that rivaled most five-star hotels in its marble and gold glory. A balcony above was fronted by a sheet of glass resembling an ocean swell. The "wave" was given definition by flowing golden inlays depicting dolphins, mermaids, and etched sea bubbles. I'd never seen anything like it. Like *any* of this.

We progressed through an archway beneath the balcony, finally emerging into a huge courtyard surrounded by more lush greenery. As we entered, Arcadian servers in gold and white livery approached, bearing trays piled with fresh-cut tropical fruit. Nearby, tables were laid out with pitchers of water and juice. Things didn't stay very quiet after that. As more of the crew filed into the atrium, excited chatter crackled the air. Between our English conversations, tentative threads of communication were started with the Arcadians. It was easy to discern the difference. Like everyone else, I'd crammed in a few lessons about the basics of their language. It was built on a Latin base, though the ugliness was sifted out with French and Turkish influences.

"Hello."

"*Merjour.* And...umm...welcome to Arcadia."

"Hey, that was good!"

"*Merderim.*"

"Merderim to you too. The fruit is...errr...good? *Bonrika?*"

"Ahh! *C'est* perfect!"

"You have a beautiful country."

"Merderim."

It made me smile to witness the exchanges. We were like kids getting to know each other on a playground. Wasn't a bad way to view the world, when hearts and minds were open— though it was a bigger step for the Arcadians than for us. We had no real way of knowing how they were taught to view the outside world, so we had prepared ourselves for every greeting between glares and gunpoint. But liveried servants and fresh fruit trays? Hadn't made anyone's radar, mine included.

Weirdly, while everyone else relaxed, Harry's tension visibly grew. I slid a what-the-hell look at him, but he responded by circling a finger in the air, a silent request to get everyone rounded up. I complied, watching the two hundred members of our team quickly fill in the atrium's empty spaces. Our number was fewer than half of what it took for a normal film crew, but it was all Arcadia would allow, so we'd handpicked everyone with care. Every person here would be covering their normal work load by double, sometimes triple. I was already grateful for their commitment.

"Settle in, everyone. I know we're all tired, so I won't take long." Harry waited for everyone to mute their chatter. Took about a minute. Tired might have applied to everyone, but so did excited. After getting the clearance from one of the Arcadians, he hopped onto the edge of a planter and joined his hands as if preparing to pray. I held back a giggle. *Paging Dr. Freud.*

"Okay," he announced with a wide smile, "we're here!" Happy but weary applause broke out. "First, I'd like to thank you all in advance for what's likely to be one of the hardest shoots of your life—but I guarantee it'll be one of the most memorable. As you know, simply by being here, you have all become a part of world history."

He spread his arms toward the soaring glass walls around us. Their shiny panels were patterned with the few clouds drifting overhead. "As you can tell, the Arcadians are just as psyched about having us here. The royal family of the kingdom, the Cimarrons themselves, have opened their home to us. The Palais Arcadia will be our main operations hub and living quarters while we are here." Another excited buzz broke out. Harry brought his arms back in. "Okay, *settle*. This isn't like your old roommate inviting you to party at his uncle's place in Malibu for the weekend. This is where the Cimarrons live and work, including the business of running their country."

One of the cameramen near the back called out, "But it's not an absolute monarchy, right?"

"Correct." Harry nodded. "Arcadia is a constitutional monarchy, run similarly to our big corporations at home. King Evrest presides over everything directly involving the 'business' of the country. Though he's been trained for the job since boyhood and his word carries extra power on all matters the High Counsel rules on, he gets no vote or veto leverage. But don't misinterpret that. 'Extra power' means *extra* power. The man has a crap-ton of challenges on his shoulders every day. We will *not* become another."

The cameraman's buddy launched into a flawless mobster drawl. "So he don't got no official vote, but *un*officially, he and Guido are quite effective, ya know?"

Everyone's chuckles rose and then died before Harry drawled, "Thanks for the lead-in, guys." He scanned the crowd again. "I doubt Evrest has a Guido hiding in the closet, but you'll find *me* breaking your knees if anyone from this team disrespects, defaces, or destroys a shred of Arcadian person or property while we're here." His face tightened. *Don't sign off on the whole diatribe yet, guys.* "It's why I'm taking a zero-tolerance line on fraternization with the locals. I know some of you will have your Harry Dane voodoo dolls out for this, but you're all ordered to stick to the beach and the north wing when we're not working. No self-guided tours of the south wing or any other part of the island. We've worked too hard to gain Arcadia's trust, and Hollywood-Gone-Wild isn't the impression we'll leave as our legacy. Shake your groove thing with each other as much as you want, but if you're caught with your pants down around Arcadian ass of either gender, you'll be sent home on the next flight out. I guarantee you won't leave with just *my* wrath on your head. The crew members who'll pick up your slack might have some choice farewell gestures too."

Two production assistants started a whispered exchange behind me. I hid my grin while picking up every word.

"Damn it. Of all places to be given a hands-off on the local boys."

"Right? Did you see the guns on the guy who helped with our luggage?"

"Did you see his *ass*?"

"And that ginger with the fruit tray over there? Get him out of that steampunk shit and into some tight black leather, I'll even let him drag out the handcuffs."

"If every man in this place is like that, I may be on a plane soon."

"Not if every *chica* in this place is like that too."

"Ssshh; he's talking about rooming assignments."

"Thank God."

I forgot about the exchange as soon as the housing arrangements were clarified. It still stunned me that the castle's north wing would accommodate everyone from the crew plus production offices. Granted, nearly everyone was tripling or quadrupling up, with the exception of Harry, myself, Beth, and her leading man, Crowe Cowan. I liked Crowe. Though he hadn't gone to Chapman with us, he was a USC theater school graduate who'd done a lot of work with Harry already. A tall, striking Irishman with a diligent work ethic, he was a perfect prince to Beth's princess in the story we were filming, a hybrid of *The Princess and the Pea* and *The Ugly Duckling* based on an original script by Harry and his writing partner, Trent Arris.

After the meeting, we were welcomed to an early lunch on the huge lawn outside. As waves crashed on the beach below, we dug in to a buffet of fresh-caught shrimp and clams, exotic salads with tangy fruit, sandwiches on bread that tasted like heaven, and desserts that were too pretty to eat.

After the meal, everyone was given the afternoon off— except production leadership. I wasn't surprised by the meeting Harry called for us in his room. I went directly there while sending my luggage ahead to mine. I knew better than to let my body hit a bed right now. Once that happened, I'd be down for at least nine hours straight.

On the other hand, entering Harry's suite was nearly enough to knock me out.

"Holy shit." The words tumbled out before I could help it. The "room" was a small palace in its own right, starting with a sitting area containing three expansive leather couches and a wrought-iron table, complimented by a stacked-stone water feature along the wall. Double doors of carved walnut opened to a bedroom with a canopy bed draped in velvet throws. The rooms overlooked a wraparound terrace with a built-in hot tub and dining set for eight. "So do you prefer Your Highness or simply *Harry, God of Everything the Light Touches*?"

"Shut up." Harry grinned while grabbing his laptop and briefcase. I was captivated by his purposeful stride across the room. Though it was clear the surroundings thrilled him, that wasn't the key source of his vigor. We were about to create a movie, and Harry Dane was a guy born to make movies. The person who knew it best was the man himself, to the core of his whole body. He'd never veered from that knowledge in his life. For that, I deeply envied him.

Harry continued out to the patio. "We need to have this meeting, but let's at least make it pleasant." He seated himself at the head of the table, waiting for everyone to settle in. There were a good dozen of us, so some stood while others dragged chairs out from the room. By the time that was done, he had his all-business face sealed in place.

Joel, our double-duty location manager and production designer, arched his bold Italian brows. "Is this the part where you tell us we have to cut two days off the shoot *and* deal with a monsoon next week?"

While he was answered with a round of chuckles, Harry's wince did little to ease my nerves. "Well..."

"Well *what*?" Beth stole the charge off my lips.

"Depending on how you look at it, this could be worse." Harry took a visible lungful of breath, anticipating the growing tension around the table. "The Cimarrons have informed me they're arranging a full Arcadian welcome party for us... tonight."

More than half the group groaned. Others, like me, expelled disbelieving sighs. "At least you said *tonight*," drawled Dottie, a friend from Chapman who'd been working on films since graduation and was already my right hand for anything involving hair, makeup, or costuming. "If we hurry through what we've got to discuss here, we can all go comatose for a few hours, right?"

I wondered why Harry's face crunched tighter. "Normally, yes. But the event is being labeled as a full state dinner, meaning we're expected to attend in traditional Arcadian attire."

Crowe leaned forward. "You mean like the doublets, cravats, and Hessians that the staff are dressed in?"

We all burst into laughter. Except Harry. "Actually, that's exactly what I mean."

Joel chuffed. "Damn it. I knew I should have picked up my medieval monkey suit from the dry cleaners before we left." He finished with mocking British inflection. "Sorry, mate."

Harry sent an apologetic smirk down the table. "They've anticipated that, *mate*. Court dressers will be coming to all the guys' rooms in three hours, with full attire for us to choose from. Girls, I'm afraid you get the 'royal treatment' in two hours. As usual, your primping takes longer."

"Imagine that," Joel muttered. Dot tossed her Bettie Page curls over a shoulder before leaning to smack his.

This time, I joined the groan fest. "I don't suppose all those action items on your screen are going to take a fast fifteen minutes to review?"

Beth looked nearly ready to cry. "Hell. I'll look like a zombie tonight without any sleep."

"Makeup covers a lot of ugly," Dottie told her. "I just hope I don't pass out into the soup."

I focused on Zen breathing toward the peaceful beach scene on my smart pad screen. Didn't help my craving to slap Harry for accepting the party invite.

And you wouldn't have done the same thing in his shoes?

The guy had to go and crank up my guilt by being Mr. Textbook Boyfriend with Beth, kissing her fingers before whispering, "You'll be nothing short of stunning, kitten."

Thank God I had a friendly email from Faye to focus on. And a chat bubble from Mom to ignore. By then, ten seconds had passed and Leif Carlson, the art director for the film, threw out a huge enough eye roll for both of us. "Can I be ill at you two now so I don't get vomit on my delicious Arcadian finery?"

Joel snickered. "Does hurling on the finery count as defiling an Arcadian?"

"Must be time to get this meeting started." Harry struggled to tame his quirking lips.

"Motion seconded," Leif said.

"I'll third." My quip was just as much a bid to stay awake as it was to get this cart rolling again. Now that my work day had been lengthened by a "state dinner" and at least three more hours, I'd need all the help I could get. I just had to weigh the etiquette of requesting a dozen espresso shots and a pot of coffee chaser along with my finery delivery.

★ ★ ★

The coffee? Not a problem to procure.

Its effects? Different story.

I stood, jittery as a misplaced Cinderella, holding up the wall of a ballroom that could fit both planes we'd flown in on. But despite the cavernous dimensions, every corner glowed with warm light, making the scene feel more like an elegant house party than a state dinner. The majority of that task was accomplished by six chandeliers, each at least twelve feet long and comprised of hanging crystals blown to resemble sea kelp.

The wall sconces in the room were fashioned in the same flowing design. Extra light was imbued by candelabras on floor stands, filled with lighted tapers that gave the room a gentle rhythm.

If only my pulse would take the same hint.

Standing between Beth and Leif, I was grateful for the glass of water braced between my hands. At least *they* had an excuse to keep still. Couldn't say the same for the vein throbbing at the base of my throat or the frantic drum solo my left foot decided to tap. The latter was the most unnerving, a reminder that despite my fondest wishes, I hadn't become a statue. I sighed, resigned to feeling this dorky and naked for the rest of the night.

"For the love of fucking Triton." Leif squeezed my elbow. "Stop fidgeting. You look amazing. Why are you so nervous?"

Bristled glare. "Everything's hinky. I feel...backward."

He yanked the glass from me. Plopped it on a waiter's passing tray. Then, as if he really hadn't just given away my pacifier, resumed his droll scan of the ballroom. "Hmmm. Explain."

"My face is covered in makeup goop and my crotch is covered in tissue paper. Clear enough?"

As he spurted a laugh, Beth leaned over. She hailed from the damn Galaxy of Gorgeous now, glossy and glam in a dress similar to mine, only black and shimmery. "Come on, Cam. The undies are a *little* better than that."

I squirmed, unwilling to admit she was right. My Arcadian stylist, a perky thing named Rosetta who looked like she really lived in a rose and ate nothing but dewdrops, had been the bearer of my new "lingerie" for the night—after stripping me all the way out of my traveling clothes, of course. The panties were an exact match to my turquoise floor-length gown, which actually *had* yanked my breath when I saw it. The combination of Grecian toga and Indian sari flaunted and teased at the same time. The blessing *and* curse about that? The fabric felt spun from the fuzz off babies' butts, meaning the panties also felt like nothing. Not the best setup for going to a dinner with several hundred other people, including everyone in the Arcadian royal family.

Hell.

Maybe, just maybe, I'd get lucky and King Built-Like-A-God would have some last-minute scepter polishing to keep him away all night.

The thought helped me sneak in a deep breath. Leif watched every inch of the move. "I had no idea you had such great tits."

I choked, wishing I still had the water. Beth slammed her clutch against Leif's chest and muttered wryly, "Nicely done, Sir Tact."

"What? They're *nice.*"

Stressed stare—right at my bodice. Damn it, it was what I liked best about the dress. A thousand tiny beads, iridescent with overtones of blue, adorned the area in swirling designs. Rosetta had stressed that bra straps would ruin the look. She'd probably been right, but my heart rate neared aerobic nevertheless. "You can't...see anything important...can you?"

"Of course not." Beth gave my hand an encouraging tug. "Cam, you look awesome. I mean it. Like a modern-day Audrey Hepburn."

"Only with great tits."

I joined Beth in whacking Leif this time. "Are you even allowed to say *tits*? Doesn't that violate your team's code or something?"

"I can admire 'em, honey, just not lick 'em."

Downhill. Fast. Even Beth emitted a combination of gasp and giggle, not sure how to save the awful plummet of the conversation.

With movie-perfect timing, fate intervened.

New energy flowed through the crowd like an incoming wave. Whispers grew in volume. Necks craned in excitement. If we were standing outside I would've looked to the sky, expecting fireworks.

"Well, well, well," Leif murmured. "Let the party begin."

"The Cimarrons?" I actually smiled about it now. I was so glad the conversation no longer revolved around my boobs, I'd be happy for the arrival of soggy hors d'oeuvres and a troupe of dancing monkeys.

"I imagine so," Beth answered. She nodded as a stunning, petite brunette crossed the ballroom, stopping here and there to greet familiar faces or accept small bouquets of flowers. "Oh, yes. There's Jayd."

"She's the youngest of the four sibs, right?" I asked.

"Yes. And the only female."

"Wow."

Shock of shocks, that was all Leif had. I stole a look at him, wondering if he really *was* considering a team switch. Wouldn't blame him for claiming the young woman as his catalyst. Her eyes matched her name, wide and honest and accentuated by lashes so long they made her seem an exotic china doll. The effect was enhanced by her heart-shaped mouth, graceful neck, and delicate steps in a pair of gold heels that were so killer, Louboutin or Blahnik were surely the culprit. Her dress, a variation of the traditional Arcadian gown, was a shade darker than the shoes. She looked every inch a true princess.

"And the guy a few steps behind her..." I stretched *my* neck for a peek now. "He has to be one of her brothers." Not Evrest but nearly as high on the *oh my God* scale. The man matched his sister's natural grace but did it with a body that could grace a Paris runway as easily as this room. He was bad and beautiful, as arresting as James Dean crossed with an Abercrombie ad, with a touch of Jonathan Rhys Meyers thanks to the traditional amber doublet.

"That's Shiraz," Beth supplied. "Older than Jayd by ten months." She giggled. "Guess those were busy years for King Ardent and Queen Xaria."

"Whatever they did, they got it right." Leif smoothed his hair. "Damn. I claim first lick."

"*No licking.*" I fired it in tandem with Beth.

"Please." Leif turned it into two syllables. "You think Dane's going to send his art director home on a goddamn plane?"

Beth arched her brows. "Maybe not all of you. But I'd think testicles would ship nicely."

I gave her props by way of a little smile. Damn it, I didn't want to like her, but the sweet spirit and quick wit were growing on me.

At the moment, she confused me in another way. By popping her eyes open so wide, I wondered if a savage had wandered in from the rainforest. I turned my head, letting my gaze follow hers...

And instantly saw how close my guess had gotten to the target.

The next Cimarron to appear was caveman crossed with nobleman—literally. Though tall as Shiraz, he was bigger...

everywhere to be seen. Joined to his proud, high chest and chin resembling one of the bricks in the walls, his flinty stare made total sense. Filling out his notable appearance was a dark russet mane of hair, groomed into a tidy ponytail and secured with a black leather thong. His doublet was also fashioned from black leather, with red suede breeches that clearly made him as comfortable as a real ape would be at a function like this. He was flanked by a couple of guys in the impressive crimson and gold of the Arcadian military uniforms. Their build—and their scowls—matched his.

"Holy shit," I muttered.

"Paging Jane. Tarzan has arrived," Leif countered.

"He was doomed from the start." Sarcasm threaded Beth's tone. "Samsyn Cimarron. Second in line to the throne—a position he never wants to fill—thereby dictating his lifelong commitment to keep the island and his older brother safe. He oversees Arcadia's military force, keeping them ready for anything from a *medicane* to a terrorist attack."

"A medi-*what*?" Leif asked.

"A medicane. It's what they call a hurricane through this region. As in Mediterranean hurricane."

I didn't say anything. Crap. Beth was beautiful, sweet, *and* smart. The complex I'd felt coming on was officially here. *File this one under "inferiority," kids.*

Which didn't hold a candle to my brain's messed-up behavior in the next moment.

When Evrest Cimarron entered the room.

Damn.

Damn.

Damn.

While Samsyn oozed caveman, the King of Arcadia himself was pure alpha wolf. Every glance was a command, every stride filled with purpose. Leader, protector—and yes, threads of predator—I saw all of that in him, though another role was palpable in every move he made.

Lover.

Shit. *Too many tabloid fantasies, Cam.* The thought belonged nowhere in my head, nor did the flush claiming my face. Thank God Harry wasn't around to witness how it got worse as I scoped out the rest of King Alpha Wolf. He was as tall as his brother and equally as broad through the shoulders, but his body tapered from there. A well-sculpted torso. A lean waist. And then—*Oh, God*—black-clad legs, so long and defined and perfect, I wondered if they'd been custom-molded by some talented descendent of Michelangelo. His black doublet was open at the top, exposing a pendant shaped like a sun and bright as the real thing, in the hollow of his corded neck. It must've been the stand-in for his crown, which was a damn good thing. It'd be a crime to mess with the thick sable waves on his head. They were gelled into regal submission tonight, combed back from the features that made his face impossible to look away from. The high, strong forehead. The eyes, as brilliant a green as the sea outside. The slender but forceful nose. The bold juts of his jaw, making his face look narrower around the sensual curves of his lips.

I was a new commercial for butter-texture limbs.

Especially as he moved closer to us.

Closer.

Followed by a throng of women.

I noticed them the same moment Leif did. My eyes popped wide, curiosity taking hold. Wasn't like we could ignore them, since they were all the epitome of classic beauty. All their gowns were the exact same shade of red, though were cut in differing styles. They were the only women in the room who wore the color, matched to the buttons and epaulets on Evrest's doublet. It was the beginning of the theme. Not only did their clothes match the king's, but their steps did too. All the women paced themselves perfectly to him, starting and stopping their progress through the room as he did.

"Tell me I don't have to explain who that is," Beth stated.

Leif grunted. "Give us a little credit."

Without looking away from Evrest—*unable* to look away—I murmured, "But who are..."

"The groupies," Leif interjected. "She's asking about the groupies in red." He added in a stage whisper, "And does *he* know about them?"

Beth chuckled. "I would hope he does."

"Why?" I so didn't want to ask it. For some reason, anticipating the answer was a lesson in uncomfortable.

"Those ten women are known as the Distinct."

Leif snorted. "Sounds like a personal problem."

"Far from it," Beth countered. "They're likely the most envied women in the kingdom right now. They were selected using an extensive screening and algorithm process as the women in all Arcadia best suited to become queen to Evrest. Every factor was taken into consideration, including genetics, upbringing, education, temperament... The list goes on and on. These ten made the final cut. They were brought to court nearly two years ago so Evrest could spend time getting to know each of them before making his final choice of a bride."

My instinct was right. I didn't like the information. Still, I conceded, "Little better than a completely arranged marriage."

Leif snickered anew. "Also sounds like great reality TV. Oh, if the walls of that man's bedroom could sing."

"Hmmm...nope." Beth's gaze emulated the knowing lilt of her comeback. "Don't think so."

I frowned. "Huh?"

"The people expect Evrest's decision to be based on affection, compatibility, and the worthiness of the woman to be a proper queen, not sex or lust. Messing around with any of the Distinct, besides anything beyond second base, would make him a complete choad in his people's eyes, less worthy of their respect and loyalty. His credibility as a leader would be severely compromised. The girl herself, branded a slut without any control, would be forced to give back her ruby of the Distinct—"

"Those are the stones in their pendants?" I queried.

"Exactly. Each was given one when first arriving at the palais. The gems are real, mined here on the island. No matter who Evrest chooses, the necklace belongs to that Distinct for the rest of her life, unless she leaves the court in shame."

"What about the girl who gets the proposal?"

"A matching ruby engagement ring is added to the booty."

"Custom designed by the island jeweler, of course," Leif inserted, "who gets to make a special guest appearance on the 'we're getting hitched' episode of the show."

Though Beth obliged with a giggle, I was still stuck on the part about choads and sluts. "But what if things just...happen?"

"Happen?" Beth's frown belied confusion. "Like what?"

"Like chemistry. And passion. And romance. What if Evrest really does fall for someone, and the moment gets away from them? And what if he refuses to let them banish her from court for it?"

"Yeah." Leif backed me with a cute scowl. "He's the king, damn it."

"I'm not sure it's ever been tried. Arcadia is a young country by most standards. Only a little over two hundred years old."

"And we're not here to help him rewrite history." I wondered why I wanted to jump my own shit about the words. Nervous and his pal Edgy simply wouldn't leave me alone tonight, starting the moment Rosetta talked me into the flimsy underwear. The panties sure as hell weren't accomplishing their task anymore. Every moment I stared at Evrest's progress across the room, marveling at every confident step he took, made me feel more and more naked...down there.

And achier.

And wetter.

Oh my hell, I was pathetic.

"So what happens to the women he doesn't pick?" Leif asked. "Do they get to slink away in shame too? Banished to the land of hawking jewelry on home shopping channels? Wait a second. *The Distincts.* Is anyone else thinking kick-ass girl group name? Maybe somebody just needs to introduce them to YouTube."

"Actually, most of them remain here in court, serving as key staff members for the new queen or getting involved in island government," Beth explained. "The pressure of being a Distinct is ample training ground for the positions. Of course, no group of Distincts has been together this long."

I tossed a quizzing glance. "Meaning...?"

"That normally, the new king has selected a bride and gotten married by now. Evrest will be thirty in September. He's required to have a queen by then or be at risk of forfeiting the throne. It's why they started the vetting process on his twenty-eighth birthday."

"So why the heel dragging?" Leif charged.

"There're a few theories. Number one, Evrest hasn't had to hurry. Samsyn has made it violently clear he wants nothing to do with the politics of running the country. Since he's not chomping to fill Evrest's seat, the king hasn't felt a need to defend it. Others believe Evrest has been too busy for courtship. Convincing the old-guard Arcadians that saving Arcadia means opening it a little to the outside world... It's been a full-time job." Beth lifted a tiny smile. "And then there's the most obvious choice."

"Which is?" Leif obliged.

"The man's simply not in love."

My pulse stumbled a couple of beats.

No, it didn't.

And those extra pretzels you sneaked on the plane were calorie free. And your origami panties didn't just become the texture of a used paper towel.

Fine. So my bloodstream decided to throw a fiesta.

Ridiculous.

Stupid.

And utterly ill-timed, considering that King Evrest Cimarron lifted his gaze right to where we stood.

And clutched my heartbeat with the stab of his stare.

And tethered my limbs with the force of his attention.

And stopped everything else in the room as he stopped where he stood—then altered his path, walking directly over to us.

CHAPTER FOUR

"Hello."

I watched every mesmerizing inch of his lips move with the word, though the sound seemed to resonate through my heart, not my ears. On the other hand, nothing in the room moved, so it was easy for me to hear both the velvety syllables.

"Hi." I didn't push it above a rasp. I didn't want to restart the world yet—though somewhere far away, a classical guitar and a harp blended in one of the most beautiful pieces of music I'd ever heard. It helped carry my soul's plea to heaven.

Please don't let this end.

Never.

Ever.

Please.

He reached. Slipped both his hands around mine.

And the certainty encompassed my heart.

I'd been waiting for this moment. For a very long time. Perhaps forever. The air in my lungs knew it. The very marrow in my bones knew it. The reaches of my soul knew it.

Why? How?

I didn't know the questions had fallen out aloud—maybe they hadn't—but as he branded his gaze deeper into mine, I knew he'd somehow heard. The corners of his mouth turn up a little, just enough to sluice all my nerve endings with high-octane awareness. Everything became him. Only him.

"Thank you for coming." The words, while seeming rote and protocol, evoked more. There was a meaning beyond his meaning, but I couldn't grasp it. *What are you trying to say?*

I hoped my eyes conveyed the question because I couldn't speak the words. Tiny crinkles formed at the corners of his eyes, as if assuring me there was an answer to that and he couldn't wait to share it with me.

"I'm happy to be here."

Nope. *Please try your connection again.* "Happy" was for free hot fudge sundaes on my birthday or a freak heat wave in January. This was something past happy. Something that didn't have a word. Something twined to the completion of my hands inside his, my nearness to him, the electricity of my whole body in his presence.

"Are you certain of that?" His thumbs caressed the insides of my wrists, shooting rockets through my belly and fireworks through my brain.

Fireworks? Seriously, Cam?

But it made sense. Weirdly, insanely, suddenly, everything just...made sense.

"It's just hard to believe this is happening." I'd caught the double-meaning virus too—and it felt pretty nice. Until now, the whole living-in-a-dream thing was confined to excitement about the movie and simply being here in Arcadia. That was before this. Before him. Before the bubble that lowered over the two of us, this strange and wonderful cocoon sealed by the bridge of our touch, the embrace of our stares, the lock of our spirits...

Not just meeting each other. Recognizing each other.

"I am Evrest." He dipped toward me, an edge of bashfulness in his voice. So beautiful. I treasured every note, gluing the sound to my memory like a precious flower in a scrapbook.

"I'm...Cam."

"Cam." He extended the last letter, almost turning the word into a silken song. My lips parted as I imagined how it would feel if he did that against my bare skin, though I didn't dare venture on what body part. Did it matter? His smile, parting wider, provided *that* definitive answer. Didn't matter one damn bit.

"It's actually...Camellia." *Yes. Go for the formality. Maybe it'll hoist your mind out of the gutter.* "Camellia Saxon. I'm the film's production manager."

"Is that so?" Like I'd just given him the coolest piece of trivia in the world. Damn, he was good. No wonder the gossip mag writers loved him so—and I yearned to splash right back into the gutter.

"Uhh, yeah. *Yes.* But...uhhh...call me whatever you like. Nobody really calls me Camellia, except my mother. And Harry, when he's in a snit with me. Which is at least once a day." I glanced away. "Shit; like you need to know that."

I slammed my eyes shut and clamped my mouth. *You did not just drop an S-bomb on the king of this island. At his state dinner. Less than five minutes after meeting him.*

He released one of my hands. Dread slammed in as I prepared for him to move on, shattering the magic bubble forever. *Way to swing it, girlfriend.*

I didn't expect a warm, firm finger at my chin, pressing until I raised my head and opened my eyes...to be consumed by the intensity of his gaze once more.

"Can I use it without being...in a snit...with you?"

I couldn't help a tiny laugh. The pauses he inserted around

the slang were blatantly innocent, an open invitation to look at the boy inside the sleek, sophisticated man. "I meant what I said. Use whatever you like, Your Majesty."

His finger stiffened beneath my chin. So did the whole of his face. My evocation of the formality had clearly pulled his tail, but ignoring the truth wasn't an option here. Bubbles were special because they were temporary. Smashable. I'd just been the first to get out the pin.

I wasn't the last. The woman closest to Evrest, clearly the alpha she-wolf of the Distinct, stepped up and looped an arm beneath his. Demure—but damn clear. *Back off, bitch.*

Got it.

The shitty thing was, she was a hundred percent justified. I was drooling all over her man—her king—like a bitch in heat, likely fulfilling every ugly preconception they had about American women.

I backed up. A lot.

Alpha Distinct didn't waste time dropping her next line. "Welcome to Arcadia." Her voice, softly accented, evoked Sophia Loren. Her big eyes, full lips, and notable cleavage supported the impression. Even modern Audrey Hepburn was no match. "I am Chianna. I believe I speak for everyone this evening when I say what a joy it is to have you in our home."

Clearly, the nine women behind her had different ideas about that—but I couldn't tell if they disagreed with all or part of her statement. I *did* know that if their glares really were daggers, Chianna would be standing in a puddle of her own blood by now.

"Thank you, Chianna." Thank God for Beth, who moved forward with a princess's grace. "I am—"

"Oh, I know who you are." The woman's smile was full of forced gleam. "Miss Beth Michele. The star of Mr. Dane's movie. Your list of accomplishments is impressive." Translation: *I know how to use the internet too—so don't test me, American bimbo.*

"Why, thank you. That is so sweet!" I doubted anyone but Leif and I could tell that Beth's smile was just as feigned. Damn, did I want to smirk. Beth didn't like Chianna any more than I did—and while that gave me yet more respect for her, it didn't help my newest dilemma. Watching Chianna cling tighter to Evrest was like witnessing an octopus wrap itself around prey.

The new tension in Evrest's stance made the ordeal worse—yet better too. I felt justifiably weird about that, not to mention my dorky hope of him tossing a glance my way again. I needed to gain some perspective on whatever the hell had just happened between us.

Or maybe...what hadn't happened.

Bingo.

That had to be it. My exhaustion had simply twisted those moments into an out-of-control fantasy. All that energy hadn't truly sparked between us. I hadn't really yearned that he'd keep lifting my chin until our mouths met. I hadn't entertained the lust that it continue further, nor seen the brilliance in his eyes, echoing the same desire. His magnetism, effortless but intoxicating, had fed the vision. He was the son of a proud leader, bred to be the same. No wonder my sleep-deprived brain took that power, stirred my wicked desires into the mix, and created a nonexistent reality.

Huge relief time. I actually sighed from it. Curious looks instantly fired at me from the ranks of the Distinct, but Chianna had already tugged Evrest too far away to hear. They headed toward a set of massive double doors on the far side of the ballroom. The crowd followed the pair and we followed suit, picking up Joel and Dottie along the way, updating classic Hollywood in their own right in ensembles evoking Sinatra and Gardner's most glamorous days. As we walked, minstrels with lutes and guitars wandered through the throng. Their tunes were similar to the beautiful melody I'd heard a few minutes ago.

Aha. No angels on high, just talented musicians doing their part to welcome us to the island. As more layers of reality were revealed, I felt better about writing off my first-meeting-with-the-king pyrotechnics as first-impression jitters.

The doors opened, revealing that the ballroom led to a sweeping, two-tiered terrace constructed of polished stone. I barely held back a delighted gasp. *Buonasera*, every romantic villa fantasy I'd conjured since sighing through *Under the Tuscan Sun*. Wisteria and sunflowers, wrought iron and balustrades...all given unique Arcadian touches of carved gold doves nesting in bouquets of freesia and jasmine. There were a thousand more candles out here, lighted in standing candelabras down the centers of linen-covered feasting tables. As more of the crowd filled the terrace, the Arcadians chuckled while the Americans damn near applauded.

"Damn," Leif muttered to Beth and me. "Is this kind of shit *usual* for them?"

"Think *I* could get used to it." Beth's smile wasn't just for the décor. Harry approached, a dashing grin on his handsome features, his hair gelled in similar fashion to Evrest's. And holy crap, did he nail the doublet look. His cobalt jerkin and black breeches hugged his lithe body in ways that already had Beth's face lighting up with sexy mischief.

"Wow." Harry murmured it while kissing her hand. "Good thing I left *you* in charge of these two while I got pretty, Leif."

"Didn't attempt a single lick." Leif ducked closer to amend, "Though I can't say the same about our tall, sexy, follow-me-to-the-seventh-circle host."

"Huh?" Harry's gaze gained a strange fire. "Who? Evrest?"

"Damn it, Leif." Beth rolled her eyes. "Did you have to go there?"

"Damn it, Leif *what*?" Harry swung his glower back at her. "He didn't—" Pushed out a bull snort. "Evrest knows we're together, B. If he tried a play for you—"

"*Down*, sparky." I called his Ferdinand the Bull with a full Xena, hands on hips. "No 'plays' were made on anyone, all right?"

Though Beth flung a glare as if to tell me I was full of shit, she pressed her lips together, remaining silent.

"Meh." Leif rocked his head back and forth. "What do I know about formal protocol anyway? And if the guy wants to play smooth operator, he has ten deterrents practically clinging to him. Except our luscious Chianna. Pretty sure she won't settle for anything less than cock."

Beth and I burst into giggles. Even Harry couldn't hold back a small smirk. "Okay, okay," he chided. "Let's all sit down and do this dinner thing so we can finally go to bed. Whatever they've fixed, it smells damn good."

Leif offered his arm as we walked out to the terrace. I accepted with a smile, happy to feel my tension ebb for the first time since putting on the gown. Things were stabilizing. We were back on track toward changing the world—after some food and sleep. Harry was right; dinner smelled great.

What a difference fifteen minutes could make.

With just a few sips of melon soup down, my stomach led another revolt. Though my taste buds protested, having heartily approved of the rich, cold bisque, my belly twisted the stuff like tension taffy.

It had gotten some hefty help.

Leif, Joel, Dottie, and I had been seated halfway down the table presided over by Evrest. Harry and Beth occupied the seats of honor to the king's right, turning the seats on his left into prime real estate for the members of the Distinct to battle over.

"Battle" being a subjective term.

As in...underestimation.

We watched as three of the women pulled the place card switch, taking advantage of the moment Chianna had to stop while Evrest greeted a group of men definitely on the event's VIP list. They all wore ceremonial sashes stitched with the Arcadian country emblem, a dove with sunbeams for wings. Like staring at the bird of peace made any difference to Chianna. When she and Evrest approached the table, she "accidentally" elbowed a waiter bearing a tray of champagne flutes, drenching the trio who'd dared cross her. As the three were cleaned up by servants, she smoothly stepped back into place at Evrest's left, voicing "concern" for her "friends" during every moment of the coup.

"Mee-oww," Leif murmured. "The kittens are feisty."

"Hey! No dissin' on the kittahs." Dottie huffed. "My Sadie and Sally wouldn't lower one paw into that kind of shit."

"While competing with ten other kittens for the attention of one tomcat?" I countered.

Leif snorted. "I'm still looking for the hidden TV cameras. Especially because Evrest baby does *not* look happy about little Chia Pet's shenanigans."

He was right. Evrest's features, schooled into a cordial smile for his dignitaries, went stormy when discovering Chianna still glued to his side. He stood and raised his glass for the crowd, but the action was stilted, followed by fast mutterings about how we all must be hungry. His "bon appétit" was almost an afterthought, punched out before his ass hit the chair again. He'd surely prepared more of a formal welcome, but his fury at the women's antics strangled him from giving it.

I hated watching him like this.

Like this? *Like* what? *You have no damn idea what he's like at all. And you shouldn't care, either. You* can't *care.*

One of the women who'd been treated to the champagne bath, a willowy blonde with innocent blue eyes, sniffed as she passed us on the way to her new place assignment—nearly at the end of the table. Her dress was soaked, and it looked like her face was soon about to be. I was moved to see that Evrest didn't miss a moment of her misery, either. His nostrils flared, broadcasting his augmented rage. His compassion for the woman's humiliation, along with Chianna's blissful blind eye toward it, made my stomach turn harder.

My spoon slid from my fingers. The soup was now as appetizing as pond scum. "Ta-ta, appetite."

Leif huffed. "You're crazy. This is the best dinner theater I've seen in years."

"Ditto," Joel murmured, practically inhaling his soup.

Dottie rolled her eyes. "You two are pigs."

"Oink, oink." Leif waggled his brows. "But clean us up and dress us right, and we're cute as hell."

I folded my napkin and set it on the table. "Well, I can't watch any longer." A waiter passed with perfect timing. I grabbed his elbow and pointed toward the pretty blonde. "Excuse me? Can you help me? That woman, sitting down over there...please tell her I'm not feeling well and retiring early. I'd like her to have my place here." As I rose, I shot a glance to Dottie. "Make sure these two behave and make that poor woman feel welcome."

"Got your six." Dot's dad was a former Navy SEAL, so military-isms were part of her vernacular.

I crossed paths with the blonde on my way out. She didn't hesitate to seize both my hands and give me a bath in her watery stare. "Merderim, sweet lady. From the depths of my heart, you have my thanks."

The warmth of her words eased the knot in my belly. "It's nothing," I assured. "And I'm sorry it's not nearer to His Majesty, but at least it's not with the kids at the card table in the other room."

Her brows bunched. "Kids? Card table?"

"With the children," I clarified.

She laughed. The sound was pretty and feminine. "Children sound nice right now. They are honest, never feeling the need to speak unpleasantries behind their hands."

"Excellent point."

Her face fell back into sadness. "I have them...every so often."

"Probably more than that," I assured. Sheez, I really liked her—but I wondered how she'd match up to Evrest as a queen. The man was a heady combination of power and sexuality. He was going to need a tigress.

Like Chianna?

Oh, God.

There had to be a happy medium somewhere in that crowd of Distincts.

"I am Novah." She extended a hand, elegant and tapered with flawless fingernails. I hid my wince at the pinky nail I'd chewed off during the air turbulence between Athens and Sancti.

"Camellia. But please call me Cam."

"Cam." Her echo was gentle and respectful, a far cry from the inflection Evrest had given it...as if he'd been contemplating how it would sound when he growled it against my ear. "I am pleased to have your acquaintance, Cam." Her face twisted on another frown. "Ugh. I should have known not to believe Chianna when she told us all you Americans were crass and selfish."

Her revelation didn't surprise me. We'd all expected some distrust from the Arcadians. That Chianna had led the charge of it with the Distincts wasn't a shocker. "Well, I hope we'll change your mind about that."

Novah squeezed my hands again. "You already have."

I left the ballroom with lighter steps. No matter what kind of drama I'd encountered around meeting Arcadia's king, at least I'd made a new friend. For now, I'd count that as a win.

★ ★ ★

I made my way back down the spacious palace hallways toward my room. My accommodations were nearly as sumptuous as Harry's, with a feminine touch to the décor. Earlier, it had taken a lot of willpower not to sink into the bed, a canopied piece of classic and modern lines topped by a comforter that looked more like a cloud. Damn, I wish I was tired enough for it now. The afternoon's espresso binge was taking revenge.

At least I could make use of the time before the caffeine crash set in. The production office wasn't going to set itself up. If I remembered right, the room was one level down and directly below mine, which meant a fast descent down the stairs would take me...

Right to the door.

I entered the room and instantly went for tonight's default on reactions. The awestruck gasp was about my five hundredth of the night—like I could help it any more than the others. Office? The place looked more like a living room designed by a billionaire sheikh and his oil baron friend. A warm combination of rich woods, lavish tapestries, and leather furniture were an invitation to settle in and read a book, not deal with the day-to-day stresses of a movie shoot. But I wasn't about to share that with anyone.

"I think we can deal with this, homies." I sat on the ledge of the aged marble hearth. In the grate behind me there was a bed of glass pieces in place of kindling and logs. Surprisingly, the choice fit the room, the amber-tinted stones forming a modern complement to the fireplace's classic Greek lines.

I peered out the French doors across the room, slightly ajar and revealing another of the palace's patios. Though the sea was dark now, I readily envisioned how breathtaking the vista would be in a few hours. The space also featured a kitchenette with all the latest appliances, plus a sturdy wood table with accommodation for six chairs—in addition to the mammoth piece that was going to be my desk for the next six weeks.

I couldn't resist another gasp of disbelief. "Toto, I don't think we're in Kansas anymore."

"Please do not click your ruby slippers yet."

My heartbeat tripled before my head snapped up—responding to the dark, silken words, issued by the equally entrancing man consuming the doorway. With the calculated ease of the Big Bad Wolf himself, he braced an arm to the jamb, his eyes glittering as brightly as the sun-shaped pendant at his throat.

CHAPTER FIVE

Ohhhh, my God.

His burnished beauty, so fitting in the grand scale of the ballroom, dominated the space in here—and crowded the words from the sudden Sahara of my throat. And while I'd yearned for the world to go away when he'd first clasped my hand, I prayed neither the floor—nor my knees—would give out as he stepped closer now.

Then sat beside me.

So close.

Not close enough.

I wet my lips. He did the same.

I couldn't look away from his brilliant green eyes. He didn't move, either.

Gazing at each other. Recognizing each other.

"You left the dinner." His words would have been accusation if not for his husky inflection. His gaze abandoned some of its glitter for an influx of unblinking focus. Either way, I was a goner. *Great.*

"Well...so did you." Amazed chuckle. I'd actually been able to speak—and even sounded a little glib. At least I thought so. The whole world was back to being surreal. "And I'm certain your exit was noticed more than mine, Your Majesty."

His brows crowded over his eyes. He really didn't like it when I went for the formal address. "Is the cuisine not to your liking?" His voice dipped as his head did, leaning in closer. "I can have the kitchen make something else. They have stocked up on many American favorites..."

I let him slip into silence, hoping he'd start talking again. The yummy blend of burlap and velvet in his voice, wrapped around that mixture of accents... I was certain the man could recite the Bible and be found guilty of verbal foreplay.

"The food was delicious. I'm just not hungry." My words were just as taut, but I had an excuse. Relaxing the tension that radiated from the crux of my thighs was damn near impossible. The man made me think of salacious things...like what the skin felt like beneath his pendant. Or what it looked like under his shirt. Or what everything would look like if he took off *all* his clothes and stretched his tall body out on his undoubtedly huge, kingly bed...

What part of "dangerous thinking" are you not getting here, girlfriend?

Likely the same part that continued right on its illicit track as Evrest pivoted his whole body in now, allowing me an inhalation of his scent. *Gah.* Yeah...wonderful. Sophisticated. Expensive. All man, bringing a rich blend of sandalwood, sage, and the sea along for the ride.

I was drawn closer before realizing what I was doing. So close, I could watch the artery in his neck beating against his rugged skin.

"Why did you really leave?" His grate was quiet...intimate. And shouldn't have felt so right...but did.

I steeled my chin. "Because I'm really not hungry."

"Hmm." He wasn't convinced. One bit.

Time for the deflector shields. "Okay. Why did *you* leave?"

He pressed a little closer. Correction: loomed. Holy shit, he was so big. And chiseled. And gorgeous. So much for the deflection tactic. My heart kicked into a sprint. My lungs couldn't catch up. And the ache in my sex was a throb I didn't even try to stop anymore. No wonder all those women concocted such crazy stunts to get closer to him.

He pulled away a little, allowing me a respite—but also breathing like he needed one himself. He leaned outward, bracing an elbow on his knee, but still looked at me as if a question brimmed on his impossibly full lips. Yet when he spoke, it was again with reflective confidence.

"A little more than three years ago, I accompanied my father on a journey to the United States. He wanted me to help select a university for my sister, Jayd, to attend." Regret crinkled the corners of his eyes. "We fought bitterly about the trip."

"Why?"

"I would have preferred dental surgery to going. I had finally earned my master's degree in Paris but done it between official duties back here and trips to Finland to check on Shiraz, who was studying science and math at university there. For many years, my life had been nonstop traveling and studying. All I wanted was some freedom before the process for the Distinct began and my life was officially no longer my own."

Curiosity stabbed. "What about Samsyn? Was he at university too?"

It was good to see him chuckle again, though I was clueless where the joke lay. "Samsyn passed through the Arcadian version of high school by the skin of his teeth and the prayers of my mother—to anyone in the heavens who listened," he explained. "And likely a deal my father made with the lord of the other side, as well." Against the background of my giggles, he added, "Syn was born to be a warrior, not a scholar, a fact

I am grateful for every day as I watch him build our military capabilities. While it is unlikely we will ever rattle our sabers in a world war, we can at least defend the island against any outside invasion."

I straightened a little. "That's a possibility?"

His expression clouded. "More than you may think."

"Wow."

"Yes." His tone edged toward grave. "Wow."

"Because you've been pushing to relax the borders?"

"Just the opposite. Syn wants the borders *more* fluid." He caught my questioning look and responded, "If we start trading our natural resources, it would make the—how do you Americans say it?—'baddies' less motivated to invade and steal them."

"Ah."

He let a long stillness pass—but didn't release me from the force of his stare, thickening with intensity...and sensuality. "I do not want to talk about war right now."

"Me neither."

He still didn't blink. Literally. What the hell was transfixing him so deeply? I'd only had some soup tonight, not enough for food between my teeth. Crap. Had I developed one of my too-stressed-out zits at the base of my nose?

My runaway nerves finally took over. "Well, make love not war, right?" *Take head. Plunge into hands.* "Annnd I did *not* just say that."

He chuckled, throwing me off yet again. Damn it, he wasn't supposed to be making me feel like the wittiest thing on the planet for that. "One of my job requirements is the ability to listen well. To *everything.*"

"Fine. Then you're hereby ordered to forget you 'listened well' to that."

There was the line he should've chuckled at. Instead, Evrest went so still, I wondered what invisible line I'd accidentally crossed.

"It is impossible to forget anything about you, Miss Saxon."

Take turbo key, insert into chest. Along with it, a thousand other senses revved. I couldn't fight the instinct that once again he spoke a handful of words standing proxy for hundreds more...hinting at a connection between us, beyond tonight, that I still couldn't comprehend. And like before, I had nothing in return but a blank stare and a frantically pumping chest— both only seeming to feed *his* serenity.

Damn it.

"Perhaps I should elucidate," he murmured.

"Perhaps you should," I snapped.

Evrest pivoted back, resting both elbows on his knees. "As I said, touring the US with Father was not my first choice of ways to spend a month." He meshed his fingers and studied their juncture. "I was young and selfish, wrapped in foolish needs to sow a few wild oats instead of acknowledging the opportunities of my life."

I shoulder-bumped him. "You're allowed, you know. Sounds like you were just a little fried."

He frowned. "Fried?"

"Yeah. You know, burned out." That didn't help. I racked my brain for the British or French equivalent. "Umm... knackered?"

That earned me a grin. "Right. Knackered. Here, we just say *bit*. It's a short version of the Turkish word for exhausted."

"Hmm. Works in English too."

"Better than comparing yourself to a basket of fish and chips." When I took my turn at a confused glance, he added, "Fried? Burned?"

I let the rest of my laugh out. "Okay, point made. You were dragged against your will. I'm sure that made things *very* interesting for your dad."

He cocked a brow. "Why do you say that?"

I pulled my knees against my chest and rested my head on them. "You don't strike me as the kind of guy who feels things halfway." I smirked. "I'll bet you were as much fun as an eight-year-old having to sit through church."

He returned the look though showed a peek of white teeth—and a devilish glint in his gaze. "Church is not so bad sometimes."

"Try telling that to an eight-year-old."

A nod, surrendering the point to me—but taking back his seriousness in exchange. "We toured a number of campuses during our trip," he revealed, "though we were discreet about it, at Father's strict bidding. His choice to let Shiraz and me study abroad was already a sore point with many of the high council members."

"The retro brigade, huh?" When his brows hunkered all over again, I amended, "The old-school funk?"

"Old!" He nodded eagerly. "Yes, yes. The...old-school funk."

As he finished the echo, I detected a bunch of meanings in his tone. More than anything, a lot of conflict. He was probably tight with many of those men, who'd likely known him since birth—but who now held his country back from surviving in a world that sped further ahead with every passing day. *Ish.* Couldn't be easy to be him right now.

"So they'd already popped a few gaskets about you and Shiraz going to school in Europe. And the fact that your dad was thinking of the same for their kingdom's sole princess, this time in the wicked wasteland of America..." Heavy exhale of comprehension. "Yeah; discretion would've been my call too."

"Of course it would have."

He said it with confidence, like confirming the sky was blue. A stupid grin tilted my lips. Weirdly, it was one of the hugest compliments anyone had ever given me. Not that my world view depended on such bullshit. Okay, so it *had* been fun to be Audrey Hepburn for a night, especially when recognizing that Evrest wouldn't gawk at me once my hair and face were back to basic makeup and a double-pencil bun—but to have him see that I could think on my own too...it felt good. Really good.

Too good.

Time to stand down, girl.

I forced myself to mean it, ignoring the carved, perfect allure of him as I straightened back to Diane Sawyer decorum. With a respectful tone to match, I prompted, "Okay, so there you were, on the great father-son college road trip..."

He broke in with a wry twist of lips. "How loose do you play with *great* in that assessment?"

"How loose should I be playing?" When both his brows arched, I plunged on, "All right, all right. I'll play along. What happened?"

His expression dipped deeper into cryptic. I fought a huff, feeling as if I worked to identify a ghost hanging out between us, waiting for the ideal moment to materialize. He'd thrown a lot of specters at me tonight, but this one was the biggest. The feeling wasn't foreign. I normally called it anticipation—

except anticipation didn't cut my breath short and make my palms get all sweaty.

Finally, in that voice like a panther treading across velvet, he answered. "Not *what* happened. *Who* happened."

Just like that, the ghost materialized.

Only it was he.

Hell. It had been him all along. It explained the enigma that really wasn't. The shadows in his words, beyond reach yet so touchable. The connection to his presence...and the clarity of what he implied now.

You *happened.*

I asked him a hundred questions with my stare alone. Evrest dipped closer. His smile was so serene, it truly belonged on a panther.

"I should be freaking out." I dragged frantic fingers through my hair. "This should be freaking me out. *You* should be freaking me out. Why am I not freaking out?"

He laughed softly—*shit, his lips looked good when he did that*—before pulling my hands down and intertwining our fingers. "You are very fascinating when you are 'not freaking out.'"

So warm. So strong. Damn it, what his touch alone did to my bloodstream...like soaking in a bubble bath at the end of a shit day. Entrancing to the point of addicting—and impossible to walk away from. "I sure as hell hope there's more to this story," I snapped.

He should have laughed again. Instead, he turned my hand over and stroked its inner lines, wrist to fingertips, over and over across my sensitive palm.

Shivers...everywhere. Good ones. Too good...

He spoke with equal deliberation, every word soft and steady. "The morning we were scheduled to visit the Chapman campus, I was an especially huge ass to my father. What we fought about, I do not even remember. It is distant, irrelevant... but seemed so important then. Important enough that he rearranged the day's itinerary to let me cool off."

Ohhh, he kept up the caresses. He needed to stop. I'd *make* him stop. In just another moment...or fifty.

Despite the torture-that-really-wasn't, I managed a coherent reply. "You know, your dad doesn't seem like a half-bad guy." I thought back to Harry's first mention of King Ardent, of his struggles to guide his people to modern prosperity despite being thwarted by a high council who couldn't pull their heads out of their asses.

Evrest's soft smile backed my claim. "He is a good man," he asserted. "Better than I gave him credit for most of the time, especially for putting up with a hothead wanker of an offspring like me."

Giggle. "Gee. Don't sugar coat things on my account, Your Majesty."

Once more, my slang clearly flew past him. My delivery in the key of snark seemed to help on the communication—though the reaction I expected was still a no-show on his features.

He gave me something better. A knowing, sexy-as-hell grin. "For the first and only time in my life, my temper worked to my advantage. Because of the change in our schedule that day, we arrived at Chapman during the lunch hour. We were walking across the plaza in front of the library just as another visitor made his way on campus—another father, arriving for a surprise visit to his daughter."

Whoa.

Chain reaction of shock, cluster bombs across my psyche. But right after the explosions, a bizarre wave of relief. Suddenly, all the jagged confusion about this man began to smooth...a connection that elevated everything into some real sense...

The memory was easy to yank up. It had been the one and only day Dad visited me at school, a surprise drop-in when a Brazilian rainforest expedition ended early. Best moment of that school year, hands down—and now that it flared so fully in my mind, every second blazed as clear as a memory from days ago instead of years. My excited scream at Dad. His shit-eating grin in reply. Then all the craned necks and curious smiles from onlookers around the plaza...including the dark, exotic stranger beside one of the campus guides, with a gaze that pierced even across the fifty feet of concrete between us... so quickly forgotten when Dad and I followed it up by walking to Old Towne Orange to forage through antique stores and suck down old-fashioned milk shakes at the Watson's Drug ice cream counter.

Scratch the "school year" designation. It'd been one of the best afternoons of my *life*.

"So was the girl surprised?" I let my grin go impish.

Evrest surprised me again with his reaction. Instead of the bigger smile I expected, his expression softened but intensified—though not back to panther mode. He was all man, hulking and masculine and edged in rough energy, as he dropped his head close once more. "She was indeed surprised. But there was more to it than that. At least to me."

"More?" I yearned to lean in just as much as him, to get lost in the sea foam of his eyes. *Not. An. Option.* Resisting him had been tough enough in a crowded ballroom, with the built-in buffer of his would-be fiancées. Now we were alone, with nothing between us but words. *His* words, filled with such sincerity and strength, about to justify why we'd really been drawn so strongly to each other earlier. If that was the case, verifying we'd just *repeated* the cosmic coincidence, I had every right to a full freak-out. And still I muttered, "What do you mean, more?"

His lips quirked again. "I will not lie. At first, it was sheer lust that locked my attention to her."

"Excuse me?" I laughed it out—past my disappointment. Maybe I'd gotten this way wrong. Maybe he wasn't referring to me after all.

Evrest squared his shoulders. "It has been a few years," he charged, voice growly, "but I shall never forget *that* part of things. Her smile... It lit the whole plaza, even in broad sunshine. The contrast of her hair, falling over her shoulders like a cascade of midnight. And her skin... It gleamed like cream turned to silk, making me wonder if it was really as soft as it looked..."

As he spoke of each feature, he studied over the corresponding one—on me. When his topic switched to my skin, he expanded the study, poring his gaze over every inch of my body. Holy shit. This man's stare gleamed like Kryptonite and was rapidly becoming that to every inch of me. Weakness in my limbs. Fire in my blood. Even the spaces between my toes were ignited.

"Okay." Rickety syllables. By divine grace, I avoided profanity—though hell, was I tempted. "L-Let's say that's the way it did go down—"

"Well, nothing fell." His brows pushed together, working to decipher my phrase. "But if you are asking about how things happened, I assure you the account is accurate."

"All right, all right; I believe you."

"But you still have questions."

"Just one." Perplexed sigh. "So for all her brilliance, the woman didn't notice *you* standing there"—*beautiful trouble, come to life*—"gawking at her? How? Why?"

There it was, without filter. While his story answered a lot of questions, it created another—so important, it counted for double points. How did he remember that day so clearly, when I didn't? When I *should* have. Okay. it'd been three years ago, but no girl in her right mind would forget eyes like his, part of a face like his, making her the sole subject of his entrancing focus...

I racked my brain once more. Zilch on the recall. My sole remembrance was the joy I'd felt at having Dad to myself for an afternoon. I didn't even tell Mom about it until months later. It had been our time, special and sacred. When one had been sired by the real-life version of Indiana Jones, afternoons like that were truly once-in-a-lifetime.

"I think you already know the answer to that." Evrest's stare didn't waver. "I see it in your eyes. They shine now just as they did that day, when you greeted your father. You did not notice me 'gawking' because Father and I were not there to be noticed. Our security team followed us at a discreet distance, and our campus guide was instructed that we required a low profile, to observe what the school was like on a typical day."

"Well, you sure did that part right."

"I was glad for it too," he replied. "Especially after that day."

I frowned. "Back in the weeds of confusion here."

He let out a little breath, not quite a sigh, while lightly venturing his fingers across the back of my hand. "Watching you with your father... It was, for me, like—how would you phrase it?—lightning? Getting...zapped?"

A laugh bubbled out. Couldn't be helped. He linked the sensation to *me*, when his touch wreaked the same havoc? "Why?"

"It woke me up. *You* woke me up, Camellia Saxon."

Hard gulp. The intensity of his words, coupled with the tingles from his touch... Shit, I was really going to melt. "But you didn't even know who I was."

"I did after that day."

Harder gulp. "You...investigated me or something?" My "freaked out" should've morphed into "creeped out"...but didn't. That should've set off alarms but also didn't. What the hell?

"No." He shook his head, dipping into boyish awkwardness with it. "I might have...asked about you. Maybe...checked on you through the internet every once in a while. That was all."

Hell. He was just as captivating without the elegance as he was in full wolf mode. That was a good thing, since my own throat seemed to be suffering a rockslide too. "You...Googled me?"

He shrugged. "Once. Or twice...when I was traveling and could get better web connection than what we had here." He averted his gaze.

"So you knew I'd be with the film crew?"

His stare locked back to me. *On* me. Like a damn laser slicing open a diamond. "No. But I sure as hell hoped it."

Ohhh, it was *so* time to change the subject.

"Tell me more...about that day. Why did you say I 'woke you up'?"

His nod was resolute. "It happened inside a moment. I looked at Father and suddenly realized something important. For the first time, I perceived him as simply a man, instead of the king of our country—who also happened to be my father. Watching the joy you shared with your father brought back the awareness of mine. His humanity...and his mortality. Though he has now passed the crown to me, he always worked too hard, drank too much, and loved his cigars nearly as much as his country." He chuckled, emphasizing the exaggeration. "He did not savor his moments...and before we all knew it, they were gone. It...zapped me." His forehead furrowed. "It still does."

Sadness crept into his eyes. My heart tightened. "Is he... still around?"

"Yes...but no." His shoulder lifted again. "He keeps his distance, even when I am not engaged in official duties. I am not certain why. Perhaps he thinks I need to make my own way, forge my own decisions and policies, but...I miss him sometimes, as if he were already gone."

I worked my fingers between his. "I'm sorry."

"Do not be." He tightened our clasp. "The Creator gave me broad shoulders for many burdens."

And for me to ogle any chance I could?

"Besides," he went on, "it makes the moments I *do* get with him that much more valuable. Times that I take full advantage of, as the gifts they are—thanks to the revelation I had that day." His free hand rose, tilting my face back up to meet his gaze. "That was all because of you, Miss Camellia Saxon of Chapman University."

Thud.

Dork factor, ten. But perfection for the moment? Equal score. The term nailed the thunder in my chest—and the nosedive my composure longed to take to the floor.

Focus on what he said, not on how he said it. Or how incredible the garnishes were, like his fingers against my cheek, his scent in my every breath, his face so close I could simply curl a hand into his doublet and tug him a few inches closer...

Oh, *God.* I was a few extra steps toward hell, without a doubt. Worse, I just kept going, using his meaningful moment of confession into a platform for my wicked thoughts—which likely would have become full, hot fantasies, if not for him speaking up again.

"So there lies my truth," he murmured. "And yes, I have remembered you through the years. The Chapman lightning flash with midnight hair and daybreak eyes, who made me see things in a new and different way one afternoon."

It wasn't a full whisper—though came close enough to count. Like it mattered. His honesty, so bold and bare, crashed the words over me like a full symphony, turning my senses into equally stunned mush.

Self-control be screwed, if only for a moment. I gave in to the music, indulging the need to touch him in return.

Forget grabbing his doublet. I had one chance, and I had to make it count. I went for his jaw, sifting fingers through the spikes of his stubble before spilling the words in my own heart.

"Like you changed everything for me tonight."

His brows lowered. A ragged breath escaped him. His fingers wound to my nape. He used the hold to drag me closer. "Tell me," he grated. "*Tell me.*"

To my shock—and horror—tears seeped out. What. The. Hell? Oh, God. *Now* the caffeine drop hit. That had to be the explanation—*not* the gut-deep honesty of my next words. "Look, I didn't accept this job from Harry out of the complete kindness of my heart. I...I came with baggage. Goals beyond just the movie. Expectations of what I wanted to achieve, ideals that might even be crazy in a few people's books."

He rubbed a thumb against the base of my scalp. "Crazy is not against the law in Arcadia, little lightning."

"Very good to know." I managed a watery smile. "Though if your loony bins are half as nice as the palais, sign me up."

"Was that how I helped, then? Do the ideas not seem so crazy now?"

"Oh, they're just as crazy. But along with all the other balls in my fun personal circus, they make a lot of noise." I pointed at my head, inciting him to a soft laugh.

"I understand."

I bet he really did. "Well, for a few seconds tonight, all of that was..."

"What?"

"Stopped." I twined my fingers into his hair to keep his stare fixed to mine. "I know that sounds weird. I also don't know how else to describe it, except that the anticipations, the demands, the baggage... In those few moments with you in the ballroom...it all went away. You—well, you just banished all of it."

He inhaled, deep and full. Slid his hand around to wick the drops from my cheeks. "And that was...good?"

"Ohhhh, yes. *Good.* I won't—I can't—stop the world very often."

"Why?"

I shrugged. "Logistical impossibility. Too busy. Too much going on. Keeping up. Keeping alive. Expectations are demanding things, you know."

"Fuck that."

Blink. Blink. "You sure as hell know *that* one, don't you?"

"Especially when I am right."

I shrugged again. Not so easy this time. "Right or not, the point is irrelevant. It's not like I can run to you whenever the circus goes too nuts. I don't even want to ask how many rules we're breaking right now, just by—"

He shut down my words by grabbing both sides of my head. His fingers stretched back, tangling in my hair, extending from my cheeks to well past my ears. His hold was hard and persistent and possessive—and I wanted more even as I ordered myself not to. My vision tunneled into him, and my head swam...as the world tumbled away once more. Just as it had in the ballroom, the room spun then stopped...and then faded. Nonexistent.

He was the only thing in my cognizance—and I in his. I didn't just sense the completeness of his focus. I knew it, as if every cell in his body sent out a homing sensor to mine and they pinged back at once. Thrilled? Terrified? I didn't know which to be.

Both?

I struggled to recall a time with Harry that had ever been like this, but even during sex, the director in him didn't rest. I'd always see him calculating artsy angles on the scene through every damn minute. Though he always left the bed satisfied, I'd wondered how much of our "passion" wound up on the editing room floor in his mind.

"Tell me now." Evrest's command was low but musical, a seduction wrapped in dominant syntax. Thunder calling to my lightning...

"Tell...you what?" I whispered.

"That I still make it all stop. That it's all gone away again." The tips of his fingers curled in, pulling my hair. "Tell me, Camellia."

I opened my mouth. Slammed it. Oh God, how I wanted to appease him. Could almost envision how his eyes would spark, how his lips would lift, how he'd reward me...with a mind-stopping kiss. The drop of his gaze to my mouth escorted the fantasy deeper in, bursting it to life in my imagination. The best thing of all about my obeisance? It would be the truth. Every word. *Yes. It's true, Evrest. It's all fallen away again. You make everything stop for me.*

"I–" The words clamored at the bottom of my throat. Clawed at me in their need for release. "Evrest–"

"Tell. Me."

"I can't." I let my hands fall just as his did. "*I can't.* I'm not even going to apologize for it. You know why as clearly as I do."

He surged to his feet. Crossed to the kitchenette in order to splash water on his face and neck. I sneaked in a glance at other things too. *Hell.* His crotch also needed the cold bath— though if he went that route, explaining the splotch between his thighs might not be the best take-home memory to give the state dinner crowd.

"Fuck," he snarled.

"Okay. You *really* know that one."

Him: simmering at the sink. Me: squirming on the hearth. *Hey, kids! Welcome to the uncomfortable-silence party!*

He finally pushed up, straightening his doublet. "I need to get back."

"I know."

"Are you coming too?"

Gaze in lap. Gaze in lap. "I don't think that's a good idea. But do me a favor?"

He turned, boyish wickedness tugging at his mouth. "Yes? Perhaps a plate I can bring you later, Miss Saxon?"

"*No*." After his smile fell, I charged, "Stop and talk to Novah. I think she's very sweet."

He didn't answer that. Just turned and left the office on heavy steps. I didn't blame him for his lousy mood but couldn't alleviate it, either. We'd already played with this fire more than we should—but thank God it was still just a pile of twigs beneath his flint and my steel. We could still smash the whole thing, leaving me to make a movie and him to form a new kingdom.

Thunder and lightning storms weren't in the forecast for the next six weeks. Nor would they be.

CHAPTER SIX

Three nights later, I stared into the sky over the ocean to behold a "storm" of a different kind. Rockets of yellow, orange, and red streaked among the stars until detonating together, illuminating the coastline for miles in either direction. As every round exploded, I joined my whoops and hollers to those of Joel, Dottie, and a bunch of guys from the camera crew. The seat next to me on the palais lawn remained saved for Crowe, who'd sweetly offered to go grab more peel-and-eat shrimp for everyone.

"Where the hell did that damn Irishman go?" Joel barked the complaint. "Did he sail back to Boston for the stuff?"

"Shiiit, dude." Suede, a cameraman who'd paid his industry dues on surfing documentaries, gave a rolling nod. "Chug a chill pill. He hasn't been gone that long."

Dottie chuckled. "It's not like they're going to run out."

One of Suede's friends, a wiry guy everyone called HD as short for Hyper Drive, nodded. "Three days in and they've already spoiled us rotten. Best damn shoot I've ever worked. *Viva L'Arcadia! Liberlük!*" He hoisted his glass in time to toast another round of fireworks. Like good movie people, we cheered the poetic grandeur of his pose, accidental or not. He repeated the chant, nearly singing it in exuberance.

"You know, HD, I hear antibiotics will clear that up fast for you," Joel drawled.

"Fuck off," the cameraman flung. "It's the Arcadian word

for 'liberty,' so it's very appoppiate. *Appipigate.* Damn it! *Appropriate.*"

We all roared again. "I'll drink to that," Joel added.

I giggled, sipping from my own glass. "I think it's the punch. You know they actually call it nectar? It's very yummy. Sort of sangria with fizz. What do you think is in it?"

Joel smirked. "Well, you know how they say Evrest isn't actually fucking any of those wenches who are hanging all over him?"

Dottie whacked him on the shoulder. "Don't go there, sparky."

"Hey, the man's in his prime. And I hear they don't waste a lot here. So all that Cimarron 'nectar' has to be contributing to the bottom line somehow."

He went there.

Luckily, another round of rockets lit up the sky. Though the group's laughter was masked, the glow illuminated the figure reentering our circle.

"Hey! Crowe's back!" I jumped up and hugged him, nearly knocking the bowls of shrimp out of his hands. "And look! He's morphed himself into Harry and Beth too!"

"Righteous, man." Suede fist-bumped the air before splaying his fingers, "exploding" at us all.

"Talented guy," HD concurred.

Joel took a different tack. "Where the hell have you two been?" he demanded of the couple.

Dot groaned. "How much have you really had to drink?"

Joel snorted. "What'd I do now?"

"It's the first night we haven't been shooting until midnight. We're in paradise. There're fireworks. Where the hell do you think they've been?"

Harry and Beth good-naturedly endured everyone's laughter and teases. Though I joined the mirth, unable to ignore Beth's freshly fucked hair and Harry's rumpled outfit, my gut wrenched. Total happiness for them was still a four-leaf clover in the field of my brain, somewhere in there but just not grasped. And...that sucked. *I* sucked. *Ugh.* I had to get over it. Despite my hugest efforts to see otherwise, Beth wasn't your run-of-the-mill actress. She'd been raised in some small town in Oklahoma, lending her a sweet accent and a level head, actually making her perfect for Harry. And damn it, sexual attraction aside, I did love Harry, so that needed to be okay with me. But it wasn't. Not yet.

Compounding my confusion in a hundred ways? The man who walked up the lawn toward us, stealing my breath more with each bold, confident step he took.

King Evrest had arrived, and the very air around us shifted because of it. And hell, was the man worth shifting for. His stride was proud and graceful, accentuated by the rugged black pants encasing his endless, beautiful legs. Shiny black boots hugged him from knee to feet—handy accessories, since it looked like he attempted to greet every Arcadian on the lawn tonight, numbering several hundred. Accentuating his lean waist, and the breadth of his shoulders in contrast, was a cummerbund-looking thing, also in black, secured by a pin bearing the Arcadian crest. The ensemble would've tipped into the realm of lame steampunk cosplay if not for the cobalt satin vest that hugged his torso, fastened by a zipper sewn in at a diagonal. Beneath it, his crisp white shirt also had an off-center collar. Though his hair tumbled more freely around his face tonight, the dark waves now had to share their real estate with his crown.

Hands down, he earned the headgear. His confident king look, mixed with a little Khal Drago and a little Outlaw Josey Wales, made me damn glad Crowe had also brought me a fresh glass of nectar. *Liquid courage, don't fail me now.* I made it my motto while joining everyone in standing for Evrest's approach.

Harry approached Evrest with an extended hand and his most charming smile. "Happy Liberlük to you, King Evrest."

"Merderim, Mr. Dane."

His gaze, circling our little gathering, didn't linger too long on anyone—until he got to me. A kick at one end of his mouth. Crinkles, oh-so-slight but oh-my-God sexy, at the corners of his eyes.

Don't look at me like that.

Don't stop looking at me like that.

I plunged my gaze into the refuge of my drink. Felt myself swaying, fast approaching the portal between buzzed and drunk. It loomed larger with every sip, but at the moment, I didn't give a shit. Out of all the men on the planet, I only wanted to jump two—and the three steps that separated me from them might as well have been galaxies.

"The merderims are all ours, Majesty." Suede grinned. "You Arcadians know how to throw down with the ragers."

At Evrest's perplexed scowl, Harry clapped his shoulder. "He's enjoying the party."

"Oh." Evrest went all boyish simplicity for a moment—like I needed *that.* Cue the flipping senses, the temporary amnesia about all the booze in my bloodstream. *Damn it.* After only three days, Operation "Avoid the King" had backfired on me. Every move he made was like water to my desert—and I was willing to stand here without sunscreen to get more.

Idiot. Idiot. Idiot.

"This holiday is similar to what America does on the Fourth of July, right?" Joel inquired.

"Precisely," Evrest answered. "In seventeen ninety, as the French Revolution began to spin out of control, a small group managed to flee the kingdom through Italy. They joined another group, already in exile, and then pushed to the coast and set sail into the Mediterranean. Their goal was relocation to Greece, but their timing was awful. They were blown off-course by violent storms and wound up going ashore in Izmir."

"Turkey." Joel nodded. "That explains the mixture of the two languages."

Evrest, back to his noble confidence, smiled and nodded.

"By that time, our ancestors were running low on supplies and food. The locals in Izmir were generous, having been no strangers to persecution, so several of them were invited to climb aboard once the ships set sail again." His shoulders pulled higher with pride as he finished his account. "When they found this island and formed the kingdom of Arcadia, they all did so with the same passions that guide her today—the tenets we still live by as its royal family. Kindness and equality to all. Determination to be the best versions of ourselves, grounded in decisions of character and fairness. Respect for our land and its gifts. And neutrality about allowing the rest of the world to pursue their happiness." A grimace tightened his face. "Or their violence."

Everyone was quiet, allowing the story to settle in. I was discreet too—on the outside. Inside? His words injected me with a thrill. I'd fantasized about changing the world, but Evrest Cimarron descended from generations who'd been doing it. The strength he took from that was evident in every majestic line of his stature—but the weight of it was also visible in the tension riding his shoulders.

He fascinated me in a thousand new ways.

Which was a thousand more than I could afford right now.

Joel's whistle finally sliced the air. "That's a tall order, man."

"Makes me understand why you've kept the goods in the cave this long," Suede added. "Bet its kept things simpler."

Evrest nodded again. "Excellent point, *dude*. But the cave is about to collapse, unless we give it some modern touches."

"I hear you, man. Get it on with your Fred Flintstone side."

Harry openly eye rolled the crack. Didn't help poor Evrest, now openly nonplussed. He recovered with a game grin before responding, "Having you all here is a giant step forward for us. I understand the first few days of the shoot have gone smoothly. That officially turns you all into ambassadors for the point I am trying to communicate to my people."

HD sidled forward. "That making movies is damn hard work?"

We all commiserated with chuckles.

Evrest kept his smile steady. "That the outside world isn't filled with murderers, cheats, and badly behaved housewives."

Our laughter dissolved into a group groan.

"The internet certainly sets a fun stage sometimes, doesn't it?" Beth offered.

"A learning experience for everyone," Evrest returned. He continued, seeming to choose his words carefully, "Guiding people away from twerking kittens and toward the benefits of education and awareness...has been an interesting journey for us all."

"What's wrong with twerking kittens?" Joel challenged.

Dottie drove an elbow into his ribs. "Please ignore him,

Your Majesty. He hasn't had his medication yet tonight."

As everyone chuckled, I took advantage of the moment to swig some more nectar. What *was* in this stuff? And did I care anymore? *Don't look a gift horse...or in this case, an open bar...*

I gratefully told my inhibitions to sit the next minute—or sixty—out. Same for the doubts about gazing too long at Evrest or wondering if my face was schooled to the right balance of decorum and respect when I did. Which, oddly, lent me the strength not to look at him at all...

Unless there was an over-coifed, fake-smiled slip of a Distinct who appeared at his side, her gaze sweeping over us like a blond beauty queen sizing up the competition.

"Oh, no," she crooned, slipping a hand to Evrest's elbow. "*Quel dommage.* Have I missed a fun moment, *chère?*"

Yikes. To laugh or puke at that? The dilemma plunged my gaze to the ground. How could a grown woman sound like an eight-year-old crossed with Snow White? When I noticed Beth sharing my reaction, laughter won over vomiting. We stifled our giggles, each inspiring the other.

"Not at all," Evrest reassured the woman. "You have arrived with perfect timing." He placed his free hand over hers yet stepped back, giving everyone a view of her breathtaking blood-orange party dress. The Greek-inspired bodice was secured by a broach matching the dove on Evrest's cummerbund, and the multilevel skirt hung exactly to the middle of her knees. "It is my pleasure to introduce Tess, who generously offered to help with hostess duties for me this evening."

"*Bonne nuit*, everyone," Tess murmured before giving Evrest a mocking slap on the hand. "Cease your silly nonsense about my generosity. It is my pleasure to be on your arm for this auspicious evening, Majesty."

Stifled giggle number two. Her *pleasure* to be on his arm? Considering how many other arms the girl had likely chewed through to get there, she had every right to enjoy the experience—and celebrate that she'd said "auspicious" without a hitch.

Evrest addressed the group again. "I requested that Tess join me here to help extend a special invitation to you all." His expression warmed. "A troupe of our youth theater members have put together a short play depicting the story I just conveyed, about the roots of Arcadia's creation. The children were excited about making certain I invited all the 'Hollywood big shots' to come see them. They are beginning the show in thirty minutes, in our palais amphitheater."

Harry's face rivaled the pyrotechnics in the sky. "We'd be honored, of course."

"Wonderful." Evrest's face lighted too. "Our children's theater performances astound me with every—" He interrupted himself, looking like any dad back in the States caught bragging about his kids. "Well, I shall let you observe and decide for yourselves...but they are damn good."

Everyone laughed while picking up their drinks, jackets, and lawn blankets. I turned from helping Dottie with her load to find myself forehead-to-chest with Harry. "Hey," I blurted, hoping it made sense past my nectar-buzzed brain. Yeah, I know; one syllable—but if there was room for error, I'd find it.

"Hey." He still looked giddy as a firework.

"What?"

He curled one of his you're-not-gonna-believe-this grins. "So...at this little production thing...the seat next to Evrest is empty. And he's invited *you* to fill it."

I squinted. "Earth to Harry? The seat next to Evrest belongs to Frenchie McTessie. And I think she has every intention of filling it."

"Earth to Cam?" he countered. "The *other* seat? It was reserved for his mom, but she just returned today from her grand tour of Europe and she's wiped. Sent her apologies down to Evrest about an hour ago."

"Or maybe she's just allergic to Tess's voice." I really wanted to let a giggle rip now, but Harry didn't crack composure, still as earnest as Cornelius Freaking Hackl. What the hell? "Harry, I'm flattered, but no. Please tell him thank you, but no thank you."

I had stronger words but held them back. Harry didn't need to hear how I questioned Evrest's nerve in all this— though maybe I'd overreacted to what we'd shared in my office that first night and His Majesty thought he was only being friendly, not nervy. Didn't matter either way. The booze fog already had my reservation for the night and was turning down the bed for me. And right now, thinking of beds and Evrest in the same sentence, let alone being inches from the man in any way, shape, or form...

Not wise. *Not* good.

Didn't Harry see that? Even one bit?

Dude...don't trust the tipsy girl with the king she's got the lusties for.

That was the end of that. Or so I thought—until Harry ripped the blanket I'd just folded out of my grip. "Damn it, Cam. You aren't Queen Xaria. *You* don't just get to say 'no thank you' to our fucking host."

I yanked the blanket back. "You're right. I'm not his mother. I'm not one of his little harem girls, either. And I'm not even one of his subjects—nor, for that matter, am I one of *yours*. So with all due respect, Mr. Dane, kiss Evrest Cimarron's ass on your own damn time. Don't pimp me out for the job."

Surprise, surprise. He actually stepped back, looking a little contrite—though in true dumb-shit style, reached for my hand. In bigger dumb-shit style, I realized he did so to steady my sway. "Cam? You okay?"

"Fine," I spat. "Let go of me."

He held on tighter. Didn't relent until I lifted my gaze back up. "Okay," he issued, "what I'm about to say *cannot* be repeated."

"You want to lower the cone of silence first?"

I expected an eye roll. Never came. He swallowed hard instead. I copied him.

"Evrest is considering the idea of letting us use the palais throne room for the wedding scene in the film."

In an instant, I caught his case of fireworks brain. "Whoa."

He grinned. "Yeah. Whoa."

"Harry, that would be—"

"No shit."

The opportunity would be extra-thick icing on the cake we were baking. We thought we'd be lucky to just *see* the throne room while we were here. The chamber was a gilt and gold work of art that had taken Arcadian craftsmen two decades to complete. Getting it on film would be not only a perfect enhancement for the film but a coup earning us thousands of dollars in free publicity.

It was also why I pushed the blanket back at Harry with a resigned sigh. "Pimp away, Mac Daddy Dane. I'll do it."

Harry yanked me close and pressed a hard kiss to my cheek. "That's my rock star."

"Yeah, yeah. But just this once, damn it. And no way in hell am I making you a sammich too, so grab your food on the way to the theater."

★ ★ ★

While Harry retrieved his dinner, I snagged another glass of nectar. Smart? Probably not. Necessary? Bet your damn ass.

I struggled like hell not to chug the whole thing as Evrest settled into his chair after handing Tess off to one of his guards for a trip to the ladies' room. I damn near groaned as my heart took a round trip from my chest to my belly. Then again when it overshot the landing, crashing into the base of my windpipe. Maybe if I stared at the stage and said nothing, he'd forget I was even—

"Camellia."

No luck. Not a shred.

I lifted my head in his general direction. *Just focus on his chest. You don't have to get anywhere near his face...or his eyes. His shirt* is *pretty cool. Look at how the buttons align with the diagonal zipper on the vest, and—*

My gaze was pulled up like it'd been waiting for this moment for three damn days—meeting his like a ship being called home by a shore beacon. In that beacon, such incredible green light...piercing me, capsizing me, making me reach to him just to keep my keel straight, so the sea of my senses would stop spinning...

spinning...

spinning...

Make it all stop again. Please.

Holy shit. How had my hand gotten coiled so tightly around his arm? Mortified and barely hiding it, I yanked back. All of his court had to be here tonight, attentions honed on him. He had to select a wife in six weeks. Curiosity had to be running high about tonight's featured candidate for the role...

...who was in the bathroom and would be back any second.

"This was a bad idea," I rasped. "A bad, bad idea."

Silence from him. Too damn much.

"Why did you do this? Why did you ask for me? Here? Now?"

He swiveled his head so slightly, outsiders probably thought it a simple act of polite concentration. Only he and I knew the truth. With the realignment of his head, he mated his stare with mine—and didn't let go.

Shit. I was in trouble. Incredible tourmaline depths of it. Demanding my truth, no matter what he asked.

And yeah, he asked.

"Why did *you* do this?"

Hmm. The simple stuff first. Or so I thought, until my reply spilled out. "Because Harry made me." *Not so fast, honey. Now the rest.* "And...because it felt nice to have him need me instead of Beth. And to help the production. To help him persuade you about filming rights in the throne room, and—"

He silenced me with a finger across my lips. I pulled back, fingertips instantly on the surfaces he'd somehow exposed to raw electricity.

Shit. Could we add *any* more hokey clichés here? The only thing we were missing was *his* dork soap opera line. *Ssshhh, baby. Don't talk.*

Instead, he stated, "The throne room is yours. Does that make things easier?"

I felt my stare narrowing. Well, *shit.* What had my drunk head left out? "Huh?"

"The issue is settled." He glanced away to nod at a passing couple. The man wore one of the fancy sashes denoting him as a high council member. "Contact Musette on my staff tomorrow afternoon. Her office is in the south wing; the switchboard can put you through. She supervises the schedule of all our government chambers. She can coordinate a shooting date that will work with your schedule."

"Oh." Jaw in the same shape. "Thank you."

"No problem."

"Huh?"

"No. Problem." It was clearer this time. And harsher. "That is the catchphrase you all use to wrap things up in America, correct?"

"When there's really *not* a problem," I clarified. "But *you*"—I jabbed him in his stiffened shoulder—"obviously still have a problem."

"I have no problem." His voice slid low as the fires in his gaze raged higher. "But if you still do, even after getting what you came for, then you *are* free to go, Miss Saxon." His jaw worked back and forth as he dropped that hot stare over my face, neck...into the V of my cleavage. "I selected you because I thought you would enjoy this show—"

"You sure about that?"

Ohhhh, damn.

This definitely beat the S-bomb drop during the state dinner reception—made doubly horrid because of its truth. He'd absolutely gone for the gawk at my breasts. And I'd absolutely liked it. Result? One heaping pile of snark, my best and finest coping mechanism.

What the hell would he do now? The blazes in his gaze were unchanged. He still leaned toward me, fanning that heat across every inch of exposed skin he could get...

"If you are uncomfortable being here...there are no handcuffs binding you to that chair."

My breath hitched. I *knew* he heard. A retaliation rose in my throat, ready to barrel past my filter—*thank you, nectar binge*—becoming the cherry on top of my oh-no-she-didn't sundae. "Do you wish there were?" *Yep, I did.* Hell. I needed to be horrified, to at least recognize that come tomorrow morning, I'd be paying the price for the words with more than a hangover, but Evrest's reaction negated it all.

I loved causing the catch in *his* breath.

"Handcuffs." I clarified it in a silken murmur, drawing out the moment on purpose. Damn, this felt *good*. "Do you wish there were really some here? And if I decided to stay, would you use them?"

"Enough." His voice was the growling opposite of mine. I savored every note of it. Slid him a tipsy smile, heady with my power.

"Awww. Sorry. Just wanted to be sure we were clear. You see, I'm a little drunk, Your Majesty. And probably full of *a lot* more questions."

I should have known he'd detect my serious intent beneath the boozy charm. Despite the primal tension still pouring off him, the rest of his face sobered. "Then ask them."

I notched my chin higher. "Anything?"

"Anything."

I hesitated for a second but kicked the insecurity to my mental curb. Vroom vroom. *Hit the throttle, Vin Diesel, the opportunity is now.* There wouldn't be another moment like this, with my inhibitions stunted and his "hostess" in the bathroom. I squared my shoulders and firmed my chin. "All right. Number one. Did you approve Harry's location shoot request because he was a Chapman grad?"

He earned props right away for not feigning that the query was an insult. His shoulders squared, his gaze meeting the determination of mine. "I wondered when you would come around to that."

I huffed out a laugh. "Well, it wasn't like I was thinking coherently the other night in my office. And strolling into *your* office is out of the question, so—"

"Why?" His brows crunched, blatant with puzzlement. "You know where my office is, yes? You can come find me anytime you need me, Camellia."

My tongue flicked across my lips before I could help it. *Define "need."* I longed to demand it simply to hear him say the word again.

"And *you* know that's not a good invitation for me to accept." I hitched up my own posture. Hell, yes. I *could* be mature, even in my condition.

"Why?" Buuut, he wasn't going to let me enjoy the victory. Persistent bastard. He finished with a little smile, affecting my body like a real caress. "We could simply talk. Like friends."

And live on Mars while we do. "Really? You think we could do the friend zone, Evrest? You and me?"

"Why not?"

"All right...what are you thinking about? Right this second?"

The parting of his lips and the flare of his nostrils were clear enough answer. His thoughts were consumed by the same image as mine. The two of us in his office, tangled together. Maybe it was on his desk or maybe I straddled him in his kingly office chair, but the puddle of our clothes on the floor stayed the same. And the lock of our lips. And the thrusts of our bodies...

He looked away and muttered something under his breath. The word was unintelligible, but the grit wasn't. Damn it, even Arcadian cuss words were alluring on his lips.

"Okay, let's put this thing back on the rails." Yes, I went for the slang just for the treat of his confused stare. "I'm distracting you with safer conversation."

A wry laugh. "The last minute has shown me something, Camellia. I am truly not certain you and *safe* will ever share the same space in my head again."

I steeled myself. Hell. He made profanity sexy but turned my name into a high art form. Yeah, right there in the art museum of my mind...next to the flawless nude statue of *him*.

"You're not making this easy."

He dipped close again. "Nor are you."

"I'm simply sitting here!"

"And your point is...?"

Uggghh. Laugh at him or hit him? "With all respect, you haven't answered my question yet. About Harry's Chapman cred?"

Though his posture remained stiff, his features relaxed back into suave monarch mode. "Ah, yes. The question."

"And now...the answer?"

"Of course. A two-part process, mind you."

"Now things are getting interesting."

"Not as interesting as the thoughts I had about entertaining you in my office."

I blushed and glared. Well, tried to. "Behave."

He inhaled slowly. Let it out steadily. "Your answer, Miss Saxon, is yes."

"Yes?"

"Yes, Mr. Dane's ties to Chapman swayed my decision about granting him the shooting rights."

I blinked. Several times. I hadn't ruled out the revelation, but the residual squirm factor was higher than I anticipated. "What's the second half of your answer?" I prayed for something logical.

"I said it was a 'help' toward the decision, certainly not the entire—what is the expression?—game changer." So much for the royal neutrality. His gaze got heavy and his energy more charged as he went on, "And I truly *never* expected you would be part of the Creator's blessing for the decision."

"Because you googled me." I smiled softly. "Just a few times."

"Not lately." He said it so simply, I knew it was the truth. "As far as I knew, you were happy and employed and settled. Never, in a thousand years, did I think to enter the ballroom three nights ago and find lightning had struck my world twice."

His finishing smile was both bold and bewildered. I felt my lips mirroring the move. Giddy rush, this magic of being near him. Joyous tumble, diving into his stare. Breathless awe, basking in his concentration...

I swallowed hard.

So did he.

I licked my lips again.

He watched every inch of the action.

"I have another question now." Amazing. The words sounded normal but felt so different. As if I'd meticulously planned every syllable. Or dreaded them.

He couldn't have looked more pleased. "Of course. I remain at your service."

"Maybe not after this."

"Fortune favors the brave, Camellia."

I looked away. Fortune favored the brave, but what about the curious who were stupid about respecting boundaries? I didn't *have* to ask this one—

"Are you really not sleeping with anyone in the Distinct?"

Annnnd did anyway.

And would probably regret the hell out of it.

I couldn't help peeking back up. Both his brows hit the high jump, but the corners of his mouth headed the same direction. I stared a little longer. Wow. Amusement really suited his face. Warmed its harder angles and emphasized the sensuous curves of his lips.

At last, he lifted his chin a notch. "Yes. It is true." Weighted pause. "Does that alter what you think of me?"

The question—well, the hesitation in it—was tough to decipher. Though his face didn't surrender an inch of confidence, the query itself said something. But what?

Despite his caginess, I answered honestly. "It makes you more fascinating, if that's what you mean."

"Fascinating?" It wasn't rhetorical. He truly didn't understand.

I was in super direct mode—*yay again, magic nectar*—so a laugh spilled. "Oh, God. Guess I backed myself into this one." I glanced up, the giggle gone. "But you're not going to make me explain it, right?" His concentration only deepened. *Lovely.* "Evrest, come *on*. Ugh; all right. So...you *are* getting *those* needs met...yes? From someone, somewhere? It's not like you have to tell me. I was just a little curious about who the lucky wench is.

Or maybe...wenches."

"Wenches?"

Finally his expression changed—though it wasn't any more readable than before. Did that strange grimace mean I'd insulted him or confused him?

"Sorry if that rankled. But you have to get it."

He looked around as if "it" was a real item. "Get what?"

"I meant you have to understand what I'm referring to." Hell. Honesty was going to be my only way out of this—again. "You're the walking justification for girl wet dreams, okay? You're like sex on two legs. Two really nice legs, I might add."

His brows furrowed. "Thank you. I think."

His perplexity made me more curious. And utterly beguiled—though I forced myself to ignore that part. *Forced.* "Tell me you know all this too. You grew up in a vacuum, but you didn't go to school in one. Someone has told you all this before, right? Maybe a few hundred someones?" When his reaction returned to the valley of inscrutable, I sighed. And prayed. *Oh, God, save me from this landmine of a conversation.* "It's really none of my business. So—"

"Why?"

"Why what?"

"Is it none of your business?"

His voice dropped as he spoke it. Descended right back to that intimate murmur he'd used with me that first night in the ballroom, a tone that felt modulated for me alone. *Silly fantasies. Dangerous thinking. Stop it!*

I'd get right on that...right after watching, mesmerized, as the man casually opened his program as a guise for covering my wrist with his long fingers. And right after he found my pulse point, then tripled its tempo with just one brush of his thumb...

"Evrest—"

"What if I want it to be your business?"

I swallowed again.

So did he.

And inside an instant, took over everything again.

My plane of vision. My pounding blood. My lungs, my limbs...my sex. It all careened over me, through me, consuming me—

Until he stopped the world again.

For me.

With me.

Yes. *Yes...*

"Miss Camellia?"

A fairy-sweet voice jabbed our beautiful bubble. I jerked away from Evrest like he'd turned into a cactus—then attempted to focus on the adorable little girl standing in front of us. Not an easy feat after a handful of peeled shrimp and five glasses of nectar, but the cutie made the effort worth it. She was about five or six, with a head of black ringlets topped by a little blue satin tricorn sprouting a yellow feather. She wore an enchanting eighteenth century costume to match. For a second, her face shimmered and doubled in my drunken vision. After a couple of blinks, I was able to return the smile she beamed, exposing a toothless gap in the front.

"Well, hello there," I greeted. "What's your name, sweet one?"

"Carissa," she replied. "Oops; I mean Lady Renata of Paris."

I held out my hand. "It's lovely to meet you, milady. I look forward to your performance tonight."

"Well..." She toed the ground and bit her lip. "That is why

I am here." During her small pause, Evrest's soft chuckles peppered the air, somehow contributing to my stomach's squirm factor. "Our opening sequence is the *Grand Fête Danse*. During it, we get to invite special guests from the audience to come and waltz with us. I have chosen you as my guest, Miss Camellia."

"Why?" *Ugh. Note to self: kick yourself later for pulling a Miss Hannigan on a six-year-old.* "Er, I mean—milady, there are so many other ladies of the land present here tonight. Look, Lady Tess is returning right now; why don't you—"

"Lady Tess talks like a constipated dolphin." While Evrest laughed harder and I worked on pushing past my shock, Carissa went on, "And she doesn't make my cousin smile the way you do."

"Your cousin?" I questioned. "Who's..." My voice trailed off as I followed her nod—back to Evrest.

"Come here, imp." He said it while pulling her onto his lap, slipping something into the pocket of her gown as he did. When her blue eyes lit up, he murmured, "That is *our* secret, Riss. If your *maimanne* learns I am sneaking you chocolate again, she shall flay me like Sunday dinner catfish. Already, we know how she prefers Shiraz to me."

Carissa had a giggle ready. "That is only because Shiraz says nice things about her shoes. You are the king now, Ev. Everyone has to love you."

He grunted at her and pushed at me. "Go. Dance. Both of you."

I was about to protest again—until I allowed myself to behold his whole face. Only one word came to mind. Joyous. His eyes sparkled like sea foam in the sun. Deep dimples dented his cheeks. I swore his grin reached to his ear lobes, and it was beautiful and dazzling and white—and meant just for us.

Then his expression softened a little—darkening with desire.

As he turned it to me.

For a moment—just one—I let a fantasy bloom. We were here, reigning over the festivities as king and queen. Everyone in our kingdom was deliriously happy, just as we were. Evrest was going to watch me dance with the children before pulling me away to our chambers, where he'd watch me dance again—while I got naked for him, layer by delicious layer.

Watch me dance for you, my king...

My nectar buzz helped the dream cling to my mind as I walked up on stage. The music began, grand and dramatic. I let the fantasy stick around just a while longer as I swirled and laughed between snickering boys and giggly girls. We "danced" through choreography that was less an actual waltz than a semblance of a party.

After a few minutes of that, I realized why the kids had been so squirrelly. The action of the play was blown apart by a gang of adolescent "revolutionaries," wielding prop dynamite sticks and bayonets, ordering that everyone at the "dance" be captured and taken to the Bastille for their trials. Along with the grown-up guest actors, I fell to my knees, held up my hands, and play-acted my screams with the prayer that my laughter wouldn't spill out, as well. No-go. By the time the "attack" was over, I lay on the stage with Carissa, joining her in fits of laughter...

Dying in my throat as soon as I looked again to Evrest.

And kicked myself at once for letting the fantasy take such deep hold.

Of course I'd noticed Tess hurrying back into her seat as the show began. Had even seen her tucking her arm beneath Evrest's, re-staking her claim. Should've gotten the damn clue then, especially when it was clear she might not stop there. Wouldn't be surprised if her next move was swooping a leg over into his lap, to use her toes on his balls.

I just didn't expect him to enjoy it so much.

Fine. It was a snap conclusion, likely prompted by my spinning vision and roiling gut. It was why I flipped to my stomach to reassess the situation.

No dice.

If anything, everything sharpened. Painfully. The twinkle in his gaze, visible even from this distance. His hand on Tess's forearm, fingers dark on her pale flesh, probably pressing into her wrist...turning every inch of her body into fire...

Damn it.

I knew the feeling.

Had known it.

And sure as shit didn't want to know *this* one. Chest tightening. Teeth clenching. The squall in my stomach now turned into a storm—especially as he threw his head back on a laugh in reaction to something Tess whispered into his ear. When she was done, she lingered. Their faces were just inches apart...

"Yay!" Carissa screamed it in my ear while jumping on my back. "That was *trés*, trés epic! Thank you, Miss Cam. Thank you!"

"Uh...okay, sweetie."

"Will you come back next year and do it again with me?"

Oh, God. "A year is a long time, Carissa."

"Just say you'll try."

"I'll...I'll try." My gasping smile was genuine, but I prayed my duty was done. *No more trés epic. Please.* My head swirled, equilibrium taking a tumble. My emotions were chaos, allowed to run too damn wild tonight.

Idiot.

What the hell had I been doing, drinking this much when knowing the probability of seeing Evrest tonight?

What the hell was I thinking, indulging that damn fantasy?

What the hell was I expecting, accepting the invitation to sit next to him—and the woman who now spread her fingers against his jaw, pulling his stare back down to her with only one message on her face?

Kiss me.

Tess's gaze proclaimed it louder as Evrest leaned toward her with hooded eyes. His jaw tautened beneath her touch as she pulled him closer...closer...

I tore my gaze away.

Didn't help.

As the carotid of my spirit bled out, I all but rolled off the stage. My head spun. My gut heaved. My face burned. Surely everyone in the place bore witness to my mortification too. Though logic jumped in to declare it was only the hooch at work in my blood, I didn't listen. Ducked my head, plowing toward the exit gate in a sea of dizziness—and yeah, a little heartache too.

Maybe more than a little.

Shit.

I softly groaned with each step, though some saint took pity on me, lending me strength to keep composed—or so I thought. When Dottie's face appeared in my vision, the concern on her face confirmed how little I'd really kept it together.

"Cam? Sweetie? You all right?"

"I think so." But as soon as the words were out, I wobbled. Laughed. Stopped in place, watching the world careen, before laughing again. "Okay, maybe I don't think so."

She wrapped an arm around my middle and hustled me out the gate. "You need to sit down."

"I need another drink."

"No way. You need five gallons of water and then your bed." Before I could even start a protest, she let out the most impressive girl growl I'd ever heard. "Don't think about going back in there, either. I've already sent Harry over to Evrest with the message you aren't feeling well. Won't exactly be rough for the man to buy. Anyone looking at you knew something wasn't right."

Another laugh. Louder. Harder. "Well, Evrest wasn't looking at me, so—"

"The hell he wasn't."

A thrill took wing in my spirit.

My raging heart shot the bastard down.

Get the hell over *this. Over* him. *He's not just off-limits. He's the* king *of off-limits. You don't get to stay and change the world when you step into off-limits. You don't get to keep your credibility with Harry, either—like, for forever.*

"Cam?"

Dottie's voice barreled in again. I yanked back, craving a long wallow in my agony. And why the hell not? I was drunk. Nectar was my new bestie because it was my perfect scapegoat. No one would ever discern the real reason for my moroseness. Nobody would guess I'd fallen into the most stupid emotional trap ever, joining the ranks of lonely cyber-trolls and delusional boy band groupies, buying the bullshit that I actually shared some mystical "bond" with the damn king of this place. On top of that, I had a damn fantasy about the man—*in public*—while he sat with a woman who might be pregnant with his child by this time next year.

Epic fail, thy name is Cam Saxon.

"I have to go." It was the only thing that made sense, a viable solution for everyone. Without waiting for Dot and her inner mama tiger to respond, I whirled and headed down the nearest empty corridor, letting the cadence of my steps wrap me in its steady hypnosis.

Fleeing. Stumbling. *Just get one step in front of the other.* I didn't care where I went as long as it put distance between Evrest and me.

Closed doors. Ornate furniture. More closed doors. Little atriums full of flowers—*pretty; let me look; no!*—all brightly illuminated at first but dimming as I kept going.

A weird panic set in. Was the nectar taking its toll? Was I so sloshed I was set to pass out in the middle of the hallway?

Oh, hell. Though it didn't officially qualify as "fraternizing with the locals," I was damn sure demerits in the Book of Harry were also in order for a blacked-out production manager in the middle of—

Where the hell was I?

This part of the palais wasn't familiar. None of this existed in the north wing. The décor, while in the same luxurious Mediterranean style, was nicer. *A lot* nicer. None of the doors here were labeled, either. Big problem. I really had to pee.

My guardian saint for the night swooped in just in time. The *whoosh* of a toilet flush sifted into the hallway. I ducked behind a giant potted palm as a palais housekeeper emerged from one of the doorways, humming and carrying a box of bathroom cleaning supplies.

With hands clasped in gratitude, I glanced heavenward. "Quick pit stop," I whispered to Mystery Saint, "and then I'll get the hell out of here." Wherever *here* was. Best not to ponder the answer for too long. I was drunk, not clueless. I was clearly somewhere I didn't belong, having likely zigged instead of zagged in my frenzy to get the hell away from the amphitheater—which had landed me somewhere in the south wing.

Freakin' great.

I tried to hurry through my business. The bathroom obviously wasn't meant for the general public. There was only one toilet, contained in a little closet formed of cobalt marble walls. The rest of the chamber contained a huge vanity formed of the same luxurious marble, accented with toiletry accessories stored in cut crystal containers. In a small room at the back, there was a chaise that would put a lot of full beds to shame, made of dark-blue velvet and piled with half a dozen pillows in various shapes. I gazed longingly at the thing while running my hands beneath the polished gold spigot.

But froze the second I turned the water off.

Footsteps clattered in the hall. Louder, louder, closing in on the bathroom door.

The doorknob rattled. I whooshed in relief. Guardian Saint—better than Allstate—reminded me to lock the door, even in the booze fog.

A woman swore softly. At the same time, keys jingled— and my gaze fell on a cell phone on the far side of the counter.

"Crap!" Of course the housekeeper was one of the progressive Arcadians. And Guardian Saint had decided to take a lunch break.

There was no way to hide in the stall. Even then, I'd likely run into the woman while doubling back. There was only one option. Glad for my noiseless flats, I retreated into the anteroom with the chaise. After sliding between the swagged curtains behind it, I prayed the maid wouldn't notice a strange lump in the thick damask fabric.

The door swung open. I listened to the maid, humming classic Madonna to herself while stepping to her phone. The device chirped with a text message. I switched up my prayer, including the plea that she not answer the damn thing here and now.

Denied.

I allowed myself a single huff. Sweat trickled down my face as I pressed back, yearning to become one with the wall.

Be careful what you wish for.

The wall ceased to exist.

Whhaaat?

I questioned the sensation, wondering if my drunken senses had turned the world upside down again, but when I reached back for the curtains, my hand closed on nothing but air.

Scream. You should scream. Really.

But my shock washed out the bridge between my brain and vocal cords, especially when a flood of fear joined in. I was pushed back, spun around, then thrust forward again, plunged into instant darkness. Alice down the rabbit hole, though not nearly as fun I remembered from girlhood. Had I blacked out? And if that was the case, did a whacked-out tea party with a fussy rabbit await now?

Wait. I was still conscious. My nose made me aware of that fact. Wherever I was, it was *not* the bathroom, with its jasmine and orange blossom freshness. This cave—corridor? tunnel?—brought a "special" mix of damp and moss, infused with a third element I could only qualify as *old*. And damn, it was cold. The temp had plunged by at least twenty-five degrees.

"Hell. If I'd known there was going to be a cave dive tonight, I wouldn't have gone for the cami and half sweater, guys."

My snark didn't yield my hoped-for comfort. It only emphasized that I wasn't in some cute little castle hidey hole but a significant cavern of some sort. Strangely, I wasn't freaked out. Hey, a constructive use for the booze in my blood, after all!

As a matter of fact, I almost giggled. A castle with hidden tunnels? *Hell, yeah.* I might have even been up for exploring around down here, if it wasn't so cold. And dark. And creepy.

Freak-out time didn't come until the next moment.

I pushed back on the wall just as I had before. Nothing budged. Pulling out my phone as a flashlight, trying to find a hidden "return trip switch," was also unproductive—and confirmed I'd been spun into a cell reception black hole. A one-way ticket underground, accessible via the bathroom. There was a really good joke somewhere in that statement, but I think my guardian saint was telling it over his three-martini lunch.

A swing of the light around the chamber revealed the area as clean and well-maintained. I chose to be grateful for that fact instead of considering the reasons why, since the only exit now seemed to lie in going forward. More inspection revealed the chamber to be a wider space as part of a corridor that stretched to my left and right. It was a crap shoot on choice of direction, since the wild ride of the trap door left me clueless about where I was.

I picked the right and started walking.

And walking.

And walking.

"And if you think the pool is impressive, let me show you the tunnels." I adopted a nasally voice that had once been an inside joke between Harry and me. We'd dubbed it Desperate Realtor Lady. "Once you see those, you'll be begging me to get an offer in for you. *Begging.*"

Again, the sarcasm didn't help. I gulped against more fear, trying not to liken myself to a rat in a maze. Shudder. No more thinking about rats, period. My luck had held on finding all the tunnels critter-free, but how long would that last? How long would *I* last?

"Stop it," I seethed. "You're not going to die down here."

But you had to go and voice the possibility anyway?

Which led to the imagining of my phone pooping out. Then my terror in the dark, solitary and shivering, praying for rescue...

"That does it. No more *Lost* re-runs." I wasn't wandering in a damn jungle. If worse came to worst, everyone would return to set tomorrow morning and realize I was nowhere to be found. These tunnels hadn't maintained themselves; *someone* in Arcadia had to know they existed...

I slammed to a sudden stop.

Pressed my hand against the wall, steadying my body, holding my breath—and hoping my ears weren't playing tricks on me.

Please, please, please; don't be a fantasy.

Wait.

Yes.

There it was again.

Music.

Guitars and soft percussion, blended into a lush melody. It became my beacon, guiding my careful steps. Every so often, I stopped. Had to keep my aim true in tracking the sound—and pray that the underground acoustics weren't playing horrific tricks on my ears.

My pulse throbbed harder as the tune grew louder.

Finally, I turned into an offshoot tunnel that led to a flight of stone stairs, descending deeper into the earth. At the bottom of the steps was a heavy wood door inset with iron detailing. I saw every detail about the portal because it was outlined by light—emanating from the other side.

"Thank you!"

My sob echoed back through the caverns. While switching off my phone, I scurried down the steps. Another prayer filled my heart as I tugged on the door. "Please don't be locked. Please don't be locked." Though if it were, I prepared myself to pound on the wood with all the strength in my body.

Not locked.

Guardian saint was back. I thanked him again, rushing it out on joyous breath—that instantly became an astonished gasp.

It was another fantasy. That had to be it. I'd actually passed out back at the amphitheater and now dreamed all of this in a toes-up blackout.

Luxurious white drapes flowed over all the walls, backlit in rich red and purple hues. The draping continued all the way up to the ceiling. There, it billowed into fabric clouds, given multicolored "stars" that shone from exotic hanging lanterns. The middle of the room was consumed by a massive platform bed, also draped in white, piled high with gigantic pillows.

Holy shit.

That wasn't the end of the goodies at the tea party.

To either side of the bed were rows of shelves reminding me of the naughty girl store Faye liked dragging me to—only stocked better. There were creams and lotions and lubes. Toys with switches and without. Feathers and leathers and even a few blindfolds.

Oh, my God.

Where the hell was I?

The answer wasn't important. I knew the two most relevant aspects of it anyway. I shouldn't be here. And I needed to find the way out of here—the *other* way out—right away.

I'd only taken two steps before jerking to a full stop again. As the hugest jolt of my night riveted me in place.

The far side of the room contained two small compartments appearing to be glorified alcoves. I wasn't certain about that, because the depths of both were plunged into shadow by half drapes. As I crossed the room, a figure became clearer in one of the enclosures. He leaned against the wall, long legs spread and braced to the floor. His black pants were unzipped enough for his sex to spring free—a long, incredible sight, enhanced by each hard stroke he gave to the swollen flesh. His veins, thick and strong, were a relief map of arousal beneath the skin, now gleaming and red from his attention.

Shit.

Wow.

Shit!

I'd never seen an erection like that before. And thanks to Faye and her filthy mind—and huge array of online hunk sites—I'd seen a healthy number of them in the last year. This man's cock would earn him top-five status on most of those sites. Size was only part of it—and just the beginning of where the perfection started. The angels had taken a little extra time to carve this part of him. From the firm, round balls to the proud hood at the top, the man was a work of art.

I was so wrapped up in that stunned assessment, I purposely didn't look up. Couldn't look up. Knowing who that beautiful flesh belonged to would *not* be a good thing, especially when I saw the guy with all his clothes in place. It was a smart tactic...

Or so I was allowed to think.

Before he spoke.

Satin. Sandpaper. Sex. It all rolled up his throat, over lips that had haunted every other thought in my head since arriving on Arcadia. He formed the words, as only he could say them, into a command that paralyzed me where I stood.

"Camellia. Stop!"

CHAPTER SEVEN

Oh my God. Oh my God. Oh my God.

I stared around, half expecting Tess to pop out from behind the curtain, though I was damn certain what I'd walked in on was—well—what I'd walked in on.

Evrest. By himself. Pleasuring himself.

By accident—I *swear*—my gaze skimmed across the huge hand that'd just been wrapped around his erection. A waterfall of heat tumbled over me, pooling in places it shouldn't be. It couldn't be.

But he was so damn beautiful.

The power of his flesh against his flesh. The tension in his sleek, sensual body. The concentration on his face, behind his closed eyes.

Was that what he looked like when he was inside a woman too?

"Shit!" With any luck, it would turn into the delete key on my thoughts. No joy. Not a speck. To make matters worse, Evrest just stood there, not making a move to zip back up—or whatever the hell his designer pants did. I looked away, a torture of effort. He was magnificent, and all I wanted to do was stare. Then dream about doing a lot more. "Oh, God," I moaned. "This is bad. Really bad."

"Camellia."

"I wasn't here, okay? I simply wasn't here. Can we agree on that, please?" I whirled toward a curtain without lights behind it, assuming it led to a way out of here that wouldn't land me back in the black maze from hell. "This is me. Leaving. Now. I prom—"

"*Camellia*." His hand closed around one of my wrists. Liquid fire shot into my arm. Traveled up, up, up until trailing across my chest and igniting through both my breasts. My camisole's built-in bra was no match for the effect of his touch. As my nipples jabbed at the fabric, Evrest tugged harder at my wrist. Understanding was instant. I lifted my gaze to his face. He cupped my cheek with his other hand, stopping my heart all over again with the amazement on his burnished features. "Where did you come from?"

I needed to push away. Massive fail. I didn't want to be anywhere else right now. All I could think about was the proximity of his lips, their curves and crevices, so mesmerizing, so perfect. "I...got lost. Then I had to pee, so I—well, I was in the bathroom, and the maid came back in, so I hid behind the drape. Then the wall swallowed me..." Damn. His lips were *really* entrancing. The top one dipped low in the middle, a carved valley that outright begged for an exploring trace.

Both those lips gained gorgeous tilts at the corners. "You found the tunnels."

How could he be so conversational, with...parts of himself...still exposed between us? "More like they found me."

"Are you all right?"

"Yeah." Damn it, *where* was I supposed to look? "I've been in darker and scarier places before." It was part of the job description when one's dad thought a great "California spring break" was exploring abandoned Gold Rush mines.

"The tunnels," he echoed, almost seeming happy about the fact—as his cock stayed its stunning course. "That makes much more sense than what *I* thought."

Unconsciously, I wet my lips. Safer alternative than what I wanted to do with my tongue. "Which was what?"

"That the heavens brought you." He meant it. Every word. The jagged rasp in his voice rubbed the knowledge into me with ruthless surety. "It was the only logic that made sense."

"Huh?"

My breaths, short and shallow, echoed in my ears as he stepped even closer. "It all snapped together when you walked in...and turned all the fantasies of my soul into reality." He stared hard, raking my face and neck as he had back in the theater. But there was no angry fire in his eyes this time. It was something darker. Scarier. "Yes. A great deal of sense."

Blink. Breathe. Blink again. My mind fought to process what he'd just said. "Wait. Your...fantasies?"

Why wouldn't the words connect?

Because you're unsure you want them to?

Of course. It was easier to keep clinging to the heartbreak from the amphitheater, envisioning Tess and him in their flirty little idyll, planning their perfect royal future. This way, I was already out of the game. The arrows to my spirit still yielded only flesh wounds.

"Look...Evrest...none of this is my business. This is clearly your space and your time, so—"

He stopped me with a ruthless hand in my hair.

Used the grip to yank my face higher, preparing me for his hypnotic kiss.

And ohhhh, how he delivered.

Fully.

Deeply.

Mercilessly.

Oh my God.

I tumbled. Floated. Burned. Needed.

More. *More.*

No. *No.*

I moaned, torn by the torment. Evrest wasn't so conflicted. Inside a second, he swept in, tongue and teeth plunging, relentless until he tore a hard groan from me. He didn't waste that opportunity, either. He assaulted deeper, grunting like he wanted to devour me, intent on toppling my resistance.

For one incredible second, I let him.

Gave up. Gave in. Gave over.

Everything I'd dreamed of granting him since his crystal green gaze had first swept over me, four nights ago...it was here, so good, so *real.* All I wanted to do was drink of him in return. Ohhh, yes...dizzy bliss, heady heat...dying in all the best ways from how delicious he was, nectar and spice and desire all twisting from his tongue to mine. I breathed him in too, sandalwood swirled with desire, a violent, perfect force in my senses.

I sighed as my fingertips tangled in the coarse hairs on his forearm before slipping under his shirt to explore his carved biceps. There was nothing soft about the man. Finally learning it firsthand started flipping every important switch in my body.

Especially the circuit of my deepest core.

When we broke apart, my lungs heaved in time to that carnal throb. Layers of nerves crashed with each other, squeezing at my most sensitive pearl, battling for control of my actions. I panted hard, so damn tempted to let them.

"Ohhh, God," I groaned. "Evrest...I have to go. I can't stay. We shouldn't have taken one step down this road, let alone gone this far."

He pulled up, his mien returning to that of a lazing panther. Sensual watchfulness on the outside, dark passion ruling his gaze. "*Have to. Can't. Shouldn't be.* So many rules, Camellia." He tucked his face against my neck and whispered against the bottom of my jaw, "Lightning does not need rules. *You* do not need rules."

"Hell." It was half gasp, half moan. His muscles tightened under my fingers as he pulled me closer. His penis swelled between our bodies, scorching my stomach through my clothes. If he bent his knees at all, he'd be lined up with the wet lips all but screaming for him. "We *both* need such things, okay? Those rules exist for reasons—"

"Nothing exists but this." He all but seethed it. His lips parted to show gritted teeth. His hands curled into my hips, powerful with demand. "Give me this, Camellia. Please. This is the moment I prayed the Creator would grant since the moment I walked into the ballroom and beheld you there. All the ways I have dreamed of holding you, kissing you, touching you"—he leaned forward, pushing his forehead against mine—"they are here, and I can barely believe it is real. Maybe I really am just dreaming."

"Then that's a damn impressive dream, Your Majesty."

I said it in reaction to the tighter press of our bodies. I didn't think I'd piled on the snark too thick, but when he grimaced, the message was clear. He voiced it in a low growl anyway. "No. 'Your Majesty' doesn't exist in here, either. It is only us. You and me, *sevette*. Locked away. No time. Only now. Only here."

I didn't ask him for a translation on the Arcadian word. Did it matter? He might've just called me a mud hen, and I didn't care. The hunger in his voice wove his spell thicker around my senses, until I began to believe him. Almost.

"Evrest." I barely recognized myself, either. My whisper belonged to another creature, hot and wanton, longing to follow him deeper down this tunnel of heat, magic...sin. "Oh, God..."

"Tell me what you want." He dragged his mouth down my neck, marking me just enough with his teeth. "What it will take to make you say yes."

My head fell back. "Weave the spell some more," I pleaded. "I love...to listen to you. Your voice..."

I hoped my shiver communicated the rest of it. The rumble in his chest was encouraging, mixed with the deep, sexy laugh he curled into my ear. "So I am your wizard now, hmmm? Shall I invoke an incantation over you? Or simply tell you about all the ways I've dreamed about having you near me like this? Of kissing you like this? Of having the chance to touch you like this..."

He drifted a hand up, under my sweater and camisole, until he cupped my breast. I gasped. It was *so* damn good. His stare never left my face as he caressed me. With every inch he covered, he gazed more intently, as if imprinting each of my reactions on his memory.

Without warning, he pinched one of my nipples.

"Oh!"

"Mmmm. Beautiful."

It was the tiniest pressure, just enough to stiffen my nipple a little, but right now, the man could read *Red Fish, Blue Fish* and make me wetter. I wanted him. Badly.

So not good.

So damn wonderful.

He did it again. On the other breast. Harder this time. I moaned and pushed into his fingers. Even the pain he gave me was...*wow*.

But then he stopped.

One fish.

Waited with intense stillness.

Two fish.

What happened at three? Four? Five?

They weren't in the book. He needed me to help write those pages. Needed the words from me. But saying them? I didn't think I could. I wasn't drunk enough to forget how many boundaries we were crossing...how many lies we'd have to tell to cover it up. And how I'd desperately hope they stuck.

There was still time. If I pushed back now and ran out of here, no transgression—loosely speaking—had occurred. Only Evrest and I would have the ramifications of the what-ifs to deal with. He wouldn't be happy with me for it, meaning he'd find ways to avoid me from now on. Probably a damn good thing.

Yes. Walking out was the best choice. The right choice.

But now it was just a thought in my head—as Evrest swept my footing from under me, pulling me up into his arms. Before I could muster any protest, he'd swung around and lowered me into the white cloud layers of the bed. The canopy billowed over my head. His big, perfect body stretched beside me. Damn. I wondered if *I* was the one in a dream, intensified by the renewed brush of his mouth over mine. Instinct curled my hand around his neck, urging him to deepen the contact, but he only smiled and kept up his featherlight taunts, tracing exquisite electricity into my whole body with every soft sweep.

I sighed. Aching. Needing. Head spinning as if the clock backed up by an hour, to the height of my nectar buzz. "Shit," I rasped. "Evrest...please..."

He trailed his light kisses into the hollow of my throat. "More incantations, sevette?"

"I—" And now, choking—in all the best ways. A gurgled sound rose in my throat as he pushed back the edge of my sweater to lick along my collarbone. Oh my *God*, it felt good. "Yes!" I grabbed his head and fisted his hair. "Yesssss."

Damn. I'd done it. Jumped off the bridge of barely acceptable and into the river Styx itself, swimming with all the other sinners, even crying out in delight as I splashed down. I couldn't help it. When Evrest added a soft bite to my shoulder, every nerve ending in my body detonated—proving he was right here in the water with me.

He lifted his head to once more meet my gaze—while his fingers did other things. Magical things. With his hand beneath my clothes, he tugged at both nipples again, spurring another high cry from the depths of my lust. I pushed my flesh deeper into his touch, writhing as I heated for him...softened for him.

I needed more.

I stripped off the sweater and the cami in just a couple of tugs. Hurled them away while smiling up at him. "Surely those incantations will work better now?"

He gazed at me for a long moment. Yes, another one I wanted to halt forever. His gaze was silken moss, his mouth parted as if poised for dessert. I stared back, yearning to be that delicacy. How would it feel to be nude beneath him, my flesh offered for his voracious licks and kisses...?

The Force is strong in this one. Well, I sure as hell was when the fantasy of the two of us filled my mind. As it consumed me more, I pushed up a little, wordlessly offering myself to him.

With a snarl that curled my toes, Evrest dropped his head again. Drenched one of my breasts and then the other in the sultry heat of his mouth while zigzagging fingertips into the valley between them...

Before he began swirling his touch lower.

Damn. The magic of his mouth was so heavenly, I didn't think anything would surpass it. But now he skimmed my flesh as if it were formed of rare rose petals, blowing my theories to dust again. His fingers spanned the center of my ribcage, fanning fire into every nerve ending, making my stomach rise and fall, faster and faster...as he continued lower...

New fantasies filled my mind. I wanted my jeans off now, torn by his passionate force, baring every inch of my body to him. I wanted his gaze raking my bare skin...everywhere. I wanted to spread myself, ready for him...

But he stopped at my navel.

Moan. Growl. Plea. Exasperation drove all of them out of me. I pulsed and ached, throbbed and yearned, becoming a worse tangle as he leaned over to bolt his gaze directly into mine—and smiled.

Big. Baaaad. Wolf.

My breaths came harder and faster—especially as he pushed his middle finger into his mouth with languorous grace. After sucking it thoroughly, he dipped it back to my navel, pressing the moistened pad into my little button, gently rolling it there.

Oh...*hell.*

The new pressure jolted heat straight through the middle of my body, ending where my womb already tightened in need for him.

"You like it, Camellia?"

His voice was as soft as it was gruff. I threaded my fingers deeper into his hair and whispered, "Yes. *Yes.* Amazing. God, Ev—" My throat clutched as he trailed his touch toward the top of my jeans. "Yes. Please..."

"Fuck." His jaw, now shadowed with stubble, tautened to hard angles. His erection, still growing, was hot against my thigh. "You call me amazing? Do you not see I am only reflecting *you*?" He dipped his head, taking my lips in a searing kiss. When he finally pulled up, he gazed with heavy eyes, as if drugged. "You are more beautiful than the conjures of my best fantasies. More passionate. More stunning. More exquisite."

I was torn between glaring at him and bursting with a laugh. Passion? Okay, I'd buy that. Stunning? I'd grant it, though harder to swallow. But exquisite? That was a word for women like Tess and Beth and other princesses, not a girl who'd been raised in sneakers and hiking boots, wore makeup only when she was commanded, and had already beaten most of the guys on the crew at burping contests. "Look, that feels wonderful to hear, but—"

He severed me short with another kiss—though made it clear, from the first crash of his mouth, that his intent was no longer gentle worship. No tender coaxes, no sweet tongues. He was a breaching battle ax, conquering every crevice of my mouth with lunges that edged on bites. And me? Deciding breathing might be overrated. Maybe thinking too. They sure as hell weren't possible when Evrest Cimarron decided to consume everything—and make it all completely wonderful in the doing.

My senses burst open like a meadow beneath fireworks. My world was full of color, of light, of noise, of passion. I was beautiful. Stunning.

Exquisite.

He finally released my mouth. Didn't stop him from continuing the assault of his own. He swept my hair back, fanning it over the pillows before licking down my neck, biting in below my ear with just enough pressure to make me—

"Ohhh, *God.*" I rolled my head to give him better access. How the hell did he know just how to do that? Just how I needed it?

This wasn't the kind of shit a guy found on Google.

I finally got bold enough to tug at the zipper of his vest and then the buttons of his shirt. Despite my naked breasts and his bare cock, we were still way overdressed.

"Tell me what else you like." He growled it while helping my efforts, tearing the shirt open and sending buttons flying. I dropped my jaw, now understanding why Faye and her book club sighed over the move whenever a book boyfriend pulled it off. It was hot. No. In Evrest's big, capable hands, it was scorching. "Perhaps this?"

I bit my bottom lip and let him see it. Wouldn't do a damn bit of good to hide the lust from my eyes and voice, either. "Yes. Oh, yes."

He slanted over me again, offering his bare flesh to my eager fingers. I explored him with both hands, gliding over the flat, bronze planes of his biceps, smiling at his hiss when I caressed his nipples with my thumbs. Damn. The man really was a wolf taken to human form, just as sleek and twice as exotic. And hard to the point of mesmerizing, no matter where my fingers roamed.

I ran my touch downward, over the twin ladders of his abs, stretching my thumbs to tease at the line of dark hair between them. Evrest hissed again, longer and rougher, making me curl a tentative smile.

"You like?" My voice was as rickety as my grin. Couldn't help it. While being near him felt like home from the moment our hands first clasped, I'd formed that impression in different circumstances than this. That crowded ballroom was nothing like *these* waters. Our course into Styx was still uncharted. And while I wasn't drowning, I had no idea which way to swim. Damn it, I was the girl who GPS'd the route to the corner store if need be. Clarity and direction had been my life vests. Without them, would I drown or float?

I didn't know the answer.

Only knew I had to take a chance on finding out.

Even if I had to swim without a map.

Evrest, with his undaunted gaze and adoring smile, made it a little easier to embrace that risk.

Perhaps more than a little.

He tipped the scale more with his answering growl. It was low, lush, seductive...addictive. "Yes, sevette. I like very much."

He ended it on a harsh hitch as I tracked my hands lower. His lungs pumped harder with every inch I dipped, bursting into a rumble as I wound fingers around the beautiful bulb at the top of his shaft.

I stared, transfixed, as his tip sprouted heavy drops of milk. Harry never had the patience to let me explore once he hit the precome stage. While my awed evaluation clearly stretched Evrest's willpower, he didn't make any move toward the rabid-boy hump. The only thing sucking up his full concentration... was me. Fascination joined the lust on his face as he rolled his hips, pushing his flesh farther into my grip.

"Fuck," he gritted. "So nice, sevette. Very nice."

"Yes." I traced down his length, finally rolling a finger into the dent between his shaft and sacs. "It is."

His eyes squeezed shut. His lips pressed tight. His breaths were heavy, almost violent, bursts. "Distract me, Camellia." It was an order, plain and simple, backed by the bestial force in his eyes. "Make me think about something besides fucking your fingers and coming all over you like an adolescent, because I swear by the Creator, you make me feel like one."

Styx just got hotter. Scalding, perhaps. It turned my senses into insane mermaids, wanting to launch into backflips of erotic exhilaration, just to see how else I could please him. All the ways I could arouse him...

"What if I take confession time?" I finally proposed. "What if I told you that I've...had some fantasies too?"

"About me?"

His amazement was genuine. *Uh-oh. Weak spot ahead.* Though the man seemed hardwired for the act of seduction, his off-guard moments drilled the deepest holes in my emotional shields. I hoped this one lasted only a few seconds, allowing me to reclaim my bearings.

"No." I went for humor as reinforcement. "About the *other* guys on the tabloid covers."

Fail-whale on the humor. That had come out all wrong— and now I had to endure his darkened stare as penance. "You thought about me before even getting here? Because of simply seeing me on magazines?"

I winced. "I know, I know. Creepy, sicko, send me to the clink. But those rags always seemed to find the hottest pictures, and—"

He stopped me with another blood-melting kiss. And a lot more.

The second our mouths slammed again, he hauled me up from the mattress, molding my body against his, stopping our clutch long enough to growl out a single directive. "On your knees, Camellia." As soon as I curled my legs in compliance so our upright torsos were smashed tight, he claimed my lips again, growing our passion with longing, plunging sweeps of his mouth. New position? Definite thumbs-up. I now had the chance to explore the sinewy plateaus of his back before scratching down the slopes of his shoulders.

Gaaahhh. He was...breathtaking. A living work of art, captivating me anew every time he moved. I longed to beg for a whole day of just touching him—though now, with his cock fitted against my cleft, the request got shoved to the bottom of the priorities list. *Impatience, almost anxiety.* Hell, how I craved him inside me, hot and huge and...

Now.

Only my jeans remained between us. Not an issue for much longer if I could help it.

I slipped my hands from his shoulders to take care of it but had only the button twisted free when Evrest grabbed me by both wrists, wrenching them over my head.

My fingers collided with something...metal? I looked up. Sure enough, he wound my grip around a shiny steel rod, suspended on chains from the bed's sturdy canopy support system.

Okaayyy. Interesting. My pulse tripled, easily acknowledging a fresh flood of sensations. Fear. Excitement. Fear again. *What the hell now?* The stare I shot to Evrest yielded what I anticipated—his alpha wolf eyes at their strongest, his rugged jaw at its stoniest—conveying his low command before he even uttered it.

"Keep them there."

My chest pumped as his just had. What a difference a few minutes made. I thought of how he'd surrendered his erection into my hands, trusted me with the most vulnerable part of his anatomy, allowed me to pleasure him...and now, stretched into a similar position, breasts jutting and body stretched, questioned why it was so hard for me to do the same.

Because this reminds you that your body isn't the only thing bared to him right now? Because with every passing moment, in bigger and bigger chunks, your spirit is investing in this too? Perhaps even your heart?

I got rid of the thoughts by plunging back into humor. "Ah. So *this* is the part with the handcuffs."

One side of his mouth lifted. Not in a smile. "No handcuffs."

My chest tightened a little more. Another battle between anticipation and trepidation. "Well, where's the fun in that?"

"No handcuffs. Not needed." His hands skated down my arms until curving in at my waist. He brought his face closer, angling over me. "You'll simply obey me, Camellia—because you want to. We both know it."

"Because I'm a good little girl?" I teased.

"Because you are *not*."

He was so close again. His breaths were full of pepper, paprika, and a touch of nectar, a blend of spicy and sweet making me a little dizzy—and a lot aroused. What he demanded of me, with this position alone...the openness, exposure, honesty...exposed so much of me in other ways. My skin was pure electricity. My muscles flexed with readiness. And my sex...hell yes, more than ready. Needing. Clenching.

And wet. So damn wet...

"Your blood sings in the key of naughty, Camellia. And your body...fuck, I can feel it...your sweet, beautiful body hums with the vibration of wicked. And your spirit longs to free it all, but you have kept it locked away, in that cage deep inside your soul, simply praying somebody will find it and open the door." As his hands slipped lower, finding the waistband of my jeans, he fit his head into the curve of my neck. "I am going to open your door, Camellia. And you shall step from that cage, free to show me who you really are. Free to give flight to that creature at the backs of your eyes, restlessly pacing, wanting her dark sky to soar in. I am going to light the stars in that sky for you... and then watch in awe as you make them all shiver as you pass."

I made it a point to breathe. *Don't lose it now, girlfriend. Not. Now.*

But even after I got air in and then out, I couldn't move. His words excavated me. Plumbed parts of my soul I'd never shown to anyone—hell, that I rarely allowed *myself* to see— locking me between floored and terrified. No, that wasn't right. There was a third choice. The one I didn't dare acknowledge, pounding at every crevice of my composure now. Because I'd kept her locked too damn long in the cage.

Karma was really a bitch, especially when your own soul dealt it.

"Damn." I gasped it, letting my head fall back beneath Evrest's hot breath, nipping lips, and worshiping tongue. He moved over my chin and the underside of my jaw, stripping more of my composure with every passionate sweep.

It was so good. Too good. Just as he promised, stars began dancing in my vision. Silver. Sweet. Vistas of such beauty. They made it impossible to protest, to tell him that this part wasn't supposed to be on the program tonight—on *any* night—which had been the point to begin with. All I'd wanted to do was scratch my Evrest Cimarron itch for good, properly expelling him from my system forever. Letting the man dive into the Marianas Trench of my psyche? Not smart. Not safe. And really not sane.

And now, not something I could do a damn thing about.

He was here against me, damn near around me, uncovering more of my soul even as he tugged down the zipper of my jeans, inch by excruciating inch. Air soughed in, tickling at the delicate nerves between my thighs, even through my panties. My gasp joined with his moan.

"Fuck," he growled.

"What?"

"They are...red."

"So I like pretty underwear."

"So do I." Every word was a statement on its own. "Especially like this. Especially on you, my fiery lightning bolt." He pushed my jeans farther down my thighs. "*C'est parmel.* You are so fucking perfect."

"Oh, damn." Pathetic squeak. Great. Some lightning goddess *I* was.

That began my official lesson about the downfalls of snap assessment. Maybe lightning *was* the ideal metaphor here. It was the only comparison that made sense as Evrest slid two fingers beneath the red silk, against my soaked curls. For the first time in my life, I thanked myself for indulging in lavish underthings. It was my guilty pleasure, perhaps a way of making up for an outward style that sales clerks referred to as "classic dressing." Like they fooled anyone with the platitude. Their averted glances always conveyed the truth about my basic piece choices. I was boring. Predictable. As easy to follow as my GPS corner store routes.

I wasn't predictable now. Couldn't claim a single syllable of the word. I was white-hot and barely tamed, prowling through clouds of need, seeking the sweet zap that would set me free to sizzle in the stars.

I fought for it. Writhed against Evrest's long, perfect fingers, silently begging him for the contact. But the banked passion in his body, even in his extended suckling at my shoulder, told me this orgasm wouldn't be an instant reward. He had plans first. Intense ones, if the energy barreling out of him was any indication.

"My sweet sevette." Though he caressed each word into my neck, his free hand got busy, raising to my breast. While palming it from below, he swiped a possessive thumb over my distended point. Yeah, he was set on taunting me. Playing with me. That intent was blatant as he drawled into my ear, "It is your turn now, you know."

"M-My...huh?" I battled amazement just to get that out. His rough treatment of my breast, now repeated on its twin, had just added a crazy revelation for me. His ruthless touch...I liked it. A lot. In the darkest coral reefs of my psyche, new creatures stirred in compliance with that message. *You want more of that. Maybe a lot more.*

"Indeed," Evrest went on. His growl was knowing and wolfish. "For now that you know about my fantasies, it is time for me to learn of yours."

Whimper.

Fitting choice. I didn't know whether to be excited or terrified—or if it mattered. Every cell in my body would still recognize that unfaltering cadence in his voice, the rhythm of a man expecting to be heeded—and willing to do what it took to earn that obedience.

"A-All right. What do you want to know?"

His eyes narrowed. "I believe you already know the answer to that."

I swallowed hard. "You want to know everything."

He nodded slowly. "I want to know everything."

I rolled my eyes. "Of course."

I wasn't certain what to expect when his face intensified, almost turning predatory. That was before I felt the new growth in his erection. The majority of his arousal might have been lodged between his forearm and my belly, but its fresh rise was unmistakable.

I almost smiled about it.

Snarky Camellia turned him on.

Probably a bad idea to call him on the revelation, though. Not now when his fingers moved closer to my core, awakening every tissue there in trembling need. I held my breath, waiting for his elegant fingers to brush me. *Yes.* Yes. *Right...there...*

Tormented groan. Consuming shudders. Then a long, aching sob as he split his caress, taunting the lips on either side of my sensitive spot.

Snarky Camellia got shoved aside.

Desperate Camellia took her place.

I lurched, breathing hard. Fought against the clenching lust in my thighs and buttocks. Forced myself to forget the tingles still spreading from my breasts—and prayed for strength as the hot bud at the apex of my body nearly dominated my existence.

Though Evrest delivered my torment, he also seemed to understand it. As if he soaked my energy right into his body, he pressed our bodies tighter together. Whoa. The new urgency coursing through his own limbs... It was intense. And magnificent.

ANGEL PAYNE

With a tight moan, he rolled his hips, sliding his erection harder against my belly. We both shuddered.

"Evrest...please. Oh, please!"

He shook his head slowly, perhaps even reluctantly. "Confession time first." His lips nestled in my ear, full of hot persuasion. "Tell me what you thought about when you fantasized about me. Tell me everything. Start from the beginning."

He wasn't going to relent. But I wasn't sure I wanted the mercy. My mind rewound to the nights when he was only my dream lover. I'd been alone, in the dark. Private...certainly never to be discovered. Thinking of it now, butted to the reality of being with him like this... It felt like I'd shot another glass of nectar, only better.

"I...was usually in bed. At night. It was usually late."

He rewarded me for that by scraping his thumbnail on one of my nipples. "Were you alone?"

I burst on a laugh. "What the hell do *you* think?"

There wasn't an inch of mirth on *his* face. "I think you must have been asked many times to share your bed. And it would not surprise nor anger me if you told me some lover did not complete his privilege of fulfilling your passion."

"So I'd turn to fantasy boy Evrest to fill the order?"

No sweet nipple tweak for that one. He raised his hand into my hair. Coiled the strands hard. Twisted me toward him for a take-no-prisoners kiss. I was actually thankful for the overhead bar now. Without it, I was damn sure I'd be collapsing in dizzy desire.

"You shall *never* be unfulfilled in my arms."

I breathed harder. Battled against the urge to point out that his promise, in all its heartbeat-flipping glory, wasn't necessary. "Fulfilling my passion" wasn't going to be his "privilege" beyond these moments.

Back to the subject.

"I was alone," I asserted. "All the times. Every time."

A canine rumble loped up his throat. "Hmmm. I like the sound of that. And were you...naked?"

"Yes." I half sighed it as my eyes slid shut. I saw the ceiling of my bedroom. Smelled the fabric softener in my sheets. The only difficult element to remember was the stillness of the condo. The world was a tumult right now. Thrumming blood in my veins. Pounding lust in my sex. And the seductive snarls of the world's most incredible man in my ear. "I was naked... and usually all it took was a thought of you to make me wet."

Evrest pressed his lips to my ear again. He was breathing hard. "What kind of thought?"

"I usually pictured you stripping me. Slowly, like a gift you'd been waiting a long time to open, your hands exploring every part of me as you did. By the time you were done, you were nude too."

"How talented of my fantasy self." His breaths harshened. "What did I do then? Something like this?" He slid his hand up my arm to wrap it over mine, meshing our fingers so he held the bar too.

I nipped at his neck. "Your fantasy self wasn't nearly this genius."

"Shame on my fantasy self."

"He was talented in other ways."

"Oh?" *Finally* he shoved my jeans down, swiftly working them around my knees before tossing them off the bed. I trembled when he was finished, because he'd left the red panties in place—and glanced down at them with clear purpose.

He had plans for the underwear, that much was certain. Not knowing exactly what was another journey into unnerving. "Such as what?" His new initiative didn't help. Instead of fitting his body to mine again, he remained inches away. Might as well have been miles. My body arched toward him. My skin pricked with need. And the little shivers that helped to drench the fabric he fixated on? Fast approaching unbearable.

But I did know one thing. Did I want relief? I needed to talk. "It was...mostly what you did with your fingers," I confessed. "Somehow, even then, I knew how beautiful they were."

His face remained dark. But my words warmed him. The trend was clear in his eyes. "And what did I do...with these 'beautiful' fingers of mine?"

"Magic." I got it out—barely—just before he hooked two fingers around the panel at the middle of my panties. He gave a little twist, turning the fabric into a silk cord that rubbed my most vulnerable flesh.

A moan tore up my throat. My whole body shook. Oh hell, was that good—and got even better. He stroked me again. Again. Again. *Ohhh, yes!*

I was bared and open, trembling harder with every second, totally at his mercy. My nipples were rocks. My body was a string of sensuality, taut and tuned—ready for him.

Surreal. This was so surreal. I'd never felt more alive, more aroused—or more distant from the person I knew as me.

I didn't miss her a damn bit.

"Magic like this?" His voice matched the command of his features.

I nodded, grateful for the excuse to stare at him.

So beautiful...

He had to be more mythical creature than man. His burnished skin, bulging muscle, and mesmeric eyes surely weren't mortal—yet here he was, honing every breathtaking iota of it on me. Into me. No matter what his hands busied themselves with, he didn't look away.

And damn, were his hands busy. While he kept up the panty-twisting torment, he used two more fingers for swiping at the outer lips of my core. He was merciless...magical. I tingled and pulsed. Quivered and needed.

Was *this* what they taught princes at European university now? And if so, why the hell hadn't I opted for a semester in the exchange program?

"Answer me, Camellia. Was this what I did in your fantasies?"

Perfectly timed. Thank God. I needed to concentrate on something other than all the exquisite shivers he brought, radiating from every new stroke to the throbbing tissues between my legs. "M-Maybe," I stammered. "A little. Oh, *shit*..." So much for distraction. He slowly shifted his fingers inward, circling the sensitive rim of my deepest tunnel. "Okay, maybe more than a little."

"I'm listening." He pushed, entering me a little. Withdrew, swirling his fingers around the entrance again. I bucked and tried to get him back inside, but his other hand clawed my ass, forcing me to stillness. "Tell me, sevette. Be dirty if you want. Let me hear the things your darkest dreams are made of."

My head fell forward against his chest. Crazy. This was crazy, right? *Darkest dreams?* Wasn't that like getting invited into the haunted house at the end of the street? Not a wise move. Not a *safe* move.

But what if the creepy guy in the house was Evrest Cimarron? And his weapon was a blade so hot, hard, and perfect, getting stabbed was suddenly the story's happy ending?

Screw wise. Screw safe.

"Y-Your fingers. Just like that," I rasped. "Only...they were...spreading me."

"Spreading you," he repeated, twisting both his fingers back inside. "You mean here? In your gorgeous little pussy?"

"Y-Yes." I moaned it. "Right there. A lot like that."

"Pushing into your body like this? Stretching your cunt?"

"Yes. Like that! Oh...*Evrest*...please...deeper..."

Every gorgeous inch of his body had already been radiating sensual tension—but when I pleaded his name, new energy unclicked inside him. Suddenly, he was a beast off its leash. He snarled against my neck before fully biting down. As I let out a high, loud shriek, he ripped at my underwear, sending it halfway down my thighs. His fingernails followed, scoring the back of my left thigh.

Do it again. Do it again.

Too late. He wrenched my senses away to a new focus. His fingers, now thrusting in and out of me, left no doubt about his purpose. I shoved my hips back, matching him pump-for-pump. *Got the message, lover?* The sooner he replaced his fingers with other body parts, the better.

"This is a very good fantasy, Camellia."

"Uh-huh." It was ragged at best. I could barely think past the heaven of his fingers, pleasuring me in brutal, hard thrusts. His palm slapped my body with every stab, setting up a hypnotic cadence. My head spun, disengaging from my body, becoming a separate entity of energy and feeling and awakening.

Holy shit. I wasn't the girl who'd "gotten around" much in my life, but I was pretty sure this was off-the-charts sex by anyone's standards—and Evrest wasn't even inside me yet.

"You feel so good. So tight against my fingers. And you smell so good, sevette. Your pussy is such a sweet flower. I want to inhale you all night. And maybe all day tomorrow too."

And *then* there were words like that. Things he said, surpassing anything my measly dreams could have concocted—meaning my "flower" was damn near ready to burst now.

"Evrest." I had to twist my hands to keep my grip on the bar. They were slick now, just like the rest of my body. I shivered as sweat trickled between my breasts and down my back. My pussy was soaked, its cream serving as lubricant for the hand he splayed across my backside, teasing into the crevice between my cheeks. Even the tissues *there* were sensitive. "Evrest," I echoed. "Damn. Please. *Please.*"

Little creases appeared at the corners of his mouth. "Please what, little lighting?"

"You *know* what. If you don't—if *we* don't...pretty soon..."

"Is that what we do in your fantasy?"

I longed to avert my eyes. Both of his narrowed, clear with command. *You will not dare.*

"S-Sometimes," I whispered.

"Sometimes...what?"

I groaned. He was going to make me say it. "Sometimes... we have full-blown sex."

His lips quirked. "Do you mean we fuck?"

I ignored his satisfied smirk when I coated his fingers with new moisture. That word...on *his* lips... It only left me with one choice of answer.

"Yes."

The hand on my ass formed into a claw of reprimand. "Say it, Camellia. You can say everything to me. Your nastiest thoughts and desires. *Say it.*"

Squirm. Wince. Comfortable and I weren't going to be buddies tonight. But at the moment, that felt...good. Freeing. The big spooky house at the end of the block? It wasn't deadly. It was...interesting. I liked exploring the dark corners, hearing the new noises. A lot.

"Yes, Evrest," I confessed. "Yes. In my fantasies, we fuck."

Shadows claimed more of his face. Somehow, his stubble had thickened in the last minute, as well.

"Like this?"

He stretched his fingers higher up into me. And, while keeping my stare fastened with the peridot intensity of his, added a third finger.

"Oh! Damn!"

The fresh clench of his jaw turned me on as much as his fingers. "As hard as this?" As he set up a brutal pace from the front, he pushed at my cheeks from the back. Everything down there turned to chaos. Heat. Pressure. Arousal. Need.

And need.

And need.

"Oh. *Ohhhh!*" He'd fully gathered the storm clouds now—and I was the downpour, waiting to break free. The build-up was unbearable. My womb ached as his fingers pounded in, electric arcs reaching out, begging for explosion. My eyes rolled back, making my head swim again. I couldn't believe he made me feel this way with his fingers alone.

"Tell me." Not a lover's persuasion. A ruler's decree, making no excuses for what he commanded. The words. I'd give him my needs in words, the filthier the better. No negotiation.

No turning back.

"D-Don't stop." I started with the easy stuff and got more intense. "Please. Oh please, don't stop fucking me. As hard as that. As deep as that. Stretch me, Evrest. Make me ready for your cock."

His growl resonated with his pleasure. "Perfect. You are so naughty and wicked and perfect, little Camellia."

"Not so hard...when done for you." The words spilled out before I could rein them in. *Shit.* Like the man needed me spewing something like that, all mushy and overcommitted and stupid, right in the middle of a stellar booty call for us both.

To my relief, he returned a generous smile—though a carnal gleam lighted his eyes. "Then my next command will be even easier to meet."

He worked a fourth finger into my tunnel. At the same time, he swiped his thumb across the most enlivened set of nerves in my body. Pressed in with expert precision. And unfurled a beautiful, feral grin.

"Come, Camellia. Come for me...now."

Whoa.

He had to be kidding. *Right?* A woman didn't just orgasm on command. I was the control freak with issues about letting go. I knew this one inside and out. And a few other ways too.

Famous last words.

As the force of the man's voice lashed through me, ensnaring every drop of my blood and force of my will, my last tendrils of restraint busted free. The pearl beneath his thumb was the first part of my body to let them go.

Turning his order for my obedience into the final latch on my cage.

I flew toward the stars.

Burning.

Exploding.

Disintegrating.

Falling.

Really falling.

"Damn it!"

The force of my climax collided with the drag of the nectar. I slipped from the bar, tumbling into Evrest's waiting arms. He easily lowered me to the pillows, still grinding his fingers into me. While stretching beside me, he kept the pleasure rolling. His whispered string of Arcadian was more beautiful in the zero sense it made. His tone built in intensity as my inner muscles clamped on him again, and I cried out in shock as a second climax hit—*surprise, surprise*—a rogue comet in the best cosmos I'd ever been to.

Floating down from the impact took me a few long minutes, as I tried to process it had even happened. That *any* of this had happened. Was I really lying in a cocoon as downy as a cloud, next to my own flawless angel, shivering in the aftermath of two soul-searing orgasms?

I turned and looked at said angel. Who was still flawless. And incredible. Yet stared back like *I* was the perfect thing, blown glass that might shatter any second.

"Evrest."

I needed to hear myself say it. Hoped it would make everything more handle-able.

"Hmmm?"

Nope. Not a chance. Not when he answered me with such reverence before stroking my hairline in the exact same way. Tingles flowed over my scalp until tumbling down my body, only confirming everything about all this was indeed real.

"Handle-able" got tossed right out the window.

Because grasping this reality...meant thinking about giving it up.

The tears burst over me like a surprise squall. Ugh. *Ding-dong; karma calling.* The wench couldn't wait to collect for the climaxes, hitting hard and ruthless, even with Evrest's fingers still inside me. From post-climax calm to hysterical sobs in under a minute.

My hands slammed to my face. Apologies tumbled out. I anticipated—hoped—that Evrest would deal by kissing it out of me, then screwing me senseless. I yearned to be tangled in him again. Around him.

He didn't kiss me.

Confusion.

Or make any move, except to yank the bed cover around us both.

Lots of confusion.

If that page out of the perfect reactions book wasn't enough, he yanked me tighter in, pulling me into the shell now formed of his arms and the comforter, crooning more Arcadian. But like before, I didn't want a translation. The litany of the words, spoken in his velvet voice, communicated all I needed. Strength. Solace. A moment, just one, of feeling completely cherished. Wanted. More than just a quick stop in someone's life before they moved on to something better.

But entertaining the thought made me start bawling all over again.

"Camellia," came his rough whisper. "*Camellia.* Oh sevette, what is it?"

His stress twisted at my heart. But I couldn't blurt the truth. Couldn't confess that I'd let this—and him—mean more than I should have.

Get to the safe route and use it.

"Don't let go." There. The ultimate safety road. I nestled against him, childlike and needy, happy not to feign that part. "Just don't let go yet. Okay?"

"Okay." He broke the word in half, two formalities strung together by the valiant velvet of his voice. It melted me even more for him. And against him.

And brought a fresh sting to the backs of my eyes.

I tried to swipe them but Evrest caught my fingers, kissing their tips. "Let them fall, sevette. I will not melt."

I pulled from his grip, letting my hand explore down, over the part of him that still throbbed, erect and ready. "Apparently not."

To my shock, he yanked my fingers back his chest. "Ssshhh. We shall get to it."

I lifted my head, firing a scowl. "Damn right we will."

He chuckled. "We have all night, Camellia."

My scowl turned into a yawn. "Damn right we do."

Shit. *Shit.* The blood that had been sprinting through my body suddenly took a rest break. I blinked, struggling to keep my equilibrium, but he pulled me into a long, tender kiss before coaxing my head against his chest. His heartbeat resounded in my ear...as he flowed his knuckles down the center of my back.

Ohhh, this wasn't good.

Or fair.

But so perfect.

Which meant that for just a little while longer, the reality outside the room could wait on the fantasy inside.

And that was more than fine by me.

CHAPTER EIGHT

Never considered myself actress material. Ever.

The next twelve hours changed that.

I walked back to my office after an executive team lunch in Harry's suite, wondering where my statue was for Best Lead Actress, the God-Awful-Hangover/Post-World-Rocking-Sex category. My performance had been stellar. Sarcasm. Smiles. Wit. Intelligence. Even attentive to the food on my plate. Nobody—not even Harry, Crowe, or Dottie, who all knew how much I truly drank last night—thought to ask me about the state of my stomach or my head now.

Just the way I wanted it.

Fate finally decided to be a pal again, cooperating with excellent timing. The second unit had a predawn call on the beach, ensuring nobody witnessed my walk of shame back to my room around six. An hour before that, Evrest had learned firsthand how I could sleep like the dead, though he'd enjoyed the numerous attempts it took to kiss me awake. Finally, he'd roused me enough to stand, before walking me back to the real world through a passage slightly more conventional than the one I'd used to find his harem hidey hole last night. When we emerged on the ground level of the palais, it was through a panel in his business office—disguised as a floor-to-ceiling mural of a lightning storm over the ocean. I'd glanced at the painting but was thankful for the mental fog of the hangover, preventing me from reading any more into it than the beauty of the image.

By the time I *was* capable of coherent thought, I was two hours behind on the day and four items behind on my to-do list. The stress was actually a godsend. Focusing on the countdown to the next three days of the shoot, involving us all traveling to the other side of the island and camping out there, gave me a walloping excuse to shunt last night—and all the burning memories of it—onto a huge mental burner.

But thoughts of the man responsible for them? Not such an easy kettle to slide around.

Evrest.

Evrest.

Somehow, in some way, he'd woven himself into the very beats of my heart. Sometimes the pound was so loud, my ears rang and my stomach ached. Others, it was just a comforting thrum, reminding me all over again of the gentle pressure he'd used to wake me up this morning...and the sweet strokes he'd used to put me to sleep last night.

Oh, God.

Last night.

Before I'd turned into a slumbering zombie on him. Probably a drooling one too.

I stopped in the middle of the hallway. My scuffs echoed against the Travertine walls, perfect cover for my horrified groan.

"What the hell do you do now?"

The tiles taunted my whisper back at me. *No escape, little bird. Try to find another window out.*

Riiight.

I shook my head. Even Google wasn't helping me with this one. I highly doubted any advice column, *Cosmo Dude* included, had dealt with something like this.

Dear Cosmo Dude: I got naked with him, screamed through two orgasms, then fell asleep and drooled on his chest. What now? And oh yeah, and my boss will cut off my nipples if he learns I slept with the guy. That's about all. Thanks! XOXO

I started walking again.

Normally, I could've handled this with a couple of careful texts. But this sure as hell wasn't normal. Even if I had his number, the risk was too great. Lesser statesmen had been destroyed by texts in the wrong clutches. He was a freaking king.

A handwritten note? *Snort. Rinse. Repeat.* Delivered by whom? Harry was the only representative from the crew allowed into the south wing, and his clearance was required for anyone else. Wasn't like I could cross that line with Evrest's "toodle over and see me anytime" coupon. I didn't know anyone on Evrest's immediate staff, much less someone I'd willingly trust here and now.

I paused again, just outside my office.

Sighed. Again.

Maybe three days away from Sancti—and him—was the best plan right now. Clean break, pull a Katniss and disappear into the wilderness—without the kill-or-be-killed thing. Before last night, I'd actually been looking forward to the adventure we were bound for on Asuman Beach. Surely that excitement hadn't gone too far away, no matter how hard Hurricane Evrest had struck. Since Harry let me handle crew accommodations again, I'd even confirmed that most of us would be "glamping," sleeping on elevated foam mattresses in semi-permanent structures along the beach. It was damn near the comforts of home...if we all squinted tightly enough.

Feeling much better, I strode into the office with new purpose.

And halted hard again.

"Uh...hello?" I stammered to the uniformed Arcadian woman in front of my desk—pushing my piles around on it. Miracle of miracles, I was cordial about it. I'd left things in a distinct order before leaving for lunch, along with standing directions to the daily housekeeping staff assigned here. Nothing was to be tidied, dusted, or moved unless I was in the room. Everything in here was too damn valuable to lose.

"Ah! Merjour, Miss Saxon." The woman's Carrie Underwood voice accompanied a June Cash hairdo, making me wonder when she'd sneaked onto the island via Nashville. That surprise was trumped when she stepped back, revealing a crystal container brimming with a stunning flower arrangement. "I am Orchid. From the palais floral design department."

"Oh." I tried a little laugh. *Guess* that *made sense.*

She motioned to the flowers. They were incredible, an array of cream, gold, and white, featuring a lot of flowers I didn't recognize—but one I did. Star jasmine, one of my favorite flowers from back home. "Is the arrangement placement acceptable?"

"Errr, yeah. Sure. Of...of course." Wasn't like I could bitch at her about the papers now. Just when I didn't think the Arcadians could blow me away more with their hospitality, they literally sent flowers. "They're lovely. I feel awful that I won't be around after tomorrow morning to enjoy them."

"Well, His Majesty's instructions were that they brighten your work space this afternoon and this evening. He mentioned you would likely be laboring late, preparing for the location shoot at Asuman."

Keep smiling. Keep smiling. It'll keep your jaw off the floor.

"His...*Majesty*? Evre—err, King Evrest told you to bring these?" When she nodded as if I'd merely confirmed the sun was out, I charged, "Why?"

Orchid shrugged. "Why not?"

"So he does this for everyone who—"

Barely sidestepped that pile of doo-doo. How the hell would I have finished it anyway? Clearly, Evrest had handpicked Orchid for his mission, understanding her innocence about the implications of his action.

Smart. But still really stupid. A huge damn risk...

"He asked me to leave this note for you as well, Miss Saxon."

Forget the risk. He'd just barreled into insane.

"Ah." Dignified smile. How the hell I managed it was anyone's guess—though Orchid likely noticed my shaking fingers while accepting the envelope. Shit. The flap was even secured with a red wax seal depicting the entwined dove and hawk of the Cimarron family crest.

I tore into the thing as soon as she left the room.

He'd written the note himself. I knew it as soon as I beheld the bold, regal cursive.

For dancing with Carissa.
And me.
Merderim...thank you.
EC

My chest began to ache before I noticed I'd stopped breathing. Even then, I resisted letting the air back in. I lifted fingers to my wobbling lips as the sweet, sexy simplicity of his words washed to the same depths he'd opened last night. The world didn't stop again...but it slowed into a moment I longed to savor as long as I could.

I woke myself up with a harsh shake of my head.

You're not in Wonderland anymore.

And this is really dangerous.

All right, I'd known that from the start. Only my focus had been the fear of Harry sending me home, not the ramifications of what this would do to Evrest. All I'd lose was a job—not even my main job—but the risk to him?

He'd lose everything.

My fingers trembled harder.

Between one breath and the next, my priorities leaped from one plate on the scale to the other—powering me with the nerve to turn around, leave the office, and head straight for the south wing.

CHAPTER NINE

My obsession with GPSing everything had a bizarre side effect. When I didn't have the tracker turned on, awareness of directions became an obsession. Thankfully, it worked even at six in the morning with a nectar hangover, meaning I was able to backtrack to Evrest's offices in less than five minutes.

But there was a huge difference now, as opposed to the situation at the butt-crack-of-dawn.

Make that six huge differences.

The red-uniformed giants of the Royal Guard clearly took their job seriously. Though their varied skin and hair coloring kept them from looking like the Stepford Guards, it was clear they'd all been sucking the same hustle-the-muscles protein drinks—and reading passages from *Chicken Soup for the Ogre's Soul* to each other.

"Shit." I paced the other end of the hall while biting several fingernails. Best tactic on this? Sweet and nice or official and professional? Maybe just a boldface lie, pretending I had an appointment. Crap, what if he already had an appointment?

Where the hell was my Arcadian Guard Magic Eight Ball when I needed it?

Maybe this wasn't a great idea.

Maybe I needed to beat feet back to the wing I belonged in. I could have done this over the phone. Not mastering the palais interoffice phone system yet, as archaic as it was, didn't constitute an excuse.

But when I looked up, a large portrait on the wall consumed my vision. The four royal siblings were in gorgeous formal outfits, the men in black and Jayd in gold, smiling from some breathtakingly ornate room. Evrest's lips, serene and sensual, tilted with the same smirk he'd used last night when we sat together in the amphitheater.

Fortune favors the brave, Camellia.

I glared. "Damn it. Fine. Message received, lord and master."

I turned. Marched toward the ogre posse. In a minute, this would be over. One or all of them could issue their most daunting Arcadian version of *shoo* and I could retreat, grumbling at his portrait that at least I'd tried. Maybe it'd be less than a minute. One of them touched a finger to his ear, likely activating a comm piece, accepting the throw-her-out orders from someone who'd seen me from the dome cameras in the ceiling.

"Good day." I made it as professional as I could. "Am I able to inquire with someone about—"

The guards closest to the doors swept them back. One of them gave an efficient nod. "Fascha will take care of you inside, Miss Saxon."

I walked forward, not certain whether to relax yet. The office lobby didn't help. The only other time I'd been surrounded by this much marble and gold was during a high school field trip to Hearst Castle, in San Simeon. Word to the spirit of Rosebud.

Behind a reception desk with stained-glass insets and gold trim was a woman with ink-dark, slicked-back hair, a perfect style for showing off the purple tint—seemingly natural—in the strands. She had matching indigo eyes, set into a heart-shaped face. I didn't even ask if she was Fascha. I'd never met a woman who matched her name more.

"Miss Saxon." She rose and smiled from lips glossed in bright pink. The shade would've turned *me* into a clown but simply added to her exotic beauty. "How lovely to meet you."

"Thank you." I tugged at my sweatshirt, a faded thing left over from a rock band shoot I'd helped Harry on. *Nine Days of Bacon*, even in an elegant scroll, looked ridiculous next to Fascha's crisp linen suit. What the hell had I been thinking, coming over here like this?

The answer wasn't pretty. I'd been reacting, not thinking. The choice was likely to bury us deeper beneath last night's mistake.

"His Majesty has cleared an audience for you." If Fascha had an opinion about the *Bacon* boys, her expression didn't betray it. "Right this way."

I followed her to another set of double doors. Shit. I really should have called first. He'd *cleared an audience*? What did that mean? I suddenly felt like an intruder, making him shove aside the business of his country just for my angry snit.

No. Not angry.

I was terrified.

Resolve returned. As diplomatically as possible, I had to teach the man about boundaries with a woman he never should've gotten naked and horizontal with.

Clearly—and adorably—he thought he was doing the proper thing. One glance at the walls in the harem hidey hole were proof that I wasn't the first companion he'd enjoyed there. Orchid had likely been delivering variations of that flower arrangement all over the kingdom. But I was a different case than my predecessors. Very different. The sooner we set that straight, the better.

I lifted my head. Strengthened my steps.

Up to the point I entered his office. For the second time today.

I'd barely glanced at everything this morning in my haste to get the hell out of here, so I looked more carefully now. Directly ahead was his desk, massive and grand, centered in front of a picture window overlooking the palais waterfalls. Adjoined to that was the room with the ocean storm mural. I saw now that it was a "man parlor" of sorts: leather couches, broad low table, full wet bar with decanters aglow from backlights. Evrest sat on one of those couches, leaning over blueprints that took up most of the table and speaking to someone on the phone in fluid Arcadian.

Damn. His voice, speaking his native language... It was like the water on the rocks outside, fluidity and strength mixed. The sight of him was just as mesmerizing. He sat in a shaft of sunlight, appearing an earthbound angel followed by heaven's favor. The light cascaded over his dark waves, highlighting the breadth of his shoulders beneath his white shirt and pinstriped vest.

Damn.

Yes, it bore repeating.

If Henry the Eighth was half this beautiful, it was no wonder women got themselves beheaded for him.

Remember why you're here. You like *your head.*

I stepped a little closer, finally catching his attention. The all-business scowl on his face transformed to a soft smile. He stood, beckoning me nearer with his free hand. Crap, *crap*. His fingers...so long, so masterful... Yeah, *there* was my Kryptonite. And damn it if the man hadn't somehow figured that out.

After I sat, he spent a few more minutes in the conversation. The subject seemed intense, but he finished with a few laughs. As his mood lightened, so did his formality. By the time he disconnected the call, his touch had traveled all the way up my arm. I got goose bumps when he brushed the bottom of my ear. The bumps turned to throbs when he murmured with pure silk, "Hello."

Deep breath. Relax.

Fat chance.

"Hi."

Okay, I'd lost the skirmish. Regrouping was my specialty. *Adapt and overcome. You really like your head. You* really *like your head.*

His gaze fell to the note I still clutched. His smile grew. "You received the flowers."

"Yes," I murmured. "Thank you. They're beautiful."

His fingers trailed upward. Combed the errant wisps off my forehead. My eyelids got heavy. *Won't do any harm to close them...to lose yourself in his warmth...for just one more moment...*

"Then I am glad."

"They're also unnecessary."

"I disagree." He spun the silk into firm command.

"That doesn't matter." I really needed to pull away. Now. But damn it, even the tips of his fingers felt so damn good...the spell of him, more difficult to resist by the minute. "They're *really* unnecessary. Listen...Evrest—"

The rumble from his chest chewed at my composure without mercy. "Mmmm." He tossed the phone to the cushion behind me while sliding closer. "My name on your lips... It is magic."

"No." I shook my head as he tangled fingers in my hair, stripping another chunk of my resolve. But not all. "No more magic. No more flowers. No more notes. Evrest—"

"Mmmm." A growl this time, low and decadent.

"Shit." Strong. I needed to be strong. It helped me push away, until I was sitting on the damn phone. I grabbed the device, flung it to the table, and then slammed my hand into his chest, nodding with pride. This was strong. This was clear.

This was also effing torture because my fingers now pressed at the sculpted perfection of his sternum. But I'd made this damn bed, so—

Great. Did I have to go and even *think* of beds and this man, together again?

Stick to the plan. Then get the hell out of here.

"We're not in the crypt of carnality anymore, okay?" I locked my gaze to his, forcing him to accept my resilience. "We're in the land of rules, mine *and* yours. We can't keep ignoring them, and we sure as hell can't keep breaking them."

Like I was doing just by being in this room. Like he *still* didn't seem to comprehend, if his twitching lips were any proof. "Wait. The crypt of *what?*"

"You heard me. Furthermore, you understood."

"Of course I did. But a crypt?"

"Fine. We can go with the harem hidey hole if you want."

He stopped snickering. Jerked up both brows. "The... harem..."

"Hidey hole." I lifted my chin, openly preening. "It was my first choice anyway. Probably more accurate."

He reared back. Seriously—as if I'd just flung burning coals in his face.

"I'm sorry." I twisted hands in my lap. "That probably

stung. The truth sometimes does, but it wasn't my intention."

His jaw hardened to the texture of solid bronze. Hell. I'd really slammed on a nerve—but my follow-up of guilt wasn't fair, either. I wasn't the one with a secret den of sin under my office. *You play, you pay, mister.*

"Is that what you think you are to me, Camellia? Part of a...harem?"

"Sheez, Evrest. Breathe. I'm not wigged. Your life is what it is. You have to have some freedom in *some* ways, and if that's what toasts your rocks—"

One second, he had reared back, pissed. The next, he was in my face—and pissed. "So that is also what you think last night was to me? A way of *toasting* my *rocks*?"

I gulped. Slid back until my spine slammed the couch's armrest. "Okay, okay. Your rocks didn't get the burn. I'm sorry about that. I'd had a lot to drink, and then you made me...well..."

He followed me right over to the edge. Pressed in against me, grabbing my nape and forcing my gaze to confront the slicing green glass of his. "I made you...what?"

"Do th-things," I stuttered. "And feel things. Lots of... things."

He loomed closer, making me lean back by default. "You mean I made you come? Hard? Two times?"

"Yes," I retorted. Damn it. Could he get any closer? I *had* to ask. He found a way, surging in with his addicting heat and broad shoulders, until I had to grab his vest just to keep myself upright. "Yes. You made me come, okay? Is that what you want to hear?"

Okay, screw staying upright. Or remaining in any respectable position with the man. He kept pressing, incessant and huge, until he had me damn near pinned beneath him. "I like hearing everything you have to say," he uttered. "But tell me more about the orgasms. Were they good, sevette?"

Deep, shaking breath. No damn help. It only made me more aware of everything about him. *Everything.* His spice and sandalwood scent. His rugged, beautiful face. His heartbeat, now lined up directly with mine. "You...you have to stop calling me that."

He demanded in a low snarl, "And about the orgasms?"

"All right! Yes. *Yes,* they were good. Right before you massaged me until I fell asleep, making it impossible to reciprocate, which has turned me into a neurotic mass of guilt, and—"

The man—and his insistence on interrupting me with mouth-crushing kisses—now straddled the line between infuriating and addicting. I weathered waves of both as he pried my lips apart with his, rolling our tongues, shooting a thousand points of fire through my chest, belly, and lower.

Yes. Lower...

Resistance was less of an option when he raced both hands up my arms—and then forced them over my head. "Neurotic mass, be gone," he rasped, curling a conspiratorial grin.

"Huh?"

"Reciprocation," he clarified. "Pretend you are giving it now, Camellia."

"*Now?*" I bit out. "Here? But—"

He meshed our lips again, not lunging as deep but adding a lot of technique to make up for it. *Ahhhh.* Even without tongue, kissing was the man's complete wheelhouse. He thrust his whole self into it, groaning against my mouth as if it were his last act before dying. "Just pretending," he finally rasped. "Okay?"

"My ass," I flung back—only to gasp as he slotted the ridge of his crotch into the V of mine. With his other hand, he hiked one of my legs around his waist. If our clothes were gone, my body would be an open portal for his. He'd be inside me in a second—and I'd be one damn happy camper with every new inch of the adventure.

"Your ass is perfection," he conceded, "but at the moment, your pussy is my focus." Shit. He had to start the hip rocking thing, now tempting me toward happy camper even *with* the barriers between us. My mouth fell open as his slow, wicked thrusts instantly turned our bodies into flint and steel. "Tell me, sevette, how it would prepare to *reciprocate* to me." He glided a hand back to my face, tilting it up so our gazes fully met. "We are only pretending. Let your imagination fly. Would you be wet for me, Camellia? And tight?"

"Yes." I was shocked that much made sense. Once the lust kicked in, my lucidity didn't stand a chance.

Dangerous. The word pounded in again, demanding I listen. This was dangerous. *He* was dangerous.

It was truer when a larger thought took hold. What if somehow, in some way, twin bolts of fate *had* struck that day on the plaza? What if they'd destined us to reunite now? It didn't add to a molecule of sense, but maybe that was also the point. Maybe "sense" had parked me in the rut back home. And yeah, it was a rut. I couldn't ignore it any longer, not after all the madness and magnificence of this week, even the insanity of— well, whatever *this* was—with Evrest. The ditch hadn't been Faye's fault or even Mom and Dad's. It had simply happened. Sooner or later, I'd have to think about it, figure out what to do.

But not now.

For another few moments, I chose to fly above the rut. And the danger. And embrace the power of the word that repeated on my lips.

"Yes. *Yes*, I'd be wet. And tight. And...and achy." I teethed his lower lip, empowered by his tight, hard moan. "And probably quivering."

His eyes flared. His erection expanded. The thunder of it pounded between my legs, as if drawing power from the storm in the mural. "Quivering...everywhere?"

"Everywhere," I whispered. "From the lips of my tunnel to its darkest corners...the places inside that'd be begging for your cock."

"Fuck." It was a filthy sound, lust caking the syllable like mud. My senses rolled in the dirt with him, compelling my body to match every wonderful thrust of his. I dug my heels into his back, wordlessly urging him to ramp the pace—right after a mental note to apologize for the Docs tread I'd likely marked into his vest.

In that perfect way, perhaps dictated by fate, he heard me.

He thrust faster. I whimpered in surrender. And throbbed. And blazed. Arousal twisted in my deepest sex, twirling up like a tornado funnel, clenching every inch of my walls while spinning toward the plains of my control.

My whimpers turned to sighs.

Sighs turned to pants.

Waiting. Wanting. Needing the instant when the tornado razed the barn...

And the world stopped once more.

"More." Evrest's charge was a snarl in my ear. "More words, sevette. What would you do...once I was inside you, filling your secret corners?"

My eyes closed as the dream consumed me. "I'd never want to let you go. Clamp all my muscles around you, keep you as deep inside as I could. Then I'd turn my mouth to your ear, and I'd beg you."

His breath caught. Oh, *God*, I loved making him do that. "Beg me...for what?"

I made him wait for it. Rubbed my mouth against the curve of his ear, letting him feel my teasing smile. Just one more second...

The phone on his desk buzzed three times.

We bolted apart. Teenagers caught on the couch in the basement.

Evrest popped to his feet. I sat up, lungs still pumping. He stalked to the desk, scraping his hair back, before jabbing a button on his desk phone. "Yes." He should've just cussed for all the wrath thrown in it.

"The architectural team for the new hospital wing is here for their two o'clock meeting, Majesty."

He glanced to me. I stood, straightening my clothes. Composure was back—barely. He took a few more seconds, grimacing while adjusting the bulge beneath his fly. After several deep breaths, he finally told Fascha to send the group in.

The team consisted of three men. Two were older, while one appeared between Evrest and me in age. He was the one who strode forward first, shaking Evrest's hand, barely able to contain his curious glance at me as he did. Though I nodded and smiled, I retrieved my note from the couch and prepared to quietly slip out.

Until Evrest turned my rule-breaking excursion into more of a complication than it already was.

He reached out to me, palm up and fingers extended. Shit. He was offering Kryptonite again, with a side dish of his come-here-and-sin-with-me command. I wouldn't resist, and the bastard knew it. Even if that weren't the case, refusing him in front of his colleagues would be a slap past rude, not to mention all the palais etiquette busted in the brawl.

"Gentlemen, before we begin, I should like introduce Miss Camellia Saxon. She is the production manager of Mr. Dane's film crew and stopped in to confirm that I shall be accompanying them up to Asuman tomorrow."

"You're *what*?" Whip-snap of recovery. "I...I mean...of course. Yes, I did."

I jabbed him with a glare without any of the architects noticing. *What. The. Hell?* I didn't know which bombshell to seethe at him for first: the hot mess of arousal I was taking out of here as a "fabulous parting gift" or the one I'd fight off for the next three days. My plan of getting over him with the jaunt to Asuman was officially blown to shreds—and not in a fun confetti popper way.

Back burner. At least for the moment. Time to pull out the "Ms. Saxon" charm and use it for quick pleasantries with the men. All three of them were excited about the plans for the new wing, which would focus on neonatal and pediatric care for the Arcadians. Focusing on them helped me cope, at least a little, with the arcs of energy up my arm as Evrest guided me out, taking my hand and tucking it beneath his elbow.

If he expected parting words, he was sadly mistaken. His hand, now digging into *my* elbow, said differently. *Damn it.* His hold was so tight that if I tried to wrench free, I'd end up making one or both of us look like asses.

His lips hardly faltered from his practiced smile while murmuring, "Meet me back here tonight. Please."

"No."

"I need to touch you again, Camellia."

"And I need to stay mad at you." Little head tilt. Sweet smile. I was getting good at this acting thing. "Why wasn't I told that you're coming with us to Asuman?"

"I was not certain I could make it until an hour ago." His expression changed. While the smile remained, it sharpened, deepened...like a wolf scenting its prey. "I planned on going to your office with the news, but then you appeared here...as if hearing my fantasies again."

Heavy swallow. Painful thud in my throat. Neither helped the molten heat he stirred once more through me. *All* of me.

"Stop that," I snapped.

"Why?" He slid closer. Gray, white, gray; I could count his damn pinstripes. Smell my arousal, mixed with his cologne. Breathe in his power, and sway from it. Hell. I struggled to stay standing while he made the whole thing appear like an innocent goodbye between friends. "I can scale mountains after making you flush like that, sevette. I can leap over oceans with the power of that pulse in your neck alone. And when you come for me, I become the ruler of the whole damn world."

Okay, forget the swallowing thing now. I was officially helpless. Locked into looking up...

To find him already gazing into me.

Intent.

Incredible.

Beautiful.

Impossible.

"Evrest—"

"Meet me. Please."

I clenched my teeth. Couldn't barely get my name straight, let alone the strength to resist him—but somehow did. "Damn it. Fate hates being tempted."

He answered me in a whisper. "Unless it is being fulfilled."

I couldn't think about how right his words felt.

Couldn't. Wouldn't.

My brain started sprinting for a gold medal headache. My body was about to jump into the race, when a tumult in the lobby yanked our sights up.

Fascha rushed in. Her *Blade Runner* glamour was marred by a clear case of frazzled. "Majesty, I apologize. I tried to tell them you were in a closed meeting, and—"

"I tried to tell your *girl* that I knew that already."

The interruption carried an accent I knew all too well. I tensed before its owner even appeared, flouncing through the portal in her gold full-skirted day dress and matching heels, looking set for a fashion shoot in Rome. Her lips were crimson and flawless, her smile dazzling yet classy.

Chianna.

Shit.

The Alpha Distinct had arrived. And after taking one look at my proximity to Evrest, narrowed her eyes with a clear message. She knew what she'd be tearing into for a teatime snack this afternoon.

Me.

CHAPTER TEN

"Evrest. Darling." The second word flowed out of the woman with the subtlety of a Siamese clawing the head off a sparrow. She flashed—well, gritted—a wider smile at us. "I was not aware you had invited...others...to the meeting."

"I do not recall inviting *you* to the meeting." His face darkened. "Miss Saxon stopped by to confirm some arrangements for a location shoot they are doing at Asuman Beach."

"Ahhh." The delight on Chianna's face actually seemed genuine. "What an honor to know my special region of Arcadia will be represented in the film. Asuman is only a few miles east of my home city, Colluss. My papa is the First-Past Regent Mayor."

"Ah." Forced smile. Half nod. "That sounds really..." Like a lame placeholder. "Regal."

"He was mayor of the city for two terms. Likely would be again, if not for the silly term-limit rules."

"We have term limits in America, as well." Sometimes, my conscious *did* work. No comment on this issue was likely the best comment with Chia Pet.

"Well." The tiny falter in her demeanor was proof I'd decided right. And if I was honest, a little gratifying. "If you should need assistance or a guide—"

"The crew has everything they need." Evrest's hand, still on my elbow, tightened as his tone did. "That is why she was just leaving. Perhaps you can be a true helpmate and show her the proper path back to the north wing?"

"That would be awesome." I maintained my smile, despite how Chianna looked as if she'd rather escort a toad back to its bog. "I'm not sane without three maps and a GPS readout." Still the truth. Sort of.

Chianna wrapped a gloved hand around his forearm and canted a practiced pout. "Perhaps Fascha can do it? You know the children's wing for the hospital is my principal passion these days."

Besides walking up an aisle with Evrest at the end?

The woman barely skipped a beat before going on, "Besides...I have brought a surprise for you."

I would've laughed again while watching the tension creep across Evrest's shoulders, but real sympathy intervened. Something told me Chianna's "surprises" had never been pleasant ones.

"Oh?" he growled.

Suspicion confirmed.

"Yes," she murmured. "I arranged it especially for this meeting."

"Oh." His tone dipped into pure dread.

Chianna slinked a bigger smile before motioning through the doorway at Fascha, as if cueing the assistant to bring something in.

Not something.

Some*one*. Times four.

The room's energy leaped as four children ran in. Evrest laughed as they all shouted, racing each other to get to him. Now dropped to a knee, he welcomed them with open arms.

A grin burst on my lips. The kids, all in red and gold school uniforms, were delighted to see their leader—but Evrest's joy was like watching the human form of New Year's Eve. He was lit from within, trading fist bumps with the boys and tugging at the girls' curls, his face suffused with open innocence despite its selected-for-sin angles.

I was enchanted. As if seeing him for the first time—and *really* liking what I saw.

When one of those girls screamed my name, I almost jumped out of my skin. I didn't get too much time to dwell on the sensation, when a head of familiar black curls plowed straight into me.

"Cam!"

"Why, Lady Renata of Paris." I bent and hugged Carissa tighter. "Fancy seeing you here."

Chianna practically preened. "The design of a children's hospital wing might do well with some hands-on opinions, Your Majesty."

"Agreed." The word was diplomatic. Evrest's tone wasn't. "But taking them out of school for it should have been cleared with my staff, Chianna. They would have informed you this was a budget meeting only." He softened as he looked to the kids. "All the boring things only, I am afraid."

Carissa scowled at him. Her eyes might have been blue to his green, but in every other way they were alike—especially when peeved. "So we have to go back?"

Evrest answered with a firm stare. All the kids moaned.

Chianna ditched her preen mode for full panic. I reined back the urge to shake her. There were a dozen ways to spin this and make everyone happy, but she was frozen after thinking she'd pissed Evrest off. Sure, he *was* upset, but the damage wasn't a bomb site. In the grand scheme of life—especially marriages—dumb mistakes like this were the minor bumps.

But the silent stalemate wasn't moving anyone along.

"Suggestion?" I hoped my smile looked helpful. "Why not a win-win for everyone? The kids go back to school, but you stop at the local ice cream joint first. There's one in town, right? I remember seeing it during our drive from the airstrip. Looked cute." I winked at the two boys, now rolling their eyes at my descriptor. "I mean, it looked cool."

The children drew breath for excited cheers but held off until Evrest ruled on the matter. When he cocked a lopsided grin and nodded his consent, they screamed—and Chianna let out a gasp of relief. All was well in Alpha Distinct land again.

Be careful what you assume.

As we followed the kids down the hall to the private entrance for the south wing, I ventured, "They seem like awesome kids. I know that Carissa is Evrest's cousin, but are any of the others—"

The woman halted short. The hall was infused with eerie silence now that her heels weren't tapping the high-fashion version of *Click Clack Moo*. "Miss Saxon." She twisted her lips, leaving Sophia Loren behind for Joan Crawford because of it. *Ew.* "Do not think for one moment that your little stunt makes us friends."

Maybe shock was a good thing sometimes. Mine prevented any other response than a stammered, "My little what?"

"*Ferme,*" she spat. "I am not interested in your pretenses."

"My *what*?"

"All right. Let me phrase it in a way you may understand. Drop the act, bitch."

She popped a haughty nod. I tried not to laugh, but the moment was too perfect to resist. "Congratulations. You've binge-watched enough reality TV bimbos to impersonate one."

The *click-clacks* returned, one-two-three, as she stepped close enough to qualify as in my face. "I will not repeat myself, Miss Saxon. I saw the way you and Evrest were pressed together when I entered his office. I also saw the way he looked at you. It was disgusting, and I will *not* be subjected to it again. If I am, I promise you shall leave this island shrouded in nothing but your own disgrace."

My laughter faded. To fill its place, I managed a believable eye roll—but as I stepped around her, refusing to further validate her threat, my knees were the texture of pudding.

At the same time, my mind and heart were still drenched in another liquid. The magic potion of Evrest's voice, reverberating four words through me.

Meet me. Please. Tonight.

Shit.

Shit.

What the hell did I do now?

CHAPTER ELEVEN

The cast and crew tried to meet for dinner every night in the north wing's airy cafeteria, but tonight, I sent down for a plate. Nobody would be the wiser, thinking me consumed with last-minute details for the trek that would take us to the other side of the island for three days.

In part, it was the truth. In a bigger part, it wasn't. I didn't know if I could face Harry right now, much less get food down with him at the table. He'd start asking about shit like logistics and arrangements and numbers, when the only numbers I could seem to focus on were the ones I'd logged with Evrest Cimarron.

Gotten naked? One.

Screamed my way through orgasms? Two.

Minutes I'd lasted after that before passing out on him? Ten. Maybe.

Minutes I'd held out before letting him climb between my legs again? About the same.

Times I'd slid my tongue with his and longed for it to never end?

The accounting got fuzzy from there. Just as my thoughts and feelings did about...

I pushed my head into my hands.

About everything.

I'd broken the rules. A whole, scary mess of them. The weirdest—and scariest—part of it all? I sat there staring at my picked-over spaghetti and tiramisu, contemplating stepping right past them again.

What the hell was wrong with me?

Rules were never my problem. I was a rock star when it came to walking the straight line, keeping the books to the penny, dotting the *i*'s, crossing the *t*'s. The rules had given me structure when none came from Mom or Dad. Gotten me through all the years at Chapman. Been the safety net for walking into Faye's office for that first terrifying job interview. The rules had been some my dearest besties.

Now I considered unfriending them all. *Wanted* to. Just for one more night with a man who should be invisible to me.

It was getting late. After ten. Perfect excuse to wrap everything up, head to my room. I needed to be on my game tomorrow. I needed sleep.

You sleep like a baby in Evrest's arms.

My eyes slid shut, fighting off that recall—and its accuracy. The man's skin, the color of dark fire, was the same temperature too. When he wrapped his endless arms and legs around me, it was heaven in more ways than one. That man, in his nude glory... *Le Sigh*, even capitalized, wasn't enough.

I wondered if he was naked right now. Waiting for me like that, sprawled across the cloud bed, waiting for me to come to him, like a wolf in his den of decadence...

My cell came alive with IZ's "Over the Rainbow." Harry's tune. This was the first time I greeted the ring with a grimace instead of a smile. I plastered on the latter, hoping to at least convey normalcy.

"Good evening, Mr. Dane."

"Hey."

I sat up straighter. His response might as well have been the F-word and his rapid-fire delivery said he knew that. I cut the formalities. "Okay, what's wrong?"

A thousand scenarios sprang in my head, from glitches with the dailies to problems with the studio. The guys with the Malibu views at Pinnacle had been happy with what we'd shot so far, but everyone knew a key exec on a bad day could combust a film shoot faster than a mouse in an elephant house.

"Can you come down here, please?" His tone, tight and quiet, didn't aid anything except the knot in my gut. He only used "please" when it was bad news.

"You still in the editing room?"

"Yes."

"On my way."

I grabbed the satchel with the majority of my files inside and headed to the editing room, located one floor below.

Eyebrow jump. Harry sat alone. His summons had me thinking this was an all-hands emergency. When I peered around and really confirmed it was just him and me, the Jack in my stomach planted a new magic bean of dread.

Great. Even tiramisu could turn to acid.

When he motioned for me to sit opposite him and then swiveled around the monitor in front of him, acid became nausea.

The image on the screen contained four elements. The edge of an ornate desk. The open doorway to an office. Two people just inside that portal, staring at each other as if deciding to kiss or simply rip each other's clothes off.

Evrest and me. From the moments right before Chianna and the kids entered his office. Faces inches apart. Eyes locked. His lips slightly open on those words that had resounded through my senses all night long.

I need to touch you again, Camellia.

I pressed my lips together. Silence was going to be my best ally right now.

If I had one at all.

Harry finally spoke, his voice flat to the point of scary. "An hour ago, a palais courier delivered a key to me from an anonymous source—with this on it from the security feed on the royal offices."

Lips still pressed—but mind on fire. *Anonymous source, my ass.* All it took to fill *that* blank space was the recall of another conversation from this afternoon.

I saw the way you and Evrest were pressed together...the way he looked at you...I will not be subjected to it again...

I ducked my head. Yeah, it was damn near an instant admission of guilt, but the alternative wasn't pretty. I couldn't meet his glare, the centerpiece of an expression drenched in accusation.

But during that moment, when all I had to look at was the tension in my knuckles, another reaction struck. It shocked me so much, my head shot back up from its force.

Anger.

Not at Chianna, who'd officially moved into a new swamp of yuck because of this—but at Harry. My amiable ex. The guy who'd pleaded me to drop my whole life for this project. My *friend.*

Or so I'd assumed.

Realistically speaking, how much did he really know? Only what he saw on that monitor. My unauthorized visit to the south wing. He'd taken a lot of liberties with interpreting the rest. A lot. That turned his allegation into one thing alone. A low damn blow.

"Gee, Harry. I'm having trouble sifting through that mess you're calling coy. What are you really trying to say, based on what you're looking at from *one* shot off a security feed?"

He had the grace to look ashamed—for a second. "One shot is sometimes all it takes, Cam. You've been on enough jobs with me to know that by now."

"Really? That's the angle you're going with?"

"And what's yours?" he volleyed. "Insulted and innocent? When I'm looking at evidence like this?"

"Evidence," I echoed, folding my arms. "Damn, Harry. So sorry. If I'd known the Spanish Inquisition was scheduled tonight, I would've brought my chains and shackles."

He surged to his feet. Angled over me, handsome features now distorted. "I resent the crap out of that. Since I was three and understood what a movie was, I've devoted my whole damn life to the art of evoking emotions through a camera lens. So look again at that screen, Camellia Diana, and tell me I'm misinterpreting that come-fuck-me-now look you're mooning at the King of Arcadia."

My wrath hit splash-down—into an ocean of sadness. The weight pressed me back in the chair. "You aren't even going to give me a chance to explain, are you?"

He stepped back, folding his arms. "Fine. Explain. Give me every chance to understand why you were in a part of the building I expressly forbade everyone from, jeopardizing our relations with the Arcadians in nearly the worst possible way. Don't think I'm unaware of who interrupted your little moment with Evrest, either. I wouldn't be surprised if Chianna was my anonymous source too. Little piece of work. I'd thank her if I wasn't so scared of her."

Oh, Harry. You have no idea.

"So saying that, you're still coming after *me*?"

He tilted his head, throwing a chunk of hair over his face. I used to call it his Flynn Rider sulk. Made me want to grow my hair fifty feet and drag him off for enchanted tower sex. Now, I just longed to smash him with a frying pan.

"Tell me that video's doctored, that you weren't really in Evrest Cimarron's office today, and we're golden."

I torqued my wrists. Shit. How deep could I really lie to him and still get to sleep tonight?

You know what that answer should *be, right?*

After flipping my conscience off, I forced my head up again. *Direct and strong. Just do this.* "Look, I had to go over some logistics...about the king's security detail...for tomorrow." Tiny exhale. Technically, none of it was a lie. I'd simply left out pieces of the narrative for...continuity. "And I knew you had a head full of insanity, getting caught up on stuff before we left, so—"

"Whoa. Time out." He shook his head. "Calling bullshit, honey. I'm the producer and director of this thing. It's my job to be insane, Cam. You know that. You should have at least picked up the phone and—"

"And I'm the *production manager* of this thing!" I yanked my hands apart, turning them into fists. "It's *my* damn job to make sure everything gets *managed*. I can't do that if I'm worried about getting your permission for a hall pass at every turn, or if you're jumping to conclusions about me before getting the facts straight—or hey, this is a crazy idea, even asking me about them." I pushed to my feet but didn't stop, letting my ire propel me toward him. "What happened to having each other's back, Harry? To a friendship that survived even a relationship? To believing in each other, even when seeing all the facts says it's something different?"

For a long moment, he only stared. I breathed easier. Just a little.

The moment didn't last. He sat back down. Swung his gaze again at the monitor again. "I don't know what to believe anymore."

"I'm asking you to believe in *me*."

"I want to, Cam, okay? But there's a lot on the line here. This really isn't just about the damn movie."

"I know."

My voice almost cracked. And yeah, I did know...but I'd conveniently forgotten. No. Allowed myself to forget. *No*. That wasn't the case, either. Forgetting implied I could remember things whenever Evrest held me...that there was a world beyond the bubble of us. But that space, carved by the universe for him and me... It was, like the stars it had been woven into, born from forever yet doomed to fall.

And sometimes, when too much was at stake, the plummet had to be nudged.

I turned, tears piercing, despite how "Ms. Saxon" cheered the fortitude of my decision. *Blegh. Fortitude.* Wasn't that a word used by pale matrons, cooing at their arfy dogs over afternoon tea?

"Cam?"

"What?" I didn't apologize for not hearing whatever he'd just said. We were both raw right now. And both at fault. His instinct about the screenshot was, after all, a hundred percent right. My guilt didn't stop me from stealing another glance at the monitor. Being able to look at the gods' eye view of Evrest and me...was mesmerizing. His head was tilted down, angled perfectly to the lift of mine. He gazed at me with passion, adoration, protection.

He was beautiful. And I was beautiful when I was with him.

The wrong place. The wrong lifetime.

The sooner we accepted it, the better.

"I was trying to apologize," Harry said. "But obviously not doing a great job."

"You're fine," I assured. "We're fine. Everything's fine."

"You know how much I believe you when you babble, right?"

I didn't laugh and knew he'd forgive me. I also didn't waste any more time defending the answer. Or myself.

It was time to take the crappy medicine. It was going to taste like shit for a while, but the alternative wasn't acceptable. When medicine didn't go down, shit got compromised. Vital organs failed.

A country got compromised.

I wasn't going to do that to Arcadia.

I wasn't going to do that to Evrest.

The words had to be spoken before we left for Asuman.

★ ★ ★

Knowing Chianna had an insider—probably several—monitoring the south wing's security feed, I took another scenic stroll past the amphitheater, behind the palm tree, and into the palais's secret passageways. While stepping back through the darkness, I forced myself to envision the catacombs of *Phantom of the Opera*, not *The Mummy*, though I exhaled in relief when the pungent damp of the tunnel was infused with Evrest's spicy sandalwood.

Small fist pump. He was still here. Still waiting. I could sense him already in the changing energy in the air, the sprinting beat of my heart, the nearly audible rush of blood in my veins.

Fine. This was the kind of crap I'd always sworn not to believe in, especially when nothing like it had ever manifested between Harry and me. Moreover, I'd logged ten birthdays since shoveling cake past my braces at fourteen. A "bursting chest" and "tingly girl parts" weren't validation for feeling "connected" to someone.

But the leap of my spirit, anticipating the way he'd see its every depth?

The race of my mind, wondering how he'd challenge it?

And the sweet turn of my heart, anticipating how he'd touch it...

How empty it would be without him in it.

Resigned breath. "Do it fast," I ordered myself in a whisper. Like ripping off a Band-Aid. There'd be no way around the pain, only the length of time for the ow-ow-ow factor.

The second I entered the room, that assessment was revised.

Ow. Capital *O.*

The same shape my lips formed, taken over—again in this room—by awe.

No colored backlighting on the drapes tonight. Instead, their folds danced in the glow of at least two hundred lighted white candles, placed around the room in tiered holders. But that bronze radiance was just the support show for the golden splendor of the man in the middle of it all. Dear God, had I actually *found* a god? No other definition made sense. His broad, chiseled chest gleaming over those endless legs, clad only in black workout pants. The ends of his hair, tumbling loose and messy to his nape, were still a little damp. Damn. He must have been fresh off a workout, explaining the shiny rivulets on his shoulders and the rapid pumping of his lungs. Perhaps I was fresh off one too. Seemed a perfect explanation for the sweat between my breasts—and the throbs that vibrated lower.

Pulses that got worse as he lifted a slow smile.

And worse again as a song of sensual longing emanated from hidden speakers.

And turned to blatant torture as he stepped toward me.

"You came."

Sawdust breath. A stumble backward, trying to keep the distance between us. Holy hell, he was magnificent. Glorious. And had done all this...for me.

This already sucked on so many levels.

"But I can't stay."

He shook his head. No. More like twitched it, as if I'd spoken words that made no sense.

"I'm...I'm sorry. I wanted to—had to—come tell you in person. Evrest, everything we've shared...this was all—" I stopped myself, banging fists on my thighs. "No. I can't say it, and I won't. What we did...it wasn't a mistake. This"—I pointed between my chest and his—"isn't wrong."

"We are in agreement so far, sevette." But the shadows in his eyes belied his forecast of my next words.

I dropped my head. *Coward*. It was true, but I wouldn't fight it. Couldn't. Staying on my feet was a composure sucker all on its own.

I hated this. Every hard, wrenching second. I wanted to make his face darken for other reasons. And God help me, I longed to dive into that darkness with him. I craved visiting those sinful corners inside myself again...the wicked desires only he'd been able to illuminate...

"Timing." There. I'd gotten it out. "It's the timing that we got wrong, okay? If this were all happening in another century...hell, in another galaxy..." The strength was too good to last. Huge swallow. *Keep going. You must.* "Our paths simply shouldn't have crossed each other." Dear God, was I trembling? *Pathetic.* I'd dated Harry for eight months and not crumbled like this at the end. "We just need to face reality now. Get shit back on track and—"

The vehemence of his growl seized the rest of it from my throat.

His stomp forward, closing the distance between us, robbed the resilience in my limbs.

"How dare you," he seethed.

"What?"

"How. Dare. You"—he jerked me harder—"speak of our paths as if they were regrettable...disposable!"

"Ev...rest." My lips parted, but even his name was split by pain, impossible to ignore as he slammed our bodies together. "I...I can't..." *Think. Move. Function. Breathe.*

"Three years. You have haunted my memories for three damn *years*, Camillia. So many times, even after my furtive internet searches, I wondered about you. Had *dreams* about you. Ranted at the Creator about why He would not let you leave my mind...my fantasies." A pained laugh left him. "I thought I was insane. Maybe I was."

"Shit." A sob, fighting past the barbed wire in my chest. Causing him this conflict... It was worse than I'd imagined. I looked down, wondering why my blood didn't stain the floor. Wanting it to. "I'm...I'm..."

"You are *here*, Camillia. *That* is the right answer. You are here, and suddenly, the insanity makes sense. When I walked into the ballroom the night you all arrived...and saw you standing there...the girl who had not left me alone for three years..."

He swallowed hard, strangling his own words short.

Before clutching me even closer and crashing our lips together.

The fury in his kiss matched every note of his words. There wasn't a second to think, to hesitate, before he shoved his tongue in and wrapped it against mine, consuming my mouth in violent heat. It was a kiss with one intention alone— to bear the truth of what he snarled at me next.

"This is not an accident, Camellia. Right here, right now, in *this* lifetime, *we* are not an accident."

Pushing away wasn't an option. He made sure of that with his eyes, his lips, his presence. His resolve cracked open mine. I adored him for it. Hated him for it.

"Wh-Why are you forcing this?"

He clutched the back of my head. "And why are you fighting it?"

"I'm not supposed to touch you."

"I know."

"And you're supposed to be touching...well...*not* me."

"I know."

Our chests were pressed hard now. I tilted my head back to meet his gaze. His eyes still held shadows, only they were different, thickening to the texture I craved so much. His muscles constricted around me. His jaw clenched into ridges of command.

Another hard swallow. But better this time. And worse.

Blissful, torqued tension.

Hot, desperate awakening.

"But you're going to touch me anyway."

"Yes." He stretched his fingers around my head to explore my jawline from behind. His scrapes, sweet but intense, spread warmth through my scalp...and new stings beneath my eyes. "And I am going to do it everywhere. Outside. Inside. As I have been dreaming of doing since I let you go this afternoon."

Damn.

Damn.

I was a maelstrom, maddened but magnificent. The heat flowed through me, stealing my breath, crumbling my defenses. "I've been...thinking about you too." More ramparts crashed. Oh shit, I needed to touch him. My fingertips roamed the ridges of his abs, the planes of his chest, the muscled bole of his neck. I sighed, unable to hide my desperation from him. "Oh, God. I fought so hard not to."

"No." He tugged harder at my scalp. "No more fighting it, lightning." The renewed plunge of his mouth was another heaven of searing demand. "Give up, sevette. Give in."

"But—"

"Tomorrow. It is hours away." More surges, made of pure fire now, as he licked and bit his way back to my ear. His hand skimmed down, beneath my jeans and underwear, forming his bare palm to my ass. "Our paths are still twined. And our reality is still only this. It can still be right. So right..."

His hypnosis, so perfect, braided with the very strands of my DNA. Cravings rose, as primal and spiritual as they were lustful. I was his wild creation, lifting my lips to lay claim on him in return. Evrest's response, a groan that thundered through us both, made me pull on his hair to deepen the connection of our mouths...the mating of our spirits.

He tore his lips away—while shoving my jeans to my ankles. After dropping to pull them all the way off, he untied my Docs and hurled them against the wall.

But when I thought expected him to stand again...he settled down there.

Ohhhh, God.

His hands ran up and down my legs, claiming, savoring, commanding. I clung to his huge shoulders for balance, breathy sighs escaping as he rained rough shivers over my skin. When I thought he was finished with the onslaught, he simply changed tactics, one of my legs high enough to kiss his way down the bridge of my foot. At the same time, he pressed his knuckles into my arch.

I gasped.

It tickled yet tantalized, blowing a shit ton of clear thoughts into the stratosphere. Correction. For a production manager who'd spent a lot of hours on her feet lately, he shot me straight to heaven.

"Oh." I half gasped it. "Oh, ssshhhhit. Yessss..."

No more words for now. I had a feeling it wouldn't be the first time tonight. Not that words mattered with him, ever.

He finished taking my other foot to paradise—and then went to work on the fabric triangle between my thighs.

"Ahhh!"

It spilled as he pressed a fervent kiss directly on that sensitive crux. "Mmmm," he murmured, trailing his mouth along the silk. "Blue this time." He kissed toward my inner thigh, turning me into a tremoring mess by the time he nipped down to my knee and back again. "Stunning, though it hardly matches your eyes."

I dug my nails into both his biceps, almost grateful for the chance at a laugh. Helped with the pressure...a little. "Are you comparing my *eyes* to my *underwear*?"

He growled, smug and sensual. Slipped his hold around to palm my backside. "Sevettc, I would recite every sonnet ever penned by Shakespeare if it kept your pussy quivering beneath my lips like this."

Stunning bastard.

"Quivering? If you mean about to slide out of my skin from wanting you, then—"

"Ssshhh."

"*Evrest.*"

He pinched my buttocks. Hard. "*Ssshhh.*" I was barely over the tweaks before he lowered his mouth over my center again—to bite me through the silk of my underwear.

"Ahhhh!"

He bit me—bit me!—again.

I held in the scream this time. I learned fast. Screaming meant he'd bite again. Not that it had been awful. I just didn't know how much more my senses could take.

I focused on twisting my hands into his hair, attempting to regain some balance. Turned out to be wise. Damn good chance I would've fallen over as he exchanged the biting for full-on licking. Yes, right through my panties.

Wow. *Wow.*

His moan warmed my mound as my body relinquished its honey to him. As he sucked in more of my essence, he moaned and licked harder. *Dear God, harder...*

"Fuck." He rasped it between harsh breaths. "By the Creator, Camellia. You are sweeter than all the fruit on every tree in my land."

I forced open my eyes. *Had* to watch him, if just for a second. His own stare, a lagoon of pure sex, already awaited. His lips were the picture of pure sin, fitted over my most private space like he lounged in that lagoon, feasting on the world's most succulent treat.

"Evrest," I pleaded. "Please, I—"

Denied. Just one second of his determined gaze did it. He wasn't listening to a damn thing I said, unless it followed the lines of *I'm going to come now*.

Not acceptable. His pleasure had to be part of mine. I'd learned it with scorching clarity when we'd stolen those passionate moments in his office. Now, it was nonnegotiable. I told him so by buckling my knees, knocking him off-balance, and tumbling us both to the floor. *More like it.* With him lying beside me, I was able to explore more of him, even suckle at his chest while dipping a hand beneath his waistband, slipped to a mouth-watering angle on his rock-hard hips.

"Camellia." His grip on my hair was as tight as the word in his throat. He ended it in a choke as I closed my fingers around his taut shaft, running my thumb through the telling liquid at its tip. "Fuck. That's—"

"Sssshhh." I gave him a saucy taste of his own medicine, following it all the way through by dropping my head...and tasting what I'd just touched.

His growl razed the air as his flesh consumed my mouth. He was perfect. Hot. Huge. Delicious. His cock swelled against my lips, turning me into a newly christened sex goddess. Powerful. Beautiful. And longing to give him more.

"Fuck. Sevette...please...I need you to—"

"Give you more?" I angled a sultry gaze up at him, caressing his cock with my cheek. "Because this is what *I* need,

Evrest. To know I affect you the way you do me. To feel *you* trembling too."

He did just that as I turned and sucked him again. The victory was heady, feeling his erection grow and his sack pulse, the essence of his masculinity at the mercy of my eager tongue and lips. As I worked his pants down, his thighs shook beneath my hands. He helped me at the end, toeing them off before using the extra leverage from his feet to work his length deeper past my lips.

"Camellia. *Ohhhh...*"

He gritted out more, long phrases in Arcadian, nasty and needy. I took in more of him, giddy with victory. Wasn't much time to celebrate it. His fingers sank to my scalp, setting a faster pace for my service. I loved every moment, feeling his pleasure against my tongue. His big body tensed and hardened, my giant wolf in sensual surrender. He was stripped bare, trusting me deeply. New tears stung the backs of my eyes with the force of my gratitude.

His grunts deepened. His thrusts lengthened. I gave back soft sighs, the ready vessel for all his heat, his hardness, his lust.

Until he ripped the air with a harsh command.

"*Enough.*"

He yanked my head up. I couldn't help staring, enraptured with the masterpiece I'd created. Didn't hurt that I'd been given a work of art to start with. His penis was as mighty, proud, and unwavering as everything else about him. It rose from his body, nearly a right angle. I licked my lips, wondering if he'd let me sneak one last taste...

No damn chance.

In one powerful move, he reversed our positions again. The world cartwheeled as he flipped me over, rolled me beneath him—and then ripped my breath out, plunging his mouth against mine.

We moaned together. Writhed together.

With equal mastery, he shoved a hand between our bodies, forcing my shirt off. I reveled in the sound curling up through him, ravenous and rough. It vibrated into the dip between my breasts before he murmured, "Mmmm. *Blue.*"

I sighed into his hair. Inhaled back in, savoring the ocean spice in the thick strands, as he nudged his tongue under my bra. I instantly stiffened for him, my nipple begging his tongue for more.

I peeked beneath my half-closed lashes as he stroked long fingers down the rest of my body. As candlelight danced along his sleek muscles, I wondered again if the man didn't have ancestors from the summit of Mount Olympus. Not that I was capable of much more thought, once his fingers slipped back beneath my panties...

And slicked through me.

And parted the depths of me.

And delved inside.

Deep.

"Evrest!"

He pushed in a second finger. "Yes, my sevette?"

"Damn it. Please. Now!" When he didn't falter his rhythm by a beat, I scratched down his shoulders and pushed up my hips. "*Please.* I need...all of you..."

He lifted his head. His stare, so brilliant, didn't waver. "You already have all of me."

My eyes slid shut as his declaration sank in. Damn it. *Not the double meanings, Evrest. Not now. Please.* Not making it sound like he was a knight riding out with my favor strapped to his lance, ready to die as I sobbed his name in the gallery.

It wasn't going to happen. Not tonight. These hours weren't for sobbing. Or regrets. Or looking back, even by an inch. We had to squeeze the magic from now...until we were both too exhausted to care anymore.

Our reality is still only this...

"You know what I mean." I gave it to him in a whisper while sliding my thigh up, rubbing his stiff length. His coiled muscles and deep growl bolstered me further. "I need all of your body, Evrest. Wrapped in mine. Hot and full. Pumping into me..."

Yikes. And *damn.*

I almost didn't believe the words were mine. While my fantasies were spun from words like that, I'd never tapped into the courage to vocalize them. Speaking them was like a magic wand, wielding an invitation to Oz. Watching what my desire did to Evrest—his huge pupils, his parted lips, his strained muscles—was like stepping from black and white into Technicolor.

More gasps. Deeper sighs. Mine *and* his.

My senses flew, part of a journey both familiar and strange, reaching higher, higher, toward my ultimate peak of empowerment. As he dipped his head, taking my mouth with his hardest passion of the night, I ascended to more beautiful. The world fell away, tiny and distant. Heaven swirled around me, dazzling...amazing.

Too amazing.

"Too much," I rasped. "You're going to...*I'm* going to... stop...*stop.*"

He didn't relent. His fingers kept pumping, claiming my channel with long, thorough thrusts. With every plunge, my pressure mounted, starting deep, spiraling outward. I gasped, fighting the incursion, unwilling to let myself fly solo at his mercy. He had to soar too. After tonight, he'd truly be my forbidden—but I wouldn't accept that without giving him release along with me.

"You need me to pump, little lightning? Harder? Faster? Talk to me, Camellia. My fingers are your servants."

Somebody still wasn't getting the whole memo. "Damn it, Evrest. What I need is your *cock*. Please!"

If that didn't bash down the door of his comprehension, I'd have to go get a real-life ax and breaching explosives. Thankfully, it worked—at least at first. Though his gaze now held understanding, the rest of his face was tight with something different. A question? A hesitation?

"What is it?" I charged. "Do I stink? I showered today—"

"Sevette." He nudged his nose against mine. "You smell so enticing, I could lick every inch of you."

"Okay." Perplexed scowl. "And I'm pretty certain your... willingness...is all here."

He laughed as I referenced his arousal. "Present," he murmured, "and—how do you like to say it?—straining at the reins?"

With my stare still bolted to his, I dared an exploring hand downward. The thick tip of his shaft throbbed against my fingers. "Then let go of the reins, my *tüsüterre*."

His eyes widened. My memorization of the Arcadian word for thunder had clearly surprised him—but not enough to help my cause all the way. His fingers slipped from my body as his forehead dropped against mine.

"Camellia. *Camellia.* Every cell of my blood, every muscle in my body, and every beat of my being is screaming at my cock to slide into you right now...to be lost in you for hours."

"But...?"

"But..." He reset his jaw and pulled in a harsh breath. "Sevette, I have taken...a royal preservation vow."

"A royal *what*?" Snarky frown. Couldn't be helped. It sounded like he was telling me about how he'd promised to save some Arcadian nature park, which made no sense, other than the angle on the birds and bees. Was this his strange way of telling me we were in his secret sex den with no condoms?

"It is an expected pledge for the Arcadian king to take," he explained. "So two years ago, I did—promising I would not share my seed with anyone other than my bride."

"Oh." It spilled before full comprehension took over. "Ohhhh. *Whoa.* You're two years into a purity vow?"

His brows crunched. "Define *pure*."

"Good point. And to be honest, thank God. But I'm still baffled." I lifted a hand, motioning at the whole of the room. "Evrest, you clearly have an...affection...for sex."

His lips quirked. "Indeed."

"That was rhetorical. No need to elaborate."

He grazed my breast with a thumb. "But elaborating can be the best part."

Shaky sigh. Damn, what the man could do to me with a quirk of his lips and a brush of his fingers. "You know what I mean."

He aligned his stare with mine, unleashing the new intensity on his face. "I would have it that you always receive the truth from me, Camellia. So yes, I have enjoyed my 'affection,' as you call it, with others. But—"

"But you've taken an oath not to consummate with anyone," I cut in.

"Not to share my seed," he clarified.

"Which means...?"

The sexy bastard countered my scowl with an indulgent smirk. "Sex and consummation... They are very different things. Carnal pleasure can lead to many things, not just intercourse." As he glided his hand back down the center of my torso, taking the languorous way toward the curls at my center, he rumbled, "Wonderful things. Wild things. A world that can bring beautiful pleasure...to everyone."

I held my breath as his fingers trailed lower. When they dipped in, rediscovering the center of my pleasure as if laser-guided there, I let it out on a violent gasp. "Ohhh..." His chest absorbed the sound. I inhaled him with frantic greed, needing his scent, his power, his potency. "You make me believe every word of that."

"As I long for you to. As I need for you to."

His fingers backed up every word of his promise. They slid deep and explored thoroughly, stopping only when they found my other button, deep inside my sex. Circles of heat, focused and firm, incessant despite how I bucked and arched...

Needing him but fighting him...

Until ecstasy gave me no other choice.

Moans and then screams. Clenches and then spasms.

Before every nerve ending in my body sizzled. And every thought in my head imploded.

"Ohhh!" I still pushed my hips up, yearning for more of the inexorable torment. Un-freaking-believable. I wanted more. "Evrest...that's so...*you're* so..." How did I pick just one word? Maybe I didn't. "Magical," I began. "Incredible. Selfless. Generous. Ohhh!" When he quickened his pace, spiraling his hand to give me even more pleasure, I arched against him once more. He'd turned me into a damn rock video hussy.

His cocky growl warmed my forehead. "You were saying?"

Slow growl. "You're unfair."

He nuzzled his way to my ear. Oh *shit*, it felt good. I hoped the man had an insurance policy on his lips. "Probably."

"And you get away with it because you're so damn beautiful."

"I get away with it because I am so damn good." He laughed at my snarl, though added in a voice sultry as honey, "And because I enjoy it. And oh, sevette...I enjoy *you* so much."

I pulled back enough to impale him with a glare. "But you don't enjoy *all* of it."

"I enjoy more than enough, Camellia." It was a directive more than a statement, backed by a rebar-strength stare. "My needs will be met. Do not waste another concern about that."

"Your 'needs will be met'?" Open chuff. *Hold up, He-Man, I can't hear past your fists on your chest.* "And don't 'waste' my 'concern' about it? What the hell does any of that mean?"

He shook his head with that sharp confusion again. The look tightened into anger as I scooted back from him—and damn it, the addicting heat of his touch—to turn and gaze at the walls occupied by the shelves of sex toys. It was an impressive collection, like a trip to Godiva for a chocoholic, and must have been like heaven-in-the-basement for the Arcadian women lucky enough to be invited for some of Evrest's time in here.

Briefly, I wondered if any of the Distinct were part of that club. It would explain why some of them resorted to the tween-tastic maneuvers to stay on his radar. There were vibrators, pulsators, and ticklers. Dildos, bead strings, and specially-shaped insertables. Sensation devices from mild massager/sensation sticks to more adventurous nipple suckers, and even big jars full of packets containing lotions and creams, all for the purpose of "Her Pleasure."

Her pleasure.

Never his.

Damn.

With new understanding, I turned back to Evrest. Stared at him, his body so hard and his eyes so tender, and let the force of my astonishment wash over my face. The change in my expression wasn't lost on him.

"Perhaps...we should talk." His words fell onto the air, leaden and ridiculous—aka, the perfect expression for the moment. But by hearing him verbalize exactly what I dreaded, I gained a hard, nervy *whomp* in the ass.

The same ass I turned upward, while repositioning myself on all fours—before starting to slink back toward him.

Impish grin. Feline suggestion. Open invitation, sluiced with my desire, as his gaze dropped to my swaying breasts. "You know, Mr. Cimarron, we have a little expression in the States about 'talking.'"

"Oh?"

The query melted the air from the heat he gave it, matching the fires sparking in his gaze. He leaned back on his heels now, giving me a perfect view of what my approach did to him. I was so tempted to dip my mouth again, taking all of his stiff heat inside my thirsty mouth...

"What kind of an expression?" His growl was full of torrid intent.

When I was just inches away from climbing onto his lap, I broadened my smile—before turning around once more. Before he could protest, I reached back his arms and slammed him tight against me. Still not enough. I slid both his hands down, plunging them beneath my panties.

His breath shuddered.

My smile grew.

For one night, I wanted *him* to be amazed once more by what could happen in this room. Taken by surprise. Taken to the place where the world stopped—to the edge of where his vow began but not over it.

It was possible—and I knew exactly how.

I just needed to keep the bold seductress vibe going.

I threw my head back against his shoulder—*imaginary tequila shot, don't fail me now*—before unhooking my bra and letting it fall away. As Evrest peered over my shoulder, rasping harder in appreciation of my fresh nudity, I finally rasped his answer.

"Talking...is overrated."

CHAPTER TWELVE

"Sevette."

I already had a list of things the man did to turn my bloodstream into a parade of need...but that endearment in my ear, whispered with that blend of aroused and imperious, turned everything into a five-keg party with a live band on the roof. And when he twisted a big hand into the elastic of my panties, yanking brutally on the soaked fabric...

Ohhh, hell.

Party. On.

I gasped hard. He growled harder. For one awesome moment, we weren't here trying to forget the bigger world above, the bigger rules we were bending. We were just a couple of dorks at a fraternity rager, hornier than hell for each other in the rumpus room. I shivered as my new arousal met the air, awakening everything between my thighs with wet, warm tingles.

Evrest hurled the torn fabric atop my discarded bra, a couple of feet away. But as he murmured again into my ear, illicit tone betraying it as more filthy Arcadian, I forgot about the clothes. The room. Maybe even my name. It was him. Only him. The only world I needed to comprehend, the only fire I needed across the landscape of my thoughts, feelings, sensations.

I showed him so by sliding my body tighter to his. My hands tunneled into his hair as he roamed his own up my body, conquering me in hot, possessive sweeps.

When he got to my breasts, he took them from below. His deep wolf's growls set the tone as he cupped me, squeezed me, savored me. "C'est parmcl. *Et douli.* My perfect, sweet sevette..."

"Yes." I arched for him, needing more of that raw canine carnality. His fingernails, marking my soft flesh, were the hungry beasts I craved. "Yes...oh please...*yes.*"

I cried out the last word, rejoicing as he finally tugged at my nipples. He'd been teasing at them for so long, when what I'd really needed...was this. Stabs of perfect pain, forcing me outside my mind...into my soul. The caverns of my own spirit called, dragging me in, echoing with my moan as he pinched a little harder.

Damn. *Damn.* Sweet, sharp pinches. Tingling, zinging aftermath. My brain strained at its moorings of lucidity...again.

"It is good, Camellia?"

From panty-ripping Conan to devoted Casanova...that was my Evrest. *No. Not yours. Not ever. Enjoy all his facets now, because this is all you'll ever get. The only night you have left.*

There was no better conclusion to firm my resolve.

"Yes," I answered. "Oh, God, yes..."

"The little stings...turning your tits into such delicious red berries for me... Those are good too?"

Frantic nod. "Ohhhh, yes. Really good."

"Mmmm." He twirled my engorged tips between his thumbs and forefingers. "I believe I agree."

I pulled in a deep breath. Windows of opportunity didn't get much better than this, especially when opened by the man who forever redefined my standards for passion. Evrest Cimarron... He'd be the one I'd never forget, as long as I existed on this planet. The lover who'd consume my mind and drench my sex even when I was blowing out the candles on my hundredth birthday cake. He was the one who got it. Who matched me. Who had walked into the darkest caves of my fantasies, peered into all the corners, and made even the dirt there feel beautiful from the light of his discovery.

Though a back pedal on all that might be part of my very near future.

What would he say when I showed him the next dark corner?

I had to take the chance. And was ready to.

I brought my hands around, covering both of his, stilling his attention to my nipples. "But it could be better."

So far, so good. He reacted how I'd hoped. With roguish eagerness, he twined our fingers. "It could?"

"Uh-huh." I emphasized every breathy note. Felt his shaft throb in response.

"Just tell me how, little lightning. You have to only say the words, and you know I shall—"

"You could be inside me."

"Mmmm." He rumbled it while dipping a hand toward my core. My fingers, still threaded with his, went along for the ride. "So true. I love being inside you. Maybe this time, you can help—"

"No." I halted us both with a firm squeeze. "I mean...inside me."

He stiffened. Another expected reaction. "Camell—"

He clutched short as I guided his fingers around my thigh, into the crevice of my backside.

"*Camellia.*"

It was definitely a night for surprises—even for myself. I didn't just keep my nerve but expanded it. With growing surety, I led his touch deeper. I didn't want him to have a single doubt about my plans.

My body rewarded me for the boldness. The rim of my tightest entrance was alive with a thousand new sensations, all brought on by just the brush of his magical fingers.

"Please tell me this doesn't violate your vow, Evrest."

His rough breath trembled the air. So did the potency of his conflict—and the weight of his arousal. No way was he hiding that from me; the swollen evidence was right there between us.

Finally he answered, "That...might depend."

"On what?"

Another heavy breath...while he worked the first inch of a finger inside me. "On what you really want here, sevette."

I hissed. Sweet invasion. I hadn't felt it since being with Harry, who'd never gone beyond pushing in a couple of fingers, despite my pleas for more. Now that the consideration crossed my mind, Harry had never been comfortable with *anything* having to do with "more." The bedroom scene in his mind was usually set before we ever got undressed, and my deviations on the script—especially the wild and kinky ones—were never welcomed.

But oh, how I longed to deviate now.

"I think you know what I really want there."

Evrest stilled his finger. I dared a peek over my shoulder, praying his inner deviant would be out and ready to play too. I had no idea what that would look like...but delighted in what I got. His face was a cross of desire and innocence, a ten-year-old who'd seen boobs for the first time. His mouth was open, but he slammed it shut, his jaw screwing tight—as twin forest fires lighted all over again in his eyes.

"Camellia—"

"Stop." I flung up a hand. Whirled my head forward. There were blazes in his eyes, but his voice had ice water of doubt. "It's all right." And it was. At least I knew he'd been interested—for a second. "You're clearly uncomfortable about it—"

"The hell I am." He backed that up by yanking at my chin, forcing me to confront the fires again. And damn...if we weren't underground, I was certain his gaze would light the sky clear to Athens. "But if I hurt you—"

"Evrest." I cut him off with a bossy kiss. "That's part of the point."

He scowled. "What?"

"Maybe I want the pain."

"*What?*"

I lifted my fingers to his face. "When we leave this room, all I'll have is memories. Letting you take me like this... It's like imprinting it deeper inside. Forcing me not to forget. Letting you brand me, from the inside out."

The confession came from my soul. Instantly, I knew Evrest's response was the same. A gorgeous sough left him, ending in his mouth's slow, savoring attack on mine. He barely pulled away before repeating it, diving his tongue deeper... grinding our bodies tighter.

It wasn't long before our crotches synced to our mouths, undulating at a pace that made my sex weep simply from the pure, primitive force of it. Evrest used the friction to spur his own arousal, dragging his erection down my ass, opening me a little more with each sensual slide. By the time he wrenched his lips away from mine, he was as hard and huge as one of the ripe bananas on the trees outside...and I was a hot mess of raw need.

Made doubly so when he opened his lips, letting me see the feral clench of his teeth.

"Get on the bed, sevette. And lie on your side."

He didn't have to tell me more than that. I knew exactly which side.

In giddy silence, I moved to comply. The bed was as soft and welcoming as I remembered, the mountain of pillows a comforting cushion as I curled to my side, away from where Evrest stopped at the toy shelves to gather "helpers" for what he was going to do to me.

Only a minute went by, but it was the longest one of my life. Once more, I wondered if this was even happening or if I hadn't just fallen asleep at my desk in the north wing and would wake up recalling the craziest dream of my life. The awful fight with Harry. Picking my way back through the dark tunnels again. Finding Evrest here again. Getting to finally taste him, only to learn he'd sworn off all real enjoyment for his poor penis for nearly two years now. And now this proposition of mine, taking us down the path to a wicked union I'd only ever dreamed about...

Bravo, girlfriend. Making damn good on that promise to make this night count.

My heartbeat tripled as Evrest joined me on the bed. Quadrupled as he pressed his warm body behind mine. Exponentially past that as he placed two tubes of lube and a condom on the coverlet in front of me.

Well. Nothing like parking the truth in front of a girl.

Lifting the packet, I managed to drawl, "You keep these around *in case of emergencies*?"

He kissed my neck and then my shoulder before responding. "They keep the toys clean."

"Oh."

Oh. It had become one of my favorite words since meeting him. Me, the girl who had at least one good line for every occasion, was now a willing servant to the monosyllables when it came to gawking at how openness, simplicity, and honesty could exist in the same man as sin, seduction, and a dauntingly thorough knowledge of all the equipment in his private kinky toy chest.

And while I was on the fine subject of daunting...

Evrest pressed closer behind me. He was so big. So warm. So hard.

Ohhhh, hell. He was...*hard*.

Amazement. Awe. And yeah, a little fear. They all added waves of crazy to my flood of desire, causing me to press back against him. Blissful sigh as he began adoring caresses, raking my whole body with his commanding touch. He didn't miss a single inch, fingers dipping, gliding, exploring...and never failing to stop and tease the curls at my core.

Forget blissful. I was now a jar of marshmallow cream, needy sighs lacing in the air with his guttural grunts, perfectly matched to the mounting intensity through his whole body.

He mesmerized me. He always had, but never so much as now.

I watched, lashes heavy, as he pushed apart my legs with his thigh. His long fingers continued melting me with their mastery. His dark skin against my pale. His conquest, my surrender. His touch...my reinvention. All the body "imperfections" I'd ever obsessed over—the linebacker shoulders, little tummy pooch, bony ankles—were the features that made him groan deeper in appreciation, murmur more words of adoration and lust.

He was utterly beautiful.

And I was beautiful when I was with him.

He hooked his thigh higher, purposely rubbing my intimate folds with the action. Then again...and again...and...

"Shit!" Heat. Need. Clenching...

"Sssshhh," Everest grated. "Breathe and push out the tension, *petite* sevette. We will climb there together."

Which was exactly what I wanted, right? Then why was it so hard to focus on anything but the quivers he brought with each swipe of his leg? The zaps of new lust from every urgent suckle on my neck? And why, *why* couldn't I think my way around the pounding desire in my core to recognize the significance of his grab at the lube in front of me?

The cold slick at my backside answered that one pretty fast.

"*Shit,*" I repeated.

"Easy," Evrest exhorted. "Very easy, little *doulée.*"

I turned a little, angling up to give him better access. "Stretch me," I begged. "Please..."

He rose a little. Rolled me fully onto my stomach. Parted my cheeks to fill me more fully with the lube. "Raise it, Camellia. Present your beautiful ass to me."

I sighed. And obeyed. I sincerely hoped he could read my mind now, comprehending what his authority did for me. The permission it gave me to step outside myself, forgetting all the lists and obligations that awaited Cam...and letting Camellia float free.

Camellia, who'd been finally set free by his touch. Camellia, who now saw the full darkness of her desires—and wasn't afraid of them.

The cold liquid penetrated deeper, brought by one of

his beautiful fingers. He slicked me gently but intensified as I moaned, taken to another mental space. It was visceral. Animal. And good...so good.

As he pushed a second finger in back there, he swept his clean hand around to give the same kind of attention to the layers at the other side.

Only now he'd brought a friend. An electrical steel cylinder of one.

Not moving. Not breathing. How could I, as Evrest slid the vibrator to my center? I wasn't lost in such a deep fog to miss the purpose in his positioning. As soon as he flipped that thing on—

"Oh my God!"

"Sevette." This time, the word wasn't an endearment. It was reprimand, snapping as sharp as the elastic band to which the vibrator was attached. The strap smacked the small of my back with a brutal *thwack*, followed by an erotic sting. "Breathe again for me. *Now*. Once more."

I wanted to snarl at him. I wanted to worship him. The vibrator hummed at its lowest setting, but I was already so close. *So close*. My thighs clenched. My walls wept. I was so damn ready. "Evrest. I...I need—"

"To breathe again," he ordered. "And focus on pushing out."

I swallowed. He didn't need to explain further. If I needed to push out, that meant he was delving farther in. Sure enough, with another gentle plunge, his fingers were seated deeper inside me.

Dull pain. Then a sweet, tight ache.

"Ohhh!"

"Fuck," Evrest grated. "So tight. So hot. My cock cannot wait to claim this."

Even without his declaration, I knew it. His erection tapped at my ass cheeks as he fucked me with his fingers, gently at first but building in passion. The whole time, he worked in more lube, making my backside as wet and ready as the rest of me. And yes, there was pain, but it was countered by his control on the vibrator, turning up its power as he pushed a third finger into my tight fissure.

There was more to come. So much more. A penetration that seemed impossible now...

"So much," I blurted. "So...much..." Stupid words, but my profound truth. I'd never teetered so long on the edge of fulfillment before. I was a thread dangled over a razor blade. And damn it, Evrest would keep me hanging as long as he wished, naked and needy and pleading to bleed for him—and then thank him for it.

"You can take it, sweet Camellia."

"*Unnhhh!*"

"You can, sevette. And you will."

Only my nod was possible now.

Because he was right.

Because I wanted him to be.

Because I wanted every inch of what he was embedding into me. The heat. The stretch. The pain. And soon, the most intimate part of his body. I'd take it all because I'd never have it again. Oh sure, I'd have other lovers. Perhaps meet a nice guy from Irvine one day, settle into a cute place where we'd sit at my stylish dining room set and talk about our dog and garden—but in the back of my mind and the corners of my soul, they'd all be compared to this...to the king who commanded my body in total ecstasy and ruled my mind with the dark mist of his own.

Never more so than the moment he reached for the condom packet.

"It is time. I cannot keep my cock from you any longer, Camellia."

As his long fingers tore open the foil, my pulse sped. As he groaned while fitting the latex over his length, I squirmed. And as he pulled me back over onto my side, this time with the head of his sex slotted snugly at my back hole, I went into kneejerk mode—and stiffened from head to toe.

"Breathe, sevette."

"I know, *I know*. You're....you're just so..."

Would words ever come easily to me again? Picking one now was like running an eighty-yard touchdown run. They *all* fit best. Huge? Impressive? A freak in the well-hung department? They'd all be right—but not very helpful in calming my sudden jitters about the erection now pressing at my sensitive rim, demanding entrance to the tiniest hole in my body.

"All of it may not fit." His voice was serrated. "Do you want to stop?"

"No!" I wasn't being noble. I meant it. I needed to be joined to him, to have his body as part of mine, even like this. "Please don't stop. Please...don't..."

The sound died in my throat, overcome by Evrest's primal groan. It was so hard to believe that I'd first met him as an urbane leader, wrapped in a fitted doublet and royal protocols. He was nothing but feral predator now, slave to the pulsing flesh he inched into my channel, invading me more fully than I'd ever thought possible.

When he slid out, I exhaled hard. The relief was temporary, and I knew it.

"Fuck." Amazement coated his tone now. "Oh fuck, Camellia. Please tell me this is just as good for you."

I inhaled. Exhaled. Forced myself to relax. For the chance to bring that wonder to his voice again, I would make it good— somehow.

He did his part for the cause. Worked himself in slowly, despite how his thighs shook from the effort of holding back. His fingers, spread across both my cheeks to keep me open, dug with brutal insistence.

He pushed in farther.

Joining with me.

Taking what he needed from me.

While my spirit and soul were thrilled, my throbbing backside wasn't. Despite the help of all the lube, his sex strained like nothing I'd ever felt.

Deep breaths. Deep breaths.

No good.

Tears pricked as I prepared to tell him this was it. "Halfway" wasn't normally a word I accepted in my vocabulary, but even a semi-nun like me knew this kind of shit normally took a let's-ease-into-this period.

When the hell had I forgotten about the vibrator?

And the fact that Evrest hadn't taken it to the highest setting yet.

Whoa.

The second he clicked the knob, I screamed. From pure amazement.

How had I not known about this? The pleasure... It was so searing and perfect, it turned even the pain of his penetration into an added push instead of an endured agony. I climbed higher, reaching for my perfect release. So close. I was so... damn...close. But I needed his help for the last few steps...

Needed every inch of flesh he could give me.

"Evrest." I mewled it more than anything, strung out on my lust. "Oh, shit. Oh, please..."

"Tell me." His voice was solid Cro-Magnon now. "Talk to me, sevette."

"Can't. Ohhhh. Need..."

"What?"

"M-More. *M-More.*"

He locked me in place while spreading me wider...filling me deeper. "Camellia...fuck...you have almost all of me."

"Then the rest!" My head arched back beneath the weight of my lust. The force of it, while twined with the physical, was so much more. I hated the thought of him holding back when every drop of my soul now tumbled in its wild, furious, feral fire. He'd unleashed me. I wouldn't be satisfied with anything less than the full, passionate beast in him too. "Set it free, Evrest. All of it. Take me how you need to. Use me. Fuck me. *Please.*"

The sound in his chest was like Zeus's own chariot wheels. Mighty. Dominating. With the same command, he seized my hips—and drove himself fully in.

The motion rammed me hard against the vibrator. My nerves were driven to the summit I'd craved. I shot to the heavens and crashed into the sun itself. I exploded—and received no mercy from the flames. The moment my first orgasm ended, Evrest tore back the vibrator to push at the top of my mons. The pressure, along with the stimulation from his cock at the opposite angle, spiraled me toward a new flame of pleasure.

"Bear down," he ordered, pounding into me even deeper. "Try to push me out. Bear down *hard*, Camellia!"

I wasn't sure what happened next—only that I'd been slammed by ten-foot Pacific breakers that stunned me less. Like one of those waves, the force built from the inside out. Vibrations from deep in my womb. Surges that intensified. Then a cataclysm, violent and pure, shattering me into a million drops of light that splintered into the sun.

I screamed, blistering and broken.

Evrest groaned, swelling—and climaxing.

He went utterly still, body tensed as his essence poured out, scalding and perfect, even through the latex sheath between us. For a moment, I wondered if I'd killed him—until a long string of Arcadian spilled from his lips.

Several minutes later, we both still breathed hard after cleaning up with moist towels he gathered from warming drawers under the bed.

As we sank back to the pillows, I winced a little. Time for ye olde twinge of uncertainty. Ugh. Hadn't done this one in a while, since my first time with Harry, but it was here—and undeniable.

Would things be different between us now? Not that "things" would exist beyond the next hour, anyhow—a fact that didn't discount the importance of the answer.

I only had to endure the fear for a moment. Evrest erased it by gathering me close and tangling our legs as he lunged his tongue into my mouth with more passion than he'd given me before. I smiled against his lips when he finally tugged away. If anything *had* changed, it was for the better.

His own grin was all puppy who'd successfully fetched its first stick, confirming the deduction more. "My sweet, sexy sevette."

I gave up a giggle, fingering the sweaty hair out of his eyes. They practically glowed with their sea foam radiance. "My lusty, gorgeous hunk."

He nipped a kiss to the tip of my nose. "So...was it good for you?"

Eye roll. "Oh, my God. You really didn't just go there."

His eyes narrowed. It wasn't a glower. He actually seemed confused. "Well, *was* it good for you?"

I wetted my lips. *Way to go, bitch-on-high.* My castigation didn't prevent me from silently cursing the girls who'd been lucky enough to share his bed at university. All this naked bronze perfection sharing their pillow, and *nobody* thought to conduct an easy lesson about the worst of the *après*-sex clichés?

"Yes, Evrest." I whispered it with sincerity. "It was pretty damn good."

As in, I've never experienced anything like it in my life—or will be likely to in the next *one.*

As in, how the hell do I pretend I'm simply in the friend zone with you now?

I refused to think of that right now. The cocoon was still intact. I didn't have to give him up yet. "So how was it for *you*?"

And why did that instantly feel like the wrong question to ask?

If his answer didn't match mine, would he step back into King Evrest mode and say the "right words" anyway? Duty above all? Or would he honor the honesty of our relationship, no matter how brutal the truth?

Neither option was acceptable. *Ish.* I should've taken his climax as the final answer on that one and been happy.

But then I would've missed the answer he *did* give. The stare he flooded me with, as powerful as a magic potion. The strength of his fingertips, spreading into my hair. And the perfect beach sand of his voice, soft and coarse blended, as he murmured. "By the Creator and all his angels, Camellia. You have shown me a glimpse of heaven."

Stinging eyes. Heavy gulp. I prayed it all wouldn't manifest beyond that. Sarcasm swooped in to the rescue. "Hmmm. Only a glimpse?"

"I do not dare say more." Real regret underlined it. He rolled to his back, bringing me along and tucking me against his chest. "If doing it *this* way was that good, I cannot allow myself to imagine what the other will be like. I would be tempted to take a shower, get right back in here, climb between your legs, and—"

"Stop." Despite how my limbs still felt like noodles, I pushed up on an elbow. Crazy, what strength a person could find when shock decided to suddenly zap. "What do you mean...'the other'?"

His answering grin was wide, white, and wicked. Normally, the look would free a herd of horses through my stomach. Damn shame I had to fence them all back. Too dangerous, considering the elephant of revelation tromping through instead.

"I think you know what I mean." He actually chuckled about it. "The *other* way. Missionary? Hitting a home run? Mounting up? Pounding in the—"

"All right; all right." I didn't need or want to know how he'd come by all the euphemisms—especially if the looming conclusion in my mind was true. And God help me, as I mated his puppy dog energy with his dark wolf idealism, that deduction felt more and more like the truth.

"Hell." I lowered my head into a hand. "Hell, *no*."

"What? Camellia?"

Damn it. I was going to ask it anyway. And was probably going to flog myself afterward.

"Evrest...are you a virgin?"

CHAPTER THIRTEEN

Yep. Flogged myself.

I could've lived with my boldness if he'd huffed with insult or gone into embarrassed, guy-style lockdown. Instead, the man cocked his head, quirked up one side of his sensuous mouth, and returned, "Should I have been clearer about that?"

Clearer about that. Like he'd just given me the wrong time for dinner or sketchy directions to the bank in town.

"Shit." I laughed, hoping it helped with comprehension. *"Shit."*

Evrest's brows lowered. "Is that a good shit or a bad shit?"

"Interesting question."

Beyond interesting. Try confusing as hell. I looked up at him, doused in the bewilderment now. What had I missed, and when? How the *hell* was he really still a—

The word wouldn't return to my brain. I didn't believe it. Everything about this man was still something out of an adults-only ad campaign for come-fuck-me booze or cologne. His godlike muscles and warrior eyes were natural extensions of his sensuality. Even his gaze, zeroed on me so intensely, checked every box under the heading of dark sin.

After a long moment, he dipped his head as if trying to succeed at his mind-reading thing. When he came up empty, he scowled. "I still do not understand."

I soothed fingers across his brow. "Me neither. But I'm trying to." The motion didn't ease his upset. I roamed my

INTO HIS DARK

touch to his jaw. "I think I threw the cake into the oven without following all the directions first."

He only frowned deeper. *Gah.* I was being cryptic, and that wasn't fair—even with this completely crazy subject.

"When you told me you took the preservation vow two years ago, I made some assumptions." Heavy breath. "*Big* assumptions."

At last, his eyes ignited a little. Thank God the man was as shrewd as he was beautiful. "You thought I had only been adhering to the vow for the last two years but not before." When I let silence stretch as my confirmation, he charged, "And what did your 'big assumptions' tell you that I did before it?"

I laughed. In full. This was worth the buy-in. "You're kidding, right?" But I already knew the answer. For all his perceptiveness about others, Evrest was a dork about the size of *his* sexual tractor beam. But I wondered if pointing it out would be like telling a wolf it was a carnivore. The creature didn't care. He was what he was. Gorgeous. Generous. Charming. Smart. Irresistible.

"Okay, so you aren't kidding," I mumbled. He blinked in silent query, flipping my senses when the candlelight caught the edges of his thick eyelashes. "Oh, come on, Evrest! You went to university in *England*. The girls—"

"Were studying as hard as I was." He stated it like commenting on the fog, the Tube, or the necessity of bangers and mash. "Camellia, there was really not time for—"

"Bullshit." The carnivore wasn't getting it. "In university, there's *always* time, especially with those randy British birds. I'll bet those girls even had your penis nicknamed."

He growled and then laughed. "They never *saw* my penis!"

"You think that matters?" I rocked my head back with cynical challenge. "Faye's introduced me to a few of them in online groups, mister. Joanne and Helen have taken creativity to a new level when it comes to naming peen. They even rate bulges sometimes."

"*Bulges?*" His brows hunkered. "Why?"

Long breath. *Really* time for a redirect. "You're *sure* there wasn't some night in a girl's dorm room, where you both had too much to drink and things just happened?"

"Things do not 'just happen' for me, Camellia." His hand tightened against my scalp. He finished in words that barely scraped the air. "Not until I met you."

"Oh?" I raced for the safety of sarcasm, despite tracing a finger dangerously across his chest. "And what exactly *happened* then, Mr. Cimarron?"

He stopped my hand, capturing it beneath his. Curled my fingers over, exposing my knuckles for the brush of his lips. He answered me in a whisper twice as soft as the first.

"Everything."

Three syllables. Three seconds.

The air joined me in a suspended breath. Not a single nocturnal sound. Even the candle flames were motionless, giving golden solace instead of flickering ovation, causing my chest to ache from the selfishness of hoarding air.

But like hell was I going to ruin this.

Everything.

Yeah. It felt like that. Somehow, not doing the "all-the-way-everything" only sweetened the sensation. What we'd done had its special space, known only to the two of us, beyond the realm of rules and pacts and propriety and procedures.

Our perfect dark.

I twisted my hands, cupping them around his. Lifted my head, sealing my lips against his. Unleashed a little more of my heart, to make room for the chunk of his that crashed down into that space. Oh...*damn*. Just like opening my body for his sex, the feeling wasn't comfortable. Not at first. I didn't know if it ever would be again or if I'd ever be the same, but the pain was eased by knowing he wouldn't be, either.

So...good shit or bad shit?

I hadn't officially popped the King of Arcadia's cherry. Good shit.

But I was pretty sure I'd put marks on something more important.

Not such good shit.

The next few days would be whirlwinds. I prayed that the breakneck pace would work with us, keeping the bad shit at bay. Or worse, a full shit storm. If Evrest played it cool with Harry and I avoided Chianna altogether, we were likely to sidestep the suckage. I wouldn't be lacking for things on my to-do list for about fourteen hours of the day...and there was also the little matter of Evrest having to pick out a bride within the next five weeks.

Oh, yeah. *That.*

"My little lightning." He murmured it into my temple, his breath warming my hair line. "Are you all right?"

I nodded but backed it up with, "Of course. I'm good. I'm... perfect."

For the next few minutes, it could still be my truth.

For every minute, hour, and day after that...I'd have to fake it.

Somehow.

God help me.

CHAPTER FOURTEEN

"Ohmigosh, stop the van. I have to take a picture."

As Beth repeated her favorite line of the day for the hundredth time, I clenched my jaw, hunkered over my smart pad, and thanked fate that I had the whole back seat of the vehicle to myself. The extra room would come in handy once I'd had enough of the photo breaks and needed to puke.

When we'd loaded up at the palais, three ungodly long hours ago, the gratitude was for a different reason. My whole body was an aching reminder of Evrest's passion, and I wanted to treat it with care—not to alleviate the pain but to sustain it. If my marked neck, sore hips, and aching ass were the only mementos I got to keep from last night, then I needed to spend as much time as possible savoring them.

And the moments that had created them.

The passion that had imprinted them...

"Look at this, you guys! Isn't this incredible?"

Beth's squeal of punctuation jerked my head up. Harry did the same from the van's shotgun position, meaning our gazes met in suffering unity. The pain in my body matched the grimace on his face, making me laugh a little. To my shock, he chuckled in return. Misery loved company, after all.

"Yes, babe," he finally offered to Beth. "It's awesome."

"You're not even looking," she snapped. "Crowe? *You're* looking, right?"

"Totally," Crowe chimed in. "Believe it or not, some

of this reminds me of County Clare, in Ireland, where my grandparents are from. The cliffs there are a lot like these, only without all the dolphins off the coast."

"Dolphins! Where? Ohhh, I have to get out and look."

"Go for it, babe." Harry already skated a finger across his pad again, likely setting up shots for tonight, after we were settled in at the beach and back to pictures-up status. The weather was going to be perfect, and we couldn't waste any second of valuable production time.

"Ugh." Beth huffed. "You and Cam live on those damn computers. Come on, Harry-bear-bear. The screen can wait. I won't have you missing heaven on earth."

"Wha?" He glanced up for a second. "Okay...right. You two go on ahead. I'll be right there."

Beth rolled her eyes but didn't delay climbing out of the van, dragging Crowe behind her. I watched them jog to the edge of the road, cameras already out. Crowe pointed toward the water, and I joined Beth in following his trajectory. Sure enough, a large dolphin pod broke through the water about a hundred yards out. Some of the creatures broke the surface to arc through the air, making the sight even more breathtaking. A breeze kicked in through the van's open door, bringing the salty-sweet redolence of ocean mist mixed with almond, poppy, and orchid blooms. The wind moved on, *shoosh*ing through palm fronds overhead and orchestrating with the splashes of the waves far below.

"She's right, you know. This place really must be heaven on earth."

It was the first non-logistical thing I'd dared saying to Harry since we'd locked horns last night. Sure, we'd both been busier than flying monkeys trying to pack up our Oz-on-wheels production trucks this morning before departing Sancti. Lists had to be checked. Cargo had to be loaded. Kittens—aka the crew—had to be herded. We'd embraced the pace as the perfect excuse not to address each other beyond the necessary. But here it was. My strange little version of an olive branch.

"Fully aware of that factoid, rock star." The reply was a plateful of snark but made me grin. *Rock star*. Back to normal by baby steps. "And I'm doing my best to make sure we capture a little of the heaven on film."

"You'll kill it." Unable to help myself, I finished on a giggle, "Harry-bear-bear."

He dug into his snack bag of Doritos and tossed one. "Look, girl. Must be pay day."

I lobbed the chip back. "*No bueno*, mister. I negotiated for the hot and spicy package. Better talk to your production manager."

"*Pffft*. She's a nut case."

I shrieked as he lobbed a handful of almonds instead of the chips. After retrieving a few, I retaliated, "Did you really just go there?" Choosing the precision of the one-shot-at-a-time approach, I aimed for his head. "Because we both know who handles the nuts better around here, buddy."

Bull's-eye. My second shot struck his cheek. He laughed harder. "Damn! Somebody's been practicing. And here I thought you'd been nutless for the last year."

That stung a little more than it should. I tried writing off the jab but leaned over to angle a shot at his crotch anyway. Though it got his stomach instead, I caught the fresh flinch of guilt across his face—perhaps his version of an olive branch.

"Not totally nutless, okay?" I went for breezy and teasy, hoping it would end our codependency party for good, getting things back to normal. Well, at least back to how they'd been before the editing room Clash of Clans.

I didn't delude myself. This was tricky. Despite all my defensive backlash, his ire was pretty damn justified. If I'd been the one smacked with that image of Evrest and me, I'd have jumped to the same illicit assumptions.

Assumptions?

Sorry, Harry. That's what you're going to keep thinking. Because, holy shit, if you ever discover that you were halfway to the truth...

Yuck. Guilt might be a quirk on his face, but now it was a full knot in my stomach. I sat back, ducking my head to let him think I'd gone bashful at disclosing my "nut" status, but in truth, stabbing the stop button on my remorse.

And telling myself—for the thousandth time—that the emotion wasn't needed anymore.

I'd seen the harem hidey hole for the last time. That portal was sealed shut for the Evrest and Cam Show. We'd gotten damn lucky. Been able to soar into the clouds and explode there without anyone seeing the flare. Attempting to ever do so again would be like swimming in a lake during a thunderstorm.

Not that I didn't think about it, in detail so hot it hurt, every other minute.

Not that time didn't taunt me with one of those minutes right now.

Not that fate didn't join the fun too, dragging a guest of honor to the van's entrance for the pure, evil fun of it. A guest who, until now, had honored my plea to stay physically away because there wouldn't be anything I could do about the torment of him in my head. A guest who looked...

so

damn

good.

Yeah, even with the tired creases at the corners of his soft green eyes. Even with the way his stare became that of an awkward teen wanting to ask me out instead of a man who'd had his fingers—and other body parts—deep inside me twelve hours ago.

Especially now, in clothes that didn't have a single stitch of royal tailoring to them.

Wow.

They needed to let the guy out of the palais a little more. Deconstructed cowboy was a *really* good look for him, starting from the top. The beat-up leather Stetson was a perfect fit with his wind-messed hair and stubble-roughened face. His chest strained the limits of a gray T-shirt, layered by a gray-and-blue-plaid shirt with sleeves shoved halfway up his forearms. I shifted back, fighting how my intimate parts tingled simply from the memories of scratching my fingertips in the springy hairs on those arms. Like that did any good once my stare raked over his legs. The denim industry needed to be paying the man a commission. What his carved hips and powerful thighs did for those faded blue jeans, falling over a pair of dusty boots, was as close to sin slipped into skin as I could imagine.

But I'd sworn sin off. I'd sworn *him* off. I'd made the message clear, even through clenched tears, after he'd walked me back through the tunnels to the ladies' room in my own palais wing. Listening to his footsteps fade into that darkness had been one of the shittiest experiences of my life—though this moment might be joining that list very soon.

He's still sworn off. No matter how his thunder thrills you or how deeply his darkness calls to you, his river is forbidden...

Which didn't explain *his* selective memory.

Why the hell was he caressing me with his eyes that way? Smiling with so much familiarity? Radiating energy that instantly made me feel stripped naked...and longing to return the favor?

Sluicing my blood into all the places it shouldn't be...

Ohhh, Evrest. Not now. Not here...

"Mr. Dane. Miss Saxon. Merjour to you both."

"The same to you, Majesty." Harry offered it with level care. Damn. He didn't miss a nuance of Evrest's gaze, which hadn't wavered yet from me. "To what do we owe the pleasure of your personal visit? Your assistant informed us that your brother insisted on other travel arrangements, that your staff and team would be driving to the beach ahead of us."

Evrest nodded. "You were informed correctly. My brother can be—how do you all like to say it?—a real dickhead about my security."

In an effort to distract myself, I'd taken a swig from my water bottle. I choked on the stuff as Harry barked a laugh. "Uh, yeah," he replied, "that's one way of saying it."

Evrest cracked a huge smile, doubling the masculine magnificence of his face. "We have just enjoyed a lengthy lunch on the cliff—during which I spiked his canteen with nectar. He was more open to the foreign relations value to me riding with all of you the rest of the way."

"Oh." I blurted it in tandem with Harry. Shock echoed in both our voices. Didn't make a dent to the relaxed country boy Evrest had become.

"The next section of the journey is especially beautiful,"

he stated, "and can be very interesting, when you have a local aboard."

Beth and Crowe had stepped back over. Beth clapped with shiny-happy-pretty delight. "Wow! 'Local' doesn't get any better than the king! Right, guys?"

The decision was sealed. Like it had ever been up for discussion.

I avoided looking at Evrest *or* Harry in the aftermath, slinking back to my seat while Beth insisted on a selfie featuring Evrest and her. Thank God it took a few tries—"Instagram filters only help a girl's skin so much," she explained—so I could compose myself with clearing a spot for Harry.

But when Harry rose, Evrest shooed him back. "*You* are the leader today, Dane. I am merely along for the sightseeing chatter. Miss Saxon has plenty of room back here for the humble local boy."

Humble, my ass. The words were half a tone shy of a full royal decree—though I seemed the only one who noticed as he swooped gracefully into the back seat. Along the way he doffed his hat, letting the full, untamed mane of his hair gleam in the sunlight. My fingers twitched, longing to touch.

I clenched them tighter around my stylus instead. Glared harder at my smart pad. That was the easy stuff. Containing my dozen huffs wasn't so simple, especially as he scooted closer.

"Guess that settles it," Harry gritted the false cheer. "Cam? You okay with company back there?"

No.

"Sure." *I'll take the fake smile special too, please.* "This'll be...fun."

As the driver restarted the van and we revved back onto the road, Beth's chatter was the only relief from the tension.

Even Crowe seemed aware that something was up, lobbing a questioning stare between Harry and me. And Evrest. Oh, yeah. *That* not-so-subtle addition to the manifest.

For a few minutes, courtesy of Beth's social media feeds, the conversation was an easy mix of the latest LA gossip and movie industry news, concluding with a dozen shots of the newest summer shoe trends.

After the footwear cavalcade was over, a cloud of silence loomed again. I sure as hell wasn't volunteering for conversation starter. Like that would be the winning moment of the day. Where was the TED Talk on coming up with safe subjects for "the morning after" with the lover who'd blown the barn doors off your libido, while your suspicious boss came to his own conclusions about every word you spoke?

I'd never been so thrilled to hear Harry's phone ring.

Harry clearly wasn't, growl deepening when he observed the caller ID. Nevertheless, he swiped the screen, answering the call right away.

"Probably studio brass," Crowe explained in response to Evrest's curious look. "He's likely to be on for a while."

"Ah," Evrest replied. But a second later, after leaning in perilously close, whispered, "Good."

Not good.

The sooner I made him aware of that, the better.

Somehow, I managed to scoot away—but not by far. *Damn it.* My body was tuned to his now, awakened by the simple call of his proximity.

In desperation, I fought to reset my libido. Aha—creative visualization. *Steamed broccoli. Cleaning the shower. Rush hour traffic.*

I didn't have a prayer.

Working on Zen breaths only doused my senses in more of him. His nearness. His energy. His sandalwood essence, now joined by the earthy mix of leather and denim... *Damn, damn, damn...*

Even averting my gaze was now an impossibility. I was riveted to his masculine glory. Even fascinated with it. Cowboy Ev was...really nice. The strong line of his jaw was accentuated by the dark scruff. His lips, so elegant before, were a soft and sexy contrast to the rough textures framing them.

"What the hell are you doing?" I fully indicted him with the rasp—and the smile that disguised it. Thankfully, everyone else was distracted for the next few minutes. Beth and Crowe decided to run lines from the change pages Trent had hit them with this morning. And as Crowe predicted, Harry was engrossed in a long phone call with Pinnacle.

Crazily, Evrest and I had been given a new bubble.

I still wasn't taking back the accusation. Or the glower I mustered with it, at least in my eyes. Or my resolve not to let *his* eyes get to me, no matter how thick with adoration they got—or how deep the temptation of their dark, sexy intent.

"I could not do it," he finally murmured. The second he did, I softened a little. His smile, a little bigger than mine, was just as counterfeit. I could see it in the edges. Sadness jerked at them, taking away the ease that normally turned my belly into a three-ring circus.

"Couldn't do what?"

He inched a hand over. Let one of his fingers edge against mine. "Stay away from you."

Double-edged sword, the Evrest Cimarron model. He sliced my soul with joy...bled out my heart in torment. "Well, you have to." I curled my pinky finger—only my pinky—beneath his. Even with that tiny contact, greedy heat coursed between us. "We agreed, Evrest. Last night—"

"Was the *last* night." He bit it out. "I remember what we said, damn it. I was there."

"Then why—"

"I want nothing more than a few minutes, Camellia. Here, with our clothes *on*, just talking."

"Despite how your eyes just got me naked in five different ways?"

One side of his mouth inched up. "Because yours were chaste about me?"

I looked away. *Blergh.* Calling my shit was one thing. But doing it in that sultry undertone, rendering it impossible to think in a straight line...

The last time he'd used that voice on me, his fingers had my backside spread open, and his erection was stretching me into a new being. *Camellia...please tell me this is just as good for you...*

Before he'd skyrocketed us both into ecstasy.

"Okay, so...what?" I charged. "Is this like letting ourselves down easy? The harem hidey hole gradual detox program? Do I get gum pieces flavored like you to help with the cravings?"

His whole face darkened. "Holy fuck, would I love gum that tasted like you." He shook his head. "As if such a thing were possible. You are a taste like no other, Camillia...and I am damn afraid that I have become addicted."

Look away. At least shut your eyes. Get him out of your sights. Maybe it will help with the rest.

Who the hell was I kidding?

Inextricably, irremovably, the man was inside me.

Every brilliant facet of his gaze, as familiar as my own

breath. Every angle of his face like a map I'd been destined to follow. Every degree of heat off his body, warmed to match what mine craved. Longed for. Needed.

The force of it pounded me like a 49ers linebacker.

I swallowed hard. Whispered back, "I think I'm addicted too."

Evrest let out a slow breath. "I know."

Unsteady sigh. Despair had never been a favorite feeling, and I hated it even more right now. "What are we going to do?"

His chin jerked up. In that moment, I watched him reach inside and access the man who'd been trained to rule a country, not the guy looking into a ravine of feeling so vast it didn't have a bottom. The ravine I now peered into with him.

I yearned to yank his hand into mine. To feel his strength instead of just beholding it on his face. To give him words that would make it better instead of questions that tangled everything more.

If only I knew what those words were.

I'm and *sorry* weren't those words. When fate gave a gift like this, even for the blink of time we'd had it, one didn't apologize for cherishing it to its fullest.

I never expected this was equally absurd. Neither of us had walked into that ballroom expecting time to stop, breaths to halt, our worlds to alter.

But they had.

And still were.

Even now, as he bent his head back down, sealing his gaze to mine with the softness of sea foam but the force of the ocean, he made everything else go away. Every*one* else.

For one more perfect moment, everything in my universe was only him.

Please make it last...

"Do?" His brows crunched as he echoed my last word. "I am not certain there is much to 'do,' sevette...except make certain I am not alone in any more confined spaces with you."

We gave in to self-deprecating chuckles.

"All right," I returned. "Noted—though I'm the last one you want to be asking for backup on that."

"Why do you think I told *only* you?"

We laughed again. It was good for the outward impression we wanted to convey but shitty for the threads of self-control I was barely controlling. Damn it. He not only looked like Dusty the Hot Cowboy but now flung one-liners like Benedict the Tasty Geek, decimating my Achilles heel from two sides at once. And hell if he didn't know it.

"Sweet Camellia." His smile tugged his stubble all the right directions. "It feels so good to make you laugh." He bit into his bottom lip, turning the look into something much more illicit. "And it feels even better to make you wet."

Annnnd, that about did it for my breath again. "Shit," I muttered. "Evrest—"

"Are you wet right now?" He leaned in, surely appearing like he simply relayed a joke. "If I slipped my hand into your panties, would they be damp? Would your pussy be slick? Would I be able to pull out my fingers and suck your sweet taste from them?"

"You are *not* playing fair."

He shrugged. "Fortune favors the brave."

"And the unfair?"

He backed away by several inches. The grin, however, stayed solid. "I like making you huffy too. I can imagine doing it while you really *are* handcuffed to my bed, and—"

"Hey." I drilled a knuckle into his shoulder. "No more trips to the hidey hole, remember?"

"Did I say a word about the *hidey hole*?"

I stewed into silence. I had nothing for that—except a growing wet spot between my legs. *My bed*. He'd said it. Not *the* bed. *My* bed. Given the chance, he would actually take me to his royal chambers. *Above* ground. With the danger of being caught by a lot more people...

We had to make sure he didn't get that chance. Ever.

No matter how potent or perfect the I-want-to-fuck-you-*now* look was on his face.

"Ohhh, hell." I slammed my eyes closed. "You're really after that wicked wolf merit badge today, aren't you?"

"Wicked wolf?"

His scowl wasn't the reaction I expected. I chortled a little. "That can't surprise you. It's been my private nickname thing for you pretty much since the second we met."

"You gave me a nickname? But...why the wicked wolf?"

"Would you prefer Little Red Riding Hood?"

The scowl deepened. "Wicked will be fine."

I let my laughter gain volume. "Glad you came around, wolfie."

He gave a boyish shrug. "It is better than others I have been subjected to through the years."

I raised my brows. "So the Arcadian press likes the cheesy handles too, hmm?"

"The press?" he rejoined. His added *pssshh* was a cute cowboy touch I didn't expect. "I would prefer them any day over the tongues of Syn, Shiraz, and Jayd."

"Now *this* is interesting." I rested my head against a cocked hand. "Sibling teasing in the royal house of Cimarron? Gasp!"

"As you would likely say in the 'royal house of Saxon,' *duh*." He ran a finger over the stitching in his hat's brim while continuing, "They were relentless—in a loving, vicious kind of way."

"Such as?" I prodded.

"Hmmm. Well. There was my favorite, 'Evroost,' a stab at my wild hair *and* birth position in one dig."

"Points for versatility."

"Indeed." He lifted that finger to his lips, evidently to spur more thoughts—or drive me crazy with how beautiful it made his profile. "They also favored Ever-Neverland, as well as *kroi-en-craquelins*, which loosely translates to king on crackers."

"Huh?"

"Arcadian humor," he supplied. "When a new king is crowned, they use the term *kroi-en-élevé*, meaning king on high, on his coronation day. It's a formality, only used in ceremonies and at high state functions."

"And as fodder for the royal sibs to keep their big brother in line."

"That too." He turned his gaze out the window for a moment. "Though Father and Mother never let me stray too far from remembering my ultimate responsibilities, either."

I studied his face closely, wondering if I'd get a preliminary answer to my next words from the depths of his eyes or set of his mouth. "Sounds like they were tough love kind of people."

"They were. But let me be clear, there was as much emphasis on love as there was on tough." A tenderness washed over his face, as captivating as any seductive stare he'd ever melted me with. "They made all of us walk hard lines but with whips of encouragement and paddles of praise. We may have grown up in a castle, but because of my parents, it was also a home filled with warmth and laughter."

"I can tell." I said it with meaning. The attention and affection of both his parents was so evident in the man he'd grown to be.

My words encouraged him to lean his head back a little and continue on. "We had silly family traditions, just like a lot of people. Frisbee golf on the south lawn. Baking around the holidays. Burying Father in the sand at the beach every summer. Even 'time outs' when we turned into little *boktards*."

"Oh, no," I teased. "Not boktards. Not *you* four."

He chuckled. "We were a handful. It does not amaze me that Mother chooses the respite of her rooms over tolerating us on a daily basis."

"Does she still have her own offices elsewhere in the palais, then?"

"Yes." The gleam in his eyes softened a little. "She is still queen, after all—though she has scaled back on her activities since Father passed the crown. But she sees that we are all grown, happy, and productive."

I kept up my smile, thought it felt more forced by the minute. "I'm sure she still keeps careful tabs on all of you."

"So she clearly declared when I went to say goodbye to her this morning."

Of course. Because that was what most moms did. They worried. Watched. Did the ardent tab-keeping thing.

Not the I'm-going-out-tonight-so-zap-your-dinner-in-the-microwave thing.

"She sounds wonderful," I said. "Actually, it all sounds wonderful."

He shrugged. "Well, typical. In many more ways than people imagine. Likely no different than many of the things *you* enjoyed growing up."

"Right."

I desperately hoped his nostalgia muted out my syllable of defeat.

Wasn't happening.

He raised his head. Cocked a solemn stare.

I may want your body with every cell of mine right now, Your Majesty, but come at me with some sympathetic psychobabble and I'll turn your balls into man prunes.

"You are an only child, correct?"

The man really did know me. With the respect beneath his tone as my safe zone, I was able to answer. "Yeah. That's right."

"And I know you care for your father..."

"And my mom too." It was more defensive than I intended, but I didn't back down. Uneasiness prowled my bloodstream. Evrest's interest wasn't malicious, but that didn't help anything. I just didn't want to do the peace-love-kumbaya on this...not with him.

He'd already seen too much anyway. Not just the getting naked shit. Too much of the other stuff, in and around that. The wicked brain that had begged him to take me last night in that illicit way. The shadows that might have been filled by Frisbee golf and beach days...

Or maybe the darkness that had turned Mom and Dad away.

Ow. No. Not there. Please.

"Look," I rushed out, "it's not that the three of us don't love each other. We do. *They* do. My parents—they're really busy. They had lives before I came along, existences that really fulfilled them. They both put it all on hold for me, for a lot of years, and I'm grateful for that. They put in their time. Now they don't have to worry anymore. It's all good. *We're* all good."

"Good?" His eyes narrowed like I'd tried to tell him the ocean was really made of angel tears. "Because they don't have to 'put in time' for you anymore? Because they can pick up their busy, busy lives that you carelessly interrupted by being *born*?"

"Shit." I should've remembered his uncanny sixth sense—and the bite in the ass that karma owed me for last night's magic. "I've said too much."

He snorted. "Save the line for someone who will believe it, sevette."

"Damn it, my life hasn't sucked, okay? I can take care of myself completely. Some of my friends still don't know how to do their own laundry! I've been very self-sufficient—"

"For too damn long."

His snarl didn't come barging in by itself. He slid his hand across the back of the seat, extending fingers to the back of my neck, compelling my gaze toward his. Once he had that lock, I was a prisoner—unwilling this time.

"Stop it." Seething syllables. "I don't need this, Evrest. I don't want this."

"This...what?" Like he knew the damn answer already. Like he knew *me*. Like he expected me to cut back *this* scab that easily for him, reopening all the loneliness and emptiness again. All the messages I'd left on cell phones over the years. All the homework I'd done alone, earning me awards bestowed in ceremonies without a familiar face in the crowd, always second choice to some important seminar, lecture, trip, or training session. All the nights I told myself to do better or perform better next time, finally landing the achievement that would make Mom and Dad sit up and notice. And then they'd finally show up. They'd finally be there.

I was still waiting. In the dark.

But nobody got to know that. Especially not Evrest Cimarron. He could fill my body, grant all my fantasies, and even twist at my heart, but nobody got in to that part of my soul.

"I'm dropping this," I spat. "Now."

"Camellia." He rumbled it so deeply, it was barely a word. "I do not under—"

"Did I say I want your understanding?"

He loosened his hold, letting me yank away. "You had no trouble beseeching it last night."

"Another time, definitely another place," I glowered. "And FYI, you're dancing at the edge of a low blow." Literally. We'd agreed that everything in the crypt of carnality would stay right where it had to. Underground. Hidden.

His jaw tensed. But shit, was I certain he'd practiced the crap out of that look, gaining maximum mileage from those wet dream lips of his. "Neither of us changed back at ground level, Camellia."

"Speak for yourself," I rasped. *Because it's what I'm most afraid of.*

"Very well." His gaze swept over my face, thick with passion...devotion. "I have not changed since I held you last night. I am the same person you trusted in that room. The same man you shared your darkest desires with. The man who held you as you shattered, over and over again, even from the inside out..." He shifted so our knees touched. My breath clutched as he pressed in again, just a little closer. "Camellia, you are always safe with me. No matter what."

Leaden gulp. "But I can't be, okay? Don't you see, Evrest?" He *had* to see. The facts hung over our heads, unaltered...

unchangeable. Before the year was over, he'd be engaged and I'd be halfway across the world. "And even if everything weren't so complicated, I wouldn't accept it if your pity came attached."

"Pity had nothing to do with what I shared with you last night."

"And last night has nothing to do with this conversation."

"But you think I pity you now." His nostrils flared, and that tic reappeared, pulsing under his stubble. "And that everything I'm saying is because of it."

"No." I jogged my chin higher. "I don't think it, Evrest. I know it." Resigned sigh. "It's stamped all over your face." I longed to stroke the noble line of his jaw just one more time—and hoped my steady, sad gaze spoke at least that much. "And that's okay."

"The fuck it is."

He ignored my glance through the van, ensuring everyone hadn't dropped what they were doing the second he'd gone from irked to pissed. We got lucky—but he still ramped the rant. "You are wrong about this. You are wrong about me. Do you dare assume I will be like everyone else? That I would default to the same convenient reaction as everyone else? How dare you, Camellia. I know you better than that. I. *Know*. You."

I bared my teeth, silently begging him to calm the hell down. "You have *known* me for all of five days!"

"Bullshit." He loomed, just inches away. "You know it. And I sure as *fuck* know it."

For a long moment, I couldn't muster any reaction beyond a tighter glare. Words would come. I'd make them. He wasn't getting the last word in.

Before I could restart the gears in my brain, the driver stomped on the brakes. The van screeched to a stop, its back end fishtailing.

Harry reacted first. "Holy shit!"

Crowe jumped in next. "What the hell?" He grabbed at Beth's shoulders. "Are you okay?"

The stench of burned rubber tainted the air as we all gaped at the three boys we'd nearly run over. "Boys" was a loose term. They were adolescents, well on their way to men's bodies but not sure what to do with them yet. Two were lanky and tall, the third a little shorter but more filled out through the chest—or so I was able to discern through the full-body wetsuits they wore.

The suits turned out to be convenient, providing ample leverage for the boys to be grabbed by Samsyn and two other men, both in Arcadian military uniforms. The officers dragged the youths to the side of the road as if carrying naughty kittens, dumping them on the retaining wall between the road and the shore, which was mostly drenched beneath a high tide of ferocious waves.

When the boys lifted their heads, Evrest snarled. Arcadian expletives followed. I glanced at him but wished I hadn't. Anger still hardened his features, but it wasn't a desperate fury anymore. It was the hard wrath—and deep stress—of a king.

"What is it?" I asked. "What's going on?"

Before he could answer, Beth spoke up. "Omigod. This is Minos Beach, isn't it?"

Evrest nodded tightly.

I still didn't know if that was a good or bad thing. "What the hell is a Minos Beach?"

"I heard some of the locals talking about it when we were

shooting on the beach the other morning," Beth clarified. "Minos Beach leads to the Minos Cliffs—obviously."

Easy enough to confirm. Just ahead, dark rock bluffs rose several hundred feet, a sight that stole my breath as much for its dangerous potential as its soaring beauty. Merely thinking of those boys anywhere near those towers turned my gut to coleslaw.

"The cliffs are home to the Cave of the Bull Rocks," Beth went on.

Crowe and Harry spurted instant chuckles. "Cave of the Bull Rocks?" Harry drawled. "Does it lead to the Tunnel of the Dog Balls?"

"The Grotto of the Walrus Nuts?" Crowe volleyed.

Beth and I traded an eye roll.

Before we finished, Evrest continued. "The label is rooted in Greek mythology, from the story of King Minos of Crete. He secured his rule over the island by negotiating a gift from the ocean, from Poseidon himself. Poseidon produced a bull from the waves for Minos, but Minos didn't honor his agreement to return the bull to Poseidon, keeping the animal for himself."

"Bet Poseidon unleashed some oceanic kick-ass for that," Crowe inserted.

"There are lots of stories about how Minos was punished," Beth stated. "Though most of them involve his poor wife being given a girl boner for the bull for the rest of her days."

I grimaced. "Gah." Crowe and Harry had more colorful feedback and weren't afraid to voice it. When they were done, I asked, "So where do the rocks come in?"

"That's where Arcadian legend takes over," Beth replied.

"Ahhh," Harry jumped in. "Okay, I think I know how this goes." He nodded at Crowe and even at Evrest, seeking male commiseration. "Minos didn't like competing with a bull..."

"Who would?" Crowe cracked.

"...so he took the animal here and hid it in the cliffs..."

"...where the poor beastie finally died," Beth concluded. "Calcified into the walls of the caverns where it lived."

I looked toward the road again. "What does that have to do with the fact that Samsyn looks like he wants to scalp those boys?"

Beth held up a finger. "Because the legend doesn't end there."

"Of course it doesn't," Harry drawled.

"The story says that the bull, being a creature originally from the sea, still yearns for his place in Poseidon's realm. His longing is so intense that when the ocean water covers him, his bones gain a beautiful iridescence. Over the years, it's become an Arcadian rite of passage for young men to swim to the rocks and wait for the tide to come in. The caves containing the bull bones are located higher up on the cliffs, so that's the only way to reach them."

"And once they swim into the caves?" Crowe asked.

"*If* they make it into the caves?" Evrest snapped. "If the waves do not sweep them off the rocks first, slamming them to the whirlpools beneath the cliffs and then tossing them like fruit in a blender? If they do not bleed out from that before drowning?"

"Right." Harry grimaced on the word, almost splitting it into two syllables. "If all...what he just said...doesn't happen, then what do they do?"

"The goal is to hack off a piece of the rock and bring it back." Beth slid a glance at Evrest, clearly wondering if there were more miracles required to survive *that* part. "When they do, certain stature on the social food chain is ensured."

Crowe snapped his fingers. "Follow the path to the popularity kwan."

"Except the 'kwan' is fucking impossible to get."

Everyone gaped as if Evrest's mutter had been a full scream. Their reaction didn't make sense until I realized they'd likely never heard an English profanity out of his mouth. It was too late to feign my own shock—probably a good thing—since the vibe pulsing off Evrest had gone nuclear with weird. He was *really* invested in every move made by Samsyn and the officers. He seemed to be waiting on his brother, looking for the moment Samsyn was done tearing into the boys, his tension ratcheting with every moment of the effort.

I wanted to grab him in reassurance, but Harry was now engaged fully in the conversation, leaning over to throw his attention on Evrest. By virtue of proximity, that sure as hell meant me too. "Sounds a lot like you speak from experience, Majesty."

"Of course I speak from experience," Evrest retorted. "As the idiot who almost greeted my thirteenth birthday as a corpse because of it."

"Holy shit," Crowe uttered.

"Indeed."

I sank against the cushion as the depth of his admission took hold. It started with an image of what he must've been like as an early teen, just as stunning but a lot skinnier—and very eager to prove that the future king of the realm wasn't going to use the chicken exit for the Bull Rocks challenge.

"Damn." It tumbled out of me, thick with emotion, but I was safe from Harry's evil eye—for now. Nobody in the van was unaffected by Evrest's intensity. "You're not kidding, are you?" I murmured to the man at my side.

"Not by a word." Evrest's huff was labored. "How I wish I was. I was one of the lucky ones. Every year, we lose three or four young men to this stupidity." He dropped his head onto his steepled fingers as if to pray. "Thank the Creator these three weren't among them."

New commotion from outside snapped our heads up. The dark-haired youth directly under Samsyn's watch had sprung back to his feet and surged forward, chest puffed. He went totally James Dean rebellion at the big man, minus the rebel yell cigarette. Shockingly, Samsyn simply folded his arms, letting the kid spiral into cartwheel arms and yo-mama chin jabs.

Evrest rose, voicing the exact same thought I had. "Is that child fucking crazy?" Then a thought that wasn't. "He was raised better than this."

Before I could piece together a question that sounded more like curious stranger and not intrigued lover—*ex*-lover—he was on his feet and bolting out of the van.

The second Evrest was out of earshot, Harry glanced to all of us again. "Show of hands. Anyone with me on voting this Bull Rocks thing as one of His Majesty's hot buttons?"

"He almost died out there, Harry." Beth gave one of her special snorts, wildebeest wrapped with woman. "That has a tendency to become a hot button."

I jumped at the chance to back the point up. "You could have been submitting your filming application to King Samsyn of Arcadia instead of Evrest."

His mocha complexion actually paled by a shade. "Shit."

"No kidding." Crowe actually shuddered. It was apparent, even during our short time on the island, where the guys' opinions fell about the royal family. Jayd was the untouchable jewel. Shiraz, the mystery ninja. Evrest was in the most enviable shoes, getting the king-style perks, living every straight man's dream with a crowd of eager women dogging his every step. But they didn't entertain any thoughts about Samsyn. Not even one. Even that felt too scary.

Which made the next minute a little eerie.

Between the van and the wall, something happened to Evrest. His spine stiffened with rage instead of a protocol. His shoulders expanded, pulling up as he formed tight fists. His pace was no longer a king's stroll. It was a soldier's stomp.

By the time he got to Samsyn's side, they could've been taken for twins.

"Holy crap." Harry mumbled the sentiment on everyone's behalf as Evrest butted in front of Samsyn, slamming chests with the youth. The boy, startled to see Evrest, relented his guard—long enough for Evrest to dig in a brutal hold, hoisting the guy to his tiptoes. He wasted no time after that, all but ripping the boy a new asshole with rage that was, to be honest, a little scary to watch. I wasn't the only one to think so. The youth's face was a rotating mix of reaction. Defiance, then hurt, then terror, before the cycle started again.

Evrest dumped the kid somewhere between fury and fear while pointing back to the wall. As the boy slumped, Evrest huddled with Samsyn, exchanging terse words and tight nods. After a minute of that, he pivoted back toward the van with his solemn soldier's stomps.

None of us said a word as he climbed in and then slammed back into the seat next to me. "I regret the interruption." He addressed everyone. "I am not normally inclined to interfere with my brother's procedures—or to lose my composure while doing so. This was an unusual circumstance."

That was easy enough to interpret. "You know that boy," I stated. "Don't you?"

He grunted as if not really wanting to deny it. "His name is Valerian. He is my cousin."

"Your..." Beth spluttered. "Huh?"

"Carissa's brother?" I broke in.

He nodded at us both. "My mother is the oldest of five, and her youngest sister married late in life. I was a teenager when Val was born, and he's been a pain in my backside ever since. If I'd had to watch Samsyn take that boy's broken body home to my Aunt Neryn..."

Everyone respected his growl of punctuation. His tirade at the boy was understandable too. God, how I wanted to wrap my arms around him, pull him near, comfort the man inside the king. Instead, I jabbed my hands between my thighs to hold them down, enduring the heavy silence along with everyone else.

"What happens now?" Beth asked softly. "Did they break a law? Are they under arrest?"

"Regretfully, no," Evrest replied. "Outlawing the Bull Rocks would heighten the allure of the quest."

"Good point," Crowe added. "The kwan gets more glamorous when it's dangerous *and* illegal."

Evrest pointed at a military Hummer that pulled up. "One of Samsyn's deputies will take the three back to Sancti. They will spend the afternoon looking over video footage and coroner's photos of the idiots who did not survive their trips." A satisfied sound prowled out of him. "That is usually the magic key into their thick skulls."

"Also spoken from firsthand experience?" Crowe quipped.

Evrest grunted. "Memories that haunt...to this day."

Crowe hummed in understanding. "So alternative kwan will look pretty good to them by tonight."

After we all shared a light chuckle, Harry declared, "I'm sure Evrest had no problem coming up with alternative kwan."

"Harry Kaimana Dane!" Beth whacked his shoulder.

"Wha-a-a-t?" he protested. "Just tearing it down to the truth. Right, Evrest?"

I pretended my boot lace was untied. If Harry wanted truth, I was certain my face betrayed a healthy chunk of it. *You have* no *idea what kind of kwan this man is capable of.*

"That might be a discussion for another time and place," Crowe inserted. "But I'll sure as hell bet Evrest has climbed a few other risky rocks in his time, in the name of a few lucky ladies."

"Maybe more than a few." Harry's supplement was practically an engraved invitation for my glare. *Crap.* He'd detected my evasion with the bootlace and now dove for my jugular—or in this case, my jealousy.

And damn it, did I burn to jump at his beat.

Which meant admitting...I *was* jealous.

Which meant admitting that I felt more for Evrest than I'd thought. Much more. Certainly more than the "this is just lust and you'll get over it in a couple of days" line I'd been force-feeding my heart all day.

Which I forgot the next moment anyway—as he wrapped fingers around mine long enough to whisper three perfect— and petrifying—words. "No. Just one."

CHAPTER FIFTEEN

I'd adored him for it—and damned him for it too. Fate wasn't going to let an admission like that go undetected. I doubted karma would, either. The pair gave us a "special treat" by joining forces, conspiring to throw us into each other's path no matter how *we* conspired otherwise.

The positive first. Asuman Beach more stunning than I'd expected—and I'd expected a lot, having gazed at hundreds of photos of the area with Joel and Leif to coordinate a workable shot list for the days we'd be here. But what we'd seen on monitors was diluted beer against the perfect cocktail of the real thing. The water was as brilliant as stained glass, the foliage drenched in Thomas Kinkade color. Even the sunlight looked retouched by the angels themselves, airbrushing the gold of their wings onto the balmy breeze. And I'd thought Sancti was incredible...

Our "glamp" bungalows were unexpectedly awesome too. Each structure was like a luxury hotel room on a platform, raised a couple of feet off the sand. Though guys shared a separate bathing house and girls another, each of the bungalows had a basic sink and vanity for its two occupants, along with writing desks and futon-style beds with pillow-top comforters. For all intents and purposes, we'd all be sleeping well tonight.

I'll take "Premature Assumptions" for the Daily Double, please?

Sleep and I weren't going to be friends tonight. Not after the first thing I saw after dropping my bag off in my bungalow.

Evrest slowly peeled his shirt off his sweaty torso while helping the crew unload the vans.

Hell.

I wasn't the only one struck dumb by the magic. Dottie, emerging from the bungalow after me, stopped in her tracks and muttered something about fucking, ducks, and chests like Mack trucks, but I was too concerned about averting my stare from the man to make sense of the poem.

Like *that* was going to happen.

By now, I wasn't alone. Female whiplash broke out all over camp. Nobody could be blamed. Angel-airbrushed sun and the V of this man's torso... *Uuuhhh, yeah*...the bronze statues of Italy definitely had a contender to worry about. His splendor was only heightened by the powerful grace of his movements. It was like watching a ballet, only the surf was the music and no man tights were in sight.

Thank God.

And *ohhh, God.*

No tights. Only Evrest and those damn faded jeans, clinging to that perfect place on his hips...high enough to be considered decent but low enough that every woman here secretly begged a few buttons would magically slip free.

But only one who knew what they'd see if that miracle occurred.

In breathtaking, burning detail.

I barely held back from licking my lips. The taste of his penis, erect and masculine and spicy. The feel of his length in my mouth, full and pulsing. Then the feel of him—*all* of him—inside my body...places that still ached from how he'd stretched them, imprinted himself on them...

"Cam." The shout belonged to Joel—who thankfully stood next to Evrest in front of the supply trucks. I could actually look like I paid attention to him.

"What's up?" I called out.

He jogged his head, indicating he needed to communicate at a distance shorter than twenty feet. *Ta-ta, gratitude; hello, dread.* Ogling Evrest from afar was one thing. Having to stand next to him and not trace those sweat rivulets down his chest with a finger? I was parched in the desert of desire, and he was the oasis—with a sign on the front reading *VIPs Only.*

But I wasn't a VIP anymore.

He'd agreed. I'd agreed.

Then somewhere in the shadows between midnight and dawn, he'd kissed me with the intensity of good night and goodbye in one. An embrace also meant to be forgotten. *Ha.* Even now, with the noontime sun casting the only shadows around, every moment of that kiss was a relentless memory.

Not good. At all.

Because as I neared, one truth screamed with abundance.

The air between us...hadn't changed a damn bit.

Every second was still a ticking time bomb of lust, every minute a skirmish of need. Who the hell were we kidding? I barely knew how I was going to keep my hands off him through the next ten minutes, let alone the next five weeks.

"Hey."

Joel's terse tone had me pulling in my chin. "Uh...hey."

"We have a slight issue."

"Other than the fact that every female out here is worth shit for productivity because of you two?"

During my walk over, Joel had pulled off his shirt too—becoming the yin to Evrest's yang in the perfect Tao of hotness.

But my praise didn't flap a feather with Joel, who normally loved strutting it like the Italian peacock he was.

"How *slight* of an issue?" I asked.

Joel braced both hands to his lean hips and peered into one truck. "How much of this equipment do we need tomorrow?"

"All of it," I retorted. "Why are you asking? We're scaled way back already."

He dragged a hand through his hair. "I know."

"What the hell's going on? For the way Harry wants to capture the light, plus the intricacies of the fight scene, we have to have full...well...everything we brought. AKS, CYA, every ABC in between."

"Well, we need to drop a bunch of letters."

I threw my stare from him to Evrest. *Ohhh, God. Looking at the view means dancing at the edge, girlfriend.* The plummet would be worth it. He was so damn delicious as shirtless cowboy crew dude. If the whole king thing didn't pan out, I wagered Faye would get him some good gigs as a steamy romance cover hero. The titles practically wrote themselves.

Arcadian Outlaw

Wild Asuman Nights

Climbing Evrest

"Shit." Forget the scenic viewpoint plunge. I was going straight to hell.

Yin and Yang construed my utterance as commentary of a different kind. After they traded a tense glance, Evrest stepped forward. "I regret this, sev— Miss Saxon, but this situation could not be helped."

His near-slip didn't help my tension level. "What situation?"

Evrest went steel rod with his posture. I cocked a brow. He'd have to try a different tactic—like getting dressed again— if he wanted to make me think of him in something halfway resembling his doublet. I humored him, forcing my eyes to his face. Not that it was a horrid chore.

"This morning, I took the liberty of sending out an advance team to pre-inspect the road you would normally use for tomorrow's shooting needs," he stated. "It proceeds through the ravine between the cliffs"—he pointed toward the highest point of the bluffs—"and on the other side, ascends to the precipice that Harry wishes to use for filming."

While every word registered, I mentally bookmarked his first sentence. "What do you mean, the road we'd *normally* use?"

His face went as rigid as his spine. "There was a reason I sent out the inspectors. We had heavy rains this spring, and I was uneasy about the stability of the ravine walls."

"Why?" I darted my glance between him and Joel. "We were told about the rains already. We were also informed that they hadn't overtly affected the ravine."

"They hadn't—at the time of the report," Joel said. "Which was nearly a month ago."

"What's changed between now and then?" I challenged.

"About twelve feet of a rock slide." Before I could fully gape, Joel flipped open his smart pad. The image that appeared, time-stamped just a few hours ago, looked like something from...well...an epic disaster movie. As Joel had asserted, the chasm was consumed by a wall of boulders, mud, and even a couple of small trees. The adjoining mountainside appeared as if a giant ogre had strolled by, dragging his ax behind.

"Damn," I murmured, scrolling the rest of the images. Where was CGI magic when it mattered most?

The facts came together fast after that. Using the vans wouldn't be a possibility—but Joel's question about consolidating the equipment already told me he was working on an alternate plan. I was grateful for the forethought and told him so with a sisterly clap on the shoulder. "All right. Let's cut the foreplay. How are we going to do this bitch?" I felt myself coloring when Evrest's brows jumped. "My...err...apologies for the salty language, Your Majesty."

His lips twinged. I was tempted to join, if only for a second. The irony *was* hilarious. I was really mentioning salt sprinkles, when what we'd said—and done—to each other last night was a hundred-gallon saline flush?

"Sometimes things need salt, Miss Saxon. And I believe you will be happy with how Mr. Bell has 'fixed the bitch.'"

Weirdly, Joel winced. "That...may be a little premature, Majesty."

"Premature...how?" I fired.

Joel pulled in a deep breath. "We can still get over the ridge tomorrow morning. Maybe even make better time than we would in the trucks. Lighter payload."

"Right." I frowned. "So why do you still look like the four riders of the Apocalypse are going to gallop in any second?"

Joel cringed again. "Funny that you brought up horses."

My turn for stiff.

Really stiff.

That was the default a girl felt kicked in the stomach, right? By a damn...horse?

Make that a Horse. Capital *H*. As in, animals that were better for me to look at than interact with.

"H-Horses?"

Joel pivoted around, looking me straight in the eye. "We

can get up and over the ridge by packing over it...on a bridle trail."

I responded like a sleep walker. Dread—the gut-deep, nerve-frying kind—did that to me. "Okay."

Translation: *shit shit shit shit shit shit shit shit.*

CHAPTER SIXTEEN

"Cam? Are you sure?"

"Yeah. *Yes*, damn it, of course I'm sure."

The words were as good as telling Joel to fuck off. I tossed him a contrite glance, and he smiled his understanding—right before Evrest pushed in, protectiveness dripping thicker than his sweat. "You do not sound sure."

I stiffened and dove my gaze to his feet. *Back off. Oh Evrest, please back off before I lunge at you and beg for a long, hard kiss to banish this damn lump in my gut.*

"She's trying to be noble."

"Joel!" Screw the shoulder claps. I hauled back and kicked him.

"Or maybe just in denial."

"Shut. Up." Slow seethe. "They're—they're nice horses, right? Gentle? Old? Named Buck or Buddy or Bart?"

Joel turned to Evrest as if I were on mute. "Tell me you've got nutcases like her here in Arcadia too, man. The ones who suck it up for the team, even when it means compromising their health—or shoving down their legitimate fears?"

Evrest snorted. "That would be my younger brother, Shiraz. Last year, he worked thirty-six hours straight, through weather that was damn near a medicane, to make certain the island's faster speed internet was installed properly."

"Yep. Perf."

I shifted backward as Evrest pressed closer. What the hell

did he think he was doing? Apparently whatever he wanted, judging by the long fingers he clamped around my wrist, halting my retreat. "Which is it for you, Camellia?" He pressed into my pulse point, a man who already knew his answer. "Your heart races like a bird fighting a window," he stated. "What are you afraid of?"

Fume. Let him have a nice view of the top of my head. Maybe my forehead. Focusing on the middle of his magnificent torso was a hell of a lot easier than gazing at the bottom of his jeans and the toes of his boots. "This isn't the time or the place." I seethed it at Joel as much as him—and meant it. One off-on-the-wrong-foot—wrong hoof?—experience with a horse shouldn't and wouldn't dictate how I related to another.

Evrest's hold tightened. I dared a look up. The same determination hardened his stare.

I wasn't getting out of this.

"Evrest! Darling!"

Unless rescue arrived in the craziest form I could imagine.

Blink. Blink again. Yeah, a third time. This was too important a sight to screw up.

Sure enough, Chianna and Novah came strolling across the sand, looking right at home in their jeans, cowgirl blouses, and boots. Both wore cowboy hats with lace bows around the brims, matching the ties on their loose fishtail braids. While shoving strands beneath the beat-up Pentatonix cap on my own head, I wondered where their stylists were hiding. No other reason explained why they appeared newly changed out of evening gowns, including the pristine pendants still shimmering on their necks. Salt and sweat were the fashion call for everyone else out here.

Evrest yanked his shirt back on—*crap*—before leading the way in welcoming our new arrivals.

"Merjour, Distincts."

"Merjour, Our Majesty." Novah invoked what seemed like a standard-protocol response. Chianna didn't echo it. Alpha Distinct, smooth and cool, was clearly convinced her first hail had done the job fine.

"Well, well, well." Joel instantly tapped into his suave Italian act. "Look what we've found. A pair of gorgeous sea sirens, trading their tails for legs, all for us."

Novah swatted him, demure and charmed, while Chianna forced a smile. Her grappling hook was already primed, ready to take aim for one person alone. And gee, were we all waiting breathlessly to find out *who*.

Not. Helping. I elbowed my inner snark into silence.

Evrest tilted his head. "To what do we owe the pleasure of your presence?"

Sweltering afternoon, meet frosty undertone. I remembered Evrest's increased tension in his office yesterday, when Chianna leaped on the news we'd be doing a location shoot so close to her hometown. There was a good chance he'd seen this coming—with dread.

"I phoned Papa to ask him if everything was proceeding well with the film shoot." Chianna looked like she'd practiced the line a hundred times in the mirror already. "As First-Past Regent Mayor of Colluss, he is still very involved with the management of our region. He has his fingers on the pulse of everything that happens here."

"I'll bet." *Had* to let the snark at least peek out for that one. Only Joel noticed, anyhow. I flew clean under everyone else's radar, even smoothly blending back to cordiality. "It's great to see you too, Novah. Do you come from Colluss, as well?"

The blonde bit her lip, looking like a blinding spotlight had been aimed at her. "I...I do."

"She hails from the far side of the city." Less than ten words, and Chianna had turned into the dad from *Dirty Dancing* with slightly better hair. In her eyes, Novah was clearly as shameful as the dancers in the cabins on the other side of the creek.

"Northern Colluss is my birth home," Novah confirmed. "I come from a little village not far from here, also located on the coast."

"Is it as beautiful as this?"

I hoped to ease her nervousness with my praise. It worked a little. She smiled warmly. "Even more so. The sky seems kissed by stars, even when the sun is out. And the water is as magical as liquid sapphires."

"She speaks the truth." Evrest chucked an affectionate thumb to Novah's chin. "Maybe that is why all the girls from Nor-Col are so pretty."

For once, the smart pad latched to my side came in handy. Checking the emails was a great excuse to cold shoulder the jealousy that nipped. If only they didn't take forever to load.

The wait gave me the chance to observe Chianna's coping method—refocusing the spotlight in her direction.

Surprise, surprise.

"Well, as *I* was saying"—as subtle as a sunburn—"I called Papa to check on all of you, and he told us about the terrible rock slide in the ravine. I contacted Novah immediately, knowing she would share my concern about doing whatever we could to ensure the film crew is successful during their time in our region. We drove up right away."

Evrest frowned. "What about Edyn? Is she not also from Colluss?"

"Edyn does not know seventy hair styles by heart." Novah's quip earned her a fast kick in the shin from Chia Pet and then a sympathetic glance from me. Solved: the mystery of the invisible stylists. Novah was a built-in advantage, Edyn, just another member of the Distinct—who also happened to have great boobs and a terrific personality.

"So." It bubbled out of Chianna with over-bright cheer. "How can we help?"

A long pause.

Much too long.

Evrest looked at Joel.

Joel stared at me.

I glared back.

If he thought I was up for princess babysitting duty, especially after the operational nuke he'd just dropped along with his "fixit" of using *horses*, he could seriously pound all of this sand. Chianna and Novah were a cute set, but they could go build sandcastles for all the use I had for them—especially in the arena of attempting to forget that I could never touch Evrest again.

Uncomfortable.

Embarrassing.

This silence was about to stretch too damn long.

"Hey, Cam!" came a sudden bellow across the sand. I looked up to see Leif in his Abercrombie ad finest, waving from an area near the crew break tents. "Hey, Cam! You have anyone free right now? Bunch of the Arcadians helping the crafties out are late because of the rock slide. We could use a few helping hands."

"*Hourra*." Novah's exclamation sounded enough like *hurray* for an easy translation.

Evrest grinned. "Merderim to you both. A favor for our friends is a favor for Arcadia."

"Of...of course." Couldn't say I didn't see Chianna's gritted smile coming—from a thousand miles away. "We are most happy to serve wherever we are needed. Errr...what are the *crafties*?"

"It's short for craft services." I barely contained my knowing smile. "You know...catering?"

The expense of a full-scale second unit location shoot? Tens of thousands.

The three trucks next to us and all their equipment? Hundreds of thousands.

The descent of Chianna's face into utter horror?

Priceless.

★ ★ ★

Two hours later, I hadn't moved very far from the spot where I'd turned Chianna as white as a catering plate. But now karma was paying me back with interest. With my butt in the sand and my smart pad on my knees, I continued wrestling with what we could leave behind in truck three tomorrow morning. Trouble was, no matter how I scooted things around, the answer hadn't changed.

We needed every piece of it.

"Uggghhh." I rubbed my aching eyes and then my hungry stomach, contemplating a break. Maybe the team hadn't decimated everything at lunch and I could find a plate of food...

As soon as the thought hit, the food found me.

A tray floated in front of me, loaded with a burger, a salad, fresh fruit, and a semidry brownie.

"Ohhhh." I didn't bother hiding my orgasmic timbre of appreciation. I followed the arm wielding the miracle, finally lifting my sights to Novah's sweet smile. "So, Novah means angel in Arcadian, right?"

She laughed lightly. "Hmmm. No. But after your generosity at the state dinner, I have been anxious for a way to reciprocate your kindness."

Reciprocate. They loved that word here, didn't they? I think I did now too. The word was definitely different after the ways Evrest had used it on me—in all the best and hottest ways—in his office yesterday.

Whoa.

Yesterday.

Sometimes, a day did make a difference. In so many ways.

"Okay, stop," I joked before noticing she really had. I grabbed her hand, frozen in the middle of popping open a can of diet soda for me. "It means that what I did for you at the state dinner was my pleasure. I wished I could've stayed, but I had a headache and jet lag..." *And a serious onset of hot and lusty for the man you might be marrying in five weeks...*

"You're being too noble again."

I nearly spat out my first bite of the burger. Would've been a damn shame because it tasted like heaven. "How the hell do you know about that?" I queried after chewing and swallowing instead.

"When Mr. Joel Bell came through the craft services line for food, he and Evrest were talking about you."

"They...were?" Curiosity and anxiety hit at once. "And Joel griped that I'm determined to show up Joan of Arc again?"

She chuckled. "Oh, *my.* He did not say that, but I am thankful he did not."

"Why?"

"Because Chianna...was already being a..."

"Bitch?" I supplied when her cheeks flared dark red. "Self-important alpha cooch?"

"Bitch will suffice." She stared at her own soda with wide eyes. I wasn't sure if I'd scared her or thrilled her. Maybe both.

"The point's made. She doesn't want Evrest thinking about too many people other than her."

She started tapping a finger on her nose. "Ding ding ding ding!"

I burst out laughing. Her response was a delightful surprise. "You're full of surprises, angel Novah."

She sipped from her drink before answering softly, "As are you, Cam Saxon."

My next bite of burger went down like a mouthful of lead. "Annnnd, you're still just as transparent as that water." I stabbed a finger at the sea. "So why the I've-got-something-juicy-on-you-now tone? What the hell else did Joel say?"

She took another sip of soda. Her pretty profile was reflective—perhaps by too much. "It was not Mr. Bell."

My stomach grinded on the lead. "So it was..."

"Evrest." Adamant nod. Could've had something to do with the astonished scowl I shot at her first. "I think... perhaps...he was trying to make Mr. Bell talk. He asked Mr. Bell something about why you are so afraid of the horses we will travel on tomorrow—"

"I'm not afraid." I stabbed the plastic fork into a slice of fruit.

"Which is why you just broke your fork on a piece of cantaloupe?"

"This is barely a fork." I shoved the fruit in by hand.

"He also wondered why you feel the need to put up a brave show for us all."

I chomped down on a grape. "Said that, did he?"

"Well...he growled it, mostly."

Another fast sip, emanating a nervous vibe now.

"King Evrest...has strong feelings for you, Cam."

Thank crap she'd been slipping glances at me. I was already girded for the assertion. "He has strong feelings about *all* of us, Novah. Think about how much is riding on this project. I know, I know. Both sides have a stake, but the risk to your country is greater. All we're doing is making a silly movie. If this experiment fails, everyone in our cast and crew gets to go back home and pick up our lives where we left them, while Pinnacle Pictures slants the story in about fifty different ways, most of them favoring us. But the future of your country's relationship with the outside world, a world you all know you can no longer ignore, begins right here."

I looked up—and my gaze automatically found Evrest. I fought the temptation to linger, but he had no idea I was staring, making it all too easy to do...and melt over so many new things about him.

He chuckled at a joke from one of the electrical crew guys, his laugh sincere and warm.

Lifted his face into the wind, as if connecting his soul to it for a moment.

Edged one side of his mouth higher, marveling at the flight of a seagull.

I sighed. Felt my breaths moving in and out, soft as the motions of his mesmerizing mouth.

Hell.

I was one step away from timing my damn breaths to his.

And I bet even that would feel amazing.

I finally looked back at Novah.

She was waiting with the same concentration I'd just directed at Evrest.

Freaking lovely.

What had she noticed?

Her soft smile didn't betray anything. Nor did the contemplative finger she twirled around the bottom of her braid. "All of what you say, Cam...it is true, of course." Another twirl. A sweeter lift to that smile. "But that does not erase how Evrest talks about *you*. And looks at *you*."

I casually reached for another grape. No way was she pulling me down that road. "Look, he's just being—"

"It is the same way *you* look at *him*."

The grape tumbled out of my grip. "I don't—"

She actually clamped a hand over my mouth. Before I could recover enough to glare, she rasped, "I know it because there is someone I yearn to gaze at in the same way."

Brows up. Jaw dropped.

She whooshed out a breath, as if relieved of a giant weight, before lowering her hand.

"Novah," I gasped. "Really?"

She dropped her head. When she lifted it, her big blue eyes carried the sheen of tears. "His name is Enock. He lives in my hometown...and he is the love of my life. We have known each other since childhood, a friendship grown into deep love. He was saving money to ask for my hand when my mother and father received the screening results for the Distinct." She swallowed hard. "Maimanne cried in happiness. I sobbed in grief."

I shoved my plate aside, no longer hungry. "I don't understand. Why did you even go to the screening, if you already knew you wanted to be with Enock?"

"It is pressed upon us as our national duty. They make it glamorous and fun, a social outing with friends. You have a phrase for it in America..." Her brow crunched, searching for the words. "*Girl bonding?*"

"Okay. I *do* understand." I peered out over the waves. Tried to envision what the last two years of this woman's life had been like. One month she was planning a future with her high school sweetheart, the next she was opening the door to find the footman outside with a golden ticket to the palais. "So you got invited to the big party. And I assume that saying 'no, thanks' wasn't an option." After her answering yip of laughter, I added, "What did Enock say?"

Her mirth faded. "The only thing he could." Tears pushed at the edges of her eyes again. "He agreed with Maimanne and *Paipanne*. Told me to go to Sancti."

I gaped. "He *what?*"

She grabbed my hand, a death squeeze of emphasis. "Cam...it was a pure, selfless act of love. I see how it is difficult for you to understand, but try to see—"

"How he was fine with your parents shipping you off to market like the family goat?"

She pushed my hand away. "The chance to marry the *king* of our land—"

"A man you don't love?"

"Love has nothing to do with something like this."

I rolled my eyes. "Is this the part where you spout bullshit about honor for your family, duty to your country, and security for your parents, your personal happiness be damned?"

"Is this the part where *you* spout something meaningful about your 'silly' movie, your personal fears be damned?"

She flashed a sugary-spiteful smirk, Taylor Swift mated with Scarlett O'Hara. I wasn't buying the act. "I'm getting on a horse for an hour, Novah, not committing the rest of my life to a life I don't want."

"Hmmm. Excellent point." More cotton candy rancor. "Because that *never* occurs in America anymore. No celebrity weddings with broadcast rights...prenuptial agreements with time limits and infidelity clauses...women marrying men three times their age because of the car in the drive and the yacht in the harbor..."

I held up a hand. "All right. Fair shot."

"Perhaps just honest." She sighed. "Which has only been my intention from the start."

I pulled my knees to my chest and dropped my head between them. "I know, Novah. I know."

It was, to the syllable, all the encouragement I dared give. Though she nodded her understanding, her shoulders sagged a little. I felt like a heel. The woman was obviously a dreamer and a romantic, a lethal combination with her observations of Evrest and me. But letting her rewrite an into-the-sunset scenario between the two of us...

Shake it off, sweetheart.

"Tell you what," I ventured. "How about we concentrate on something we *can* control? Would you consider...holding my hand through this whole horseback riding adventure tomorrow?"

Her face lit up. "I would be honored."

Alarm jolted my stare back over. "Wait. You know a little about horses, right?"

She giggled. "In Colluss, everyone learns to ride nearly before taking their first steps. The terrain on this side of the island makes it necessary."

"Okay, good." I smiled my relief. "That's good."

Novah reached for my hand again. "Cam, I know you are frightened. That something happened to make you this way. I do not require the details. The memories must be difficult for you already. But together, we will make sure that tomorrow is not a repeat of your past."

I tackled her with a thankful hug—not just for what she promised but how she made the vow. Novah might look like she was made of porcelain, but her spirit and heart were as formidable as the sea she'd grown up with, ousting the doubts I'd had about her Evrest-worthiness the first night we'd met.

Irony really was determined to be my best buddy today.

If only willpower could be, as well.

Because, damn it, no matter how much extra work had just gotten piled on my plate due to the rock slide, my coping method seemed to involve stolen glances at Evrest throughout the afternoon.

Correction: stolen, *lusting* glances.

Which wouldn't have been so torturous if he hadn't started to notice—then give back as good as he got. Wicked half smiles. Peeks through his thick lashes, angled from beneath that *chapeau-le-sex* leather hat. And on a few occasions, using the bottom of his T-shirt as a sweat rag, ensuring the fabric clung to a lot of his jaw-dropping abs.

By the end of the day, all I craved was a cold shower. If not that, then my vibrator—even if it was several hundred miles away, tucked into my other bag in my room at the palais. Okay, stupid move—but when one was packing for a couple of nights in a camp with a hundred other people, Mr. Vibe wasn't exactly the first name on the necessities list.

But as the horizon welcomed the sun and everyone washed up for dinner, I was a hotter mess than the poor crafties trying to keep the meal rolling.

I needed some solitude.

After dropping everything but my phone back in the tent, I walked out toward the water. It felt natural to follow the berm, letting it guide my steps as I allowed the crazy pieces of my life out of the mental box they'd been stuffed into.

The life I'd built at home, far away and foreign.

The world immersing me now, equally alien and confusing.

But the work, familiar and invigorating. The pace, the urgency, the camaraderie—likely the closest experience I'd ever have to being in a real family. Undoubtedly, the feelings were heightened by being here, on Arcadia.

Arcadia.

Had I ever thought the word would come to mean so much?

An island that had captivated my soul.

Ruled by a man who'd awakened my body.

No.

A lover who'd shaken my world.

Opened me. Exposed me.

Made me see...the beauty in me.

Only now, I didn't know what to do with that awareness. Or who to even talk to about it. Despite the bonding time with Novah, she was hardly a confidante—and God only knew what maneuvers Chianna would pull to make her spill about it anyway. Mom? *No.* Dad? *Hell, no.* Harry? *Hell to the freaking no*—ruling Beth out by default, as well. And Faye? Well, *she'd* be thrilled by the call, even if I dumped every intimate detail on her—but did I want my boss to know all of this? Or any of it?

"Shit." It ripped up from my gut, into the balmy brine of the wind.

The ridge dipped, making way for a rocky outcropping. Curiosity prodded, I peeked around the edge, discovering a small but deep cove. Its rock walls soared like a cathedral, protecting a pristine white beach leading to a cave framed by bougainvillea.

The rising tide tackled the shore as I walked, erasing my footsteps with each retreat. Even after I stopped to dig my feet in deeper, every wave wiped away the indent. New elements redefined the sand. Rolling seashells. Scuttling sand crabs. Bits of sea kelp. Every time, the pattern was different yet the same... or so I thought. Over centuries, these tides would change the shoreline. One look at the colored striations in the cliffs was proof of how they'd once been part of the ocean's floor.

Slow change...brought by stability first.

Sometimes—maybe a lot of the time—that was how people had to change too.

To know the shore was still going to be there, even if they let the tide carry them a bit.

To know they had a friend to watch their back while they got on the damn horse.

To know their king wasn't going to rip up *all* the treasured traditions—like, say, how he picked a bride—before he asked them to break with others.

"Shit."

It didn't come from my gut this time. It echoed from my heart.

Like the tide exposing a fresh swath of sand, the universe gave me a fresh shore of understanding. And humility.

I'd been so arrogant. Cavalier. Coming here with the mindset of some noble visitor from the "civilized world" to help change these "backward savages"...

When I was the one now changed.

The realization tumbled in, my mental ravine caved in by a rock slide of insight. But instead of falling beneath the weight, my head lifted with it. *To* it.

Maybe because my soul already knew the sight that awaited me.

Evrest emerged from the depths of the cave, wind lifting his hair, sunset burnishing his skin, and surprise popping across his features—before determination marked his every step toward me.

CHAPTER SEVENTEEN

"Hello." The edges of his lips curled.

"Hi." I was pretty sure mine did too—but at the moment, with the sun turning his eyes into peridots and the wind turning his hair into temptation, I could barely remember my own name.

"Fancy meeting you here."

His exotic accent, rolling over the trite words, granted me a welcome laugh. "First time you ever tried that one, mister?"

He didn't return the laugh. "Sounded easier than asking the Creator why He brought a fantasy to life on my beach."

"*Your* beach?"

My intention? Wit and charm. Actual result? A pair of quivering sighs, courtesy of the man himself. His fingertips brushed my cheek as he caught errant strands of hair and tucked them into the space between my ball cap and ear.

"Hmmm. On most days, yes." Just like the night we'd met, his tone hinted at extra meanings—though now, there seemed more sensual intimation. Likelier explanation? I simply knew that all the good stuff came in the lower registers of his voice now.

Oh, God. I *was* changed. But unlike the shore, this had all happened in less than a week. Or had it? Had the tides of my life been at work long before now, readying my mind and heart for all of this? Preparing me...

For what?

Not for him. He has his own shore to change. An entire country. Rules he must live by in order to break others.

"Well, I certainly didn't mean to trespass." *Self-high five.* I'd actually been composed. Even professional. "I'll just turn around and—"

His mouth on mine, sudden and warm and demanding, sucked the rest of the words from my head.

So much for composed.

At least I still had professional.

Sort of.

Like he was going for it at all himself. In less than ten seconds, he transitioned from sauntering wolf into grinning puppy, twining our fingers and tugging me toward the cave. "Guest," he asserted, "not trespasser. Come."

As I followed, I wondered if it was a good or bad thing that his switch-up didn't unnerve me. That it actually felt normal, expecting the unexpected whenever he was near.

"So what's on your mind, Mr. Cimarron?" The formal address felt wrong, but I had to make the effort. *Your Majesty* was definitely not happening. My substitution felt halfway acceptable.

"How do you know *anything's* on my mind?"

Hmm. Valid question. "Gut impression?"

I glanced over in time to see the corners of his lips curve up. "Or maybe you know me that well."

I should've objected. But it felt too good to let the comment simply sink in. The next second, I wondered if I'd regret the decision. He tightened the connection of our fingers before murmuring, "I want to know you just as well."

Okay, not regret. But definitely...*Anxiety, the pilot episode.* Maybe a step into cute would help. "Errrm...you know me pretty damn well."

"What happened to make you so terrified of horses, Camellia?"

Gah. He wanted to know me *that* well.

A realization struck, sudden and stunning. I wanted him to know too. But *wanting* and *doing*, especially in this case?

Don't you want to trust somebody again in your life, Cam?

Bullshit. I trusted lots of people, in lots of different ways. Just not in this way. Not with the one who could be, if I wasn't careful, my *ultimate* trust. The cathedral walls for my beach. A shore for my tides. The safe keeper for all my secrets. The person I'd pretty much given up on finding, so had learned to deal and move on. *Way* on. My corners had stayed dark. The rules were locked in place. My heart, secured and safe.

But he'd been into all those corners. One by one, had snapped all the rules. And my heart? Cartwheeling on a tightrope with no safety net in sight.

Which did nothing to explain why he still felt like the ultimate vault for my secrets.

At the same time, it explained everything perfectly.

Deep breath. Another. "It's...not a big deal. Really—"

He stopped me with another kiss. "Nothing about you is a small deal, Miss Saxon."

Long sigh. Longer melt. Resigned head shake. "Fine; okay. So, in our junior year at Chapman, Harry got offered his first outside directing gig. A music video for a friend's band."

Evrest's brows hunkered. "An outside gig?"

"A film project not related to a class or a grade. Totally off campus."

"An actual job, then."

"Nice idea—but not in the film business. Not for a director still in college, paying his dues. This was strictly a Doritos-for-pay thing." I ignored his skeptical frown. No use trying to justify that truth now. "Harry needed the work for exposure, especially because the band had some label interest due to internet buzz. In other words, the video had to rock out loud."

"Rock out loud." Confusion tripped through his echo. "Is that not what videos do?"

"Go with it for now." I squeezed his hand, resisting the urge to giggle. His unfamiliarity with my slang turned him into a mix of erotic and adorable at the most inopportune times—like now, when I had to confess to something like this. "To make the shoot happen, we had to...well..."

Evrest stopped. Turned and gathered my other hand into his. "What?"

Just get it out. "We...borrowed some equipment from school...without them knowing about it. It was a Saturday. We were sure the cameras wouldn't be missed if we returned them on Sunday. One of the guys in the band knew some people and was able to reserve a ranch north of LA for the day. It had been used in some film and TV shoots, with some of the sets still standing, so we figured we'd get all the shots we needed. We were right. The day went really well, productive and smooth—until around sunset, when Harry decided he *needed* to take advantage of magic hour."

He canted a cute smirk. "Do I want to know what 'magic hour' is?"

"Not as much fun as it sounds." I smirked. "Movie folk way of labeling the light between sunset and total nightfall. Doesn't last a whole hour, either. If you're lucky, you get twenty to thirty minutes. But Harry concocted this shot and spiraled from intrigued to obsessed about it inside a minute—"

"Ahhh." He nodded, a man clearly familiar with Harry in "obsessed" mode.

"He wanted a realistic, jerky shot from a high angle. We probably could've done it from a ladder, but then Harry saw the stables, and it was all over from there."

"And he wanted you to do the shot?"

"Ohhh, no. While I know my way around a camera, I'm not a pro. I was only in charge of prepping the horse. Me, the girl who only knew horses from parades and petting zoos, now had to figure out how to put a bridle and saddle on one, then get it out of the stall and into the street—"

"In less than twenty minutes."

"Oh, yeah. There was that part too."

Recounting the story now actually made me laugh at it. Evrest wasn't so keen on sharing the mirth. To my shock, his features turned thunderous. "*Battarde.*" No translation necessary. "What was he thinking, demanding you endanger yourself like that?"

I crunched my brows, touched but confused. "You mean what was *I* thinking, volunteering for the task?" Another dry laugh. "Evrest, we were really young and super stupid. Making the footage sparkle was the only thing that mattered. Moreover, I didn't know any better. I lumped horses with puppies. Thought I could feed them a treat, talk nice to them, and I'd be the center of their world. For about four steps, the horse let me hang on to that illusion. But after the poor guy saw all the lights and flex reflectors—"

"Hell." His eyes conveyed how he narrowed down a list of the ways my tale might end, none of them great.

"They say I was thrown about ten feet. Felt more like twenty. A bunch of the lights and a camera were destroyed too.

We got in a shitload of trouble for it. Chapman talked about suspending us, which would've messed up my scholarships, but instead let us work off the debt by scrubbing bathrooms on campus for the rest of the year. I felt awful about it."

Damn, I still did—though that remorse took a back seat to fresh nerves as darker emotion descended over Evrest's face.

"Damn it." It was a steel pestle drilled into the mortar of the air. "Cameras and lights are replaceable. *You* are not."

"And I'm still here." I yearned to lift a hand to his face in assurance, but his hold had become damn near a death grip. The tips of his fingers trembled against my palms. "Look. See? Still all here. Still ready to get the shots. Just a little skittish about my horse karma now..."

It felt like a good excuse for another little laugh.

Or maybe just another log on Evrest's pyre of tension.

Gee. Discomfort was so fun when a girl had a whole beach to jab her toes into. "Maybe...I should just go." When his grip only tightened, I blurted, "Hey, I didn't mean to bunch your boxers." Which could or couldn't be accurate. I had no idea if he rolled boxers, briefs, or...nothing. *And isn't* that *the unneeded thought of the day?* "It's probably just best if I—"

"*No.*" He unlocked one of my hands but kept his shackle grip on the other. "Come."

He headed for the cave again. I followed, but in a different mindset than before. Much different. A darker place, defined by a new heat in my blood, a definite tightness between my thighs—both made more unnerving by knowing exactly what had caused them.

The image of him going commando? Incredible—but fightable.

But the moment he'd given me total commands instead of charming requests?

Hell.

I was probably stepping into trouble.

Ten steps into the cave, that speculation became fact.

It wasn't a cave at all. It was a tunnel, leading first to a little grotto, where a small natural waterfall tumbled into a subterranean creek. Shafts of the lingering sunlight filtered in, dancing on the water and texturing the striated rock with golden swirls. Suspended from a hook overhead, a large basket chair faced the pool, padded with a thick pillow that all but begged a visitor to sit for an hour—or three—of reflection.

"Whoa," I blurted.

The strain eased—a little—because Evrest's did. With one side of his mouth kicked up, he asked softly, "Good whoa or bad whoa?"

"What do *you* think?"

A full grin took over his face. It made him appear a celestial half breed as the sunlight gleamed over the top half of his head, haloing his hair and irradiating his eyes. "I actually come here when I need to do just that. Think. The water quiets my mind. Centers my soul."

"So I guess you come here a lot."

"Not lately." He prodded a finger beneath my chin. "Not even this calms me more than watching you sleep in my arms."

I was going to castigate him for that—as soon as I pried my throat open enough to do so. He beat me to the punch, turning and walking again, leading me deeper into the tunnel. The sunlight faded and the floor dipped, though I could still hear running water. I thought of telling him a little boat and some candelabra might do some good for sprucing the place up, but considering how well that worked out for the Phantom of the Opera...maybe not.

We kept walking.

It got darker.

I wound my other hand around his forearm and dug in, unable to control the trembling beneath my fingers.

He stopped. Pressed his other hand around mine, emitting a rough huff when confirming my shivers.

"Camellia?"

It wasn't that I didn't trust him. He clearly knew every bend and curve of the passage. I just couldn't deny the allegory of it all any longer. We'd sworn off the dark together. His. Mine. Ours. Now here we were, literally immersed in it again.

And I never wanted to leave.

"Sevette? What is it?"

"Could I address that once we reach some light?" Where I wouldn't have a damn issue anymore. Where the temptation of his scent, his nearness, and these shadows wouldn't be such a perfect concoction, luring every naughty part of me...

To do exactly what he did.

One second we were just walking. The next, a stone wall bit into my back while every muscled inch of him molded to my front—and his mouth smashed over mine. He tore off my hat and then dug demanding hands into my hair, angling my face up, forcing me to take more of his raw passion. It was only the beginning. In seconds, his hands were dipping, scraping, and ravaging lower...

lower...

Yessss...

He was beneath my clothes, locating all the parts of me that ached and pulsed and needed—*Oh, God, yes, I need*—partnering with the blackness to take over me, overwhelm me, surround me...

And oh, how I let him.

Without the light, the world was another place. Everything, heightened. The scent of him, sweaty and spicy. The taste of him, masculine and rich. The feel of him, slick and huge—hard and demanding. Pushing into every curve of my body with the blunt edges of his own, not stopping until I acquiesced, parting my legs to let him take over that space with his steely heat.

He lunged his mouth in again, sieging in full, demanding access to depths I didn't know I could give. But that was based on the assumption that I was still *me*. This creature inhabiting my muscles, my body, my will... I wasn't certain who she was. *What* she was.

When the dark made everything safe, what would I dare to be? To do?

What would he do with me?

"Fuck." He snarled it the second our mouths broke apart. "So good. You feel so *fucking* good, Camellia."

I sighed. Moaned. Attempted to squeak a protest. But every time he dunked my senses beneath another caress, another touch, another suckle, I drowned deeper in his perfection. I couldn't breathe. Couldn't think. Couldn't remember what I'd been doing five minutes ago or why it wasn't supposed to be this.

Thinking. Wasn't I supposed to be thinking? Alone? Getting my head on straight again? About *him*? About the fact that—

"Th-This isn't supposed to be happening."

His hands, huge and sure, shoved beneath my jeans and then my panties. Cupped my backside...to angle my crotch more perfectly against his. "Have you been able to think of anything *else* happening, sevette?"

"That's n-not the p-point. Evrest"—oh, how he opened me, woke me anew, right *there*—"we swore we wouldn't—"

"Just a taste." He pushed my clothes down, baring everything to his questing fingers. But in the dark, did it qualify as *baring*? Where was the line between covered and naked? Between fantasy and reality?

Between a vow and a sin?

"Let me sip you just one more time, Camellia." He spread me from behind and rocked me along the heavy ridge in his jeans, spreading arousal through my core, making me moan from the tight, hot ache of it. "Fuck. How the Creator tortures me with this want. With feeling you...smelling you...so tangy... so perfect..." He pressed in, making my sex quiver against his pulsing shaft. "Your beautiful cunt is begging me for a taste, little lightning."

His whispers tumbled me farther into the dark...and strange conflict. His embrace was so safe but his touch so wicked. I whimpered, yearning for both, doubling the desire by racing my hands beneath his shirt. *Ohhhh, God.* The stiff buds of his nipples. The defined ridges of his abdomen. The thick ends of his hair, so perfect for my clutching fists as he trailed lips down my neck, over my ribcage, and then even farther down...

down...

down...

His mouth struck me like electricity.

His tongue slid over me, liquid light.

His teeth scraped me, delving deeper.

His lips treasured me, sucking my very center.

"Ohhhh!"

My frantic breaths. His relishing moan. My high gasps. His countering growl. And darkness, more darkness, not just around me anymore but inside me, swirling like smoke, building like thunder, climbing higher with every tantalizing, demanding curl of his tongue.

My head kicked back. My hips arched up. I bowed toward him, mindless and primeval, needing...needing...

"You are so sweet." He kissed his way along one side of my aching cleft. "So succulent."

"Evrest. Ahhh. *Ahhhh.*"

His hands clawed at my ass, anchoring me in place. The black ops torture masters had nothing on this man. His mouth dealt my illicit waterboarding, making me tremble and sob as he selectively flicked and nipped. With every teasing tap of his tongue, I edged toward the brink of explosion before falling again into the darkness.

When I'd turned the texture of paste, he slipped one hand away from me—only to delve those fingers between my back cheeks. With steady rhythm, he taunted the quivering rim of my back hole.

"Oh...my...*God.*"

"Does it still ache a little, my sevette? Here, where you begged me to fuck you last night?" He pushed in with extra determination. "An answer, Camellia." And just as demanding a snarl. "Now."

Holy shit. *Can't I take a pass, professor?*

"Yes," I squeaked. "Oh damn, yes...it still aches."

"And you have thought about it, yes? At times, during the day, in little moments when you thought nobody would catch you staring...as your mind filled with what it was like to have me inside you, fucking your breathtaking body?"

Hard swallow. Careening senses. "Y-Yes. I-I've remembered you...fucking me...oh, Evrest...please..."

He clearly remembered too. His strained growl came with the grind of his descending zipper and then a discernible rasp of skin on skin—his free hand sliding along his freed erection. Oh, damn. *Damn*. Just the memories of what that cock looked like, felt like...

I was instantly wetter. Hotter. Achier. Ass tightening. Thighs trembling. Everything else...needing.

He pushed a second finger into me, plunging harder from the back as he stabbed his tongue into my channel, fucking me from the front. I clenched and shook, squeezing out more cream for him. He devoured every hot drop, groaning with harsh satisfaction.

How the hell did my legs still hold me up? Or were they? Had I tumbled completely into the blackness, adrift like a feather in tar, simply waiting for the pitch to suck me under? And would I care?

Likely not.

Not as the perfect sin of my release finally burst, claiming my body in waves of complete, carnal bliss. Not as my scream consumed the tunnel, high and raw with my ecstasy. Not as I felt Evrest pump harder on his cock, exploding a minute later, his seed smacking the packed earth as he snarled against my center, still hungrily devouring me.

I waited for reality to return. It didn't. The frightening thing? I didn't know if I wanted it to. I yearned to stay with him, melted and sated and anonymous, into tomorrow...and the next day...and the next...

What the hell was wrong with me?

I'd always been a girl of the sun. Dawn was my thing,

relishing the hours when the day was new, looking forward to the hours I'd have for crossing everything off my to-do list. Shadows were for rats and vampires and hiding.

Except for now.

Except with this man.

Except for *his* dark...where I'd finally let the girl of the sun become the woman of her truth. Pushing past the rules. Taking hold of her strength. Celebrating her beauty. Believing that maybe she *could* change the world...because she'd let it change her.

Only what did I do with her now?

I couldn't stay here forever. But couldn't return to the girl of the sun, either.

And right now, I could barely stand.

Confused. Lost. *Damn it.* Where was the GPS? I needed to get somewhere important. Back to me. Now.

A sob. Another.

"Shit," I stammered. "*Shit.*"

"Camellia."

I wanted to fight as he righted his clothes and mine. Even wanted to know how he did it at the same time, but my coherent dialogue had scuttled to the same hidey hole as the strength in my legs. When he straightened and then lifted me up into his arms, whispering soft Arcadian praise against my forehead, I acquiesced without a peep. *Heaven.* His chest was a wall of welcome strength against my head, his heartbeat steady in my ear.

I was only tempted to object as he started walking—*please; I don't want to leave; can't we just hide out a little while longer?*—but resigned myself as the path angled upward, back to the light. Back to reality.

Reality?

Perhaps I'd rushed that one a bit.

Maybe more than a bit.

The ocean was audible again, meaning we'd emerged somewhere near the shore again. I listened closer, picking up the tired laughs and sarcastic conversations from the crew, though they were a good distance away. We were somewhere near base camp but not right next to it.

Everything else was *not* familiar ground.

By loose interpretation, we were in a tent—though even "glamping" seemed a silly word for what I beheld. The square footage alone likely rivaled my condo, including the garage. The swooped canvas ceilings met support poles wrapped in ivory fabric, accented by arrangements of tropical flowers in hand-painted urns. The "room" was divided in half by a rectangular fire pit, flames leaping from black glass stones, smoke curling up a glass-walled chimney that disappeared through an overhead opening. Directly in front of us was a four-poster bed with drapes of dark-red velvet, matched by the pillows atop its ivory coverlet. The same crimson shade was repeated in mantles that covered the leather couches on the other side of the room, all stitched with the Arcadian emblem in brilliant gold.

I was tempted to dig up my voice long enough to ask Evrest if he called this the mini palais.

That was before two men stepped out from the kitchen area behind the couches—both wearing condemning glowers.

Aimed right at their brother.

Who still held me in his arms—bearing all the signs of the nasty things he'd done to me.

CHAPTER EIGHTEEN

"Brothers." It bore the same command as if we were all in the ballroom back in Sancti instead of a tent across the island. "*Bon aksam.*"

"Yes." It was the first time I'd heard a word out of Shiraz. His voice was calm and cultured, though less exotic than Evrest's. "It *is* a lovely evening." A knowing smirk. "As you have apparently discovered for yourself, Ev."

Samsyn whacked the side of Shiraz's head while surging forward, his glare preceding him. "Family sobriquets do not belong in the presence of strangers." The last word was a snarl.

Evrest shifted, pulling me tighter to him. "Camellia will not share our privacies."

"Because she is *not* family!"

Samsyn pounded a fist into a pole. The whole tent rocked. I gasped. *Shit!*

Evrest swore in a lot of Arcadian. Shiraz jammed hands into his tailored khakis and rolled his eyes. "For Creator's sake, Syn. Calm the fuck down."

He was wasting his breath. Samsyn juiced his advance, venom flashing in his pale-green eyes. Damn. How could someone look so much like Evrest but throw off such different energy? His anger threatened to suck me in, the Kansas twister to Dorothy's house.

"Have you fucked her?"

"Oh, my God." I kicked out, forcing Evrest to set me down.

Not that my legs thanked me for it. "Maybe I'd better just—"

Evrest clamped a hand around my wrist, though his glower never left Samsyn's face. "How dare you." A bare notch of volume. A huge seethe of wrath.

Samsyn gave back as good as he got. "I do dare, Evrest. And you know damn well why." He pressed in, silhouetting his face with Evrest's against the fire pit flames. Their profiles were nearly mirror images. "Answer my question, brother. Did you break your preservation vow with this American *rosputé?*"

"*Syn.*" Shiraz stomped forward. "Sobriquets and manners, my lord hypocrite?"

Again, like he hadn't spoken. Samsyn didn't break his concentration from Evrest. "Did. You. Fuck. Her?"

Before I could get out half a cry, Evrest plowed a fist into Samsyn's jaw.

I had time to get the job done as Samsyn fell to his backside. Furious Arcadian spewed from the big man. No freaking kidding. I sobbed while throwing a frantic stare between him and Evrest, like they paid a shred of attention.

In desperation, I looked to Shiraz—who beamed like a bookie at a title bout.

"Shit!" I gasped.

Shit shit shit.

The two oldest brothers of the House of Cimarron were going to kill each other, and it would be my fault.

Evrest's chest heaved with his breaths. Unbelievably, he still gripped my wrist. I hadn't fought the hold but reconsidered the logic as he shifted, clearly waiting for Samsyn to rise before lunging again. "Evrest. No!"

"Ohhh, *yes.*" Samsyn grinned—*grinned*—while planting his feet. "Come on, little kroi-en-craquelins. Come on!"

Shiraz gave that a fist pump. "Well done! Half a point to Syn. Damn, I wish Jayd were here. She is much better at point-keeping than—"

"Stop it!" I fired. "Stop. *Stop.*"

The words clearly caught him aback. Samsyn and Evrest shared the reaction. I took advantage of the surprise to wrench free from him. Didn't mean I was done with him—or his human battering ram of a brother.

"Camellia—"

"*Don't.*" I smacked a hand to the center of his chest. "You are the damn *king.* Show it. Control your shit, Majesty."

His mouth fell open.

Samsyn grunted—I think in approval. "Well, well."

Shiraz snickered. "Full point for Camellia."

"Shut. Up." I yelled it this time. Swung back toward Samsyn, slamming *his* chest. "And you"—mounting fury twisted my fist into his T-shirt—"are next in line to the throne. But more than that, you're his damn *brother.* You want to try a little tact and respect?"

If my hand weren't curled into the middle of his chest, I'm sure he'd have beat on it. "You have admirable spine, woman. Just be certain you bring your head along with it—to tell you where to tread."

I kicked up one side of my mouth. "Said the pot to the kettle."

He gained an inch of height while stiffening beneath me. "The progress of our country depends on the honor behind its crown. Can you understand *that,* Miss Saxon? Evrest has made a vow—"

"And has kept it!" I released him by shoving him. "Take your brother's advice. Calm the hell down. The precious royal cherry is still in one piece."

He gave me a scathing once-over and sneered, "Forgive me for assuming otherwise."

I shook my hands out, fighting the itch in their palms. *You aren't too big to slap, Bam-Bam.*

"No," I finally muttered. "So not worth it." Wasn't a lie. It had been a long damn day. Running mitigation on the Arcadian royals, especially over the subject of me, wasn't an ordeal I cared to add on the list. "I'm going to bed. You boys have a real nice night."

Without another look back, I pivoted and walked out what I hoped was the front door. One couldn't be too sure in a mansion masquerading as a tent.

Behind me, footsteps scuffled. After that, heated mutterings and growls, almost yanking me back to yell at the boys again. And yeah, right now I meant *boys*, all three of them.

But weirdly, I didn't want to dilute my fury. It helped keep other thoughts at a distance—all the shit that should have stayed in the darkness of my psyche, instead exposed by the darkness I dove into with Evrest.

Because of Evrest.

Of what he did to me.

No. Of what he exposed in me.

The lightning bolt that had stayed hidden in my clouds. The anomaly in me—the *glitch*—that had been the reason for clinging so hard to the rules. The rules kept everything held in, defined. Even Harry had been an adherence to those boundaries. He liked the rules just as much as I did. The world was a film frame to him. A safe box.

Evrest wasn't a box.

He was beyond any boundary I'd known. My battling ions turned into lightning. My glitch turned into a power surge.

My wrong become right.

Comprehension slammed like a tidal wave. I stopped in my tracks after passing the Arcadian guards outside the tent, drenched in the glory—and despair—of it.

What the hell did I do now?

How the hell did I ignore this? Ignore *him*?

The answer was a ruthless blare in my mind.

You can't.

You won't.

We were right but still so wrong. Power trapped behind the trip switch. Thunder and lightning—in separate storms.

Never meant to be.

Which meant life was about to get real painful.

Not even anger could help me now. I stumbled across the sand before finding a little crevice in the cliffs. Tucked myself into it and then sank to my ass. Buried my head in my hands.

Let the pain squeeze in on my heart.

And the sobs crash over my composure.

By the time I finished bawling and made my way back to main camp, mostly everyone was asleep. I fell into my bunk, too exhausted to change, welcoming the lead weights that fell over my eyelids too.

★ ★ ★

The moment of truth arrived way too fast.

After sleeping for what felt like a minute, I was roused by Dottie, who told me breakfast service wouldn't wait. Like there was room for anything in my stomach except acid and nerves. *Terror. When a juice cleanse just doesn't do the job.*

I finally did make it out to the beach—where I stood awaiting my doom.

"Stop it." Gritting my teeth on the words didn't help. Maybe I should have gone to breakfast, if only for the chance to beg a cocktail from craft services. Maybe Novah had some she could bring...

Breathe, damn it. Enjoy the day. YOLO, baby. Eat the red velvet cupcake.

Okay, right. The good stuff. Time to make a list.

If possible, the weather was more spectacular than the day before. The air was clean, bright, and crisp. The sunshine was warm amber touched with gold, more angels reporting for duty. For the millionth time, I still wondered if I'd be pulling a Dorothy Gale, waking up to learn this whole week had been an elaborate dream...

Until Harry, Beth, and about a dozen of the rest of the team appeared, mounted up and ready for the journey over the ridge. In their midst were a pair of horses with empty saddles. Novah walked between the two animals, a lead line for each in her leather-gloved hands. She wore a similar ensemble to her outfit from yesterday, only her jeans were tucked into tall riding boots now. Her smile grew as they approached.

Yeah, I wondered if the executioners at the Tower of London smiled too.

"So...everyone's come to watch the ax fall?" I cracked as they all stopped. The Tower of London thing was clever. Might as well get mileage out of it.

"Bitch, please," Leif teased. He sat atop a gray dappled mount, saddlebags bulging with his supplies. "If I can do this, so can you."

"We're here as the cheer squad." Harry smiled, and I knew he was sincere. More than anyone, he knew what I was overcoming today. He'd taken me to the ER after the accident, clenching my hand through every poke, prod, test, and x-ray. He'd been scared...maybe terrified.

In my strange brain, that memory actually boosted my courage. If I could conquer my anxiety and ride the damn horse up the stupid hill, we'd be full circle. Could put that awful memory behind us. And maybe banish the lingering tension from between us too.

Beth, mounted next to him, waved with enthusiasm. "You can do it, Cam!"

Sheez. I officially tossed out the remaining molecule of my plan to find anything worth hating about the woman. Not worth the stress.

Especially when there were bigger things to freak about.

Like the horses Novah pulled even closer.

Damn it. *Damn it.*

I stared at them and then her. Which one was mine? Like it mattered. They were both white with cream-colored manes. Beautiful.

And huge.

"Do I get to beg the king for my life first?" The line didn't make Evrest appear...as I'd hoped. Instead, Novah laughed out loud while stepping closer.

"Funny girl!" she quipped, approaching Glinda the Good Witch for prickly sweetness. I stared at her—*what gives, woman?*—before letting her crush me into a "friendly hug." Into my ear, she quickly rasped, "Evrest is already on the cliff, watching through binoculars." Shifting to the other as if giving me double sugar, she added, "We had a long talk this morning. I told him of Enock. He is releasing me to return home tomorrow, for good. He confessed your priority to him too. He wished to be here to support you, but...conditions... have prevented that."

She stepped back, but I riveted my stare to her. *Priority?* What did that mean in Evrest lingo? And *conditions?* What conditions? What the hell was that all about?

I had to accept that the answers weren't coming soon— just as I had to relent that fate wouldn't be opening a trap door in the sand for Chianna to disappear through. Didn't stop me from continuing to wish for it as she and her mount, a sleek chestnut mare, came forward to join Novah and me.

"*Bon sabah,* Miss Saxon!"

"Good morning." I barely contained my envy of her too-graceful-to-be-real dismount. Novah's words from yesterday echoed to mind. *In Colluss, everyone learns to ride nearly before taking their first steps.* Chianna had simply learned to do it with the flash of a Cirque performer gliding off a trampoline.

"Mmmm. Smell that air. I *so* love riding on mornings like this. You?"

The woman's knowing wink told the whole story. Somehow, she'd learned about my Achilles heel. Or at the least, my Achilles butt—which hesitated more about this "adventure" by the minute.

"Yes. It's a beautiful morning." Sticky note smile. "You know, I just heard that Evrest is enjoying it already. He's ridden ahead, up to the ridge..."

"Oh?"

I already sent a telepathic apology to Evrest for giving him up but didn't know if I could do this with Chianna watching my every move. She'd only come over sniffing for him anyway. Now that she'd secured a target lock, she wasted no time swinging back up into her saddle and eagerly peering to the area we were bound for...

The cliff that looked too damn daunting, even from here.

"Hmmm," Chianna crooned. "Perhaps he would like some company..."

"Perhaps he would." *Sorry, wolf man!*

I pushed the contrition aside, knowing he'd want me to. Besides, he could hold his own with Chia Pet. I wasn't so sure about my chances with—

Damn. I didn't even know my horse's name. Maybe that was a good place to start.

I forced in a deep breath. Turned and approached Novah. She was waiting with another warm smile. "Come and meet your new friend." She lifted my hand, guiding it to the horse's— what was the nose part called?—the muzzle. That was it. As I petted the big guy—at least I thought it was a guy—he bobbed his head sharply. I flinched.

"Oh, *this* is going well."

"It is all right." Novah giggled. "Fiyero is just saying merjour. Go ahead; pet him again."

I reached for his neck this time. No more bobbing. A gruff snort this time. As friendly as it sounded, I still went slow. There was no mistaking the power beneath my fingers or the knowledge that this creature could easily destroy me, outweighing me at least ten times over.

"Fiyero, huh? Well, hi there. I'm Camellia—with a *cah*." Another snort. "I know, not funny. I tried, right?" I accepted the carrot offered by Novah, letting him munch on it as I petted some more. "What do you say, buddy? You want to do this? I'll be good to you if you're good to me, all right?"

I really hoped his soft whicker meant *yes.*

CHAPTER NINETEEN

"Look. You made it to the top!"

Novah's praise pulled nothing out of me but a weak smile. Why had I conveniently forgotten that getting on a horse meant suddenly being higher off the ground? Great recognition to have while climbing two hundred feet, up a path only a little wider than a hiking trail, atop a "vehicle" with a mind and will of its own.

Not to mention a testy temper.

Which only worsened with every calming effort I made.

I hadn't come into this thing blind. Skipping breakfast meant I had a few extra minutes to Google the basics of becoming besties with a horse. I'd whistled into Fiyero's nose. Petted the tops of his eyes and kneaded his withers, praising him the whole time. Couldn't bring myself to do the "peach fuzzy" thing, though. I didn't scratch my own ass and wasn't about to do it for an animal I'd just met.

For a while, Fiyero bought it all. The picture of equine contentment. I'd been able to relax a little too, marveling at the vistas that unfolded through gaps in the cliffs. Arcadia truly had a little of everything: beaches and cliffs, mountains and forests, valleys and meadows. My initial impression from the incoming flight held true. Sometimes it hurt to look at it all.

Right now, my head pounded for a different reason. Like wondering if there really was a burr beneath Fiyero's saddle. His sidestepping and snorting was getting worse.

ANGEL PAYNE

"I never get weary of the view from here." Novah finished with a wistful sigh. "The cliffs... They breathe with the wind."

"Thanks for the description, Maria Von Trapp." I felt like crap for being her Baroness Von Schrader, yet as I grumbled it, Fiyero's head jerked up and down a bunch of times. "But I'm trying to figure out if Fiyero's deciding to be a bull instead of a horse today."

"Because he feels your unease. Rein him in, Camellia. Instruct him who the leader is once more."

Though Fiyero complied once I heeded the direction, I kept scowling. "Something still isn't right. He started out as a Porsche. Now I'm trying to steer a Yugo."

"Because he is not a *car*, Camellia." Her rebuke carried a hidden giggle. "Breathe deep. Speak calmly. All will be fine."

I glared again. Novah smiled back with rosy perfection, shirt still crisp, posture still prim. *Thanks, Santa. Just what I needed. An Equestrian Barbie.*

I berated myself for the snark as we continued across the plateau. The path widened here but would narrow again soon, as the hill in front of us escalated once more. I already wasn't looking forward to that part. The cliff wall would be to our right, with another to our left.

As in, sheer drop to the sea—into the same kind rocks and whirlpools we'd seen around the Bull Rocks cave.

"Don't think about it," I muttered. "Don't think about it. Don't think about—"

Fiyero grunted, a horse version of *back off, bro,* when another horse bumped his backside. I leaned over and stroked his neck, an equally soothing move for my jacked-up nerves and slightly dizzy head. Hell. Maybe I should have considered eating this morning. I'd given up dinner for the opportunity to be on Evrest's "plate" instead, not even thinking of a snack before bed after everything that had gone down with Samsyn. Even the cap on my head felt too tight, a poor substitute for the one left behind in the cave.

I stayed down a moment longer. Even gaining this small progress toward the ground was a relief. Besides, the sun had warmed Fiyero's coat, another visceral comfort.

Downside? The position magnified every note of the strange sound that spilled out of Fiyero now. Not a whinny. Worse. Not a snort. Higher.

Angrier.

"What the hell?" I jolted upright, making him skitter even more. But what had irked him to begin with? I peered around. Our pace, deliberately slow because mostly everyone in the caravan had saddle bags, hadn't altered. But the animal beneath me acted like he'd been bumped and bitten by every horse in the vicinity. "Whoa, boy. Fiyero, you're all right. *We're* all right." Where had Zen Girl suddenly come from? Best to just be grateful. It allowed me a unique ability to see a bigger truth. *This isn't your fault, Big F. Whatever's wigging out your horsey hormones, we'll figure it out together.* "Easy, boy."

I repeated it—even as he went up on hind legs for a couple of seconds, repeating that furious squeal, tossing his head. As he did, I looked to his eyes—and saw mostly white. His ears zipped backward.

"Camellia! By the Creator!"

Novah. Shouting now. Somewhere behind me. At least I thought so. Which way *was* back? Forward? I was so turned. Where had everybody gone? Okay, the sky was still up, the ground below.

And the edge of the cliff—directly ahead.

The center of my chest thudded. Made its way down to the middle of my belly. *Zen Girl, make way for Terror Bitch.*

"Camellia! Hang on!"

Why was Novah screaming now?

Educated guess? Wasn't because Channing Tatum had suddenly appeared on the ridge.

Conjecture confirmed as soon as I heeded her by clinging hard to the pommel, my sights thrown to the ground in the process—and onto the scorpion there, poised to strike as soon as Fiyero came down.

Now I was glad for my empty stomach. Even a breath mint would've come back up as I braced myself for the inevitable—that this horse, rage already spiked and fear already stirred, was going to go for the gusto in a full bolt.

Damn it, I hated being right.

It wasn't zero to sixty in three seconds—though close enough for rock and roll. Or in this case, bile and prayers. "Oh God, oh God, oh God, oh God." I gladly repeated the refrain again, just in case the guy upstairs—or the animal below me—weren't clear about my desire to live. I broke the litany for a fast apology to Fiyero, before grabbing his mane in instinctual desperation. No way in hell was I going on a search for the reins, long lost from my sweaty hands.

The world turned surreal.

Wind tearing into my cheeks and eyes.

Breath crashed in my ears.

Lungs pumping against my ribs.

None of it as bizarre as the ground beneath us, whooshing by so fast, so fast, so fast. Why did it look so pretty? So soft? Like a multicolored blanket, billowing beneath us. Could it hurt that much if I decided to just jump off?

Fiyero kicked up a rock. Not that big. Maybe? I wasn't sure. My only certainty was how it felt like a punch in the face when hitting my cheek. If my body hit the ground at the same velocity...

Jumping wasn't an option.

I could only

hang

on

and

pray.

Dear God, I don't want to die. I don't want to die. I don't want to die.

God was apparently off making a peanut butter sandwich.

Because when I finally looked up, all I recognized were two things.

To the right, the vertical cliff up.

To the left, the vertical drop down...

And the sea, so beautiful. Simply waiting for Fiyero to take one wrong step.

CHAPTER TWENTY

Screaming wasn't an option. Not with panic swelling everything in my throat, pure dread sealing the deal.

Me. Speechless. There was a first.

I was so fascinated by that fact, I almost forgot about the world still blasting by at a speed that shouldn't be legal on this insane precipice. For all I knew, it wasn't. Either way, Fiyero didn't give a flying damn, emphasis on *flying*.

Oh God, oh God, Fiyero please, just listen; just—

Just ahead, the cliff jutted out farther.

Did that mean the path got narrower?

I didn't know if I could bear the answer. With eyes squeezed shut and face turned into Fiyero's neck, I treasured every breath—each one joined by a memory.

My fourth birthday. Rainbow Dash cake.

My tenth birthday. *Hannah Montana* cake.

First bra. First period. First day in braces.

The day Dad moved out. The day Mom moved her first boyfriend in. What was his name again? I'd pretended not to care.

The day Harry came for all his stuff. What was in that pile anyway? Still pretended not to care. Really good at it by then...

But then, Evrest.

Oh, God...Evrest.

Hello.

Hi.

The crinkles at his eyes. The wine-on-velvet curves of his lips. The reverence of his touch. The magic of his words. The imprint of him on my heart.

I cared again.

Ohhh, shit. I cared.

How the hell had that happened?

I can't care. I can't care.

I can't die!

But the scream in my soul wouldn't pass through my lips. I clung harder, hating every passing, terrible second. Hoping Fiyero might tire out before we tumbled over into the waves and rocks. Praying for a miracle but only getting harder hoofbeats beneath, louder chaos all around, thunder that rattled the very roots of my teeth.

"Camellia!"

Lightning joined the thunder. *Evrest!*

I instantly banished the joy of it from my heart. *His voice.* I hadn't remembered the powerful perfection of his voice, but the agony in my soul verified why. Remembering his voice, beautiful even on the harsh blade of the wind, only made this torment worse.

"Camellia. Look at me!"

Hell. He wasn't going to leave me alone, was he?

I wasn't pathetic enough to obey. Or so I told myself. But there I was, twisting my head around, inch by stupid inch.

My eyes banged open. Throat closed even tighter, which was probably a good thing. God only knew how much dust I'd already sucked in by letting my jaw plummet at the sight of him, galloping beside Fiyero and me on a coal-black stallion...

On the outside edge of the trail.

"What"—holy shit, I *did* still have a voice—"wh-what are you—"

"Give me your hand."

I stared at his outstretched arm, clothed in a brown long-sleeved shirt. No. A white shirt turned brown by the perilous ride he'd taken to catch up to us. The dumbass wasn't out of the woods—well, off the cliff—yet, either. What the *hell* was he thinking? Doing? To make matters worse, I'd never seen him look hotter. Much sweatier and dirtier than yesterday. And way angrier than I'd left him last night.

Not angry.

He was just as terrified as me.

Gee, Cam, ya think? Because he'll *now go over into the brink first? Because he's riding at the same illegal speed as you, only secured to his mount by one damn hand...*

Now ordering you to do the same?

"Are you insane?" I yelled. "Evrest, this is—you're—"

"Not asking," he bellowed. "Give. Me. Your. Hand!"

Doubling down on aces. Sunday at the beach. Extra whipped cream on the latte. Should've been a no-brainer. "Scared shitless" was already a speck in my rearview. Left it behind when I'd asked God for a fast death, along with passing the message to my parents that I'd faked all those I-don't-care moments. Now the big guy in the sky had given me a savior angel, brave to the point of stupid, gorgeous to the point of unreal, and commanding to the point of...

Shit. I really didn't have a choice.

I was really going to do this.

Turning my face back into Fiyero's neck, I rasped, "Bye, big guy." *Please don't run over the cliff, okay?*

I untangled my hand, finger by finger, from the flying cream mane. Then, yearning to cross myself first, I swiveled and reached out. And prayed like hell that Evrest would catch me.

I got in two words of the petition before he latched on, sliding his grip all the way to my elbow.

I screamed. Then again, even louder, as he hauled me out of my saddle and into his.

As soon as I was mounted in front of him, he worked the reins and relaxed his thighs, slowing his mount. In a daze, I watched Fiyero race on, disappearing around another curve in the path. I hoped that without my panicky ass atop his, he would calm enough for someone to treat his sting—and get him a few months of "Post Camellia Stress Syndrome" therapy.

Evrest curled his body around mine, huge and protective. His lips pressed hard to my forehead. His breath flooded my face with his ferocious breaths. "Fuck," he growled. "Camellia. *Camellia.* My sweet sevette. Dear fucking Creator, I thought I was going to watch you die."

"I'm...I'm still here."

I'd intended to get in a laugh. Instead, I reached for his arm, clawing into its steely strength. My fingers trembled. My breath faltered. Hell, he felt so good. So warm. So *alive.* I wanted to tell him about the trip I'd taken down the this-is-your-life tunnel—and his importance in it—but this seriously wasn't the time or place. I hoped I'd get it soon.

For now, I let myself sag. Sank back into the blissful reality of his embrace. As I surrendered, his chest rumbled with primitive satisfaction.

This was what I'd clung to Fiyero for. Prayed to get back to.

He'd made it happen. Almost dying himself as he did.

Crazy idiot. Beautiful hero.

I was conscious of him turning the horse at some point but didn't realize what that meant until the terrain again looked familiar. Sure enough, we rounded a curve onto the ridge I'd first climbed to with Novah. She was still there, pacing beside her horse, panic distorting her face. Harry, Beth, Leif, and another dozen crew members hung out nearby, chatting up Samsyn and a crowd of his officers.

I waved as she cut the air with a joyous shriek. As we neared, I observed the streaks on her face. Had she been... crying? My heart twisted. I needed to go to her, to hug away her fear.

I was about to ask Evrest to stop and help me get down when he yanked on the reins. That handled the first part of the equation. The latter? Not so easy. Before he even swung down, I felt it in the tension through his body. The impression was confirmed when he shot a glare up at me. "Stay here." *And don't brook me.* "This will not be pleasant."

Huh?

"What? Why? Ev—"

"Talk." He loomed over Novah after barreling at her like a bull. If she'd been wearing a red cape, I would've feared for her life. "*Now!*"

"Evrest!" I struggled to swing my leg over and jump down but gulped and hesitated. If getting on Fiyero had taken me to the fifth floor, this horse was the fifteenth. "Sheez and rice. What the hell are you—"

"Majesty." To my shock, Novah's sob cut me off. She collapsed to her hands and knees before Evrest, her shoulders shaking. *What the hell?* "I am sorry. So, so sorry. I promised you she would be safe. I have failed you deeply."

"*Fail* is only the start of this," Evrest snarled. "Do you know what that animal almost did with her? *Do you know?*"

"Evrest!"

Oh, sheez.

Still without a second to cross myself. I slid down anyway, giving everyone a gawky clown act in the doing. Bad, *bad* decision. The second I hit the ground, my noodly legs gave way. I braced for impact—but my humiliation was stayed by a pair of arms, bolstering me back to semi-dignity. "Thanks." I met Harry's gaze, letting him know I meant it—stunned at the glower I received in return. Had *he* been that stressed about me too?

"No problem." He issued it in his editing room tone. Tight. Accusing. "Guess your boyfriend can't be in two places at once."

Three, two, one. My rage rockets fired on all burners, presenting a plus/minus thing. Plus? I needed the extra fuel in the energy tanks. Minus? I had no idea if the tanks were even functioning right now. "Really, Harry? This? Right now?"

So much for the friend who'd held my hand in the ER years ago. He was replaced by a stranger with a dour pout and a stick up his once-charming ass. "Everyone saw how he held you on that horse, Cam. *Everyone.* Do you know the implications of that? What everyone will be saying now?"

"Yeah." Forget the rockets. I launched the spaceship of ire now. "That King Evrest just saved my damn life."

"And...?"

"I don't have time for this."

I really didn't. Not when it looked like Evrest had caught the asshat virus too and was about to tear Novah's head off for reasons I still wasn't clear about. Worse, she was going to let him. Had everyone been snorting lines of insanity while Fiyero took me on the joyride?

"Majesty," she sobbed. "*Rahmié*. I beg your mercy." When he gave her nothing but a harsh laugh for that, she stammered, "You know about me, Evrest. You know *everything* about me. What reason do *I* have to wish Cam harm?"

I stepped around Harry. "She has a good point. Evrest, listen to me. I think there was a scorpion on the trail—"

"Before or after he tried throwing you off?" His tight nod followed my telling blinks. "Exactly." He wheeled back on Novah. "Which leads back to the beginning, Novah. To you."

"I picked him up from the stables at dawn, Majesty. They had him fed, saddled, and ready for me, told me he was precisely what you'd requested for Camellia's mount. Calm, well-trained, happy."

Her face crumpled again. *Wrong. Something was so wrong here.*

I threw my stare to Evrest. Wasn't tempted to smack him now that I glimpsed how he'd gotten to the anger—but he was still due for a hard poke if he didn't see the truth soon. If only his shoulder wasn't so fuzzy. If only I wasn't so damn dizzy. Two skipped meals, one *wow* of an orgasm, and a near-death experience later, I wasn't the same girl as twenty-four hours ago.

"*They* who?" he demanded, low and determined.

"The boys at the Colluss stables." Novah gave it with the immediacy of honesty. She met his gaze directly too. "The ones who work there, for Merlyn."

"Did you see Merlyn when you were there too?"

"Briefly. He came over to be sure everything was fine with the horses. He seemed to be rushing, but there were many horses to prepare for this day, so I thought nothing of it."

"And Fiyero was fine then?"

"Polite as a prince, Majesty."

"He was a gentleman when I got on too," I cut in. "It wasn't until we made it up here that things got hinky. The poor guy probably realized what a novice he had on board and—"

"*Camellia.*" That and an upstretched hand, like a jerk-ass hailing a waiter, and he had me shut up. *You. So. Did. Not.* As I fought my swimming senses for a creative alteration of *go fuck yourself,* he pivoted toward Samsyn and the guards. "Where is Merlyn now? He came with the caravan to assist with the horses, did he not?"

One of the soldiers advanced and then pointed. "Then why is he tearing back down the ridge?"

As everyone swooped their gazes to the switchbacks leading back down the cliff, Samsyn roared, "Get him now!"

Half a dozen guards sprinted, turning the cliffside into a strange combo of the Tour de France and Super Bowl. While it only took them a few minutes to tackle the guy and haul him back up the ridge, it was the opening I needed to get back to Evrest's side. "Never figured you for a witch hunt kind of guy."

He whirled on me. Both of him. Then all three. *Whoa.* Maybe copycatting the guards on the rushing act hadn't been such a great idea. I blinked hard to realign my vision, though one of him, glower still in place, was just as intimidating—and stunning—as three. Ahhh, hell.

"Damn it, Evrest!" I clenched my fists, refusing to let his incensed allure get to me. "There's nothing hinky going on here, okay? Stop looking for someone to blame! Fiyero drew the short straw and had to carry my sorry ass for the day. My tension was probably as thick as a fog bank. Horses have ESP for that kind of shit. He was likely looking for a reason to bolt, and my crap-ass horsewoman skills provided him with motive, means, and opportunity. Period. End of story."

"Rahmié!" The shout pierced the air as the guards dragged forward a man about my age, dark hair messed and dirty clothes rumpled. "Rahmié; I plead you, King Evrest—and Miss Saxon—I did not want to do it. Deep in my belly, I knew horrible things would happen if I did. I swear I did!"

Karma poured liquid lead down my throat. As the shit oozed into my stomach, I forced my gaze toward Evrest. The brutal tics in his jaw confirmed the new stab of dread in my gut.

Hell. Something strange *was* happening in Oz.

Evrest amazed me by becoming the walking picture of calm—until I caught the raging elixir that glinted in both his eyes. Damn. This was what his anger really looked like. It was no longer scintillating. It was scary. "You did not want to do *what*, Merlyn?"

The man quaked. I barely held back a grimace on his behalf, hoping the scene wasn't about to take some a Tarantino-esque turn. *Nearly met my maker less than an hour ago. Please, guys, no soggy pants or wrenching groveling.*

"M-My family owes hers some money, Your Majesty." He weighted *some* enough to mean *a lot.* "She... She told me the debt would be paid in full if I gave Fiyero the sedative, enough to make him seem docile for a while."

Painful gulp. Strike that. Swallowing scorpions would've been easier. "You mean he's not docile *all* the time?"

"N-Not exactly."

"Not *exactly*?"

Merlyn could barely look at me. "By the Creator, Miss Saxon, I never thought you would be in danger! I swear I shall never be so cavalier again."

"Damn right about that." Evrest lunged forward, hands aimed for the man's neck, but Samsyn held him off.

"It was all supposed to be a jest," Merlyn whimpered. "She made me think it was just all in fun."

"She who?" I asked—though after Evrest and Novah traded a knowing look while he helped her up, I had my answer.

Evrest whirled to Samsyn, shoulders coiled with tension. "Find Chianna. She is surely lurking around here somewhere."

My senses careened again, zigzagging like the seagulls on the currents above. *Chianna*. Was she that loose of a nutwheel? Or...was she that jealous of *me*?

The concept made my head swim again, but I self-corrected. What kind of a world changer would I be if resorting to the Spanish Inquisition, guilty until proven innocent instead of the other way around?

I turned to Evrest. Yanked hard on his elbow before murmuring, "Promise me you won't jump her shit right away." He feigned confusion due to the language barrier, making me add fingernails to the hold. "Knock it off. Give her the benefit of a—"

"Evrest? Darling?"

Chianna approached with round eyes, clasped hands, and voice to inspire a diabetes onset. Annnnd I instantly kicked myself for the last twenty words out of my mouth. The woman lasered on Evrest like I wasn't there. Her performance was so over-the-top, a high school production in Podunk, Idaho, would cut her in first auditions.

Evrest stiffened. "Chianna."

"Are you all right? By the Creator, how fast you sped off during our chat on the hill." She flattened fingers to his chest. "I hardly breathed while watching everything. You were so brave and—"

"*Chianna.*"

She looked to her hand—hardly believing he'd just shoved it back at her. "What is wrong? Why are you so tense?"

Tense. Perfect word choice. *I'll take some too, please. With a side of massively pissed.* While I didn't expect to get Chianna's first nod of attention, being treated as invisible was another story. At least the recognition served one purpose. Nothing like the cold-shoulder treatment to expose the glaring, awful truth. Too bad it didn't ease the stab of hearing Evrest growl it the next minute.

"Look at me, Chianna. And speak the truth. The horse, Fiyero. Did you bribe Merlyn Xandon to sedate him before Novah picked him up for Miss Saxon's use today?"

"Excuse...*me*?"

"I will not stand for a lie, woman. If you do not speak, I will have the matter investigated. And if I then learn that you deceived me to my face—"

Her wail interrupted him. "Oh, Evrest!" She flung herself at him, burying her face in his chest and wrapping arms around his waist. "I am *not* deceiving you, I swear! I...I was simply frightened—so, so scared of what to say! Merlyn and I... Our hearts were in the right place. We have been silly pranksters together since our school days—"

"She de-winged the butterflies, and I took the blame," Merlyn muttered.

"—and we thought it would be a little fun jest. To give Camellia a horse that really *was* docile as a lamb. You see?"

"Certainly." His tone belied the polar opposite of the word. "Except that you purposely picked a temperamental horse for your *little fun*." He stepped back like she'd come down with leprosy. "That was not 'silly,' Chianna. It was cruel. Purposely so."

Her face twisted as hard as her new fists. "In everything I have said and done in the last two years, it has only been with you in my mind, Evrest."

He blinked. The thunder vanished from his face—washed away by an emotion nobody was likely to misread. Sadness. "Then I am frightened for you, Chianna. And me."

She stumbled at him again. At least I think she did. I wasn't feeling great. The tension between them, nearly a pall on the air now, wasn't helping. I stared at Chianna's face, so pale and devastated now, wondering if she was going to puke. Or maybe that was a little projection...

"Evrest." Fat tears plummeted down her face. "Please—"

"Your remorse falls empty with me, Chianna."

"Hey." I tugged at his shoulder. "Maybe she's really... umm...sorrah." Damn. Why did I suddenly sound like I'd pounded five tequilas? No salt or lime, either. *No bueno, amiga.* "Maybe thish was all a big mishtake."

Something whooshed between us, whacking him away from me. No. Thrusting *me* away from *him.* Buh-bye, balance. I fell back, grunting as I landed. And I thought Fiyero's saddle was the crappiest thing to happen to my ass today.

"*You.*" Chianna's face, vicious and leering, filled my vision. "Have you not ruined things enough since you got here? Keep your hands *off* him, Camellia Saxon!"

She was hauled back at once by Samsyn and one of his guards. "Stand down," Samsyn bellowed, "or I shall force you to do so with a good sleep in Censhyr Prison."

Chianna hissed at him, "You would not *dare.*"

Samsyn smirked. "Would I ever."

"I am a member of the Distinct! One of His Majesty's chose handmaidens, and—"

"Not anymore."

Evrest's growl cut her off. Chianna snapped her head up, eyes wide. "E-Evrest? Wh-What are you—"

"I wouldn't propose to you now if both my balls depended on it." He extended his hand, palm up. "Samsyn, remove her pendant—and give it to me."

Incensed fish was a new look for Chianna. She sure worked it, jaw undulating up and down, not a word coming out even Samsyn complied with his brother's wishes.

I watched it all with a weird feeling in my stomach. A part of me couldn't wait for the show about to go down, as soon as Chianna found her voice again. Another part dreaded it. Deeply.

Our family owes hers some money, Majesty.

I suspected the Xandons weren't the only ones Chianna had secrets on.

My stomach lurched harder. My senses spun wilder. A hand waved in my vision; one of Samsyn's men was offering to help me up—but no, I needed to stay here, closer to solid ground, where the world didn't whirl so badly. Even then, the blackness kept closing in on me. Beckoning with its perfect, cool completion...

"Miss Saxon? Are you all right?"

I managed a smile at the officer. "Yesh. I simply...need to rest...for a bit..."

The darkness was so nice. So peaceful. Only thing that would make it better was Evrest in here with me. Oh, now wouldn't *that* be awesome. Not restful anymore, but awesome. I almost giggled. *Black. It goes better with a Cimarron.*

Maybe I'd even go looking for him...

Hey! That nice, nice guard was helping me too!

"King Evrest! Come quick! Miss Saxon...she's—"

"Camellia? Camellia!"

There he was. Just in time.

"Camellia? Sevette? Fuck!"

He smelled so nice. His arms were so strong. *Yes. This is nice. Think I'll stay.*

"Samsyn! Hail the medical team, *now*. I am losing her. I am—*fuck*!"

No. I'm not lost. Right here, Ev. Right...here...

Why couldn't he hear? Why did he keep up that rapid-fire Arcadian, interjected by only one line of English that chilled me to my core?

"If she dies, Chianna, you'll pay for her life with your own."

CHAPTER TWENTY-ONE

His words pounded at my consciousness, forcing my eyes back open—once. He wasn't going to have blood on his hands because of me, even if it was Chianna's. I couldn't deal with that. I wouldn't. *That's not the way we do things in the modern world, King Evrest...*

But now he was gone. So was the ridge. I was falling but cushioned. There was warmth and softness. Light and then shadows. Voices and faces...

"She's fine...just a concussion...dehydration..." Harry, looking like a bus had hit him.

"Send all of the bitch's belongings back...not allowed in Sancti again..." Evrest, looking like a train had hit him.

Blackness again. Feeling so good. Then another burst of the dream.

"Of course...call you with another update soon, Tan..." Harry again, upgrading the bus to a sixteen-wheeler. Talking to *Dad*?

"Better now...vitals good...merderim, Kerrie; I shall do so..." Evrest again, exchanging the train for a damn ocean liner. Talking to *Mom*?

What the hell was happening? This was such a strange dream. Why was I walking around in San Jose again—in shorts? Was I still fourteen, on summer break? Had the last ten years just been a product of my subconscious, or was I having that crazy life flashback again, on the cliff with Fiyero? My favorite song of that summer echoed through my mind. Green Day. Fuck, yeah. *She's an extraordinary girl, in an ordinary world...*

The song transformed, becoming another. A tune I didn't recognize. So beautiful. A voice humming it in my ear, a musical magic spell. Whispering my name like a prayer. Telling me to go back to sleep.

Okay...

No. *No.* I had to open my eyes. People needed me. I needed them to need me. It was time to go back to work. To make a movie and change the world.

"Mmmpph."

I pushed harder through the cloud, shoving back the mist. *Have to...open your...eyes...*

A frown took over as soon as my vision focused. Where was I?

Dim lights. Gentle wind. *Shoosh*ing waves. A tent? Near the ocean?

Shit. Evrest's tent. His "backup palais" at Asuman. I wasn't just in it again. I was *in it*—as in, tucked in his bed.

And turned to behold his perfect face, watching me from inches away. A fantasy come true...

"Gah!"

A boundary we couldn't break.

I shoved up. Groaned. No wonder I'd been dreaming of buses, trucks, and ocean liners. They'd all really hit me. Oh, hell. Everything hurt.

"Welcome back." Evrest smiled as if I'd just gone to the damn kitchen to fetch a glass of water. Which reminded me...I was really thirsty. And hungry.

"Wh-Where'd I go? What am I doing here?" It smelled like nighttime, smoky and misty. The darkness beyond the canvas bore out that fact too. "Shit. What time is it? Did I miss anything?"

"Sevette." His tone firmed. "Calm down. All is well."

"All is well?" I retorted. "I'm in your tent, in the middle of the night"—another moan spilled when I looked down—"dressed in nothing but your *shirt*, and...and..."

I sputtered into silence. Couldn't go on about how many ways we were laughing in karma's face with this. And damn, that bitch had a long memory.

"The medical team did not want to risk transporting you to hospital. I refused to let them put you anywhere else. After you blacked out up on the ridge—"

"After I *what?*"

He sat up as well. No help whatsoever for the mush of my thoughts, now draining their way to the gutter with the searing-hot sight of him. Though he was on top of the covers and I was underneath, all he wore was another pair of workout pants, sending my imagination into overdrive. Thank God my aches and pains inventory didn't include my tongue—or a few other key body parts.

"Do you remember anything about what happened yesterday?"

"*Yesterday?*" Plummeted jaw. Attempting to do the math on that while keeping a decent distance from him... My head *really* hurt now. I pushed fingertips to my temple and rubbed. "I blacked out? Why?" *Zap.* Comprehension. *Heads up, Seven-Up.* "*Wait.* Up on the ridge. Ohmigod. *The ridge.* Oh, shit! Fiyero! Is he all right? Did they find him?"

Evrest shook his head, chuffing and smiling at the same time. The blend, ridiculous on anyone else, just made him hotter. "You're worried about the horse that nearly carried you to your death?"

I snorted. "It wasn't his fault. Merlyn and Chianna slipped him the trail ride roofie."

"So you do remember."

"It's coming back in weird pieces." I sighed. My heart ached for the horse, an innocent pawn in yesterday's fuckery. "And yes, I'm worried about Fiyero. He must've been more terrified than I was when that crap wore off. And ohhhh, shit... Ev, it got worse. I think a scorpion stung him too."

His lips parted on a wider smile. His gaze softened to the texture of sea foam. "He is fine, sevette," he soothed. "Samsyn sent out a team of his men. They found him on the far side of the cliff, closer to Minos Beach, and took him for treatment there." He pulled my fingers into his. "You are still troubled. Why?"

With reluctance—a lot of it—I untangled our hands. "Not troubled. Just thinking I need to get out of here."

"At four o'clock in the morning? After two days without food and surviving a concussion?"

The man had surely practiced the glare on his face, concerned intensity mixed with his mussed hair, nearly unraveling my resolve. *Nearly.* "You really never did sneak out of a girl's room at university, did you?" I sighed when he remained intractable. "I need to go back to my tent. I've been lying in here nearly twenty-four hours, without bathing or—" I looked down, examining things again and taking a tentative whiff. "Hold on. I smell good. I smell...like *you.*"

I gaped.

He grunted. Then lifted one brow. "Even kings wash their own balls, Camellia. I know how to use a sponge and some soap. Now close your mouth."

I actually obliged—before deeper horror set in. The kind

brought on by humiliation. "Ohhhh, shit. What else have you seen?"

A smirk traced his lips. "Nothing I have not tasted before."

"*Not* what I meant." I went ahead and groaned. "I talked in my sleep, didn't I? And drooled on the pillow?" One glance at his face confirmed everything. "Lovely." Head-in-the-hands time again. "We're swimming along nicely on this whole hands-off thing, aren't we? Sponge baths, sharing pillows... annnd, I just called you *Ev*."

He yanked my hand back into his. "That was the part I liked the best."

For one more second, he took my breath away. Just a week ago, in a ballroom full of candles and people, our hands had meshed like this...and every moment was threaded by hidden meanings, things we were thinking and didn't dare speak. No more double messages now. No more polished, PR-perfect king. No more King Evrest. Just tangled, unshaved, half-naked Ev. Smiling at me like that. *Staring* at me like that.

Dropping his wolf's gaze to my lips, as if he knew exactly what he wanted to do to them.

And God, how I wanted to let him do it. And more...

I pushed against him—before it was too late. "It's *so* time for me to leave."

"Camellia—"

"No. Please...Evrest—"

"Ev."

"*No*." It escaped as a soft whine instead of the order I intended. Damn him for letting me get the shove in, only to retaliate with a steady grip at the back of my neck. He fingered the tiny hairs there, already knowing the electric shocks that would jolt through my body. "Hell." I gasped. "No..."

"Why does that 'no' sound a great deal like *stop and you die?*"

"If you don't stop, we're both dead." I wasn't sure I used the term as simple symbolism. "We can't ignore repercussions anymore. All the chaos Chianna caused yesterday...and she only inferred things—"

"Chaos only scratches the surface." He didn't stun me with the growl. But the viciousness beneath it? In an instant, all the heat from his touch was canceled by a stunned chill. "Camellia...when you did not wake up for me..." His jaw turned to granite. "I have never known such fear in my life."

My hand lifted to the dark edge where his hair met his temple. "I know."

Okay, fine. I'd just been vowing to get the hell out of here, but the turmoil in his gaze was too wrenching to resist. My touch seemed to ease it a little. He exhaled softly, let his lips part in that sultry combination of question and assertion before grating, "You do?"

"I felt it," I confessed. "Somehow. Even in the darkness." Contemplative smile. "Maybe because of the darkness." I wandered my fingers into his hair. "Was that you...singing to me?"

His thick lashes lifted again. "Only because you sang first."

I giggled. "I did?"

He nodded. "I copied the tune you hummed but made up my own words."

I didn't hide my perplexity. "I've never sung in my sleep before." Until yesterday, I hadn't nearly died before, either.

"Well, that was after you talked."

He glanced away before finishing the assertion. Hmm. *Evasion, party of one.* "Oh?"

"Hmm. Yes. You said, 'Evrest, you mighty stud, come here and be my big thunder.'"

I pushed him off in order to fall back to the pillow, giggles bursting into laughter. He followed, grinning down at me with cocky triumph. I conceded at least the moment to him, grateful to do so. The tightrope of sexual tension we always walked— could we get through another second without mauling each other?—was especially taut now, and the humor let us tumble to a safety net.

For all of ten seconds.

We were both lying down now. Separated only by the bedclothes. Waist up, he was naked. Waist down, so was I—and the moistening folds there let me know it, drop by excruciating drop.

The safety net was gone again. And the tightrope was twenty feet higher.

But Evrest was so much closer. Bigger. Harder. Everywhere I looked, everywhere I breathed, like—

"Thunder."

On the tremble of my rasp, it was no longer a joke. It was the statement of my spirit, the declaration of the soul he'd captivated since our eyes had first locked...and the heart he now possessed like a thunderhead did the sky—powerful, dark, magnificent.

So...what was that I kept blabbering about, about leaving ASAP?

You're too late. You're too far under.

Getting my body out of here wouldn't do a damn thing for where my heart decided to stay.

And now, you're too screwed.

Tears burned as the full truth of it sank in. Evrest gazed at me, into me, already seeing it...his face transforming because of it, forehead crumpling, lips parting on harsh breaths. He dipped toward me, swiping a thumb across my cheek as if compelling himself to look deeper, demand more. I winced, longing to look away; he wanted depths I couldn't possibly have, let alone give...

But he found them. Then, without compunction, took them. "Lightning," he grated. And just like that, turned all of the magic around, giving it back to me. "My Camellia. My lightning."

So many things in his voice. Potency. Possession. Passion. But all I heard was the desperation. And all I knew was the desire to banish it—using whatever means I had.

Without a word, I twisted a hand into his hair again. Yanked hard, crushing his mouth down to mine.

Hot. Wet. Primal. Animal. We devoured each other, taking with abandon, feeling without care. Why had I tried to fight this, to pretend we could make it go away simply by ignoring it? Why had I tried tricking fate into tipping the scales for us, turning it into a blessing instead of a punishment?

This—*us*—wasn't either.

I was the lightning to his thunder, the shore to his tide—not a gift or a curse, a right or a wrong, but something bigger than those ideas. Something that simply *was*. Like a wolf scenting a deer, he needed to hunt, slay, consume.

And I needed to fall, surrender...perish.

The wind rushed past the tent, bringing new energy to every touch we exchanged while evoking the impression we were caught in a vortex all our own, as wild and fierce as the ocean crashing so close. Nothing we'd done in the crypt or inside the cave had been like this. As Evrest slid his mouth to my neck and bit down, I let my sigh join the wind. As he ripped at my shirt—*his* shirt—exposing my nudity in one tear, I arched. As buttons *ping*ed off the lamps and tent poles, his gaze flared at my puckered nipples.

"*Bezelle.*" He lowered his lips to one. "So beautiful." He glided to the other—and sucked in hard.

"Yes." I practically fisted his hair as he pulled my aching tip between his teeth. *Bite it. Use it. Feast on me.* "Yessss!"

He suckled into the valley between my mounds. "My naughty little sevette. You like that...letting me take from you, even if it hurts."

"Yes," I managed. "Take more...please."

He lifted his head, nipping his way up to my neck. With his long fingers splayed along my jaw, he shoved my head to the side, exposing my neck for a more brutal assault of his tongue, teeth, and lips. "Everything I have for you? *Anything?*"

I didn't give him an exact answer, figuring the question more than rhetorical. When he kicked off the covers to fit his thighs between mine, words spilled anyway. "Oh," I moaned. "Ohhhh, yes. Anything!"

His hand hooked into my hair, pulling me up for another kiss. Every pore of my nudity turned into shivering expectancy. My breasts scraped against his chest, zinging with higher arousal. My thighs rubbed against the cotton encasing his legs, making me officially declare a love/hate relationship with the fabric. I skated hands up the burnished crests of his shoulders, cherishing every ripple I encountered along the way, until digging fingers into the perfect sinew of his back. I kept them there even as he pulled away, hovering his face inches above mine, mingling our heavy breaths.

"What about my cock?"

I bit my lip, flashing a coquette's smirk. "Especially that." A thought barged in. I peered around. "Errr, do you have a stash of lube here?"

Evrest, meet enigma—resulting in Cam, meet confusion. He was really, utterly unreadable. Strange but...awesome. The quivers in my sex turned my brain into a ping pong match between what-the-hell and let's-not-argue-a-good-thing.

Just before I conceded to the latter, he hitched down his sweats enough to set his erection loose. His tip slid easily against my most sensitive nub—before kissing the entrance of my shivering vagina.

"I do not think we shall need any, sevette."

Huh?

"Huh?"

He captured my mouth beneath his again. Twined his hand deeper into my hair...while bracing himself above me, as if he longed to stay there for a while.

"I want to be inside you, Camellia...just like this. Taking you as I am meant to. Fucking you with everything I am."

"But—"

"Ssshh, ssshh." He cut me off with a gentle kiss. "I know what I am saying. What I am doing." Once more, his entire face compressed with that painful crunch of emotion. "I also know what I felt, when I thought you might die yesterday. The first time, I pushed it off as the result of adrenaline and stress. But the second time, when you were unconscious in my arms, I knew..." His whole body shook—and I knew at once that lust wasn't the only cause. "I may have to move on from this, from us...but nobody else will be my true bride."

Inner scream. Outer sob. Until the boulder in my throat

made even that impossible. I managed to choke, "Evrest..."

"It is you, Camellia. Only you."

Don't say it. Please don't say it. Thank God the inner scream was still functional. *If you say it, this will become the best and worst night of my life. I can't bear that now, damn it. I can't!*

"Just for tonight...be my one and only bride. Make me forget what my life will be, has to be. Make me forget it all and fill it up...with you."

CHAPTER TWENTY-TWO

He might as well have said it. The blow hit just as violently in my heart, a head-on collision with the blood, guts, and trauma to match. My soul was wreckage I no longer recognized, my body a fiery twist of need, my resistance his helpless casualty.

He was going to make me take it. All of it. His body. His virginity. His passion. His completion. And God help me, I'd eagerly accept every moment—and wouldn't regret one. Would know, as I pulled these memories out of my life's treasure chest in the years to come, that they'd be the lovingly hidden gems at the bottom, taken out only in those moments when I longed for him the most...

So, all the damn time.

It hurt. Bad. In truth, it had hurt from the beginning—but I'd been able to control the pain by simply slamming it out of my thoughts. Didn't work that way now. The ache was stitched into my heart...and the incisions still bled. I wondered if they would...or if I'd want them to.

I framed Evrest's face with my hands. Dug my fingertips into his thick stubble. Adoring him. Always. Yes, now I knew... always.

"I never asked for this." The words sounded like defense. They felt like it too. I guess, for some crazy reason, I needed him to know.

His forehead pressed to mine. "I know, sevette. I know."

"You've changed me."

"As you have changed me."

"I'm a damn mess!"

"Then let me help."

"*Help?*" I laughed through my tears, unable to process the insanity. "You have a space shuttle parked out on the berm that you haven't told me about, mister? A way to get us off this rock, to a planet where a whole kingdom isn't waiting on you to—"

He kissed me harder. Harder still. He shuddered, sweeping even deeper, even as his thighs trembled from the strain of holding his cock in check at my entrance. When he lifted his face, shattering me anew with the peridots of his gaze, he rasped, "Let me take it all away, Camellia...just as you shall for me."

I writhed, conflicted—but even that little move worked his tip inside me by a fraction. We moaned in tandem. His head was already wet, expanding and surging, begging at the tender gateway to my deepest core. To have him there, joined to me, connected at last...

"*Hedrir moi,*" he gritted. "Give this to me, Camellia. Fuck, I need this. Need you..."

His face, strained and sensual and beautiful, was my final undoing. I scraped my fingers to his nape, gazing without shame at him now. "As I need you."

A harsh breath left him. He pushed himself in, just an inch more. "Yes?"

"Yes, Evrest. Yes..."

If I had any more words, he ensured they'd all be forgotten, giving me everything in one carnal, incredible stroke.

I cried out in ecstasy.

He groaned—hopefully in the same. As a litany of Arcadian tumbled out of him, fervent and rasping, I made a leap and assumed the best. And felt even more. The stretch of him inside me... It was more amazing than I'd dreamed. More huge against my walls. More hard. More powerful.

That was before he even began to move again.

As he did, thrusting in time with every breath he took, I gripped his shoulders and gasped against his neck. He bent his head, pressing his lips to the sweet spot beneath my ear as he rolled his hips with increasing force.

Fine. So it was *really* too late for the protection chat. But the two booty call boys I'd indulged between Harry and now had included raincoats, and Evrest sure as hell hadn't been playing around, so I decided to wait a few minutes on crossing the second bridge of that concern—especially when he murmured against my skin in a nerve-melting mix of rasp and growl.

"Fuck. *Fuck.* My Camellia." Forget the nerves melting. He seared straight through them with the utterance. "*Mat paradise.* Mat *cielle.* Mat *amkim...*"

I didn't want a translation—because I already battled the echo of the words through every corner of my being, kicking back the English version of everything...all the words I craved to give him in return. *Shit.* Of all the times I refused to grab for heat-of-the-moment as a perfectly viable excuse, this had to be it. Didn't make sense, when the man made *every* moment "the heat."

And right now, even more.

He trailed his lips to the dip between my breasts once more. At the same time, his hands glided down too, finally gripping at my hips. His fingers dug in, but then, after a moment, loosened.

"No." I practically read the thoughts in his mind. "Don't be gentle." He protested with an empirical glare, forcing me to demonstrate. "Mark me, Evrest Cimarron." I punched my nails into the top of his back and then gored my way down to his ass. "*Make me* remember you."

Fast learner. And hell, was I grateful. He returned the favor with a gritty sound, seizing my hips and turning me into the pinned vessel for his harsh, hot lunges. Soon, he pushed up a little higher, using the hold to piston my body onto him, round him.

"Push up on your elbows," he instructed. "I want to see your nipples dance while I fill you."

Joyously obliged, my king.

From the new angle, I could better see every salacious shadow that crossed his face...every hungry twist of his beautiful lips...even every inch of his dark, dense shaft as it plunged and then pulled from my swollen, soaked sex. I was alternately awed and aroused by him. This gift he gave, mine alone, of sharing this occasion with him... It humbled me. At the same time, I had trouble believing it. How had a man with such passion to give, with a body so clearly crafted for sin, nearly gone until his thirtieth birthday without doing this to a woman? It was almost a crime.

But damn, was it my honor to give him the intro to the dark side.

For which he was clearly suited.

"Now reach in and pull on them," he growled. "Your pink, perfect nipples. Make them red. Squeeze until you want to scream. Mark *yourself* for me."

Who the hell had I been kidding? *Me*, induct *him* to the dark side? The man had invented the place. Nothing told me that clearer than the points I tugged and pinched for him, commanding the blood to swell both nipples until I clenched my teeth against shrieking from my self-induced torment. But every moment was worth it. As the pain charged my blood, Evrest's stare fired over my body, greedy and hungry, open and lusting, adding heat to my stings and arousal to my agony.

I watched his breaths and purposely matched my own to them, needing him as part of me in any way...in *all* the ways. My senses keened backward and then forward, down and then back up. My only equilibrium was him. His cock, burrowing deeper with every moment. His arms, flexed and straining. His thighs, powerful and taut.

"Does it hurt, sevette?"

"Yes," I rasped.

"Make it hurt more."

I abided, my brow furrowing and my lips parting on a long, harsh hiss. Evrest's exultant grunt was my perfect reward.

"You like it like this," he gritted. "Tell me that you do."

My head fell back just before I whispered, "I like it like this. Yes, yes; I do."

"When I make you hurt?"

"Yes, Evrest."

"When I fuck you hard?"

"Yes, Evrest!"

"Then hedrir moi *hertout,* my Camellia. Give it all to me now."

"Yes. *Yes.*" His flesh pounded a spell over mine. His voice wound the same magic through my senses. "Tell me how."

Anything you want.

Everything you want.

"Spread your legs wider. I want to see how much you like it. How wet my cock has made your sweet little cunt."

I opened for him, rejoicing in the look on his face as he fixated on the juncture of our bodies. "Parmel," he growled. "Bezelle. So pink and wet...needing me right here."

"Yes." I must've sounded like a lousy GIF on repeat, but it was the only word that made sense, the symbol of the surrender he craved. "Need...you...yes...ahhh!"

I cried out as he brought his hands in from my hips, bracing them to my upper thighs—and shoving them farther apart. With his fingers spread up to my abdomen, he used his thumbs on the lips of my sex, opening me fully—including the strip of my most sensitive nerves.

"*Here* you are." His murmur carried deep male satisfaction. It braided with the thrum from my bloodstream, louder and louder, as he teased toward my clit with tiny circles of his thumbs. Dear *God* and all the angels, he was good at that. Joined with the rhythm of his lunges, I was a sitting duck, waiting to be annihilated by the bullet of his prowess.

"Evrest! Shit!" My arms went limp, making me plummet back to the pillows. Wonderful madness as Evrest followed, pressing to me, stabbing inside me, rocking my damn world like no other lover ever did—or likely would again.

He was the wind over the canvas, power and magnificence.

He was the waves against the rocks, force and beauty.

He was the night itself, dark and perfect, plumbing every shadow inside *me*...and conquering it.

Making me his virgin as much as he was mine.

"Fuck. *Camellia*." He groaned and kissed me with soft desperation. "What you do to me..."

I smiled and scratched back up his spine. "Is that a bad thing?"

"It is when I long to come inside you."

The moment the words left his lips, a decision snapped into place. Unfaltering. Undeniable. Irrevocable. "Yes." It wasn't the GIF on repeat. It was the desire of my heart. "That's what I want too." When his mouth opened, I threw two fingers over it. "Shut it, Your Majesty. As a wise man told me in this very bed, I know what I'm saying. What I'm doing."

It didn't earn me even a snort of snark in return. Instead, a low, tormented growl prowled up his chest. "And if there is a ch—"

"If there is, then I'll handle it." *Whoa. Backpedal stat, girl, before he glare-skewers you into next year.* "Okay, *we'll* handle it. My condo has a second bedroom. It'd convert nicely to a nursery. You can come visit. We'll dress you up in funny disguises and then go visit the 'magical mouse' up the street."

He didn't capitulate. But he wasn't glare-skewering me anymore. A good sign? His new kiss, dragging at me with longing and hunger, sure said so. But when he concluded with a ragged moan, still holding himself away, I had to tamp a frustrated groan.

"You want to take me the way you were meant to?" I charged instead. "Then *do it*, Evrest." I ran my hands back down, pushing his pants so I could cup the firm, tight muscles of his ass. "Let me take you in. Squeeze every inch of you. Feel the scalding cream, exploding from your cock, deep ins—"

He cut me short by pulling my hair. With his fresh angle on my exposed neck, he bit down again. I gasped in anticipation—but broke into a wail instead. Was he going for king of the vampires as well as Arcadia tonight? "Tit for tat, little lightning," he rumbled. "You show me no mercy with your mouth, I show you no mercy with mine."

Two can play, Your Majesty. Two. Can. Play. "Now show me no mercy with your cock."

He moaned. Moved his bite-fest to the bottom of my ear. "Ruthless enchantress."

"With a pussy that's shivering." I lifted my legs, wrapping them around his waist. "Needing you. Dripping for you." I sneaked in a hot lick across his Adam's apple. "Evrest...I'm so damn close..." It wasn't too far off the truth. "And I'm so damn wet..."

"And I'm so damn—"

"*No.* Don't!" The new reverence in his tone had given up his game—and thank God for it. Leaving him behind after this was already going to be damn near impossible. If he gave me those words on top of it, he'd cripple me. Worse. I'd be without bones, period. The structure of my life wouldn't just be in shambles. The structure of *me* would be. "Show it to me instead," I pleaded, failing abysmally at keeping the sob out of it. "Give it all to me with your body. Please. *Please!*"

He barely let me get the last of it out before melding our mouths once more, sucking my tongue inside him before letting me have it back, coated in his heady taste. Oh, *hell.* Shivers and quakes, then hardly recovering in the moments he pulled back just enough to utter three coarse words.

"Creator help me."

Then I knew—*knew*—what he meant by truly taking me.

The erection that had first rendered me awestruck? I thought my body knew what the full force of it felt like by now. Between one thrust and the next, he rendered me wrong. Really wrong. My teeth knocked as he plunged deep, deeper,

deeper,

pushing, straining, opening...

marking, hurting...fucking.

Words fell from him, unintelligible but clearly nasty. I returned the same in sighs and cries, surrendering to his consummation. With every thrust he became more primal, even his words giving way to the growls of his purest lust. The sounds pulled more pins from my own control. As they filled my head, they turned my body into liquid. I was certain I'd never ridden a wave of arousal so far before. It brought on a strange predicament.

Don't let it end.

Oh God, I need to come.

But he burned even those words away, turning my whole body into a lava flow, consumed from the inside out by his power, his heat, his force. My arms slackened, falling away from him, tumbling to the pillows over my head. The second they hit, Evrest locked down, pinning me by the wrists before pumping even harder. I let my head jack back too, clenching my teeth to prevent myself from giving us away to the whole damn camp.

"Yes?" He panted it against the column of my neck.

"Yes." I gasped it into the darkness. So good. This was so damn good. My thighs trembled. My ass convulsed. And the tunnel he filled...pulsing pressure, building, burning...needing to release...*needing*...

"Give it to me, sevette. All of it."

My orgasm didn't bother sneaking up on me. It burst in with violence and light, C-4 to my senses, exploding, *im*ploding, razing everything in its path, white-hot demolition until I shuddered and screamed from the impact. But Evrest was there, absorbing the sound with his mouth, letting me cry into him—before thrusting it back into me with a vicious groan as his body tautened and stopped, a solid band of ecstasy. When he snapped, scorching me deep with the flood of his seed, I moaned in rapture, welcoming every drop.

We'd ridden the wind together...to the stars. It took a long time to find the earth again. I wasn't complaining. Didn't think he did, either. During the descent, Evrest turned the connection of our mouths into long, tender kisses. Released my wrists, only to keep sliding his touch up and down the lengths of my arms. Kept his sex inside mine, protecting the heat he'd brought...maintaining the seal of our dark dream for just a few minutes longer.

I needed it to be hours. Days.

Longer.

Forever.

Stop it.

I backed up the thought with a grimace. Should've known Evrest would not only read it but counter it with a soft, lingering kiss. "My first," he finally whispered. "And always my best."

My adorable—and observant—hunk. By being the tender one, he let me be the snarky one. "That's a mighty significant promise, pard'nah."

"Everything has been significant since you got here, Camellia."

I looked away. Not even snark could help how that one punched in, tearing at too many corners of my soul.

At the same moment, his body slipped out of mine. *Lovely.* Karma had gotten in her little joke after all.

Hard swallow. It lodged at the bottom of my throat, not such a bad thing. Focusing on the pain helped me keep the tears back—at least until Evrest rolled to his side, pulling me around with him, until we were face-to-face on the same pillow. His gaze, like the Northern Lights in the dimness, pierced me. His fingers, strong and adoring, brushed the hair from my face.

Hard swallow. Again. Tight breath. *Snark, don't fail me now.* "Okay, not-so-virgin boy, let me enlighten you about how this part of things goes."

The hills and valleys of his lips undulated into a smirk. "Hmmm. This should be interesting."

"Not really. Just the basics. Number one, I'm really not required to spend the rest of the night."

He scowled. "In my bed, you are."

"You're breaking the rules."

One eyebrow cocked up. *Really, sevette? You are going there* now, *with* me? "Move on."

Sexiest growl I'd ever heard from him. Arguing was going to be impossible. "Fine. Second point is more important anyhow."

"Which would be?"

"You have to say something really asshat-ish now."

Both brows jumped now. "*What?*"

"Yeah. Come on, it'll be fun. I'm sure you've heard a few of the classics already. 'This was great, but I have an early meeting.' Or maybe, 'Can I get your number? I'll call; I promise.'" I forced a game smile. "Okay, your turn."

Hell. He searched every inch of my face as if I'd told him I had Ebola instead. Then again, as if praying the force of his gaze could heal me.

"Stay here, Camellia. With me."

I made a game show buzzing noise. "That wasn't asshat. Not even a bit. Please try again, sir."

He kissed me. No tongue, but it fried every cell in my bloodstream anyway. After pulling away, he rasped again, "*Stay.*"

Intense, amazing man. "Fine. You win. We still have a couple of hours. I can sneak out right before dawn, and—"

He silenced me with another kiss. Like before, no tongue. Also like before, blazing bloodstream. *Not* like before: prickled suspicion. Then cresting awareness.

Ohhh, my God.

"You mean...stay *here*? In Arcadia? When everyone else leaves?"

Every inch of his face was a steady affirmation. "With me. For me."

I shifted to my back. *Whoa. Hell.* I needed some space. Maybe a lot of it. "As...what? Not your queen, right? You still have to pick her out from the lineup back at the palais." Now down by two. I thought of Novah, hoping she and Enock were into double-digits on the reunion sex orgasm count by now. I didn't spare a single thought for Chianna.

More solemnity rolled off him, deepening the confusion for me. And the heartache. "So I'd be your *mistress*?"

He continued to meet my gaze—but he didn't deny the accusation. "I will not insult you, Camellia. You must know I am not the only king who has been in this situation."

I twisted on him, yanking the sheet across my chest. Gave me something to form a fist around. "Yeah? And how many of your ancestors proposed opening the borders of the country to a world where gossip travels the world in three seconds and then goes viral in an hour?"

"The internet is new, but discretion is not." He reached for my free hand. "The family owns a villa under another name in a little town south of Sancti. The property is large, and the beach is private—"

"*Nothing* is private." I jerked back. Bolted from the bed altogether, dragging the sheet with me. "You don't get to have 'private' anymore, Evrest."

He was shockingly undaunted. "We would only have to be careful for a few years—"

"A few *years*?"

"But we could see each other every day. You are so skillful at so many things. You can work at the palais, in the offices with me. Fascha already confessed how much she likes you—and I know everyone else will too."

For a long moment, I could only gape. I wanted derision to be my pal right now, maybe bring along a bag full of insulted for the ride—but this was one of those moments where the sheltered king and the sexy wolf bashed each other. He truly saw nothing wrong with what he proposed. Hope actually tugged the edges of his lips.

"No," I finally murmured. "No, Evrest, I can't."

"Why not?"

Thank God he pushed. At least I could grab at some irritation. "Because in everyone's eyes, even Fascha's, I'd be your whore. You want to talk about the raised eyebrows when we go into a 'closed door meeting'?"

He bounded from the bed now too. Stalked at me, all naked sinew and regal stealth, turning my throat dry yet my sex into a puddle. "I shall eviscerate anyone who calls you a whore."

"Then sharpen your knife and get ready for the bloodbath, because the whole country will be on that bandwagon."

Should've thought that one through a little more. It only fueled his advance. But I wasn't thinking right now. At all.

"Camellia—"

"Don't." I flung up both hands. "Please don't." If he came any closer, he'd snap me again. *I'd* snap *him*. He'd already smashed one vow because of me. I couldn't—wouldn't—let him shatter anything more.

"*Camellia.*"

"I won't do it, Evrest." I blinked against the tears on my lashes, turning into rivers down my cheeks. "You were born to be a great king. You *will* be a great king. I refuse to be the bruise that ruins your reign."

"Bruise?" It choked out of him like a gust of grief. "How can you—"

"Because it's the truth—and in your gut, you know it as well as I do."

"Damn it!" His eyes flashed fire. His teeth bared white. "I'm in love with you!"

CHAPTER TWENTY-THREE

My eyes slammed shut. That only made the tears heavier, bursting past their trembling dams and rushing over my twisted lips.

Hell.

He'd said it. Smashed open every Pandora's Box of conflict in my heart in the doing too. Declaring total surprise would've been a lie. Half of me had already steeled myself for it, though it hardly made the agony of answering any easier.

"I'm in love with you too."

So...there. We'd done it.

Shit.

I closed the space between us with three slow steps. Reached a hand up to caress his perfect jaw. There was no reason to keep him at a distance anymore. Even if we jumped back into bed and he sank his sex inside mine again, the great wall we'd just stacked and sealed would still be there, looming between us. This connection we could no longer hide...this love we could no longer deny.

But had to. Somehow.

Somehow.

The options for that definition were very slim. As I stood on tiptoe to brush Evrest's lips with mine, I'd already made the choice. The best one—no matter how it gashed my heart apart like razor blades. His composure, ramrod stiff and ominously quiet, proved he'd stabbed a guess at my decision too.

I forced myself to whisper it aloud anyway.

"I love you, Evrest Cimarron...which is why I have to leave you."

★ ★ ★

Damn the dawn.

It came too soon, stabbing through the tent walls, breaking into the hours we spent lying in each other's arms, simply staring...savoring...memorizing. I promised to post regular pictures to my Facebook page. He promised to let the paparazzi get a good candid every now and then. We accepted the words for the emptiness they were, knowing nothing would ever be like this. Knowing the hours of our time had slipped into minutes...

the minutes into moments...

the moments into a kiss.

I stood in the center of the tent, staring at the shaft of light he'd stepped into after giving me that kiss. Pressing fingers to the lips that still vibrated from the desolate urgency of it. Fighting for air in the chest that had shut down as his lips took mine for the last time, unwilling to taint the moment even with breathing.

There was just one catch to letting the air back in again.

Doing so meant conceding to time once more. Admitting I had to move forward, step ahead—and yet back. To real life. To the rules. To the condo. To the job. To Faye.

Maybe all of it was an "up" side. All of it was safe, familiar, what I knew...

With the exception of one thing.

I didn't know *me* anymore.

Or maybe, for the first time in my life, I actually did know. Which was why I couldn't move.

One week. One man. Waking me up...in his darkness.

Making me crumble in the emptiness of the light.

My knees gave way as the tears fell, hard and huge. My chest heaved, a conveyor belt of stabs and sobs. I pushed a fist against it, fighting to rub out the pain. Useless. So was the palm against my head, fighting the pressure there. Where was the instruction manual for this kind of sorrow? There had to be one, right? Filed in life's "Heartbroken" section, subheading "Kings You Can't Have"?

I was lost. Helpless. This had to be the worst ugly cry of my life—

Meaning, of course, that *someone* had to catch me in the middle of it.

Silver lining? At least it wasn't Chianna, though Harry definitely wouldn't have been my go-to nom for the moment. Nevertheless, I was damn glad I'd thrown on some clothes before Evrest left—if the wrinkled T-shirt and khakis from my duffel still constituted clothes.

"Hey." His murmur was gentle, his touch equally so. "Cam...sweetie..."

Past swollen eyes and tears, I realized he'd tossed down his satchel to kneel in front of me. When he tugged, offering his shoulder as a cry towel, I willingly fell against him, blurting the first things that sprang to mind. "Oh, shit. Oh, yuck. Oh, Harry..."

He cradled the back of my head, muttering in resignation, "Damn. Yeah. This is a giant yuck."

He wanted to say more. I felt the words pushing at his chest, his throat. The *I told you so* practically hacking at him, righteous in its truth. But this week had changed him too. Matured him to the point of even having a little class.

I took the pressure off him, spilling it all myself. "You were right. All along. I broke the rules, big-time. I couldn't keep my hands off Evrest Cimarron, and now I'm paying the big-daddy penalty for it. I'm sorry, Harry. So damn sorry."

Lots of reactions scrolled my list of expectations. A sympathetic smile? Definitely not an odds leader. Yet there it was, lighting up his handsome features before he replied, "Funny. Evrest told me *he* was the one who couldn't keep himself in check."

Snotty sniffle. *Ew.* I gratefully accepted a tissue from him. "He...he told you that?"

"He told me everything." He laughed when my eyes bugged. "Okay, revision. The cleaned-up version of everything. Chill, rock star. We didn't *compare notes* or anything. But there was a lot of time to kill between checking on you and keeping your parents updated."

"So you bonded by talking about me?"

He shrugged. "Tried to wrangle him into a debate of Tarantino versus Ang Lee, but he preferred you." Quick wink. "Imagine that."

My stunned stare didn't falter, even after blowing my nose again. "And you're...not pissed?"

"Was at first. A whole damn lot. Especially when you played evasion tactics on me that night in the editing room."

I winced. "I know. And I *am* sorry."

"Accepted. Don't lie to me again."

I nodded. We hugged. Hell, it felt good to really have the fog cleared between us again. "I went to him that night," I offered. "And we agreed to douse the fire."

He snorted out a laugh. "Cam, the two of you are a couple of matchsticks on bone-dry kindling—in a Santa Ana wind storm." His reference to Southern California's brutal brushfire starters gave his words extra weight. "I knew it as soon as I saw you together in the back seat of the van."

I glared. "Come on. We weren't *that* obvious."

He tapped at his temple. "Trained eye."

I relaxed the look, silently giving him the win. *Trained eye.* Well, no shit. His director's perception had probably picked up on every glance, touch, and nuance between Evrest and me—during a thirty-minute car ride. And Evrest thought we could be "discreet" beneath paparazzi lenses for a few years?

"He's in love with you, Cam."

There wasn't a shred of judgment in the statement. I smiled up at him with appreciation. "I know."

"You're leaning in the same direction, aren't you?"

Bit lip. Massive effort to look away. *How's that for your trained eye, Mr. Dane?* "You mean *leaned.* Yep. Hard. Knocked over the whole damn display while I was there."

His answering exhalation was heavy. "Glad I told Joel he might be inheriting your duties for good."

I locked my gaze back to his. Weird. Maybe *my* observational eye was off, but Harry seemed...discomfited. For enforcing his own rule?

Hopefully, my smirk relaxed him. "Guess I owe Joel a shitload of wine when you all wrap, then."

"Yeah." Harry chuckled. Thank God. "Make it the good stuff."

"Tell him it'll be on his doorstep."

Long silence. Harry drummed fingers on one of his knees. Peered around the tent, seeming baffled that nobody else was around. "Well...I came to see how you were doing. Guess I know now."

"Probably more than you wanted to."

"Nah." He contradicted the retort with a tight hug and heartfelt growl. "Never."

He kept up the squeeze for a really long time. I was the one to finally break away—a first for us. "Don't you have an award-winning movie to be making?"

He rose to his feet and then pulled me up too. "Errr... yeah. The team's packed up and ready to head back to Sancti. They're waiting on me."

I smiled my approval. "Evrest has arranged a car for me... to the airport."

His brows arched. "Now? Today?"

I nodded, using it as a distraction against more tears. "Yeah, now. Today. I...I can't stay here any longer, Harry."

Comprehension washed his face. He cupped a hand around my nape and squeezed but didn't go for another hug. The coolest thing about becoming friends with an ex? They knew when you didn't need the touchy-feely as well as when you did.

"Be safe, rock star."

"Kick ass, Mr. Dane."

It wasn't my final farewell of the day. Ahead was the drive along the coast to the airport—and the goodbye I'd have to give to Arcadia itself. I swallowed hard, already knowing the trip wouldn't be easy. This beautiful island and its enchanting people were woven as deeply into my heart as their king.

I sighed while gathering my bag from the couch. The rest of my things, packed up from the room in Sancti, would be waiting in the airport transport.

Before I closed the duffel, something pulled my attention between the cushions of the couch. I yanked on the black material, discovering it to be a man's T-shirt.

Tentative whiff. Then long inhalation, my eyes drifting shut.

Driftwood. Ocean. Spices. Sage. My man.

No. Not anymore.

I'd thought I was all out of tears.

Wrong. Wrong. Wrong.

I palmed the moisture off my face, unwilling to dilute the scent in the shirt—because it was so going home with me. After carefully folding the fabric, I reached in to make sure it had a secure place in the bag, toward the bottom...

Where my fingers knocked against something hard. Something *I* hadn't put there.

A box?

A...*velvet* box?

With a frown, I pulled the square-shaped container out. Slid my fingertips across the luxurious black velvet along its top, as well as the symbol embossed in shiny crimson there. A dove with wings that turned into sun rays.

I pressed my other hand to my lips, capturing my gasp of awe. With an evening gown, elbow gloves, and better hair, I'd be ready to rock the *Pretty Woman* take-off—only without the opera trip and an orgasmic ending to my night.

But there is the man who wants to take care of you forever...

I replaced the gasp with a snort. "Taking care of me doesn't mean hiding me."

Bravado aside, there was no fighting the curiosity about what lay in the box. Evrest had clearly wanted me to find it later, but that wasn't washing with the girl who dealt with sealed gifts as well as unmapped driving routes. In short, not well.

As soon as I pushed back the lid, gasps were in order again. When I remembered to breathe once more.

Lying against the ivory satin inside, a shimmering gold chain supported a delicate pendant fashioned out of light-green tourmaline...the exact color of his eyes.

The glittering stone was carved into the shape of a lightning bolt.

Beneath its place on the satin, words were embossed in gold.

Fortune favored me.

I closed the box. Clutched it to my chest as I sank to the floor next to the couch, struggling to suck down air...wondering if breathing was ever going to be a natural function for me again. And not really caring if it was.

All I had to do was tell him yes. Just direct the driver to take me on to Sancti, where Evrest would give me the keys to the villa fashioned of fantasies. The life of my dreams...

Where I'd always be the king's dirty little secret.

His true love but his life's afterthought.

That wasn't a dream. It was an excuse.

And somehow, in some way, I'd face each day without it. Without him.

No matter how impossible each of those climbs felt now.

"Creator give me strength," I whispered.

Then hit the repeat button on it constantly during the next half hour.

Right after climbing into the Sprinter, in which I was the only passenger. Again after my call to Mom, which had rung straight through to her voicemail. After calling Dad, same result. And again, unsuccessfully, before pulling the square jewelry box back onto my lap—then taking the necklace from it and fastening it around my neck.

Clutching the pendant in one hand and my phone in the other, I hit the speed dial for Faye.

I had no idea why I dreaded the moment she'd picked up—until she did. Before she was done gleefully gasping my name, the now-familiar sting invaded my whole head and spilled out my eyes. "Cam? Honey?" Her tone switched from joy to alarm as soon as she heard my sniff. "Oh shit, girl. Are you okay? What's going on?"

I grabbed a tissue—these transports literally came with everything except the kitchen sink—and honked into it. *Gawd. I* was as much of a mess as the weather. A sudden squall had blown in off the sea since we left Asuman, now slashing sideways rain against the speeder's windows. "I... I'm coming home, Faye. Now. Today. Will you be all right with me taking my files back sooner than expected?"

A nonplussed huff. "Well...sure, dear. But why? Cam, talk to me. What's happening?" More pathetic whimpers from my end led to: "Or dare I ask this...*who's* happening?"

I half expected her conclusion. Faye could turn a run to the store for tampons into a full-on romance novel starring her own swarthy sheikh. It shocked me that her money came from the polar opposite, a world of ledgers, pinstripes, and Dow trends. The contradiction normally made me giggle. Today, it was my solace—and a reason to bawl harder.

"Oh, Faye. Oh, God. It's...such a mess. And it hurts so much."

She joined a little sob to mine. "*Honey.* I wish I was there to help right now."

"I know." I dumped the words out with a little shame. But the truth was, given a choice to magically teleport anyone here right now, it'd be her.

"Okay. Start at the beginning. What's his name and how did you meet him?"

I hoped she was sitting down. After ensuring the driver really *was* into the newest Coldplay tune on the radio, I murmured, "Evrest. His name is Evrest."

Silence.

Until now, a word I'd assumed as nonexistent in Faye Mellencamp's world.

"Errr...Faye?"

"Your 'mess' is *Evrest Cimarron*?"

Her outburst was oddly therapeutic. I actually giggled. "You need a second to process?"

"I may just."

Her words were obscured by the Sprinter's screeching brakes. "Holy shit!" I cried as a drenched figure ran into the middle of the road, arms stretched out, pleading with us to stop. I burst the words out again when taking in every detail of the fool. A woman. Blonde. Huge eyes, tiny boobs. Panic so potent, it'd made her suicidal. "Holy *shit.* Novah?"

"Stop!" she screamed. "Please! Stop! Help us. Help us!"

"Faye, I'll call you back."

After clicking the call off, I threw the phone onto the seat and bounded out of the van. Rain instantly pelted, temporarily blinding me. Still, I shouted, "Novah? What the hell are you doing—"

She practically tackled me in a desperate embrace. "Thank the Creator! Camellia! I do not know what to do. I...I cannot think—"

"About what? Why? What're you doing out here in the middle of this muck-fest? Come on, get in the van and—"

"No." She jerked back, face crumpling. "I cannot. I cannot! He is out on the rocks. He is trapped there!"

"Damn." I peered across the road—at the turnout we'd used a few days ago, on the way to Asuman. Minos Beach again. And those huge Bull Rocks.

"Th-The s-storm," Novah babbled. "I was trying to get to him myself, but the weather turned so fast, kicking up the waves—and now he cannot swim back in." She grabbed both sides of her head as if her brain would explode. "Oh, Creator. Dear Creator, help him!"

"Whoa. Okay sweetie, calm down." Her panic was like a living creature, scaring the crap out of me. "*Who's* trapped out there? Enock?" Crazy notion. Grown men were supposed to do the thinking with their big head, not the little, but entire YouTube channels had blooper reels as proof of the opposite.

"No." She slammed it back with irritation born from sheer panic. "*No*. Not Enock. Tochi. My son."

CHAPTER TWENTY-FOUR

"Your *what?*"

My comeback was meet with bared teeth. "Can we speak of this later? Camellia, I will not *have* a son if we do not *do* something!"

She was right. One look at the huge waves across the street was proof enough of the point. But I also observed a weird rip current pattern between the breakers. Maybe, just maybe, a strong swimmer could use the flow to their advantage, getting pulled to the rocks without expending a lot of energy. The return trip was going to be the bitch. Yeah. A really strong swimmer was needed.

Good news? I pretty much knew where to find one.

That was also the bad news.

But another look to the rocks, and the small boy huddled atop them, left me no alternative. With the right wallop from the right wave, that boy was going to be swept right off his perch—into one of those dangerous whirlpools.

I raced to the driver's window and motioned for him to open up. "Call emergency response services. An extreme emergency call is code red, right?"

"Yes, ma'am."

"Use it. And...you'd better call the airport too. I'm going to be late for that charter."

I grabbed Novah's hand and dashed over to the beach. We hopped the guardrail and sprinted along the sand, the wind kicking wet sand and sea spray at us. I barely noticed, my head too full of more prayers—and a silent plea to the boy all alone out on that big boulder. *Hang on, kiddo. Please.*

At least he had the sense to hoist onto a bigger rock, though now that we were close, I noticed another *ugh* factor about the situation. Black moss, shiny as the green stuff but worse because it blended, coated the whole boulder Tochi had claimed.

"Damn," I muttered.

"What?" Novah volleyed. "*What*, Camellia?"

I refocused her—and me. "How old is he?" I demanded while peeling off my T-shirt. I didn't want to face the possibility of those rocks in my bra but couldn't afford the drag. My leggings and Doc Martens would have to stay. Needed them for essential footing.

"T-Ten." She got the answer out between chattering teeth. It wasn't that cold, but she was that scared. "M-My aunt has raised him as my cousin, but he is mine. He has such a fiery streak. Wanted to prove his worth to the older boys at school, so they dared him into an initiation of conquering the Bull Rocks by himself." She erupted in fury, hissing hard. "Little boktards. Bratty fools!"

"Ssshhh." I yanked her into a fierce hug. "He'll be back in your arms in minutes. I promise it, Novah."

I meant every word. Her tears, iridescent blue against the gloom of the storm, shivered in her eyes. For the first time, she seemed to comprehend my purpose. "Wait. Camellia...you cannot mean...to try this—"

"You know how you grew up around horses? Well, I grew up at the water's edge—in Central California." At her confused scowl, I assured, "I'm no stranger to big rocks, my friend."

Conflict still twisted her face, but she nodded and let me squeeze her again. "Creator bless you, Camellia."

The sweet trust of her words brought a shit-eating grin to my face. After thumbs-upping her, I turned for the water, amped by a surge of adrenaline. In contrast to the despair I'd been swimming in since this morning, the energy felt—well, awesome.

It didn't stick around for long.

Very quickly, I learned that that energy had a knack for morphing into fear—the kind that could consume a body and shake a lot of muscles. Though I was right, to a degree, about using the strength of the rip current, I'd neglected to think about the tricky eddies they left behind. Crevices that were probably just puddles when Tochi came out here were now hidden pools leading to make-out sessions with razor-edged rocks.

As I inched closer to Tochi, I could already see that he'd learned that—the hard way.

No wonder he clung to that boulder like a damn tree frog.

Which meant my real work hadn't yet begun.

"Tochi!"

Sure enough, when I yelled it from the rock just beneath him, the kid barely moved. A tiny jog of his head was the only sign he hadn't passed out or died. Thank God.

"Tochi...your mom sent me."

Better response. By a little. He turned and shot me a terrified stare, but that was all I got. About twelve feet of sheer black rock separated us, all at a sixty-degree angle. It felt like the side of El Capitan to me, and I wasn't a scared shitless ten-year-old.

"My name is Cam. I'm here to help, okay?"

He struggled to keep his grip. I actually hoped he'd lose it, since I was now ready for the catch—and we had to get out of here soon.

"Don't want any help!" His falsetto sliced across the wind.

Calming breath. Or at least what I could manage under the circumstances. "Why not?"

"I broke the rules. Maimanne and Paipanne told me how dangerous it was, but I came anyhow."

"Because of the boys who teased you at school," I retorted. A wave bashed in, harder than the others. *Damn it.* Tide was rising. "So it's not entirely your fault."

"Is too!" A shrill wail now. "I broke the rules. I deserve to die!"

Sheez. Boys and their pissing contests and the really ridiculous results. But I couldn't fling that at him now.

How to get him down by making sense too?

"Hey, buddy. I get it, okay? You wanted to prove your honor to those guys. And you were willing to face danger for it. And yeah, you went yes-yes to a big no-no by doing it—but it all sounds like a decent break-even in my book."

Tochi tilted his gaze down again. Kept it fixed on me this time. "You speak like Spiderman."

Yay, internet. "Well, you look like him—but the web is wearing off, Spidey. If we don't get you down from there, the Goblin's going to make one of these waves into a force we can't fight, and then we're both going down."

Good sign. At least I got a conflicted grimace now. "I...I'm scared."

So am I, Tochi. So scared, even my bones started to chill because of it. As another wave crashed in, feeling three times worse than the last, I searched my brain for some more brilliant nuggets of ten-year-old wisdom. *Nada.* The light had gone out. I was dark.

But I should've realized something about my new relationship with darkness.

At its blackest point, it gave back the best shit.

Like a brand on my skin, I suddenly remembered the pendant against my chest. I fingered it with a mischievous smile. *Thank you, Evrest.*

"Can you see this?" I yelled.

"Kind of," Tochi replied. "Is it a lightning bolt? Like the boy wizard?"

"It's a lightning bolt—like the power of Minos."

His eyes widened. "*What?*"

Note to self. Tell Novah that Minos trumps Dumbledore.

"Yeah. The...uh...sorcerer who gave it to me said he cut it straight from the Bull Rocks themselves."

"How?"

"Sorry. Didn't ask. It would've been rude. It was a gift." I held the bolt a little higher. "But he *did* tell me I could wear it to the Bull Rocks and be granted total safety—though the power would only last for fifteen minutes." I let the pendant drop. "So the clock's ticking, buddy. You ready?"

It was now or never.

Thank the Creator, Tochi realized it too.

As he slid down the boulder to me, I swore I heard Novah's scream on the wind.

After that, it was nothing but a lot of water. And yelling at Tochi to hold on tight—like he needed the reminder. And struggling, rock by rock, stroke by stroke, breath by breath, until my feet hit sand—

Right before a wave rammed me with linebacker force. Toppled. Tumbled. Flooded. Off my feet. Into the sea...

I latched on to Tochi and prayed again. Hard. For a long, crazy minute, we were ice cubes in Poseidon's blender, grinded and tossed and pummeled by a force we couldn't see or control. The wave was too huge for any kind of defensive footing. It had swept us at least eight feet off the ocean floor.

When the world stopped whirling, we'd either be beached or dead.

Whump. My fingers spread against solid ground. I took a tentative breath. Another. *Ish*. Sand in the teeth. Shells in the bra. Kelp in the hair. My girlhood dreams of becoming a mermaid definitely didn't include this.

The adventure still had the happiest ending I could imagine. I smiled while watching Novah clutch her little boy, raining zealous kisses over his dazed face. Tears welled. For the first time in a long time, happy ones.

My expression fell as Novah turned and pointed frantically at me—directing a trio of medical guys. *What the hell?* Was I bleeding? Missing a limb? Quick glance down. Everything seemed to be here. Wow, my boobs had even stayed put in the bra. No blood on the sand, either.

"Guys," I protested, "hey—I'm good. *I'm good*, okay? Tochi's the priority. He has some bad nicks on his arms; looks like the sharper rocks got in some digs at him—"

"*Miss Saxon*." The lead medic shot a don't-fuck-with-me scowl. "As you can see, we have colleagues attending to the boy. Ellis, Roarke, and I have orders to make certain you are fully checked out before we transport you to the hospital."

"Hospital?" As lovely as their manners were, especially their efforts not to look at my chest, I shoved to my feet and pushed them back. "Ohhh, no, no, no. I don't need the hospital, just the transport van. There's a plane waiting for me at the airport."

I spun, trying to even *find* the transport again. *Whoa*. How much time had really passed since Novah stopped us? The road was a totally different scene. Emergency trucks. A couple of cars bearing the logo for the kingdom's newspaper. Another for the blog. At least a dozen town cars. Sheez, even a military Hummer spewing a few of Samsyn's guys.

"Wow," I muttered. "Talk about a splashy entrance."

But I only wanted to make an exit. Quietly. Quickly.

"Miss Saxon." The burly one—I think he was Ellis—pounded over, blocking my way while thrusting a clean T-shirt into my hands. "We have to insist."

Peeved glare. "No. You *don't*. Just tell Novah thank you for her concern, but—"

"Our orders are not from Lady Novah."

The way he folded his arms, with an air of serene authority and a regal twist of lips, didn't make my follow-up query necessary. I knew exactly who called their shots now but couldn't figure out how to feel about that. Miffed? Touched? Exasperated? Excited? Every time I tried to step out of Evrest Cimarron's way, he insisted on stepping into mine.

And God, did I love him for it.

As if the chaos of my thoughts willed it, there was a fervor up on the road—a black town car weaving through the others, Arcadian flags flapping from the front bumpers, tires spraying water as it came to a sharp stop. A second later, he bounded out the back door.

And holy shit, did he look *good*.

Clearly, he'd come from duties at the palais. Though he'd shucked his suit coat and tie, his dress shirt was bespoke to the inch, his dark pants equally perfect. They flowed with him as he hopped the guardrail without a break in stride—and kept coming down the sand like he had the first night we met. No sideways glances at anything else. Not a care about the press members, now running to keep up. Not a backward look at his dozen staff members, doing the same thing. Not concerned about the rain that drenched him, plastering his shirt to that magnificent torso, dripping in his thick eyelashes as he blinked hard...

Pure pain etching every plane of his face.

Even then, he still looked amazing.

But my stomach wasn't getting the same memo. "Wh-What's wrong?" I managed.

His chest heaved. Once. That was enough. "*Wrong?*" His eyes flared. His lips parted. Hell, his teeth were clenched.

"Evrest. Whoa. What the hell?"

He raised a hand toward the Bull Rocks. His fingers shook. "You could have died. *I* almost died out there!"

"And your mother would have been destroyed, just like Novah would be now."

"So you jumped in? Without waiting for the damn rescue teams?"

Time to break out the inner Elphaba. "Waiting wasn't the right thing to do. I'm a strong swimmer, Evrest. It wasn't like I was—"

"Thinking?"

"Stop it!" My own teeth were clenched now. Despite how he'd flown off the proverbial handle, I was more than aware of the press taking their fun little notes just a few feet away. "You don't get the right to stress about me anymore like that."

"The fucking hell I do not." He stepped—correction, stomped—closer. "You. Could. Have. Died. For *what*?"

"For my son, Your Majesty."

Novah had come over, one hand on Tochi's shoulder, the other tangled in his dark-blond hair. She attempted a small smile at Evrest, for which I silently thanked her. It mollified him, at least a little.

"King Evrest, this is my son, Tochi." Her eyes welled once more. "I am so, so sorry...for not being forthcoming about this. My family has kept him a secret since his birth, when I was fifteen. To avoid the scandal in our little town, my aunt and uncle feigned *her* pregnancy and then raised him as their own."

"And Enock is his father?" I asked.

She nodded. "Since we were all so close, Tochi has been raised by the two of us as much as my aunt and uncle...behind closed doors. We knew that once we were married, we could be more open about Tochi's true roots. When I was chosen as a Distinct, we intensified our guardianship of the secret." Her voice cracked. "And it was hell."

"A hell you no longer have to endure," Evrest assured—but his next words broke apart worse than hers, joined to his taut gaze back into mine. "Sure as the Creator lights the sky, I understand the hell of hiding your heart."

"But you should not." Novah pushed forward by another step, her head held higher now. "*Why*, Majesty, does it have to be this way?" A harsh sound erupted from her, half harsh cry, half outraged grunt. Though the burst was unique, it didn't prepare me—or clearly Evrest—for what she did next. "Can anyone answer this question for me?" she shouted to every person gathered on the shore. "Why the lies?"

Just as the rain died down, the confused mutterings of the crowd swelled. I wondered why it seemed so loud, until noticing the group wasn't just emergency responders and court personnel anymore. The remaining ten members of the Distinct had caught up to Evrest. About fifty Arcadian civilians had stopped to watch the circus too.

Circus. A pretty good descriptor now, judging by how things were proceeding.

Until Evrest raised a hand.

By the time he reached the height of the move, fingers poised at elegant command, even the wind fell silent.

"Lady Novah has issued an excellent protest—one I happen to agree with." As he moved out, the crowd shifted back, creating a semicircle of space—as if they already knew he was about to shift more than sand on this beach today. "If it is time for Arcadia to move forward and open ourselves to the world, why are we not open with each other? Why are we all sacrificing ourselves for rules and laws that have no place in our heads, our hearts?"

He watched the questions race across each face in the crowd...returning those questioning gazes with the unflinching belief in his own. I stared at his profile, never more awestruck—or proud—of him as I was right now.

"My duty to Arcadia has always been the priority and joy in my life. As her king, I have been passionate about making her into someplace better, bolder, happier, more prosperous for all. I also know that my duty begins with honoring the laws of her traditions. All my life, I have studied those traditions, making them part of my heart, my spirit—which is why I would never break one of them without deep, thorough consideration."

I swayed on my feet. Damn. *Damn.* He was *not* going there. *Here.*

Yeah.

Yeah, he was.

I was forced to open my eyes as he reached a hand back, beckoning toward Novah and me. The little blonde nodded at me with knowing encouragement.

My knees turned to quicksand as I stepped forward.

My heart turned to thunder as our hands locked.

My soul...turned into peace.

I looked up, letting his gaze lock mine down. If anything could get me through this moment, it was going to be a shot of the conviction in those beautiful eyes. Too bad I couldn't order a chaser of bone-melting sex along with it.

Behave.

With our hands still twined, he pivoted toward the crowd. "With all here today as witnesses, I, King Evrest Cimarron, hereby propose a new law for our land. Let the Distinct still be honored for Arcadia, though these amazing women will be chosen for their talents of serving our country, not just its king. They shall all be free to love whom they choose—as will their king."

He turned back toward me. Tripped my heart up all over again with the strength in his stance, the adoration in his smile, and the possessiveness of his touch. "I can only rule this land as a true and devoted leader with the woman I love by my side...a woman with the boldness, bravery, and generosity of a true queen in her heart. Camilia Diana Saxon, you are that woman. You have been that woman since the moment I walked across that ballroom and slipped my hands around yours. I know you have only been here a week, but I am going to feel this way in a year. In ten years. In ten thousand years."

I gasped. The crowd did too. As my heart burst and my soul soared, he dipped his head, taking my mouth as passionately as he could without tempting my hands toward his ass. How did he know *just* that breaking point...

We pulled apart, breathing hard. The throng was so rapt, they could hear us.

"Stay with me, Camellia," he murmured. "In my home, in my bed, in my heart—"

"In *our* hearts," Novah inserted.

"In our land." He sealed that with another kiss. "Together, my love, we can change the world."

Long moment.

Once more, not able to breathe.

Once more, not really caring.

Was this really happening? Had he really just said all that? Vowed to change his life, his *rules*, for *me*?

Hell. The very least I could do was vow he'd never regret it.

This time, *I* leaned up and kissed *him*.

As I did, the crowd went ballistic. Even more so when Evrest took advantage of the liplock, sweeping his tongue in to properly ravish me.

My giggle finally broke us apart. Awesome timing. The wind started carrying the squall away, bringing rays of golden sun across the beach—and Evrest's noble, beautiful face. Envious of the light that danced in his hair, I joined in the fun by threading my fingers through the thick waves too—then jumped up to wrap my legs around his waist, launching the press into a photographic feeding frenzy. With my lips against his, I whispered, "Take me home, Your Majesty."

A gorgeous grin parted his lips as he wrapped both hands

around my thighs. Hell, what that grin did to so many parts of me. Had I really thought I could survive across the world without that smile? These arms? This man?

I didn't want to think it. I didn't have to anymore.

As he carried me back up the beach, he spun me around and around until I screamed with dizziness and joy...and a love I never thought I'd realize. A love so powerful, it made the world fall away, the shadows into magic, my life into lightning.

Destiny? Some, perhaps many, would speculate about that in the days, perhaps years, to come. I wouldn't go there. Didn't matter. Evrest and I would be too busy changing the world—and loving each other.

And oh, how I loved him. Completely. Passionately. Obsessively. My lover. My partner. And now, my king. Commanding my heart. Ruling my body. Loving my soul...

Even the dark parts.

Especially the dark parts.

EPILOGUE

My fingers shook as I signed my name on the last page of the Realtor's packet that had been dropped by courier plane yesterday.

"Done." I released an equally unsteady sigh, looking past the veranda of my office to the ocean. *Zen, find me now.*

Gah. I'd really done it. Finally cut the ties on a huge piece of home—though a little over three months to the day I'd arrived in Arcadia, I couldn't fathom California being "home" again. Sure, I'd been a little homesick when the movie finally wrapped and everyone left, despite Harry keeping me on the production team as an under-the-radar "consultant" at Joel's earthier-than-usual insistence—but Evrest ended my funk in his wonderful train-without-brakes way. A week into my funk, he'd ushered me into what used to be the film production office, freshened with new décor and a stack of new files on the desk. I'd met his gaze, as dazzling as the sun on the waves outside, wondering what the hell he was up to.

Time to get to work, little lightning.

He'd handed over a key card on a lanyard—my security badge for the palais employee entrance. His reward was my squee, and an *attempt* at a kiss. I was on the clock. No PDA until I clocked out, he explained.

Devastating. Mesmerizing. Stacked like an MMA fighter. Hung like a porn star. And now, cunning as a tech mogul. Since we were waiting on announcing an engagement until the laws governing the Distinct were officially abolished, I couldn't go to work for Arcadia as his fiancée, so he simply put me on the payroll. Since then, my days never lacked for challenges to tackle, ways to make every minute count...

Opportunities to change the world.

"Regrets?" Novah murmured it while taking a sip of her tea. Thank the Creator, she'd accepted my offer of staying on at the palais—Enock and Tochi in tow, of course—to be my personal assistant.

Gawd. "Personal assistant." It sounded a lot better than "show the new girl everything she needs to know about this place, and we mean *everything*"—but it amounted to exactly that. Novah had been indispensable in that capacity and so many others.

"No." My answer was sincere. "There are just moments when it all feels more real, you know? Or maybe surreal."

She set down her teacup. Contentment tilted her lips. "Or maybe too good to be true."

Her expression was clearly justified. On the sand below, Enock and Tochi played catch together. It still weirded me out a little, looking at Enock. He seriously could've been Novah's brother, his tousled hair just a shade lighter, his lanky body matching her Twiggy frame. No wonder Tochi looked like a walking piece of driftwood with a spray of yellow wild grass on top.

I laughed. "Yes. That too, *arkami.*"

She smiled in approval. "You learn new words every day— but that one is very pleasing...arkami."

I grabbed her hand and squeezed. Very soon, I was certain she'd even be my *bonamie*—best friend, not just a pal. We had the total beginnings of a Rachel and Monica, proved out this morning alone. The hours had flown while we finalized plans to turn the palais into a Christmas wonderland soon, complete with new books as presents for the children and island vendor gift certificates for their parents. I was stunned it was already noon.

Better surprise? The man who walked into the room, stopping the air a little more with every prowling, perfect step he took. As every drop in my bloodstream responded, including the teasing pulses between my thighs, I bounded to greet him.

"Merjour, Novah." Though his tone was casual, he stuck to decorum in kissing my cheek. His gaze? Way different story. It already had me sprawled and screaming on the desk beneath him.

Woo-hoo.

"Merjour, Majesty." Thank God the woman was bright. She already had her binder and phone packed up. "Stopping in for a midday meal break with your queen?"

I shot her a glower. Explaining the law of jinx hadn't gotten to Novah. She still insisted on using the term, despite my discomfort with it.

"Hmm?" Evrest's head jerked as if she'd startled him from a dream. He'd barely heard what she said anyway. *Good.* "Ahhh, yes," he finally mumbled. "Midday break. Of course."

"I believe I shall retire to our cottage, then," Novah said. At the end of the north wing were a dozen private cottages for preferred royal staff members. "It appears my men will be famished soon."

"Famished." Evrest growled it suggestively, never taking his eyes from me. "I know the feeling."

He continued the theme the second she left, delving his mouth against my neck until I moaned from the arousal he drenched through every inch of my body. "King Evrest," I managed to gasp, "for shame. What have you told me about behavior while on the clock?"

He snarled harder, whipped the lanyard off my neck, and hurled it out to the patio. I was beyond caring as he suckled down between my breasts, turning my nipples into rock candy and my sex into a puddle.

"Okay then...just fire me."

If so, this was a damn great pink slip. Good thing I'd unpacked all my clothes from home over the weekend and discovered this wraparound-style blouse, instantly sensing the royal approval it would receive. His savoring snarl, vibrating through my left breast as he nuzzled, confirmed the view. *So hot.* I could watch him like this, savoring my skin with his head to my chest, for hours.

In anticipation of his next move, I quivered to my toes, ensconced in my favorite pair of platform heels. Yes, it was crazy but true. I was now a regular heels girl. Guess it had to happen sometime. The look *was* more grown-up, and—

Who the hell was I kidding? I just liked what the sight of my legs in heels did to him.

Though somebody had hit the disconnect button on that one today.

To my bewilderment, Evrest straightened and stepped back. "I actually did come over...in an official capacity."

"Oh." I couldn't wean out all my surprise. If we needed to discuss "official" things, he usually called me to his office, not the other way around. His noncommittal tone didn't give me any more clues. "Should I be scared?" When he didn't match my chaser of a snarky laugh, I pressed, "Evrest? *Should* I be scared? Is it Chianna? Did you find her?"

"No."

He rushed it out in reassurance. A week after news had gone public that Chianna had been stripped of her pendant, the woman had gone to ground. Though Samsyn's elite forces were taking their woman hunt seriously, she'd truly vanished, likely into the wilderness at the far side of the island. If there were any new developments, I wasn't getting them out of the king today.

At least it cleared the way for a new realization.

"You're here about something bigger, aren't you?"

He kept up the purposeful cloak. I fought the urge to grab his gorgeous red silk tie and strangle it out of him. He was in full power suit mode today, the tie offset by a three-piece Armani set that had me yearning to strip it off him before he even left our suite this morning.

He reached up, running one elegant finger along the pendant at my throat. My tourmaline lightning bolt. I hadn't taken it off since the day I put it on.

"You know, Tochi still thinks this has magical powers."

I smiled. "Well, he's right. It does. It was given to me by a man with great powers."

Even my suggestive glance at his crotch didn't shake him. What the hell was going on?

Not easing the confusion: the way he pulled me over to the leather couch, making me sit down next to him.

"Maybe it should have a companion piece, then."

The confusion cleared. It had no choice about the matter, making room for how I now felt the pound of my heartbeat through every cell in my skull. The cadence made its way into my chest as he lowered to the floor in front of me, dropping to one knee...

And holding up a ring that blew my damn socks off.

Okay, my pumps.

Oh, hell. Whatever!

My mouth dropped open. It was...incredible. Beyond incredible. A tourmaline stone, at least a couple of carats, surrounded by diamonds shaped like wings. Despite the honking size of the thing, the gold band was fashioned to look delicate, a braided alloy filigree.

"I have been in meetings with key high council members all morning." His voice emulated his face, ebullience mixed with pride. "They have given me their support for revoking the practice of the Distinct. As soon as the Council takes a final vote in three months, the laws will be officially changed." He leaned in, aligning the ring with the tip of my right ring finger. In accordance with Arcadian tradition, the ring wouldn't move to my left hand until...

Oh, God.

Until our wedding day.

I bit my lip like a dorky kid. Just thinking about it made my senses swim—in all the best ways.

Somehow, Evrest didn't get that. He kept the ring hovered there, over my fingertip, until I finally peered up at him, perplexed again—to find him watching me, seeming awed and breathless himself. When I intensified my stare, silently urging him on, he finally spoke.

"Yes?"

"*Yes.*" I laughed it out as he finally, *finally*, slid the ring on fully. The second he did, I twined my arms around his neck, welcoming his lips on my own, his moan through my senses, and his tongue, at last claiming my mouth with heated possession. I opened for him. Sighed for him. Surrendered for him. Anything he wanted. Everything he needed. *Let me be it for you. Give it to you.*

If ever I was certain the man could read my thoughts, it was now. His growl, pure and primal, answered my words with a message of his own. *You are, sevette. And you will. Oh yes, you will.*

"Fuck." His utterance startled. I was barely aware we weren't really kissing anymore. His hands could be blamed for part of that phenomenon. Pawing beneath my clothes and then clawing at my skin, they were the wolf in his hottest, hungriest form. I writhed and whimpered, accepting the scrapes, needing his unique brands across my most tender skin.

"Ahhh!"

His fingers, one and then two, found my core.

Especially *that* tender skin.

"Fuck, fuck, fuck." He jabbed my skirt to my waist in a pair of urgent shoves. "I just proposed. I am supposed to order champagne, bring you a rose, kiss you with rom—"

He choked into silence as I scooted forward to palm the huge ridge beneath his pants.

"Do you want that, My Majesty?"

I rasped it against his Adam's apple on purpose. It drove him crazy, evidenced by his consuming shiver. He wasn't the only one going nuts. The naughtiness of gazing at him in his corporate finery, knowing what I was doing to him underneath...

Oh, hell yes.

"I am yours, Evrest Cimarron. Just for now, let this ring around my finger act as your collar of ownership. What do you want to do with me? How do you want to play? With champagne and roses? I can certainly do—"

He cut me off with a roar, mostly muted to the rest of the

ANGEL PAYNE

palais because he shot it into my mouth, practically punishing me with the assault of his lips, teeth, tongue. By the time he set me free again, he'd torn one side of my panties, pushed the rest halfway down the other thigh, and began working on my wettest petals with one hell of a demanding thumb.

"I shall play with you with my cock, little *douleé*. And you shall let me."

I let my thighs fall open for him, arching in the way I knew he loved, exposing more of my intimacy for him. "Yes, My Majesty." His gaze flared as my sex unfolded for his full, unfettered view.

"By the Creator." His grate was finished by the scrape of his zipper. "Look what you do to me."

He didn't have to tell me twice. I actually licked my lips at the sight of his erect bronze flesh against the black of his suit, drops of shiny milk dotting the swollen head before dripping across my own glistening arousal. I gasped with their scalding impact.

"Clean them up," Evrest ordered. He fisted himself, rubbing in slow anticipation. "With your finger. Wipe the drops off your pussy and then lick them."

Hell. Maybe that ring was as magical as the pendant it matched. We'd been having some great sex but mostly in the crazy-new-positions department—not to mention Evrest's desire to make sure I "toured" every room in this place with *his* special seal on the deal. Not since he'd popped his cherry with me, that first night in the tent, had he gotten this wicked with the ol' missionary.

I adored him for it.

I loved him for it.

I let him see the force of that love in my eyes despite gliding my finger into my mouth with the sensual seduction of a porn star. His brilliant eyes flared. His hand pumped faster at his cock. *Perfect.* He might have just put a down payment on the cow, but I wanted him to know the milk was always going to be this hot. And lusting. And wanting...him. Always, only, him.

"Holy fuck. My sexy sevette."

I slid the finger out. "Always." After that, I traced my touch down my chin, over my pendant, into my cleavage...and then waited, yearning for him to read my mind again. *Tell me to expose my tits. Order me to play with them for you.* I'd never get tired of that one. Ever.

With a shit-eating grin, he shook his head. "No. Keep going. Slide that wet finger into your pussy. Roll it there. Tease your clit for me. Let me see."

Maybe that *was* better than playing with my nipples. Just a little.

Or a lot.

As he watched me, he returned the favor. I stared at his long fingers, working at his penis in long, captivating strokes. Holy hell, he was magnificent, even with the rest of his body still clothed—maybe because of it. If demigods were a real thing, I'd just gotten engaged to one. *Luckiest. Girl. Alive.* I vowed then and there that we'd never make a sex tape. If it was ever leaked, every Hollywood producer would be on the next plane to Sancti, contract in hand. It had already been rough enough, confronting the ten "spurned" Distincts after he outted us on Minos Beach that day.

My body began to throb. Pulse. Strain. Sensation mounted beneath my finger, torrid and tingling, demanding I let it out. Deeper inside, my walls clenched, primeval vibrations turning into screams of need, begging for the fill they usually received at this point.

"Camellia...hang on tight, my love. I need to do this hard."

Thank the Creator.

One stroke and he was all the way in, his length invading, pushing, flowing...crowding so much inside my body that my mind tumbled into the surrender of it too. The surrender to him. Breathing him in. Tasting his flesh. Becoming his plaything. Being his lover.

I toppled fast now. I told him so with my panting moans in his ear, my clawing grip in his hair. It all just made him pound harder. He knew I loved it like this, taking me like he couldn't get enough of me.

Because I sure as hell couldn't get enough of him.

Even when I was exploding around him.

"Evrest!"

He grunted, cupping my ass to fit my body tighter to his. "Yes?"

"Yes!"

I screamed it about twenty more times—or maybe it was two hundred; counting was difficult when one's senses were shattered—before he finally slowed, bringing us both back to earth with gentler thrusts and soft kisses.

Just before his phone rang.

Reality. Yay. *Not.*

With a naughty smirk and his body still encased in mine, he reached into his jacket pocket to answer the call. Ridiculous as it was, I blushed clear to the thigh he caressed with his free hand.

"Syn, what is it?" he barked. *Shit.* Much *deeper blush. Did it have to be his brother, of all people?* "What I am up to is none

of your damn business. Do you have progress for me or not?"
He nodded tightly. "All right. I am on my way."

I smiled in heartfelt empathy as he pulled away with
a grimace of apology. "Duty calls. Has Samsyn learned
something new about Chianna?"

His face was blank—once more on purpose. "No. It is
something else. Nothing to be concerned about, but nothing
I can speak of."

"All right." I tidied my clothes. "I understand, *betranli.*"

He turned back with a smile like a tethered sunbeam.
My heart leaped. *Score.* Such little things tickled him, like my
learning the Arcadian word for fiancé. I longed to learn all
those idiosyncrasies about him—and be with him to create a
lot more of them too, private ones for just the two of us.

"Dinner underground tonight?" He said it with a wink
while giving his tie a corrective yank.

Things like that.

I twirled my ruined panties on a finger. "Yes, please."

"Lose those."

I giggled. "That's a given."

"I mean before dinner tonight, as well."

"That can be arranged too."

He stopped and turned just short of the door out to the
hall. "Now that I think about it, just dismiss the fact that you
have panties."

"Permanently?"

"Permanently."

One long stare at the command in his face, and pure, illicit
delight took its turn at tugging up my lips. "Okay."

"And sevette?"

I stood for him. Tried to be demure and classy about it as

I could. *Note to self: ask Novah how one behaves like a queen when all they want to do is jump their king's bones.* "Yes, My Majesty?"

"Do not be late. The days are shorter now...and the nights longer."

I only had three emphatic words in response.

"Thank. The. Creator."

Continue The Cimarron Series with Book Two

Into His Command

Available Now
Keep reading for an excerpt!

INTO HIS COMMAND

BOOK TWO IN THE CIMARRON SERIES

PROLOGUE

"Happy birthday, Prince Samsyn."

The curvy blonde batted her big brown eyes, curled her full dark lips, and then opened her purple satin robe.

She was naked underneath. As he had expected.

His body responded with cold nothingness. As he had also expected.

It was almost midnight. He had officially been twenty-one years old for four hours.

He felt older.

So much older.

Officially, the world was now supposed to be his—how did they say it in America, those "crazy kids" who would be his peers, if he lived there?—his bitch. Yes. That was it. The world was now his bitch, ready to be molded to his will, commanded at his whim. The Ferrari, McLaren, and Jaguar in the garage downstairs would help him do it faster. When he was done, he could return to this twelve-room suite, on the top floor of a palace, with just as many servants to see to his every desire. He could relax on his own terrace, with a view of the

Mediterranean arguably better than that of the king's.

Best aspect of that? He *wasn't* the king. On the island of Arcadia, where the twentieth and twenty-first centuries balanced on an interesting teeter-totter, second in line to the throne meant the best of both worlds. All the fun, none of the responsibility.

Or so they said.

Somebody forgot to let fate in on that joke.

As fate liked reminding him, with floods of glee, during moments like this.

He eyed the nude beauty over the rim of the scotch she'd brought. From the moment she entered, he'd known the expensive liquor was just the beginning of Father's "extra" birthday gift. His gut still roiled because of it. He had nearly taken the bottle and then tossed out the woman, but what if Father's minions were watching, ensuring she performed the assignment? He hated how much that made sense.

The scotch bloomed to a burn throughout his mouth and throat. He yearned for the warmth to seep lower, into the ice between his thighs. By the Creator, how he craved just an hour of turning his mind off for the throes of a good fuck—but tonight, it simply was not to be.

Tonight, he could take the hypocrisy no more. The sham of a birthday party Father and Mother had thrown for him, with that room full of people—his brothers and sister included—gazing at King Ardent and Queen Xaria like they were the couple who damn near walked on the sea outside the windows. Like they adored each other as much as they did their beautiful children. Like they couldn't wait to end the party and be in private chambers with each other—instead of Mother summoning the pool boy between her thighs, and Father...

Well...Father liked to have choices.

A fact Samsyn should have been more peaceful with by now. He certainly had not discovered the sham yesterday, after all. Three years was a long damn time to live with lies.

Yes. He was old.

And angry.

And tired.

And needing to forget.

Praying to forget.

He took a bigger gulp of the scotch. It loosened him enough to speak to the woman.

"What is your name?"

She blushed prettily. "Arista, Your Highness."

"You are lovely, Arista."

"*Merderim*, Highness."

"Did my father say the same thing when he fucked you?"

She confirmed his suspicion as soon as her gaze dove for the floor. She feigned insult. "I...I cannot..."

"Cover yourself, Arista." The patience in his tone only came from clenching his teeth. "You are not to be blamed for wanting to make your king happy."

She softly stepped closer. "I would greatly enjoy the chance to do the same for my prince." Slid between his legs. Guided his touch to her naked hip. Before Samsyn could process a protest, she knelt and pressed her mouth to his groin.

He shoved to his feet. Released a ruthless growl. "I said cover yourself." A deep breath reined his rage back in. "You can stay the night, Arista," he muttered wearily. "The scum who sired me does not have to know we never fucked."

Her tiny sob sliced the air. "You are a good man, Prince Samsyn. Honorable and decent and—"

He interrupted her by hurling his glass against the hearth.

As drops of liquor sprayed, the flames hissed and spat like fuming demons. Perfect. Fucking perfect.

Honorable. Decent.

He was anything but either. Hiding his parents' filthy secrets, even from his siblings, had changed him. Tainted him in ways that would never be clean again.

Aged him.

A shrill ring blared through the room. His cell phone. The ring for his most private number, designated as his *must answer* tone. Tonight, he'd never been more thankful for it.

"What?" He gave no further greeting. It would either be Tryst or Cullen on the line, considering the late hour and the number of pissed-drunk mates he had stepped over when exiting the birthday party an hour ago.

"Highness." The deep timbre was all Tryst. The formality was not. Samsyn's skin pricked, not all in a bad way. "Your father begs your pardon for interrupting your birthday celebration—"

"Debatable," he snarled, knowing Tryst understood. The man only looked like a dumb giant. T had seen and heard enough to deduce the truth about the king and queen on his own. "What is it?"

"He requests your personal attention...to something."

"All right." He gave it too eagerly but didn't care. The hook was out of his mouth. No lies would be necessary about how he had handled the situation with Arista.

"We have...a delicate situation."

He almost laughed. Tryst and the word *delicate* were hardly a logical match. "Creator's fucking toes, T." When no commiserating snicker came from his friend, he paced off his disconcertment—and dread—by walking out to the terrace.

"Has the *éslik* gotten some poor thing pregnant?"

"No." Finally, there was a laugh in the man's voice—though the next moment, he went straight back to cryptic. "But you had best get here anyway."

"Good enough." He looked out to the darkness of the sea, ordering it to yield Tryst's nonexistent details. No such luck. "'Here' being where?"

"The airport."

"The *airport*?"

"Your Highness, with all due respect, just get your ass over here."

This story continues in
Into His Command: *Book Two in The Cimarron Series!*

ALSO BY ANGEL PAYNE

Cimarron Series:
Into His Dark
Into His Command
Into Her Fantasies

The Bolt Saga:
Bolt
Ignite
Pulse
Fuse
Surge
Light

Honor Bound:
Saved
Cuffed
Seduced
Wild
Wet
Hot
Masked
Mastered
Conquered
Ruled

Secrets of Stone Series:
(with Victoria Blue)
No Prince Charming
No More Masquerade
No Perfect Princess
No Magic Moment
No Lucky Number

No Simple Sacrifice
No Broken Bond
No White Knight

Temptation Court:
Naughty Little Gift
Perfect Little Toy
Bold Beautiful Love

**For a full list of Angel's other titles,
visit her at AngelPayne.com**

ACKNOWLEDGMENTS

Evrest and Cam never would have made it without the incredible love, support, listening ears and encouraging hugs from some truly amazing people.

THANK YOU ALL!

VICTORIA: You are there through thick and thin...even when I lose it in airport parking lots. I will not ever find the words to tell you how grateful I am.

ELISA: How can I express how amazing you are? Oh, wait! I Can! Cornelius Hackl!

Shannon Hunt: For being there at midnight, at 6 am, during the tears and heartaches and anxiety attacks...just for being there...you are, and always will be, so neurotically, awesomely, precious to me.

The Original Beta Reading Goddesses:

Lisa Simo-Kinzer

Angela Barrett

Leagh Christensen

Carey Sabala

Thank you to everyone who has loved and supported this crazy new world through the years. It's a dream come true to share the Cimarrons with all of you!

ABOUT ANGEL PAYNE

USA Today bestselling romance author Angel Payne loves to focus on high-heat romance starring memorable alpha men and the women who love them. She has numerous book series to her credit, including the popular Honor Bound series, the Secrets of Stone series (with Victoria Blue), the Cimarron series, the Temptation Court series, the Suited for Sin series, and the Lords of Sin historicals, as well as several standalone titles.Angel is a native Southern Californian, leading to her love of being in the outdoors, where she often reads and writes. She still lives in Southern California with her soul-mate husband and beautiful daughter, to whom she is a proud cosplay/culture con mom. Her passions also include whisky tasting, shoe shopping, and travel.

Visit her at AngelPayne.com